# THEO'S STORY

Ron Rhody

# THEO'S STORY

Ron Rhody

Academy Publishing/East

THEO'S STORY

Published by Academy Publishing/East
Pinehurst NC

Printed and bound in the United States of America

First Edition

ISBN 978-0-578-00760-1

Library of Congress Cataloging-in-Publication Data

Rhody, Ron.

Theo's Story/Ron Rhody

p. cm.

Library of Congress Control Number: 2009901277

For Dad

# ONE

The death of Benjamin Dannan was the driver.

What happened to Michael, what happened to me, Benjamin Dannan's death was at the root of it.

Michael and I were nine.

That was thirty years ago.

Lord, what I wouldn't give to be a boy again, back in that time with everything just beginning.

It was late October of 1941.

Mr. Dannan's body was found just after daylight, covered by snow and lying on the side of a road up in the mountains of Breathitt County.

There had been a big storm that night and a Kentucky Utilities crew was out checking for downed lines. It doesn't usually snow so early in the year up there, or anywhere in the state for that matter, but every now and then it does, and this was one of those times.

At first they thought it was a deer that had been hit by a car and tossed up on the shoulder.

But it wasn't. It was Benjamin Dannan.

No one knew why he was there.

Or how he got there.

There were no houses or buildings within miles. His car wasn't found.

He was in his shirtsleeves. He had no coat, no hat.

Prominent men don't walk around coatless and hatless on a mountain road in the middle of a snowstorm in the dead of night.

It was a very big story.

Benjamin Dannan was a power in his time, one of the best-known men in the state and one of the most outspoken. Foul play? Accident? The hand of God working in mysterious ways?

The local sheriff and the State Police put everything they had into it. The newspapers, too, especially *The State Journal*, Benjamin Dannan's own paper.

The story played nationally for a while. But that December the Japanese bombed Pearl Harbor and World War II came. The story was pushed aside. By spring, since nothing had been found to keep the investigation alive, the police closed the case.

In the end, all that was known was that Benjamin Dannan, loving husband of Rhae, proud father of Michael, publisher of *The State Journal*, was found dead, lying in the snow on the side of a lonely road in the mountains of East Kentucky over a hundred miles from home.

Though the coverage ended in the papers, people continued to wonder. Benjamin Dannan had powerful enemies.

All the conjecture made good cocktail conversation, but nothing ever came of it. Over time, the story evolved into one of those standard features that newspapers do when appropriate anniversaries occur. On the occasion of the 25th anniversary, I did a story for *The State Journal* myself.

As I think about it now, Benjamin Dannan's death made almost as intense an impression on me as it did on Michael. Michael was the direct recipient and I saw the real grief he bore. Neither of us had experienced a death and had no thought that someone close to us, someone loved, could be taken from us in such a way.

As I watched Michael deal with his pain and his anger, I, too, felt threatened and unsure. I became uncommonly attentive to the health of my own mother and father. I was certain that only my prayers, said in a precise form while I knelt in exactly the same spot at the foot of my bed each night, kept them alive.

This was a heavy responsibility for a boy. The weight of it accounts in part, I suppose, for my feeling, even now, that it is up to me to watch out for things, to make things right.

## TWO

No one expected Michael to come home.

When he called to tell me he was leaving his job, his only explanation was "there's something I have to do."

"What?" I asked.

"I'll tell you when I see you," he said.

We didn't get a chance to talk about it until the morning after his big homecoming. Rhae Dannan staged an evening at the New Capitol Hotel that made the Governor's Inaugural Ball seem ordinary. This was just a week after Michael said goodbye to his colleagues at McKinnon headquarters in San Francisco and climbed on the corporate jet for his last flight as CEO.

The Governor came, and even though the Legislature wasn't in session, so did most of the members of the House and Senate from districts within driving distance. All the city fathers turned out, and the county courthouse crowd. And the big businessmen from Louisville and Lexington. And Bluegrass society – the people you had to know to count at all. They were there partly out of deference to Rhae, who had the influence and the financial wherewithal to be a person you wanted on your side, and partly out of curiosity. They wanted to size up Michael.

No one gave grander parties than Rhae Dannan. She had taken over the hotel, the best and the largest in town, on Main Street, right in the heart of Frankfort, where anyone who was out that fine June night had to be aware, with the cars pulling up and the tuxedoed and gowned couples being disgorged, that something very special was going on. There was an orchestra on the lobby floor, and dancing, and eight bars, and waiters circulating with oysters, and shrimp, and country ham on beaten biscuits and small cups of burgoo. And anything… anything… you wanted to drink.

The ballroom up on the fourth floor had been made into a dining room and by the time the crowd sat down to table in the candlelight with the white-gloved waiters gliding about, a nice rosy glow prevailed.

Rhae said a few simple words in welcome about how proud she was of Michael and how glad she was he had come home and how much she looked forward to whatever it was he had in mind for the rest of his life, and how she hoped it was here with her and in this place that loved him and that she knew he loved. Then the Governor seconded all this and we all fell to.

After dinner, Michael was prevailed upon to say a word, which he did, modestly, and as I remember, making the tired old idea about how there's no place like home sound moving and eloquent. Nothing more. Nothing about his plans. But it was enough. Everyone was relaxed and satisfied.

The event was as if Rhae was staging a coming-out, getting Michael properly introduced to all the right people and making sure everyone appreciated who he was and what he was.

Michael was superb.

In a room mostly full of strangers to him, all curious, a few jealous, many already conniving for what benefit to themselves might be in the offing from the evening, he was gracious, self-effacing, and charming.

Charm was Michael's stock in trade. It is a hallmark of certain boys, boys from the Tidewater of Virginia, from the Lowlands of the Carolinas, boys from the Bluegrass of Kentucky – a charm polished by their adoring mothers and burnished in the small liberal arts colleges they attend and mellowed by the ritual of the privileged Southern culture in which they move, until it is as natural as sin – and as seductive.

There are not many so favored, but when they come along, they are deadly. Their presence is such a pleasure, their company so comforting that they are irresistible. They put a strong hand on your shoulder, smile with such warmth and look you in the eye with so much understanding that you know you have found a friend for life – a true friend, loyal and brave, a friend you can trust and rely on. That was Michael.

Allie wasn't there.

I had seen that she was on the list, but she didn't come. It could be that she had no one to come with. Her marriage had lasted longer than any of us thought it would when she eloped at Christmas of her senior year at the university. It was beyond comprehension that she was attracted to the boy she married.

His family had a little money, but hardly enough to be the worth of her.

Whatever had drawn her didn't last. She had the baby, a girl, almost right away, and when the baby was old enough to be left with a sitter, she ended the marriage and went to work. Under the pressures of single parentage, she dropped out of contact with all but a few of us, and even that was infrequent.

Or it could have been that the child, now a young woman, a strikingly beautiful young woman almost as graceful as her mother, was simply too ill to be left alone.

In any event, Allie wasn't there.

If Michael missed her he didn't mention it.

The evening went on until almost dawn. It was a success in every conceivable way that Rhae might have hoped.

Finally only Rhae and Michael and I, and Paul Isham, the Managing Editor of the *Journal*, Rhea's close friend and advisor as he had been Benjamin Dannan's best friend and advisor, were left.

We had a final glass of champagne. Michael danced to "Goodnight Sweetheart" with Rhae, and we all adjourned through the early morning streets and out the darkened lanes to the farm.

It was after breakfast that Michael told me.

I have a particularly clear memory of the discussion. It was Saturday morning, June 13, 1970. We were in the library having coffee, just the two of us. Paul Isham had returned to town and Rhae was on her way to bed. We were standing at the big window looking out over the meadow to the tree line that borders the creek. A half moon risen late was still in the sky as dawn came. Pale blue light lay on everything.

Michael said into the silence, "I told you I had something I had to do."

"That's right," I said and turned my gaze from the window to look at him

He was smiling broadly.

"How does the idea of Governor Michael Dannan appeal to you?"

"What?"

"I'm going to be Governor."

"Of what?"

"The very state we're standing in, old buddy. Your birthplace and mine. The grand and glorious Commonwealth of Kentucky."

He's making a joke, I thought.

"Be serious."

"I am being serious."

"Why would you want to be Governor?"

"It's a step I need to take to get to where I want to be."

"You were already one of the God-like creatures as CEO of McKinnon. Being a governor can't top that."

He didn't hesitate.

"The Presidency can."

There was that grin on his face that he gets when he knows his cards are going to beat everybody's, especially those still raising.

"What the hell are you talking about," I said.

Here we had gone from a very fine evening to a very fine morning and I was feeling relaxed and satisfied and ready to hear about this thing he had to do and all at once I get this nonsense.

"That's why I'm here. It starts here."

"You've got to be joking," I said.

Outside it was getting lighter and the first strands of ground fog were beginning to reach up from the creek.

Michael took a sip of coffee and kept smiling.

"You want me to understand that you gave up what you had at McKinnon to come back here to run for Governor?"

And then it got through to me what he really said…"the Presidency…you're aiming at the Presidency of the United States!"

"Exactly," Michael said. "This is the first step and I need you with me. I want the team again, you and me. Kings."

He sat his cup down and put his hand on my shoulder in that way he had of drawing you in. I was absolutely flabbergasted. Not amazed, stunned, or speechless. Flabbergasted is the only word that describes my reaction.

So, with me amazed, stunned, speechless, and flabbergasted, while the morning mist rose softly from the fields and the sun fingered feebly through, we sat at the table in front of the window in the library at the farm and Michael told me how he was going to take "the grand and glorious Commonwealth of Kentucky," and how that was only the first step.

It turned out that what he had in mind was a thoroughly reasonable approach – so cynically right about what would deliver the Governor's office that its simplicity overshadowed its cynicism.

In the proven tradition of Bluegrass politics where the only sure thing is to buy it or steal it, he was going to buy it.

I had to admire the logic. He would be in no position to steal it, he didn't have an organization – but buy it? Damn right! Others would be out there trying to buy it, too, but Michael was convinced, and he convinced me, that if his own personal family fortune wasn't enough, he had powerful friends upon whom he could call who would very much like to see him Governor and on his way to bigger things. These friends could open the purses of the nation's biggest corporations and could conjure up more money than the Democratic Party in Kentucky had ever dreamed of, more than it could possibly raise and spend on any candidate of its own choosing. Enough money to carry off the Governor's chair like a piece of old furniture at a garage sale.

If the plan was well executed and he caught a little luck, it had every chance of succeeding. Politics is the art of the possible. Is everything possible? Michael could make you think so.

There was nothing uplifting or inspiring about the technique. There has never been anything redeeming about hardball politics...except winning. I had no doubt it could work.

Part of the trick, a very big part of the trick, is to have the right people doing the buying. Everything may be for sale, but the price is not always money. Pride and power have remarkable currency. So do revenge and envy. Avarice, too, and lust. Any of the things that make men men can be traded upon. But there is a certain protocol that must be honored. Certain conventions to be observed.

Michael needed me because I knew the game and the players. I knew the "who" and the "how." I could uncover the "what." People can never keep secrets. They always have axes to grind, and since my column was read widely throughout the state and enjoyed a reputation for being on the side of the little man, I got told lots of things by lots of people who were after this or that and soon had so much information that I didn't need to be on the inside. Most of the time I didn't even have to work at finding out who the buyers and the sellers were or what was for sale. Their enemies told me. I had knowledge, the kind of knowledge that can be enormously powerful in knowing hands. Michael wanted that.

And he needed me because he trusted me.

Clearly his plan had been put together long before he came home, with Rhea's obvious blessing, probably even her enthusiastic encouragement, and with Paul Isham's endorsement.

It was unfair of him bring me into it this way – even manipulative. It was a hell of a story, maybe the biggest of the year, but if I wrote it, I would kill any chance he had of getting the idea off the ground before he could even begin.

I told him this and he seemed surprised

"You're not going to write it," he said. "You're my best friend."

I hadn't expected that.

We were best friends when we were boys together. We kept in touch over all those intervening years, but Michael had been all over the world. He knew great and important people. I did, as well, I suppose. Not quite that great, perhaps, or that important, but heavyweight enough for the world I lived in. But his best friend still with all that universe before him? The thought flattered me.

"Newspapermen don't have best friends where big stories are concerned," I told him.

"You do," he said.

"And it smells like it's on the edge of being illegal."

"Nothing illegal. Everything by the rules."

It was full daylight by then. The fog still lingered, but the sun was up. I needed to be getting back to town, grab a few hours sleep before it was time for me to be back at work.

"You're only looking at the negative side, Theo. Look at the possibilities. I can be a fine Governor. You know I am smart enough and you know I am tough enough. Nobody can buy me.

I'll do what I think needs doing and to hell with what the special interests want. I can do *good*. I know you, Theo, you're for *good*."

He smiled that damn you-can-trust-me smile of his, and sitting there watching him work on me, because I knew exactly what he was doing, I had to admit I did think he would make a good Governor. Possibly even a great one.

"Well?" he said.

I didn't answer. A silent moment went by. I said, "I am due at the paper soon. I have got to get some sleep." And I left.

## THREE

The dilemma was a real one. Would I help Michael take the state? Was I willing to become part of the process from which I made my daily bread as the public's honest surrogate – the people's fearless protector and defender? Did I want to get into a game I knew to be dirty, but, in truth, sometimes ennobling, played by people I knew to be venal, yet on occasion selfless and courageous? Did I want to become one of them rather than the relatively noble creature I saw myself as, standing watch and protecting the public interest? Did I want to be a player in the only absolutely indispensable game played in this country?

If I did, in conscience wouldn't I have to give up my role as a newspaperman and columnist? Could I be objective while promoting the Dannan agenda?

But I didn't want to give it up. It was important to me. I was somebody. Not a monumentally big somebody, but big enough for the pond I swam in. I was someone with a name people knew and respected, sometimes even feared – important people. I had a job that paid well and in which I probably took more pride than I should have. You would be amazed at the rush that comes from seeing your byline on the big story of the day, the one you know everyone will be talking about – the Governor or some high-ranking department head God-damning you, and your colleagues of the Fourth Estate envious that you got it first and they didn't.

The weekend passed. The party was still being talked about, becoming grander in the telling than it actually had been, but remaining still a great success however it was described. I hadn't been in contact with Michael since that Saturday morning at the farm. I still wasn't sure about how I would to respond to him.

On Monday morning a call from Michael woke me. I'd gotten in bed just before daylight. Michael apologized for waking me, didn't bother with small talk, and said he had something curious he wanted me to see. Could I come out to the farm for lunch?

Those of us who toil for morning newspapers do most of our work at night – and we become addicted to it. Night is when secrets are told and hidden doors open. Out of the glare and the chatter, night is when the big decisions are made, the ones that count, the ones that change things. In the darkness and the shadows, in the whispers and the stillness, the unknown is always waiting. The knives are slipped in at night.

So our breed, abroad and hunting in the dark, doesn't get to bed much before dawn and isn't afoot much before mid-afternoon, or at least I'm not – except that day.

I made it to the farm in serious need of coffee. I'd driven out there not fully awake, but I knew the way so well it didn't matter. Up East Main Hill past the cemetery overlooking the river, and the Negro college beyond it now morphing into a desegregated facility in a reverse kind of way if they could only get the whites to come, left at the Green Mill on the east side of town where the road forked to Georgetown, past the new homes sprouting up on the farmland around Black's Pond, and then left again out twisting Steadmantown Lane. Head for Peaks Mill. Look for a long, tree-lined gravel lane on the right and follow it up a gentle rise to the farm.

The main house sat on small hill overlooking a broad Bluegrass pasture where two young thoroughbreds played. There was nothing pretentious about it, no Greek columns or sheltering portico or any of the mansion touches seen so often in the Bluegrass. It made no attempt to be anything other than what it was – a gracious two-story home of sprawling dimensions built in the old style and held in the embrace of a big porch that wrapped it on all sides. It was painted white and matched the white plank fences that marked the meadows. It had a black slate roof, unusual for this part of the country, and the look of a place of enormous comfort and confident stability. Swinging in a wide bend just beyond was Elkhorn Creek, bubbling over riffles and sliding past boulders where, I knew, big smallmouth held in the shadows.

On summer nights, with the windows open for the breeze, the gurgling of the creek would lull you to sleep. I remembered summer nights spent there as boy with Michael, the fireflies blinking over the meadow and the sound of Michael's grandfather's rocker on the porch.

Michael was waiting for me there, a cup of coffee in his hand, watching the colts. He came down the steps, looking serious, but smiling.

"Hungry?"

"Coffee."

We went inside to lunch. Michael let me eat and come awake. There were no questions about what I had to say about his proposition. No questions at all. Instead, he talked. About how good it was to be back ...back at the farm and home again...about our old school buddies and what they were doing.

"Did you miss Allie?" I asked him.

"Allie?"

A silence.

"She was invited," I said.

More silence.

"Why didn't she come?" he said.

"Did you miss her?"

He let a beat go by.

"I wasn't expecting her."

He didn't ask more, not about how she was, or how she looked, or what she was doing.

Bess, the cook, came and took the dishes away and poured us more coffee. We sat in silence, satiated, though Michael seemed impatient. After a few minutes, he handed me an envelope.

"Is this the curious thing you wanted me to see?" I said taking it.

He nodded.

Had I known then what I know now about where its contents would lead us, I would have burned it on the spot and scattered the ashes to the afternoon wind.

Inside the envelope was a letter written in a delicate script in blue ink on ivory stationary that bore the letterhead of Mountain Home. The penmanship was graceful, the kind that spoke of well-bred young ladies from exclusive schools where thank-you notes are never late and where manners count as much as mind.

The letter read:

*"Dear Mr. Dannan,*

*"My name is Marne Young.*

*"I help with Miss Hanna Collins, Aunt Hanna everyone calls her. Do you know the name? I hope so, because she says she must see you.*

*"She is ninety-four and very frail. Her condition is quite serious. Our doctor thinks the end is near. She is not afraid. She has said her goodbyes and seems ready, but she says she cannot go in peace until she has settled something with you.*

*"Will you come see her? <u>Please.</u>*

*"Come soon. There isn't much time."*

Miss Young's letter went on to explain that Mountain Home was a sanctuary for a few special "guests." They must be natives of the county who had a terminal illness of short duration and no family to care for them. Preference was given to people of Melungeon heritage. The home had accommodations for fourteen and was run by The Appalachian Baptist Society on an endowment made by an anonymous benefactor whose generosity supported its operations. Those who could pay, or who had relatives who could, did so. Hanna Collins was in the latter category. She was not a charity case.

The letter went on:

*"Aunt Hanna has been with us for almost four months and had never mentioned your name until she learned from the news on television that you were returning to your home in Kentucky. She prayed with our chaplain, then called me to ask me to write to you for her. She is too weak to hold the pen herself.*

*"This is all quite a mystery to me, Mr. Dannan, but please come see her. It isn't a long way. Your kindness will be so valued as to make whatever sacrifice of time and convenience that may be involved more than worth it."*

Miss Young closed the letter with her phone number, driving directions to Mountain Home in Breathitt County and *"the prayerful hope"* that Michael would *"honor this dying request."*

I put the letter down and looked across at him.

"I have no idea what this is all about," he said.

"The name Collins doesn't ring any bells?" I said.

"None."

"Any chance your old company could be this anonymous benefactor?"

"No. We don't give gifts anonymously. It defeats the purpose," he said.

"Melungeons?"

"I don't know what that is."

Benjamin Dannan's body had been found in Breathitt County. I couldn't remember when anyone had last mentioned his death. Michael and Rhae had dealt with it privately and together and had put it behind them and moved on. All of us had. It was just a memory, faint, like an old-time story told late at night. But still....

"You suppose this has anything to do with your father?"

He didn't reply.

"Rhae or Paul Isham have any ideas?"

"Mother doesn't. I haven't asked Paul. She said she would."

"Even so," I said, "a favor done Hanna Collins or her family, a debt that needs to be repaid? They pay their debts in the mountains."

"After thirty years?" Michael said.

I felt the wash of it coming back. I got the news at school. The last bell had rung. It was curious that Michael wasn't there. He was never late. We had all taken our seats in homeroom, still jazzed from the running and scuffling, when the teacher made us sit and be silent...and kept us that way for what seemed forever. Then she told us that Michael's father had died and that we should all be silent and say a prayer together. None of us knew what to think.

Dead? Nine-year-olds don't want to know about dead, don't know what to think about people who die. Poor Michael. No father now. But what did that mean? None of us had ever been without a father, couldn't imagine such a thing. We just wanted the uneasy feeling to go away and for the day to get started like always again.

I was the only kid in the room who knew Mr. Dannan as anything other than a name. I liked him. He took me and Michael fishing in the creek in the summer and was planning to take us quail hunting for the first time as soon as the season opened…we were big enough to learn to handle guns, he said. I got very cold sitting there in that old brick school on Second Street by the river, waiting.

"We never knew why he was up there in Breathitt County," Michael said.

There was nothing to say to that.

After a moment I said, "I wonder why she put in that mention of the Melungeons?"

"What's a Melungeon?"

"Mostly a myth, I think. They are supposed to have been living deep in the mountains long before the first white settlers arrived. No one knew where they came from. They spoke a strange form of English, full of old, odd words, but didn't look English. They were dark skinned, like Turks or Egyptians. Kept outsiders away. Great hunters. Made magic. That sort of thing."

I had never met or seen a Melungeon or know anyone who had.

"Did you ever hear your father or Rhae mention Melungeons?"

"Never."

"Then maybe there is a connection with the mine wars. Your father was up there during the big mine battles of the thirties, right?'

"He was ambushed once. A bullet through the windshield of the truck he and Paul Isham were in. Missed them," said Michael. "I should go see Miss Hanna Collins, I imagine."

But it was too late.

Hanna Collins passed in her sleep that very night, peacefully it seems, though who can actually know such things.

She had left a small silver box locked with a silver key, Miss Young said in the call she made to tell Michael that Hanna Collins had died.

The box was for Mr. Dannan. Would Mr. Dannan come and pay his last respects and fetch the box himself, or should Miss Young ship it to him? She would do the latter, but she imagined Mr. Dannan might want to see where Hanna Collins lived and is buried, even tour Mountain Home.

It would be such a comfort for all of them if he were to do so. The funeral would be in three days, on Thursday, at the Baptist Church in Jackson, the Breathitt County Seat. The visitation would be Wednesday afternoon and night. Then, after the funeral, her remains would be brought back to the little cemetery at Lost Creek.

Aunt Hanna's only known living relative and what few of her friends still alive would be there for it all. If Mr. Dannan had questions perhaps these others might have answers. Would Mr. Dannan please let Miss Young know as soon as possible?

We were in Paul Isham's office at the *Journal* when the call came. Miss Young had tried to reach Michael at the farm, but when she found he wasn't there, had insisted on being told where he could be reached. It was an emergency, she said. So Bess, the cook, knowing Rhae and Michael were to meet Paul and me in Paul's office before moving on to a dinner party at the Governor's Mansion, gave her Paul's number.

Michael took the call and listened politely. He thanked Miss Young for her thoughtfulness and told her that he would have to call her back. He then repeated the conversation for us.

"Funerals are taken very seriously in the mountains," Paul Isham said.

Rhae nodded, "Everything stops when the cortege goes by. Did you know that? It is the most striking thing. People on the streets stand still. Cars on the road pull over to the side and stop. Even farmers working in their fields, they take off their hats and stand respectfully until the whole funeral party passes."

"Don't go," I said.

They all looked at me in surprise.

"In a town as small as Jackson and an area like Lost Creek, everyone will notice, and everyone will be curious. You're an outsider. You would attract too much attention."

"It seems a small enough thing," he said.

"Until we know what Hanna Collins left for you, the last thing we want is Miss Young telling the story of how you are there in answer to a dying woman's request."

"The last thing *we* want?" Michael said.

"If you're serious about being Governor, "I said, "you don't want to attract any attention right now. And you damn well don't want to go opening any doors without knowing what's behind them."

"So it's *we*!" Michael said. "You've decided. You're with me." He laughed and clapped me on the shoulder and said. "It's all over but the shouting, now, buddy! We'll cut a swath through this state like never seen before, and then on to Washington. Washington, Theo! Think of it. The two of us in the White House. How you're going to like that!"

I can't pretend the power Michael offered wasn't tempting. It was more than tempting. It was seductive. On one level I saw what might happen if I took this road. I had been around powerful men long enough to know that beyond any millimeter of doubt power rots virtue, that the strong always take advantage of the weak, that self-interest almost always wins over public interest. I had lived with myself long enough to know I detested this, couldn't abide it, that I had to fight it. And yet, and yet....

Michael would be a good governor, with my help possibly a great governor. And later, in Washington, well...

"This is a chance to make an impact that really counts. Directly. Yourself!" Michael had said to me when we first discussed this.

I can't say I arrived at the decision through any rigorous thought process. My dad used to say that we make the important decisions with our gut and everything we go through after that to explain to ourselves or to others why we have chosen what we have chosen is simply rationalization. For those things that really make a difference, we decide with our emotions.

"You're going to leave the *Journal*?" Paul Isham asked me.

"No," I said, "not unless you insist, and if you insist, I'll have to rethink my plans."

I then went on to lay out for them what I had been thinking about, unconsciously, I suppose, though as I spoke the idea took full form in my mind. I wouldn't give up my job, my column. They were too important to me. I had to have the independence, the liberty to be my own man. But that didn't mean I couldn't advance Michael's cause. I could be a confidant, a counselor, helping lay strategy, taking advantage of the information I would have, or could get. There were honorable precedents for what I had in mind – Kroc of *The New York Times* with Roosevelt;

Bradlee of *The Washington Post* with JFK – well respected newspapermen who sometimes served as alter egos to political leaders. As important, I could be more effective for Michael if I wasn't a direct member of the team but continued to be seen as a newspaperman who had the public interest at heart – which I was and did.

I wouldn't hide my preference for Michael Dannan. Columnists are expected to have opinions, to take sides. I would be up front about that, but I would still be looking out for the public interest. Wasn't that stronger?

Rhae applauded. Paul Isham smiled and did the same. And Michael took my hand and shook it.

I can't explain how inordinately relieved I was after this. I didn't realize what a strain I had been under. Of course I had to help Michael. Of course it was the right thing to do. And of course I had to have my independence.

I could have it all. We were going to be a team again.

I didn't stop to consider whether the boy we each remembered and were counting on was still in us.

When we were young, strangers often thought we were the sons of twin sisters. We were both about the same height. We both had black hair that we kept close cropped in a crew cut like the Marines wore back then. Regular faces, not handsome, but serviceable enough, and blue eyes the girls seemed to like. Michael was the sole heir to the fortune that his mother's family, the Hopkins, had been building from tobacco and thoroughbreds since the Civil War. My dad was a beer still operator at the distillery. It was the best hourly job at the plant, but still not the landed gentry. My mom's folks were small farmers.

Michael was stronger. I was quicker. I was the captain of the football team. He was an all-state running back. We were both good students, not normal for jocks. Michael was brighter, but I worked harder.

We did almost everything together...hunted, fished, dated, and though it seems immodest to say so, excelled. It is true. We excelled. We liked to win. We expected to win. We insisted on winning. We didn't care so much which one of us won. Only that one of us did.

Together, we were kings.

After high school, we took different paths, but stayed as close as distance and circumstance permitted. Michael went to Centre College, a fine little liberal arts school nearby at Danville, then on to graduate school at Stanford out in California. I went to UK, the University of Kentucky at Lexington, twenty miles up the road from Frankfort so I could commute every day and get back to work each night at the paper where Rhae Dannan had gotten me a job to help pay my way through school.

The Korean War erupted at the end of our freshman year in college and I got called up with the Marine Corps Reserve unit I had joined because I needed the extra cash. Michael didn't and hadn't and so he stayed in school.

With roughly two years out for the Korean exercise, I graduated with a degree in journalism from UK at about the same time Michael was getting his master's in marketing from Stanford. I went to work full time at the *Journal*, first as a sports reporter, then later became its political writer and gained modest fame as a columnist syndicated around the state. He joined McKinnon Industries, one of the stars of the multinationals then carrying American industry's banner around the world, and became its president at age 30 – the youngest president ever of a *Fortune 500* company. In time it bored him. He came home too.

I say too because I also left for the brighter lights of the big city. To New York. Two years was enough.

We both came back. First me, then Michael.

For different reasons, but back.

"I am so happy, Theo," Rhae Dannan said, breaking my reverie. "You two were always together. I feel so good about this." She put her arms around us both and beamed.

Laughing, Paul Isham said, "Come on, now. We'll be late at the Mansion. We don't want to keep the Governor waiting."

Outside, the streetlights were just beginning to come on. Paul's car was in its reserved space in the small Courthouse lot off the alley. We left through the back shop, making our way past the row of job presses on which the *Journal* did much of the State's contract printing, and let ourselves out the carrier's door. Yes, the *Journal*, too, fed at the State trough.

# FOUR

*There is a girl. A country girl. She goes to the county high school. City boys don't date the county girls and county boys don't date the city girls. A comfortable territoriality prevails. But for this girl we would have gladly broken the rule and shattered territoriality like a piece of glass. We see her from a distance...at games, at festivals...like hunters watching a doe at daybreak, never revealed, never suspected by the prey....*

*She moves with a ballerina's grace and the poise of a princess born of the blood. She seems demure and unassuming. She has a figure that takes our breath. Her face is so beautiful it makes us shy. She is seduction and innocence and by mutual agreement, the most desirable girl we have ever seen. We never learn her name, so in the way of young romantics we give her a name – Roxanne.*

*It is Saturday night in the spring of our high school senior year. We are in Michael's car on the way to a party in Lexington. We aren't drinking. By agreement, we won't start that until we get to college. But we don't need liquor. It is the sort of night that has our blood up – a crescent moon riding above the tree line in an ink blue sky, the cool of the evening fresh on us, juiced with the juices of being eighteen, laughing and joking happily.*

*We are on Jury's Lane. Michael has decided to take it because it is a fine night and the drive will be good. Jury's Lane is one of the small back roads that cut through the Bluegrass, not much wider than the wagon path it originally was, dipping and curling over the rolling fields, crossing back and forth over a winding creek, tree-lined in spots, rock-walled in others. Small farmsteads are sprinkled along it, nudged in among the larger holdings of the big tobacco farmers and horse breeders. The few houses sit well back from the road.*

*As we round a curve and come into a straight stretch of road, our headlights flash on a spot of white drifting toward us.*

*The spot seems to float, weaving erratically, moving slowly.*

*"What is it?" I lean into the windshield. Michael slows, shaking his head. "Beats me."*

*As we come closer, we see it is a girl. She is dressed in white. Michael slows further, almost to a crawl.*

*The girl moves haltingly toward us. She stumbles in the loose gravel on the narrow shoulder of the road, falls to her knees, catches herself from falling prone with stiff, outstretched arms. She seems not to see us.*

*Reeling, she stands up slowly and starts toward us again. Michael stops. She is fully in the headlight of the car now, her eyes reflecting like those of a deer frozen in the spotlight of poachers.*

*The front of her dress is streaked with blood. The fabric, a satiny material that is shiny in the light, glistens. Her face is battered and her mouth bleeding.*

*She stumbles past us as if we are not there.*

*The white form shimmers through the glow of the taillights and on into the dark while we sit in the middle of the road with the motor idling, too stunned to move.*

*Suddenly, Michael puts the car in gear and shoots forward.*

*"Jesus, Michael, you're in the wrong gear," I yell. "Put it in reverse!"*

*Michael speeds up.*

*"Stop!" I shout again, "that was Roxanne!" I am banging on Michael's shoulder. "She's hurt. Turn this thing around."*

*Michael pushes me away and keeps driving.*

*"Shut up," he growls. "Think!"*

*He takes a curve very fast and I bounce to the side.*

*"We stop and pick her up and take her home, if we can find out where home is, she didn't look in any shape to tell us. Or we take her to a hospital."*

*We speed over a small rise, the car lifting and bouncing down on the pavement.*

*"One of her, two of us. City boys. She is beat up and bloody." Michael brakes for a downhill curve, then straightens and keeps going fast. His eyes are focused on the narrow road. He sounds angry.*

*"What are people going to think? And what does she say? Maybe her boyfriend did it and she doesn't want to blame him? Maybe she was somewhere she wasn't supposed to be and doesn't want to admit it. She doesn't know us. We would get bloody getting her in the car. Get blood in the car. How do you think her family is likely to look at that? Father? Brothers?"*

*Michael keeps checking the rear view mirror as if he thinks we are being chased.*

*"Or at the hospital. Two city boys bring in a girl in shock. She is bloody and battered. They've got blood all over them. Use your head, for God's sake, Theo!"*

*I can't believe he is saying this.*

*"You're serious! You're goddamn serious! You're worried someone will think we're responsible! Stop this thing and let me out. I am going back!"*

*"No," Michael says and speeds up. "No grandstand plays tonight."*

*The car is moving too fast for me to jump out and each minute puts us further away. I slam back against the seat in a withering rage.*

*The next Monday afternoon we are walking back from spring football practice, trailing behind the rest of the group. The graduating seniors always work out with the next year's team. It is a way to stay in shape and to assert our dominance for a while longer. We're not talking, just walking side by side. We haven't had much to say to each other since the Saturday night. I am still angry. I feel ashamed and embarrassed, and feeling so makes me even angrier. I don't know how Michael feels. I don't much care.*

*We have just turned up Wapping Street past Liberty Hall where the antebellum homes sit back on broad lawns when suddenly, savagely, as is if by mutual agreement, we are at each other. Maybe it was a look I gave him. Maybe he bumped me. Whatever the trigger, we ignite. Hit the bastard! Hurt him! I concentrate on what I'm doing. No yelling or talking. The only sounds are the grunts we make as our bodies strain, a muffled crack when a fist hits bone.*

*No one tries to separate us. The rest of the group lets us fight, at first for the sheer excitement of watching it, and then, when it seems it should be stopped, because no one is bold enough to intervene.*

*Finally, when we have tired, one of the biggest boys steps in. As we cool, he asks, perplexed, "What happened? You guys never fight."*

*My cheek is bruised and my lip cut open. Michael has a hand-size blue mark on his forehead and a cut over his eye. His pants are ripped at the knee and he is bleeding from his nose. I stare at Michael and our eyes lock and we almost start again. Then he says to the boy between us, "Nothing. Forget it. It's over."*

*We begin to clean ourselves up. Michael takes a handkerchief from his pocket and offers it to me. I hesitate, then take it.*

*Michael says, "I did what I thought was best — for both of us. Let it go."*

## FIVE

There was no mountain funeral for us that week the letter came.

We all agreed we had to know what secrets Hanna Collins kept, but they would have to wait.

Michael called Miss Young and gave her his regrets. He was so sorry and was sure that Aunt Hanna Collins' passing was a big loss to them all. He would have been pleased to be there to pay his respects but the schedule of events arranged by his mother and others and already committed to made it impossible for him break away. He would come soon, perhaps the following week. He was looking forward to meeting her and to visiting the grave and to retrieving the box Hanna Collins had left for him. He would be in touch.

Our attention turned to the campaign.

The Party had already unofficially decided its candidate. There had been no formal announcement, but every one knew that Jesse Bristow was the anointed. Bristow was a power in his own right and with the Party's muscle and money behind him, the odds that anyone else had a chance were zero. Michael had no organization behind him, no name recognition, no political experience, nothing. Somehow in this compressed time frame we had to convince the power brokers that our man, not Bristow, was the man for them.

Or force them to that conclusion.

Or decide to ignore the party and make our run as rebels.

Our man!

An unknown, an innocent.

A would-be politician who had paid no dues, whose loyalties were obscure, and whose submission to the will and discipline of the party would be suspect at best.

A man who had never attracted a single vote, cut a single deal, walked a single precinct.

Our man! The Pride of Peaks Mill! The Amateur!

That we even had the balls to consider it still makes me wonder.

More important than winning over the Party was the ability to win the hearts and minds of the voters. We could talk of buying the election, and we would buy what we could. But the buying is done at the margins – offering enough of whatever is necessary to flip a County Judge in our favor, to help the local Superintendent of Schools see things our way, and, yes, to buy an extra vote or two in a precinct where it is needed. I am not proud of this – everyone does it, it has to be done, and I accepted it as necessary. We would spend whatever was needed and be glad we had the money.

But the voting – that's the thing. No matter how much money or favor or influence is spread, you don't get elected unless you get the most votes. And the great mass of people – voters in the numbers needed – vote for you because they believe in you. The Party can deliver the faithful, but the candidate has to deliver the rest. We would have to make Michael the most attractive candidate in the race.

And we had to do all this by stealth. We would have to slip up on the Party unsuspected – whisper in the right ears, apply pressure in the right places, persuade and cajole and intimidate and be off and running before they realized what was happening. No, we hadn't much time, and yet that was part of the plan, too. The less time there was, the less opportunity we would be found out before we were ready.

You can see the challenge of it.

Which is why Aunt Hanna Collins' mysterious letter and box had to wait.

Our first task was to test the waters…to try out the idea of a Dannan candidacy with a few of the Party's kingmakers and see what reaction we got, a few whose influence might move the rest, whose approval would open the way.

Dace B. Havershamp, late of Golden Pond, now of Aurora, in West Kentucky, was the Baron of that end of the state. The oldest of the power brokers now, Dace had made a fortune with the velvet moonshine of Golden Pond that became famous from New York to New Orleans during Prohibition.

With the money from moonshine he had built a political apparatus that delivered West Kentucky counties for Democratic politicians like clockwork, even in years the Republicans won the state. At first his little machine was a matter of survival to him. He had no interest in politics then. He played it to make sure he had no interference from the local law and due warning of what the Feds had in mind. Later it became a matter of power and ego.

For the southern tier of counties it would probably be Judge Ormand Blue of Somerset. Blue knew every County Judge in the state, was on good terms with them all, and was known by Rhae to be a man who could and would keep a secret.

We would have to find a man with behind-the-scenes influence in the mountain counties almost as great as Jesse Bristow's up there. Jesse Bristow was mountain-born-and-raised. He was a hero of the mine wars, pulled up by his own boot straps. Rich now, and powerful. Sattis Arnow was the man we settled on. His Miners & Merchants Bank of Ashland had most of that end of the state in its debt.

We would look for one or two others that could be approached with confidentiality, someone influential with the business interests. Jonathan Winston, the head of Elkhorn Distillers, president of the Bourbon Association, and as blue-blooded a member of the Bluegrass aristocracy as there was, would be our first choice.

Rhae Dannan would be our way in.

When the riveting shock of Benjamin's death began to ease, she looked for escape, for anything that would distract her mind from her loss. There was Michael and she devoted herself to him, but she soon saw that such smothering would be unhealthy for them both and she looked for more. She found it at her doorstep – in the *Journal* and the farm.

The newspaper was new to her, and the farm's other businesses, the tobacco and the corn. But she sank into them and pulled them around her. Between that focus and her devotion to Michael, she began to heal. She hired good people and gave them their head. She didn't meddle. She set her standards and expected them to be met. Whether it was the economy of the times, or her style, or luck, everything prospered. As time went on, she began to be asked to serve on boards, to chair committees, and over the years, with no intention of doing so, she had become a very influential woman.

Now that influence would be put to work for Michael.

We had an indication of what the reaction to her plans for Michael might be at the dinner party at the Governor's mansion the night Miss Young's phone call came telling us of Hanna Collins' death.

There were only the six of us – the Governor and Mrs. Parsons, Rhae and Paul Isham, Michael and me.

I earned my place there on my billing as Michael's good friend, but not wholly without regard to my relationship with the Governor. In a way I had played a role in his successful election, for which he was not ungrateful. Though I had from time to time been critical in my column of both his policies and his conduct, I halfway liked the old goat. He knew that and harbored illusions that some day in some way he might be able to use that leverage.

As such things go it was a pleasant enough evening.

Hunter Thompson's story on last month's Kentucky Derby was still very much on the Governor's mind. Thompson was building on his notoriety as the "gonzo" journalist and had cobbled together a rambling piece reported mostly from the beer-soaked partying that always goes on in the infield at the Derby. He titled it, "The Kentucky Derby Is Decadent and Depraved."

"Did you see it, Rhae," the Governor said. "How dare that smug little hippie. We should have ridden him out of the state on a rail."

He said it smiling but I knew he meant it.

"I don't think the article did much damage, Governor," I said. "Not many people read *Scanlon's Monthly*. Anyway, most of the talk is about Lee Brown and his female jockey."

That turned the conversation.

Lee Brown, the chairman of Brown-Foreman Distilleries, had put a girl named Diane Crump up on his entry, Fathom – the first woman rider in the history of the Kentucky Derby. Whether he had done it to flout convention or because he actually thought she had a chance of winning, no one knew. But everyone suspected the former.

Miss Crump finished fifteenth in a field of seventeen, but rode a decent enough race. The thought of a woman riding in the Derby alongside jockeys of the stature of Willie Hartack and Willie Shoemaker, indeed, riding in the Derby at all, was a certifiable scandal to some. But to others it was another welcome poster that a woman's place was anywhere she chose.

"Lee thought she had a chance," Rhae Dannan said. "I congratulated him on his courage and good sense and told him I might consider the same for next year's Derby if I can develop a horse I confidence in."

The Governor considered that.

"How about you, Michael," he said. "How do you feel about women riding in the Derby?"

"Governor, I feel that women ought to have the chance to do anything they think they can do," Michael said with a grin, "and so far as my experience extends, that's everything."

Rhae Dannan laughed. "That's absolutely right, young man."

"Indulge my curiosity further then," the Governor said. "You're a big mystery to the folks here who flit around the rarified circles of Bluegrass society. Now tell me. You can trust my discretion. What are your plans? You're much too young and talented to be satisfied just sitting around watching your fortune grow."

Michael took his time responding. He looked to Rhae, and then to Paul Isham, and finally to me. Then, smiling, he said, "Why, Governor, I've barely closed the door on corporate life. All I have in mind at the moment is to relax and enjoy myself."

He lifted his glass in a half toast, "And to savor every moment of being home. Such as tonight. Thank you."

The Governor smiled in return.

"Yes, yes. You're entitled. You've earned that. But a man with your talent and your drive – that can't be wasted. That has to be put to use. Maybe you just need a short furlough. There are great opportunities here for the right man. You could start a new company. The state needs the jobs. The strip-mine wastes! Yes. That could be it. Reclaiming the strip-mine wastes of East and West Kentucky. This is a monumental undertaking. There are state and federal subsidies that will absorb most of the risk. You would be doing a real service to the state and the profit opportunities are considerable."

The Governor was grinning earnestly at Michael and I could sense as he built enthusiasm for the idea that he could see a role for himself in such a company when he left office next year.

"Governor, please," Rhae interjected laughingly, let the poor boy rest. I'll have more than enough to keep him occupied for a while with the newspaper and the farm and the stables."

"Well," the Governor replied, "a short rest, maybe. All that energy and experience can't be wasted. How would you feel about the university? President of the university? That could be arranged."

You could see he was sizing Michael up and had no doubts that whatever plans Michael might have, retirement was not among them. It was equally clear that of all the things he might imagine Michael doing, entering politics wasn't among them either.

He hadn't asked about Michael's party affiliation. He knew that Rhae and Paul Isham were Democrats and must have assumed that Michael was as well, though I doubt he would have thought that made any difference. My experience, his, too, I was sure, is that most businessmen are whatever they need to be.

As the evening wore on we left the table and adjourned to the library upstairs for coffee and brandy. It was a beautiful, high-ceilinged book-lined old room on the northwest corner facing the Capitol building, comfortable and quiet. Two leather couches faced each other across an aged cherry table that had belonged to Henry Clay. High-backed winged chairs, also covered in leather, were arranged in a semi-circle at the top of the little alley the couches made. In the wall at its foot, an oak fire burned in a fieldstone fireplace.

We talked a while of nothing in particular and then, knowing the Governor's wife was from East Kentucky and because I was curious, I asked her if she had ever head of Melungeons.

"Well, yes," she said with a little laugh. "Melungeons, oh my. I haven't heard that name since I can't remember when. Our parents used to scare us with them, you know. Strange people who would come out of the hollows and get us if we weren't good. They handled snakes and could put a curse on you that would turn you dumb if you made them mad. Oh, Melungeons. However did you happen to think of them?"

I mumbled something about a feature story I was working on.

"Did you ever see one?" I asked.

"Oh, no. But we knew they were there. Way deep in the mountains. Back up the most remote hollows. The scary tales were just made up, I imagine. But the Melungeons were real. They lived in very tight little groups. They were very secretive. Our fathers and brothers, deer hunting back in the mountains, or sitting around their fires at night while their hounds ran coons said they sometimes would see a dark figure on a ridge top looking down at them, or sense a presence at the edge of the firelight on those fall nights, ghost-like, there and gone. They had yellow eyes. Like wolves. I don't know if our men felt threatened...but there was always an air of unease whenever Melungeons were mentioned.

"Oh my, now you'll give me bad dreams in my sleep tonight, Theo. Why did you bring this up?" she said laughing, but you could hear the echo of a child's worry in her voice.

I told her not to fret. I would get to the bottom of everything and my story would set all her fears to rest.

"Well, find out if they're Republican and if they are, you make sure you tell our folks so they can get up there and register them to vote," the Governor joked.

Michael looked at me with a little smile I'd seen a lot across a poker table and said, "Politics. I hadn't thought about that. Do you think I ought to consider politics, Governor? It seems interesting and I don't imagine there is time to get bored."

The Governor laughed out loud. "Absolutely not! Go with your talents, Michael. Leave the politics to the politicians."

"You're right, Governor," Rhae said. "Michael, stop teasing. Such a thought gives me a headache."

By then it was time to go.

As we walked to the car I asked Michael, "How do you think you're going to like living there in the Mansion?"

"I'm going to get rid of all that leather," he said.

## SIX

The following Monday we were on our way to Kentucky Lake.

We decided to begin with Dace Havershamp. Rhae knew him well.

"Dace is secure enough in his own power not to be nervous with the seditious idea we're going to present to him," she said, "and he's enough of an opportunist to see the possibilities."

She made the contact and set the appointment as a favor to herself in getting for Michael "the benefit of Dace's advice and experience" as Michael began the process of trying to decide what to do with the rest of his life.

"Theo is coming along," she told him, "partly to keep Michael company, but mostly for an interview I hope you'll give him for the first in a series of stories the *Journal* plans to do on the state's political leaders."

This was all a flattering and blatant appeal to ego and Dace Havershamp recognized it for what it was, but he was not above a little flattery. Accommodating Rhae Dannan on such an easy request would give him a marker for future use that would cost him practically nothing to acquire.

Michael picked me up at the paper just as the first copies were coming off the press and we were beyond the Bluegrass when night began to let its grip on the landscape ease and we could see the dawn coming up.

Michael drove, left hand on the wheel, right arm laid easily across the back of the seat. I sat back comfortably, content with the sound of the tires on the asphalt and the sights of the fine summer morning. We spoke very little. That was a very good thing between us. We didn't need to talk to be companionable.

But though we weren't talking that didn't mean we weren't thinking and I was still mulling the question of why Michael had given up a life of power and prestige to come back here and start on what seemed such a Quixotic quest.

"When did you decide you wanted to be President?" I asked into the silence.

Michael smiled, "That's what every red blooded American boy wants, isn't it?"

"No. They want to be pro baseball players, or fire chiefs, or jet pilots."

"None of that seems to have appealed to you, Theo. What do you want to be?"

"When I grow up?

"Yeah, when you grow up."

"Michael Dannan's *Eminence Gris* in the White House."

He laughed.

"Seriously," I said. "Why do you want it?"

He answered without hesitation, as if he'd expected the question. "I owe it to my father."

"Your father? How does he figure into this?"

"He was a great man. He would have been greater if he'd lived. I'm obliged to be great, Theo."

"You were nine when your father died."

"I've been given gifts that I can't waste. I've got the mind. I've got the skill and the will. I've got the money. And I *can be*, Theo, I *can be* President."

He turned his eyes from the road to look at me. The expression on his face was one of absolute certainty.

"Kentucky is just the first step. I have the backing of some of the most powerful men in the country. We'll put together whatever it takes to get me the rest of the way. And I can win people to my side. You know that."

He turned back to the road.

"I can be President. I'm going to be."

He was smiling a peculiar, half ravenous smile. For just the flick of a moment I felt a chill.

"Then what will you do?"

"I'll do good, Theo. Just like you want. I'll do good."

He laughed and slapped me on the shoulder and turned back to the road.

His mood was infectious. I laughed, too, and settled back to watch the morning grow. The fields looked fresh and newly washed. Down the fence lines, every possible hue of green glimmered in the rising light. On the curve of the hills that rolled gently out before us, dew sparkled like little diamonds. The day was new and eager and though I didn't have a real answer to my question, I felt that tingle of excitement that used to come when we were boys setting off on the bus trip for the first away game of the season.

We turned south at Louisville and dropped down to Elizabethtown, then west again through Big Clifty and Caneyville and Beaver Dam and Dawson Springs, skirted the top of Lake Barkley, and over the big dam across the Tennessee River at Gilbertsville that forms Kentucky Lake

We figured we would be at Dace's boat dock by noon or so. It was a long drive, but Michael had wanted to see the country and to begin his re-education for the run upcoming.

Betsy had filled a thermos with strong coffee and sent along a basketful of homemade doughnuts, fried crisp and dusted with sugar and cinnamon and the crust still warm. We ate and drank as we rode and felt superior, like time-travelers in a special craft sagely observing the ways of the folk, but making no mark by our presence.

So we lazed down the road in the happy grip of caffeine and dextrose.

After awhile I poured myself another cup of coffee, licked the sugar off my fingers, and said, because I had been thinking about it for a good part of the drive, "When did you see Allie last?"

He glanced in the rear view mirror, turned his head to look at me, then back to the road again, and said, "I'm not sure. Long time."

"Did you ever meet her daughter?"

He glanced at the mirror again.

"No," he said, "I never did."

"Beautiful girl. Almost as pretty as her mother. She's dying."

"I heard. I am sorry."

"It must be an awful strain."

He nodded, not commenting.

"You're not curious?" I said.

He turned to look at me again, then back to the road.

"About what? How Allie is doing? How she looks? About her life? You're a romantic, Theo. Sure, I'm curious. But I haven't the time to be interested."

I sat back.

"Even so," I said.

"I don't get involved with other people's lives. Mine is complicated enough."

## SEVEN

*It is a Sunday afternoon in the winter of our junior year in high school, bitterly cold with dark coming on and a heavy snow falling. We're on our way to a movie everyone is talking about – "The Gun Fighter" with Gregory Peck as Johnny Ringo, the fastest gun in the west.*

*As we start across the broad intersection in front of the New Capitol Hotel, Michael notices a boy and girl standing next to the bus stop, shivering in the snow. Nothing is moving on Main Street. Through the snowfall, the movie marquee glows dimly and I can barely see the street light at the intersection. Nothing is on the street except a cab in front of the hotel, its motor idling to keep the heater working for the dozing driver.*

*"Those kids must be freezing," Michael says.*

*I have my head down into the wind paying attention to not stepping into snow over my shoe tops.*

*"Probably waiting for the bus," I say, glancing up.*

*"Let's see."*

*"Aw, come on. We'll be late for the movie."*

*"Only take a second."*

*The kids are scrunched together for warmth against the wind. The boy is dressed in a thin red windbreaker and jeans. The girl has on a knee-length coat. Her legs are almost blue with cold. Neither have gloves or a hat. Their canvas tennis sneakers look icy stiff.*

*"Hi," Michael says. "I'm Michael Dannan and this is Theo Clarke. What are you doing out here in the middle of this snowstorm? Looking for a job as snowmen?"*

*The boy looks at him, uncertain what to say. He might be twelve. The girl, younger still, moves closer to the boy. Through chattering teeth the boy manages "Waiting for the bus."*

*"Missed the last one?" Michael asks.*

*"Guess so."*

*"When's the next one?"*

*"Don't know," the boy says nervously.*

*"Where do you live?"*

*"Thorn Hill," the boy says, a note of concern in his voice. I thought of the distance all the way out to that section on the edge of town.*

*"The bus might not be running with all this snow."*

*The boy just looks at Michael and brushes his nose with the back of his bare hand. The girl stays close to the boy's side, shyly watching.*

*"How are you going to get home if the bus isn't running?"*

*I see the anxiety in the boy's eyes.*

*The pair have probably been to the Sunday afternoon movie, their big treat, something they look forward to all week. They've either missed the bus, or the bus isn't running. Maybe they have just enough money for the movie and bus fare and can't call home to say they missed the bus because they don't have enough money for both the pay phone and the fares. There is probably no phone at home, anyway. And no car. By now the mother must be beginning to worry. Kids late. Snowing hard. Dark coming on.*

*Turning to me, Michael says, "How much money do you have?"*

*"Enough for the movie and Milk Duds."*

*"Lend it to me."*

*"What for?"*

*The little girl snuggles closer to her brother, watching him silently with eyes beginning to tear.*

*Michael doesn't answer, he just smiles at her. He holds out his hand. She looks to her brother, hesitates, then reaches her hand out to Michael's.*

*Michael walks them down to the idling cab, opens the door, speaks for a moment to the cabby, gets my money, puts it with his own, puts the kids in the car, and sends them off.*

*It is dark by then. And colder.*

*Still no one on the streets but the two of us. No sound except the sound of the wind and the cab pulling away.*

*"There goes our movie," I say.*

*Michael has his shoulders scrunched up and his head pulled down against the blowing snow. He watches the cab drive away until its red lights fade to pink, then fade completely in the snowfall.*

*When he can no longer see it, he turns to me. "Couldn't you feel it, Theo? Lord, I'd hate to be cold and scared with night coming on and no way to get home."*

*His face opens in a smile and he throws his arm around my shoulder.*

*"Don't you feel good right now?"*

## EIGHT

I turned back to the road. The sun was up behind us and the long shadows of morning reached out ahead.

The only intrusions on the landscape were the squadrons of black pumps thrusting up and down in barren pastures to bring up oil or natural gas. A little further along ugly gashes marked where strip-miners had torn off the topsoil to get at the easy coal seams just below and dumped the overburden like black offal back in the cuts. The land all about was desolate.

Michael slowed and pulled over on the shoulder. Even though the sun was shining and the sky was blue, everything seemed blighted. No birdsong, no insect sound. A dead land.

After a moment he shook his head and said, "Governor Parsons thinks there is money to be made off this wasteland?"

"He's having a bill introduced in the next session of the legislature to put a special tax on strip-mined coal," I explained. "The money raised will be matched by the Federal Government. It's all to be used to reclaim the areas ruined by the stripping operations. Some small fortunes are going to be made by the people who get the contracts to do the work. And guess who will decide who gets the business?"

"The Governor," Michael laughed. "But surely there will be competitive bidding?"

I smiled.

"Absolutely. The law demands it. But in this case the competition is about who will kick back the most."

"You know this to be the case?"

"Everybody knows. The players get sloppy enough sometimes that some of it gets exposed. A few go to jail. Some fines are paid. Not enough of either to be much of a deterrent with the kind of money that's available."

"I think I am really going to enjoy this, Theo," Michael said.

He put the car back in gear, pulled onto the roadway and we sank into a kind of depressed hush as we watched the tortured land roll by and waited for the wastelands to end.

It was, as I said, a beautiful day and once through the mine fields the countryside flowed lazily to the west on the gradual slope that takes the state from some 4000 feet of elevation in the eastern mountains to a little over 600 feet of elevation on the western border at the Mississippi River.

We were to meet Dace at the Owl Point Marina, the only marina on the upper end of Kentucky Lake, attendant to the state park there and operated under franchise from the state. The lake and its sister, Lake Barkley, cut across virtually the entire length of the western tip of Kentucky and together make up the largest tourist playground in middle America. The marina franchise was a goldmine, and to no one's surprise, Dace Havershamp was the franchise holder.

Fishing boats were anchored in the river below Kentucky Dam as we crossed, lines out and probing deep in the current for the monster catfish the pool below the dam produced. We lost sight of the boats as we turned left at the end of the dam and onto the road into the parking lot at Owl Point.

The inlet that sheltered the marina was filled with boats – sleek cabin cruisers, ski boats with high-powered outboards, a smattering of houseboats, even a couple of graceful sailboats, floating at anchor off buoys. The four long floats that made up the dock tethered the 18-foot V-hull and 14-foot flat-bottom aluminum runabouts that weren't out on rental. The flat-bottom boats were painted a dull non-reflective green so as not to spook the fish when they were worked down the banks. The V-hulls, meant for speed, flashed sunlight off their anodized aluminum skins.

Dace Havershamp was waiting for us at the end of the dock in the kind of boat Jay Gatsby might have kept for his pleasure at his place at West Egg – a graceful mahogany-sheathed cruiser so sleek and glistening that I had to stop and admire it.

He had on a faded blue cotton work shirt that looked freshly pressed, starched khaki slacks with a pleat like a razor's edge, a red Murray State windbreaker, and deck shoes.

I had met him several times before, suited and polished at political events. He was what was meant by the phrase "a big man." Not fat...big, a truly big man in all respects – head, hands, shoulders, legs, and belly. He must have stood six-foot four, weighed probably 240. Michael and I, both at just under six feet and weighing about 180, seemed like kids beside him. Don't let anyone tell you size doesn't impress.

He couldn't have been more affable.

"Boys, you're practically right on time." He shook our hands and guided us aboard, smiling and gesturing to the rear of the boat. "I thought we would run down the lake a ways. Give you a chance to see some of the water, Mr. Dannan. You haven't seen it, have you? Best damn crappie fishing in the U.S. of A. Not half bad for bass, either. We'll anchor in a little cove I know. Private. Be a quiet place to talk."

We took the seats he indicated, he got behind the wheel, started up the engine, and we eased slowly through the no-wake zone out onto the main lake.

The lake was absolutely flat – no wind ripples on the surface, smooth as glass, our wake behind us dancing green and white into a widening V. The countryside around us was fairly flat and the banks mostly grassy to the water's edge, and bushy. We ran south down the lake and after a while began to pick up a few hills. We were moving fast and the wind noise made talking difficult so we didn't try. I watched the sky and the water and the wake and felt almost hypnotized. A long point came up on our right. Dace slowed, eased into and then around it and we found ourselves in a deep cove with sloping banks and pin oaks shading the water. He idled the engine and maneuvered us slowly into the cove, looking for markers and when he found them, he cut the engine, threw over an anchor, and we glided to an easy stop.

"Here it is, boys, my secret crappie hole, the finest on all of Kentucky Lake. If you can find it again, you are welcome to fish it," he said with a grin.

We laughed, stood, stretched, and looked around. The way the cove angled and in the spot we sat we wouldn't be visible from the main lake. The trees gave us shade, but weren't so thick we didn't get sunlight, and the sloping banks cushioned sound, so we had silence and privacy and a setting as relaxing as anything I had experienced.

Dace went down into the little cabin and reappeared with two ice-chests.

"Lunch time," he said.

He opened the one chest. "I can offer you Coca-Cola, Falls City beer, or Dr. Pepper. I imagine you city boys favor coke or beer, but I am a Dr. Pepper man myself. "

"Now I hope you don't mind making your own," he said, opening the other ice chest. From it he took a long, unsliced salami, a length of bologna of the about the same size, a loaf of white bread, two large onions, a half dozen boiled eggs, a jar of cucumber pickles, two cans of sardines, and a box of fig newtons.

"The Food of Kings, boys, the Food of Kings," he said. He laid out everything on the top of the ice chest which he had put behind the wheel along with a couple of knives, some paper plates and napkins, and small jars of mustard and mayonnaise.

"There," he said with satisfaction when everything was arranged. "Now, what'll it be? Want me to go first? I'll show you how to make the best sandwich in the world."

He took two slices of bread and slathered the side of one with mayonnaise, and the other with mustard. He laid the bread down on the ice chest top, then peeled one of the onions and cut three large slices from it with a filleting knife he took from the chest. He put the onions on the mayonnaise side of the bread. He then took a can of sardines, opened it with the little attached roll-up key that came with it, and, with great care and clear anticipation, reached in with his fingers and layered the onions with the sardines thick enough so the onions couldn't be seen. Atop this he put the mustard sided bread, smashed it all together and grinned, "Guaranteed, the best!" To the plate he added two boiled eggs and about a half dozen cucumber pickles.

"The famous Dace B. Havershamp Raw Onion and Sardine Sandwich," he announced, "Boys, there's nothing like it!" He took a seat at the side of the boat and said, "You want to try your hand at this or you want me to do it for you?"

We looked at each other.

I have never been a sardine eater and raw onion hasn't been high on my food list, but I shrugged what-the-hell and pulled out two slices of bread and started. Slicing the onions made my eyes water and I lost a couple of sardines on the deck, but finally managed to get the thing made.

Michael watched as I did this, looking amused, then took his turn. He managed the onion better than I did and lost no sardines.

"Better have a Dr. Pepper with those, boys. Beer don't cut it," Dace said.

I took an exploratory bite, not too big, but big enough not to seem finicky. The onion was firm and sweet and the clean fish taste of the sardines with just the hint of salt water was so good in combination it surprised me. A bite of boiled egg chased by a couple of the slightly sweet cucumber pickles and then a swig of Dr. Pepper and I couldn't have been happier.

Michael seemed to be having a similar revelation. We nodded to each other and smiled our appreciation.

Dace did the talking while we ate – about the crappie run, the best anywhere in the South, hand-sized crappie "you call 'em newlight up in the Bluegrass" ready to spawn and so active you could limit out in a couple of hours if you knew the right spots; then basketball prospects at Murray State –not good, but getting a little better with the new coach. He had a special place in his heart for Murray State, he said, and felt it was unjustly slighted when time came for the legislature to apportion money out to the various state colleges.

"The area is growing fast now that the Land Between the Lakes is catching on and Murray can be a real asset in helping build the economy in this end of the state," Dace said. "But dammit, UK gets all the money."

We nodded, asked the questions that seemed to be in order to keep his stream of words going, laughed when it seemed appropriate. He talked. We participated.

The fig newtons made dessert. They were cold and crisp from their time in the ice chest and just sweet enough. I have had grander meals, but none more pleasant, sitting in the shade on a balmy afternoon with oaks arched above and sparkles of sunlight glancing off the surface of the big lake, the water lapping against the boat, beating rhythmically like a gentle pulse.

When we had finished and had everything cleaned up and put away, Dace eased back against the wheel and put his hands behind his head and his feet up on the gunwales and studied us for a moment in a relaxed and curious way.

"Well now, boys," said, "you've got sardines on your hands and onions on your breath. They may not let you back in the Bluegrass." He chuckled and stretched and then said in a friendly tone. "I knew your daddy pretty well, Mr. Dannan. He was a good man. What can I do for you?"

I didn't think he would figure Michael for a man who needed advice about what to do with the rest of his life. I imagined he had a fairly good idea that he was going to be asked something unexpected. I don't think he had any inkling what, but I was sure he didn't imagine it had anything to do with helping Michael decide what he ought to do now that he had left McKinnon.

Michael looked straight at Dace and held his gaze for what seemed a long time. Then he nodded his head as if deciding something. "I want to be Governor, Dace," he said, "and I want you to help me."

Dace took his hands from behind his head and his feet off the gunwales. "Governor?" he said.

He leaned forward slowly to get his face closer to Michael's. He studied Michael, silently, intensely. There was no question he was surprised. He pulled his face away and leaned back against the wheel again.

"You were aware of this, Theo?" he said, looking at me. "Rhae, too?"

Now Michael leaned in toward Dace.

"It shouldn't be too hard. I have the energy. I have the ability. I have the money. But I don't have legitimacy. There needs to be a laying-on of hands. I need to be anointed."

Dace ignored Michael. He turned to me again. "Is Rhae dreaming?" He shook his head from side to side and smiled to himself wonderingly. "Of all the people I would never suspect of wishful thinking, Rhae Dannan would lead the list."

"Not my idea," I said. "But interesting, isn't it?"

"And what does Paul Isham say?"

"He's for it," I said.

I couldn't tell whether Dace was intrigued or amused. He could have been both.

"Well, well," he said, "what do we have here? What are you all seeing that I don't?"

We spent the rest of the afternoon gnawing it. Dace poking at why it wouldn't, why it couldn't work, making the same arguments I had made – an unknown, no organization, no experience, no claim on anyone's heart or mind, a carpetbagger, and so on and so forth and don't you know.

And Michael countering. The Dannan name was known. We would build on that. Michael's reputation as an executive, as a man who got things done was well known. We would build on that. With money no object, we could assemble the best organization the state had ever seen...fast. As for experience, well, it was true he wasn't experienced at politics, he didn't know about backroom deals, or lining your pockets from the public coffers, or buying and selling men's reputations, no offense meant, Dace.

"But I'm experienced at getting results, at getting people to work together to make things happen. All the key businessmen know me. I got excellent contacts in Washington that I've built over the years through my work for McKinnon Industries – Senators and Congressmen from all the states McKinnon operates in, including Kentucky; the heads of Federal agencies and their staffs; think-tank scholars and the high-octane law firms; I've got them. And there's this – this most important thing. I'm on no man's payroll. I'm obliged to no special interests. I can't be bought and I can't be blackmailed. No other candidate out there can say that, Dace. Michael Dannan comes with no strings attached."

Dace took it all in. Stayed quiet. Then after a moment, he said, "But if I step in and give you my backing, won't you be obliged to me?"

And that was the nut of it...the "what's-in-it-for-me?" proposition. We knew it had to come. We had made the trip expecting it, had even gone over the possible enticements with Rhae and Paul Isham before we left. What were we prepared to offer in return for Dace's imprimatur and endorsement, how much was Dace's end of the state and his influence within the party worth to Michael's ambitions?

In this sort of situation, you never say what you're prepared to give. Once said, all you can do is negotiate up from that. No, you make the other party reveal want he wants, and then you try to negotiate down from that.

But Michael didn't.

I doubt Dace had anything specific in mind...this idea had been sprung on him so unexpectedly. But every politician has a standing wish list. It is made up of those things he wants and will not rest until he has and those things that rightly ought to be his by virtue of his hard work and suffering and dedication, ought to be his, by-damn, if there is any justice anywhere in this old green-eyed world.

"I would be risking my reputation, you understand," Dace said. "They might even laugh me out of the Party. It's a big risk you want me to take."

"It's a risk worth taking," Michael said. "We'll control the state. We'll control the Party. You'll control it. I would put you at the head of it."

I was as surprised as Dace. The Party Chairman controls the patronage, controls the purse strings of the party, has a major say in who gets the lucrative contracts for work being done for the State. It is an enormously powerful position – second only to the Governor's.

Dace was already a power in the party, but he wasn't *the* power. This would make him so. I knew the Party Chairmanship would be one of the things on the table. We had discussed all the possible enticements before we left. But Michael's decision to offer this prize so early in the game with so little sparring seemed rash to me...made us seem too eager.

Never let a person know how much you want him, how valuable he is to you. It puts you in a position that can be taken as weakness.

Anyway, I wasn't convinced we needed Dace that badly. There were others. I had a middling preference for Ormand Blue. I thought he would be easier to handle, ready to get with the program with no other agenda than the one we gave him. I doubted Dace would be as pliable. But I didn't know that Michael and Rhae had already decided that Dace Havershamp was the man they wanted at the head of Michael's party...the only person they thought strong enough to fight off Jesse Bristow in the early rounds leading up to and through the primary, and then tough enough to protect our turf once Michael was in the Governor's chair.

Dace didn't say anything. He rose and walked to the bow of the boat. A light wind was blowing in off the lake and had swung us on anchor so that the boat faced out toward the mouth of the inlet. A few small whitecaps were flecking the main lake surface. We saw a sailboat on the far side working its way on a western tack back toward the dam. The long shadows of late afternoon were beginning to stretch out on the water.

Dace stood with his back to us, looking out over the lake. He stood that way for what seemed a long time.

When he turned back to us he said, "You would have to win to be able to make good on that offer. So the questions are do I think we could work a miracle and make you Governor, and if we could, would I want the job? I'll have to ponder that, Mr. Dannan. It's tempting. It's also dangerous. You're a stranger to me.

"I don't know whether I should trust you. I don't know what kind of Governor you would make. I don't know that I would buy what you have in mind for the state, particularly this end of the state. I don't know whether you're here to help us or to screw us. We need jobs and schools and roads, basic stuff, nothing fancy – the whole state does. I am for the little man, mostly. I don't know you, Mr. Dannan. Who are you for? What are you for?"

Michael started to reply, but Dace stopped him.

"No, I don't want to hear it from you. I imagine you're pretty good at telling people what they want to hear. I need to do some thinking and get some questions answered. I need to talk with Rhae."

It was almost dark by the time we got back to the Owl Point Dock. We made the ride back in silence, companionable enough, not tense, the three of us off in our own little worlds. The wind had died again and the surface of the lake was like an immense pane of darkening glass, deep shadows rimming the edges, the part open to the sky a shimmering oval of muted light.

At the dock we shook hands.

"I'll be in touch," Dace said.

"Soon," Michael replied. It wasn't a question.

"Several days," Dace replied.

Dace turned to me. "What about that story you were going to interview me for, Theo? You forget about that?"

I felt the needle.

"Soon," I said.

We all laughed.

As a matter of fact, I did do the interview later and I did write the story. It played statewide and was of some considerable help in building the kind of image we wanted for Dace when the time came to go public.

I thought it was a plus that he had stopped calling us "boys."

I thought it curious that he had not asked Michael why he wanted to be Governor.

## NINE

I took what Michael told me at face value. He had plans for the state, commendable plans. I accepted that. I accepted as well that the governor's office could be a launch pad to the White House – if we were very, very skillful…and very, very lucky. But I had no concrete idea of what Michael might have in mind for the Commonwealth, or for the country, if we made it that far. I assumed we would work all these things out as we went along and that they would be right and good.

I had no reason to believe otherwise.

There was that situation in Jamaica, of course. McKinnon had been found to be putting mercury-laden waste from its mining operation there into a lake that served as the only water source for a local village. There was nothing illegal about it. Jamaica had no specific laws against dumping discarding mercury-laden waste anywhere.

McKinnon stopped the practice when workers started turning up at the plant infirmary with strange complaints of stomach cramps and nausea. The company built a fine water treatment plant for the village to make sure safe water was available to all and provided technicians to make sure the plant ran well. But I had to wonder, didn't anyone bother to check to make sure that what they were dumping in the water was safe? No one died. But no one knew what the long-term damage might be to those who drank the water, especially the children.

I gave Michael the benefit of the doubt. The CEO can't know every little thing his people are doing. When the practice came to light, responsible action was taken.

And there was that town in Oregon, the one that had to roll up the streets and turn off the lights when McKinnon bought the timber company that ran the sawmill there and closed it down.

The sawmill was the reason the town existed. It was the only employer for miles around. The mill wasn't profitable the company said. Two hundred and fifty families without income, out in the cold and the dark in the forests of upper Oregon, and nowhere to find work.

McKinnon gave them all a nice little severance, two months' pay, and said it would try to help them find jobs elsewhere. I appreciate that you can't run a successful company by holding on to units that lose money. Still, the act had a Scrooge-like quality to it.

No one inquired as to whether anything could be done to make the sawmill profitable and thereby save the town and the jobs. I didn't. It wasn't my story and I had no stake in the matter other than my association with Michael and at the time there was no hint he'd come home or that we would be doing what we were now setting off to do.

I didn't know whether Michael made these decisions or they were made by underlings and he stepped in when he found out. That was my assumption. I knew Michael could be hard and sometimes take actions that were cold and calculating, but didn't we expect that of leaders, weren't such strengths necessary for leaders?

Yes, I told myself, and yes.

Besides, I'd be there.

After leaving Dace Havershamp we drove down to the state Fish & Wildlife Department's camp on an isolated cove on the west side of the lake. The Department opens it in the summer as part of its conservation education program and hosts kids from across the western end of the state. They fish and swim and learn about things intended to make them good stewards of the state's natural resources.

Mr. Fleming, the caretaker and unofficial grandfather to all the kids who came to the camp, would find a place for us, I was sure. I'd done a story on the camp and the conservation education program years ago and became good friends with him in the process.

Mr. Fleming was working on his dinner when we arrived. He put out a couple of extra plates for us and we sat around the table in his cabin sipping bourbon while he finished frying a couple of bass he caught late that afternoon and then we had dinner and talked.

Mr. Fleming treated Michael like one of his boys and Michael seemed genuinely interested in Mr. Fleming.

Perhaps he was. But Michael was so effortlessly engaging it was often hard to tell. People were so flattered by his attention that they never gave a thought to whether he was really there or not.

We talked about Murray State basketball. Murray was a big topic on that side of the lake as we knew from our time with Dace, and Michael inquired about Mr. Fleming's family and what he thought about all the changes taking place because of the development going on over at the Land Between The Lakes.

Mr. Fleming didn't like it. The area was already drawing too many tourists dropping their trash in the woods and zipping around in high-powered boats on the lake.

"It's like the punch-line to that old joke," Mr. Fleming said. "I've lived a long time and I've seen a lot of changes...and I have been agin every damn one of them."

We laughed, and talked a little more, then went to bed.

Mr. Fleming put is in a little cabin out on a point overlooking the lake. Lying there, with starlight coming through the windows and listening to the whippoorwills calling, I felt as safe as a kid in my own bed at home when Mom and Dad were alive and we were a family.

I slipped off to sleep thinking of Allie.

Next day we headed for Somerset to see Judge Blue.

The drive took us across the Pennyrile, that peaceful strip of rolling country paralleling the Tennessee border from Kentucky Lake all the way east to the upsurge of the Cumberland Plateau. In the spring the whole area is in bloom with the little blue flowers of the Pennyroyal plant...so striking and distinctive that the section came to be called for the flower. Over the years, Pennyroyal became Pennyrile in the lazy way people have with words.

We had been driving for almost three hours, watching the country, talking about what Dace would do, getting our strategy in hand for the meeting with Judge Blue. Michael was concentrating on the road, which was two lanes and twisting. We lapsed into silence for a while, drifting in and out of talk.

In that silence I asked, "What happened between you and Allie?"

The question took him by surprise. It took me a bit by surprise, too. I had no conscious intention of asking it. I knew it had to be asked at some point, but I expected to find a right moment and a natural way to bring it up. Once said, though, there was no option but to follow it.

"All you ever told me was in your letter that Christmas I was in Korea. You wrote that Allie was getting married and that you had been accepted for graduate school at Stanford and would be moving to California. No elaboration. No explanation."

"Damn, Theo," Michael said.

"I thought it would be the two of you."

Michael shook his head, looked mad.

"That was a lifetime ago. She was at UK. I was at Centre. I had another two years of school ahead. We would never have lasted that long."

"You didn't want to try?"

"It wasn't going to work!"

"There was a letter waiting for me when I got down from Chosin. From Allie," I said.

"What did she tell you?"

"Not much. Nothing about the two of you. Nothing about when you broke up, or why, although the letter couldn't have been written long after that. She wanted me to know that she was going to marry John Andersen. I didn't know she had ever even noticed John Andersen. She said they'd make their home in Frankfort and that John would take over his father's Chevy dealership. That she would have kids, go to the country club, take winters in Florida and spring trips to the Greenbrier. She said she would have a very satisfactory life, and hoped I would, too. 'Satisfactory.' That sounded so damn sad. Lord, Michael, what did you do? How could you let that happen to Allie?"

He turned a cold glare on me.

"I told her the truth."

"Which was?"

"That it wasn't going to work."

"How could you know that?"

He moved his attention back to the road and in a quietly fierce voice said, "I knew."

And I knew from his tone that he did know, that he knew what was in his own mind then and that nothing she might do would change that. I knew that once Michael Dannan had made a choice, nothing would put him off it.

"What a shame," I said.

"You saw her after you got back from Korea?"

"Once," I said. "She'd had the baby by then. Then a time or two after her divorce. Then I went away, too. I've seen her since, but she hasn't volunteered anything and I haven't pushed it. She wouldn't talk about it, anyway."

"You never asked me about any of this before. Why now?"

"It wasn't any of my business."

"What makes it your business now?"

"Because you're aiming at being Governor."

"I don't understand."

"I need to be prepared for any surprises that might be coming."

"Meaning?"

"That Allie's daughter might be yours."

Michael kept his eyes on the road and both hands on the wheel. He glanced over at me for a second with a look I couldn't read. Finally he said, "Do you think I would get her pregnant and run out on her?"

"She might not have told you," I said.

He still didn't look at me.


It seemed to take forever to get to Somerset.

At the first stoplight, Michael shook himself, as if coming awake. While we waited for the light to change, he turned to me, "Don't make problems where there aren't any, Theo."

If Michael said there was no problem, then there was no problem. The fact that he hadn't reacted at all when I suggested that Allie might not have told him she was pregnant – if she was – seemed off-key, but then I realized that he would expect that. He would expect his women to protect him. They always had.

So I pushed the matter of Allie away for the moment and began concentrating again on the meeting ahead.

To my mind, Judge Ormand Blue was pivotal.

Under our system, a county judge is the monarch of all he surveys. We have one hundred twenty counties in Kentucky and in each county the county judge runs things. Road building and maintenance, the county health department with its doctor and nurses, the social services with its welfare and social workers, the disaster and emergency services, the people who keep the weeds down along the sides of the winding little county roads and spread the cinders and pick up the trash, all the people and funds necessary to run the county are under the control of the county judge. Jobs and money. The judge controls them. That's power. And since he is elected himself, and must keep getting elected term after term, he is the county's most adroit politician. He is the man who knows where the votes are. And how to get them. And how to deliver them. Regularly. Election after election. If you're running for Governor and have the county judges on your side, that's power squared.

Somerset seems an unlikely power base, sitting as it does just above the Tennessee border at the tip of Lake Cumberland in the foothills of the Cumberland Mountains – a market town of no particular distinction in an area of relatively sparse population. But the Judge had made it so because that is where he was.

A self-effacing, prematurely gray Somerset native with a law degree from Yale and the courtly manners and natural grace of the old Southern aristocracy (of which he was not), Ormand Blue, at 45, was the dominant force among the judges. He had become so by dint of his personality, a record of absolute integrity, and a reputation for fearless, and, in some cases, relentless pursuit of ends he felt beneficial to his county and himself.

He had been President of the County Judges Association. It was his intent to establish a personal relationship with all the other county judges in the state and to whatever extent possible, put them in his debt. For the most part, he did. Not all of them, by any means. There were a few equally ambitious men who resented his power and envied his reputation, but they weren't as smart or as cunning and none of them was willing to challenge him

This time it was my contact, not Rhae's, which was the opening.

I had come to know Ormand Blue nearly twenty years earlier at Toktong Pass that deadly December in Korea.

I was with Charlie Company of the 1st Marines. We had pushed ahead of the rest of the Division to Yudam-ni, a nothing village on the western edge of the Chosin Reservoir in some of the most forsaken country God Himself ever created. We were there executing Gen. McArthur's grand strategy to get to the Yalu before the Chinese.

Only they were already there. In numbers that were completely overwhelming. The result was that we were in major danger of being surrounded and cut off.

Captain Ormond Blue's Fox Company had the job of holding the door open through the pass so that we could get out and join the rest of the division down at Haguru.

If the Chinese had cut us off, we would have been isolated so far north that no force could have extracted us. Even from Haguru it would be a long bloody way back to the sea, but if we didn't get through the pass, we didn't get out at all.

I was on a ridge-line shivering in the snow and laying down covering fire when an officer crawled up beside me and told me to get the hell out of there.

"You're through the gap," he said. "We'll take it from here."

Before I could move, a mob of Chinese in their padded jackets and tennis shoes flooded the ridge above and pinned us down. We held, though, and when it got dark we slithered away, dragging our dead and wounded out with us.

Inside the perimeter at the aid tent in Haguru we got hot coffee and had what was bandageable bandaged. I had a nick on my cheek. I hadn't felt the round – it was that cold or I was that scared. It's only a little scar now...on the right side, just above the cheekbone.

The officer came looking for me at the aid tent. He and I had been the last two down off the ridges. We took turns covering each other. He introduced himself as Captain Ormond Blue of Somerset. That's when we discovered we both were from Kentucky.

"You were on that ridge line all alone when we got there, Private, did you know that?"

I hadn't. I had gone up as part of a platoon-size team meant to keep the Chinese off the high ground while the rest of the company came down the road. It was an almost vertical climb through snow and ice to the top of that ridge. A few lost their handholds and fell to their deaths. More were knocked off the face by rifle fire. Those of us who made the top strung ourselves out and started laying down fire like good little Marines. I didn't see the others once I got in position.

"Well," he said, "good work."

He checked the bandage on my face and said, "That wound?"

"Never been better," I said.

He smiled. "You weren't very pretty anyway."

I saw him twice again as we fought our way back to the sea. And once we made Hundang, waiting for the troopships to take us off, he looked me up and we had a drink together. I didn't see him again in Korea.

Much later, I did a story on him when he was elected to head the County Judges Association. A good story. We both liked it. Afterwards, we got together sometimes when he came to the Capitol on county business. We weren't friends, but we were acquaintances and we shared a pride and camaraderie from having been Marines together at Chosin.

I was using that to open the door for Michael.

## TEN

Judge Blue was easy. It was almost as if he had been waiting for the opportunity.

We had read his ambitions right. He wanted to stand for United States Senator when the incumbent's term was up. We would back him. We would get it for him. None of the other potential candidates would, or could. Never mind that the incumbent was an honored name in the state, a distinguished and able servant of the people with a fine record and important committee posts. We would trade him for Judge Blue's muscle in a minute.

The Judge thought Michael a reasonable gamble.

Michael impressed him. Judge Blue thought we could pull it off. He liked the boldness of our plan, the arrogance. He liked taking on big odds for big stakes. That's one of the reasons he had been such a fine combat commander.

After Korea, the Marine Corps sent him to Yale law. He served two years with the JAG in Washington, then came home to Somerset a hero – to an area in which manly skills are highly prized and what could be manlier than success at mortal combat? He ran for county judge against a man who'd held the seat since Capt. Blue was a boy, won easily, and now saw himself on his way, in time, to take the place he knew he deserved among the nation's guardians.

Judge Blue had no inkling of Michael's grand scheme, but his ambition couldn't have fit better with Michael's plans. A senator beholden to him would be no small thing when Michael made his bid for the White House.

We returned to Frankfort the next day, feeling fairly pleased with ourselves. The drive north that morning took us through knobby hills of scrub cedar. We cut back into the Bluegrass at Danville and stopped awhile there at the Centre College campus. On the lawns, scattered among the white columned buildings of old brick, a few students in ones and twos were lounging on the grass with books open before them. Michael seemed more peaceful there than anywhere I had seen him except the farm. We didn't intrude on the scene, we just walked and looked.

I wanted to take over the driving chores and give Michael some rest, but he wouldn't relinquish the wheel, so we headed home past the old log fort at Harrodsburg where the first permanent white settlement west of the Alleghenies had been established and from there on to Bridgeport in the Bluegrass, then east on Highway 60 down the hill into Frankfort, across the river, then back up the hill on the other side and out the road to Peaks Mill.

Rhae Dannan and Paul Isham were waiting lunch for us. We sat on the porch looking out to the creek having lemonade and tuna sandwiches while Michael and I recounted our meetings with Dace Havershamp and Judge Blue.

Rhae was sanguine about Dace Havershamp.

"He'll take it," she said. "The power we're offering will get him. Or the prestige. The prospect for an old bootlegger from Golden Pond to lord it over the snobs of the Bluegrass and make those mountain coal millionaires come to him for favors is too rich to resist. Oh, he'll take it all right."

She smiled that beautiful smile of hers, a sixtyish woman, still handsome. For most of my life I had known Rhae Dannan as Michael's mother and, although she was my employer, as a friendly and benign presence. She was a successful businesswoman who could be as tough as she needed to be, and as demanding. I knew that. I knew that she had power and was counted among the people whose good opinion you needed if you hoped to get important things done. I knew she knew her way around politics and used her money and influence for issues and candidates she favored. But I hadn't thought of her as a player. I had seen no evidence of it, though I admit I wasn't looking.

Watching her now, though, listening to her, I knew she had the instinct for it, and, I suspected, the ruthlessness as well. She had selected the bait that would catch Dace Havershamp. You could see the gleam of satisfaction in her eyes.

Paul Isham smiled and nodded to Rhae in agreement. "Dace will go for it all right. And with Judge Blue already committed, we're more than halfway home. As for Wilson and Arnow, when they learn that Dace and the Judge are on board, they'll want to be a part of this, too."

"Let's not count unhatched chickens," Michael cautioned.

"Arnow and Wilson? Paul's right," I said. "They'll sign on."

"Well, let's not celebrate until we talk with them."

That was planned for the following week. Michael and Rhae would meet with Jonathan Wilson in Louisville on Monday. The next day, Michael and I would head east to Ashland to enlist Arnow.

On the way, we planned to stop through Lost Creek and find out what Hanna Collins had waiting for us.

I had a nagging unease about this. I had the feeling that it had something to do with Benjamin Dannan, though I couldn't fathom what, and I couldn't conjure anything that could be negative. From all I knew about the man from the research I had done for the story on the 25th anniversary of his death, Benjamin Dannan bordered on being revered

He stood for things.

He believed that government ought to serve, not make servants of, its people. He thought that the rich ought not take advantage of the poor, or the strong abuse the weak. He demanded that people be treated decently, regardless of their station, and insisted that opportunities ought to be open to all – no special privileges, secret handshakes, or hidden doors that opened only to certain colors of skin, or wealth or power. From the pulpit of the *Journal* he fought for these things.

The people whose wrongs he helped right loved him. Those whose ambitions he thwarted were not so kindly disposed.

There is no doubt Benjamin Dannan had faults. Too quick a temper, a weakness for the taste of bourbon, an air of cockiness that could be taken for arrogance, and perhaps a touch of a messiah complex. No one said the latter to me in exactly that way, but there were comments like "He thought he was God Almighty, sitting in judgment," and "he wanted justice for the common man and he was going to see they got it, whether they wanted it or not."

I can attest to none of this, only to the fact that some of the people who knew him said these things.

It *is* a fact that in the section of the Cumberland Mountains where the bloody mine wars were fought Benjamin Dannan was revered. This can be verified even today by mentioning his name at any union hall in the area.

Benjamin Dannan went up there and took their side and told their story to the rest of the state and the country – the only newspaperman to do that. He took the miners' cause, at considerable personal risk, against the mine owners and most of the rest of the state's business and political establishment, none of whom wanted to see unions established anywhere. He did not do it from his desk at the *Journal,* safe in the Bluegrass, but from a pickup truck and a small hotel room in the middle of the war zone in Harlan. Yes, the miners and their families loved him. He was one of theirs.

And he made a difference. He brought so much public attention to bear on the outrage being done the miners and their families that finally the state was forced to step in, and honest elections were held, and the miners won.

Hanna Collins lived her whole long life in that country. If she didn't know Benjamin Dannan, at the very least she must have known of him. It seemed to me there was reason to be edgy about the little silver box she had left waiting for his son.

## ELEVEN

The road to finding out led east through Lexington to Winchester, then out of the gentle pastures of the Bluegrass up Hwy 15 past Stanton and Slade to Bethany and Jackson, into the Cumberland forest and onto the edge of the Cumberland plateau – oak and pine, maple and fir, rising ridge on ridge to become the mighty Appalachians.

The first Europeans into these mountains were probably Spanish. Some of Hernando DeSoto's men could have ranged this far north as they searched through the Southeast in the mid-1500s, burning Indian villages and killing hostages. Certainly parts of Juan Pardo's expedition twenty years later did.

The French, coming out of Canada, trapped down this far. So did the English and Dutch and other adventurers after hides and game. A few settlers ventured in, braver or more desperate or more seduced by illusions and dreams than most, moving north from the Carolinas, pushing west from Virginia – the Scots-Irish mostly, and the Germans – threading the valleys, scaling the ridges, finding land to clear for homes and farms, edging their way in to unknown territory.

Then, just before the Revolutionary War, Daniel Boone opened the door to Kentucky through the Cumberland Gap. The path to the new West lay open – except for the Cherokee and Shawnee who would contest it bloodily, and the French who wanted as much of the American continent as they could grasp, and the British, who, though they had lost, didn't give up easily.

The mountains that Boone found his way through, the country we were heading into, is different in ways not explainable by words. There is the feeling that you are intruding, that this is enchanted ground. But the land – the mountains and forests, the crispness of the air and the quiet of the backcountry – the land is so majestic that unvoiced apprehensions dissolve finally into only a casual foreboding.

We estimated about three hours to Lost Creek and had asked Miss Young to meet us at The Mountain Home around mid-afternoon.

We decided to take Rhae's 1955 Thunderbird – a red convertible, a beauty – figuring its size and cornering abilities would be just the thing for the roads we expected on the way to Ashland. Rhae drove it rarely, had purchased it on a whim as a birthday present to herself in a year when she was feeling frumpy. That passed rapidly. She put it in a garage at the farm and only used it in the spring with the top down and the dogwood blooming. Michael sometimes took it on his infrequent visits home. At McKinnon they insisted he use a company car and driver. His time was too valuable to be wasted on driving and his person too valuable to be chanced in the hands of someone other than a professional on the freeways around San Francisco. He suffered that and thirsted for the freedom and excitement of the T-Bird when he was home.

Michael was a natural behind the wheel. He was a natural at most things.

The mountain roads didn't disappoint.

Once out of the Bluegrass we were on a narrow, twisting two-lane road that hugged the creek beds where it could and cut along the sides of the ridges where it couldn't. The curves were demanding, tight loops bending back upon themselves or s-ing and z-ing, and the straight-aways were narrow and pocked with holes. This was pay-attention kind of driving where you had to be careful to leave enough room for a coal-truck across the centerline on the curves and be always aware of the condition of the berm and the depth of the drop-off. We had the top down and a balmy day and the rhythm of swaying with the road got us both. It was lovely.

But we were conspicuous. A small red car with no roof scooting down their blacktop wasn't a usual sight for people in the area. Heads swiveled in the vehicles we passed. Oncoming coal trucks slowed down. A few pickups behind us tried to close the gap to get a better look, but weren't up to it.

I knew as soon as we cleared Lexington that we were going to attract attention. And fairly soon, after we had made our stop in Lost Creek and become identified with the car, the mountain grapevine would work and we wouldn't be unknowns anymore. I imagined that by the time we made the turn to Ashland, people would be lining the highway waiting to watch us pass.

In fact, we weren't that much of a spectacle, but I wanted to get in and find out what Hanna Collins had waiting for us and get out with as little notice as possible – and the same with Arnow.

No chance of that with our little red car. We had taken the Buick down to see Dace Havershamp and Judge Blue – solid, respectable, unexciting transportation, exactly the right cover. Now we were working our way through the Cumberland Mountains in about as conspicuous a way as could be managed.

But Miss Young was pleased. The little red T-bird easing over Lost Creek on the one-lane bridge had a strangely exciting effect on her, she told us later, and she was almost immediately taken by a surprising urge to ride in it. Her excitement was obvious when she greeted us.

"Oh, Mr. Dannan, I am so glad you are here...and Mr. Clark, welcome." But her eyes were hardly on us. They were on the car. "It's a Thunderbird, isn't it? I have never been in one."

Miss Young could barely have been in high school when the T-bird was built. The '55s became classics, collector's items, incarnations of what cars ought to look like. No one who ever saw one ever held any other idea. No one who ever rode in one ever thought another vehicle better. And that's what Marne Young wanted – she wanted to ride in it. She was so obviously taken with the car, that Michael, right there on the porch of Mountain Home before we had even properly said hello, feeling her interest and playing the gallant, offered her a ride then and there.

She blushed slightly and apologized. "Do please forgive me. I don't get excited about cars. They are just something to get you from here to there. I don't know what got into me. But it is such a pretty car. All you see around here are pickups and station wagons. Yes, thank you, I would love to ride in it. But not now. That's not what you came for."

She was a very appealing young lady. From her letter I had expected a middle-aged woman resigned to spinsterhood and bolstering her self-esteem with the sacrifice of service to others, proper and plain, well-schooled, well-mannered, not from the region, but attracted here by the nobility of Christian effort in the backwoods of Appalachia.

Marne Young looked to be in her mid-twenties – a slim, smiling brunette far prettier than any aide in a home for the terminally ill ought to be. I couldn't imagine why she was at Lost Creek.

She took Michael's hand in a totally unaffected way, smiled into his face and said, "Let's go see Aunt Hanna's room."

The Mountain Home sat back on a shelf above Lost River. The shelf was about 100 yards wide and ran for perhaps a quarter of a mile along the east bank of Lost River as it worked its way north to meld into the East Fork of the Kentucky just this side of Jackson.

It was a big wood-framed two-story house with a long front porch under an overhanging roof. There were swings on either end of the porch and rockers on both sides of the entrance door. The porch looked out on a wide, grassy lawn. A large black oak rose off to the left offering afternoon shade. Several sycamores flanked the river line. Flowerbeds put color in front of the porch and climbing vines trailed over a split-rail fence that lined the outer edges of the lawn. Off to the right near the bridge, there was a small Baptist chapel with an Episcopalian-like steeple. A softball field anchored the other end of the property. I doubted the residents of the Mountain Home played softball and assumed the field was part of the youth program of the church.

I could imagine sitting on that porch in the warming sun on autumn afternoons with the big oak turning color and how pleasant that must be. I hoped Hanna Collins' passing was easy.

Her room was on the second floor, on the front corner, looking out to the oak and the ball field. She could have watched the kids at play from here...and the leaves turn. The room was furnished simply – an iron bedstead covered with a blue and white quilt in a star design, a rocker by the window, starched lace curtains, a chest of drawers, a small desk and chair, an old steamer trunk – the kind people used to use when they took long trips by rail or boat. There was a King James Bible on the small lamp table by the bed. No pictures. No personal keepsakes. Those must have been collected and packed away.

"Isn't it dignified," Miss Young said, "just like her. Quiet and dignified." She explained that a new "guest" wasn't expected until next week, so the room had been left as Hanna Collins had arranged it.

"The bed and the rocker and the chest are hers," Miss Young said. "I don't know what we'll do with them. Mr. Bristow doesn't want them. There aren't any other relatives."

"Mr. Bristow?"

"Mr. Jesse Bristow," she said. "Her nephew. Do you know him?"

There could be more than one Jesse Bristow, I thought.

"The one who is the head of the Mine Owners Association?" she said. "He is such a lovely man."

I stammered.

"The names fool you," she said. "Hanna Collins is, well, was...no *is* ...death doesn't change the fact, does it? Hanna Collins is Mr. Bristow's maiden aunt – his mother's older sister. The mother died young, TB they think, the medicine up here was so bad in those days I doubt they really knew. The father was already dead, lost in a mine cave-in.

"When Mr. Bristow's mother died, Aunt Hanna took Mr. Bristow and his baby sister to raise. Mr. Bristow was about 14, I guess. He had to give up school and go into the mines full time to help earn a living for the three of them. Isn't it such a typical mountain story?

"Sometimes it seems God isn't paying attention to the poor people in these mountains. They take on such sorrow. They don't lose their faith. They take care of each other and they keep on. Surely He has something wonderful in store for them...here or in the hereafter. He must."

She had turned to the window. Her gaze was fixed on the sky. The way she had said "He must" sounded more like a demand than a statement.

The tone surprised me. Miss Young was turning out to be nothing like what I expected. I came expecting to be in the midst of the fundamentalist sects that people these mountains – the speak–in–tongues, fall–into–trances, drop–into–fits, dance–and-shake-and-handle-snakes, heal–by–the–laying–on–of–hands Christians I had heard so much about, but had never experienced. If Miss Young was of such a persuasion, she was shattering my illusions. She said something under her breath that we couldn't make out – a prayer? a bargain? – then smiled sadly over her shoulder at us and turned back to Michael.

"But the things Aunt Hanna left for you, Mr. Dannan. You must be eager to see them." She led Michael to the steamer trunk.

Taking a brass key from the pocket of her skirt, she opened the trunk and stood back. The scent of violets drifted up. Inside there were blankets and bed-clothes neatly folded, what looked to be a flannel robe and long white nightgowns, and several sweaters of muted color in cardigan style.

"Her things," Miss Young said.

On top of these lay a blue envelope and a small oblong silver box.

Michael took the box and the envelope from the chest, pulled the rocker over closer to the window for more light and sat down.

"You would probably like a little privacy," Miss Young said. "Come on, Mr. Clark," she said to me, "I'll show you the grounds and the rest of the house." To Michael she said, "When you're ready, we'll be on the porch.'"

We left him there sitting at the window, the box and the letter still unopened.

Miss Young led me down the stairs, out the door, and across the lawn to the edge of Lost River. It was a somnolent afternoon, a drowsy buzz of little winged insects in the air, a light breeze, warm and pleasant.

No one else seemed to be about ...napping, I thought, or sitting peacefully in a rocker in the sun.

"Can you imagine a lovelier place to die," she said

I looked at her, unsure whether she was being sarcastic or bitter or artless.

"I mean it," she said. "Can you imagine a lovelier place to die? If He is going to take us, and He will, can you picture a more beautiful place then this? This is where I would like to be when my time comes."

I had no thought of dying, not on such an afternoon.

"What are you doing here?" I asked her.

"What?"

"How do you come to be here? Why are you in this lonely, isolated, practically unknown place?"

"Isn't that a personal matter?"

"You're not one of those sacrifice-and-prayer, suffering-and-denial, I've-given-my-life-to-Jesus-women, are you," I said.

She smiled. "Well, perhaps some sacrifice and prayer, but no, I am not a religious kook, if that's what you're asking."

I laughed. "I guess I was. So...?"

"So?" she mimicked.

"Why are you here?"

"Let's talk of something else," she said.

I was smart enough to know to drop it.

"Indulge a newspaperman's addiction to curiosity then and tell me something of yourself."

It turned out she was a daughter of a section of west Kentucky known as The Barrens, the child of a well-to-do family of fundamentalist Baptists whose land holdings outside Glasgow had grown from a small grant made to an ancestor for service in the Revolutionary War to cover a sizeable portion of the county. Now, with aged parents and no siblings, she would be the first woman to inherit it all. I gathered it was not a prospect she savored. Like most of her peers, she had gone South to university and was a graduate of a very proper girl's college in New Orleans named Sophie Newcomb (I had been right about the manners) with a master's degree in cultural anthropology from the University of Georgia (which possibility would never have crossed my mind). She had come to Appalachia on a folklore study grant. How she came to Lost Creek she didn't say and I didn't press any further.

"And this is where you met Hanna Collins?

"She was such a remarkable woman. I was so blessed to know her."

"What will you do now?

"Stay on here. I am needed and I have work to do."

"Are there other patients?

"Guests? Just two. Another comes this weekend. There is only the Reverend Jamison, he runs the place, the cook, a nurse and me. Caring for the dying is hard, hard work. It is all we can do to help the few we have here. If more come... Yes, I am needed. I can give a little comfort, help with the chores, ease the load. And I can still find time to do the work that brought me here. Lost River is a perfect location for that. Did you know it was the first settlement in the county…one of the first on the Cumberland Plateau? It was an important community then. It is nothing now, not even a crossroad, just a post office and place-name, but it was the beginning in this county."

"Your work…?

"My doctoral thesis. The Melungeons. I am trying to gather what's known of the history of the Melungeons. Do you know about them?"

Just then we heard Michael calling to us from the porch.

As we walked toward him, he moved to the swing at the end near the big oak tree and sat waiting.

Miss Young took the seat beside him. Michael leaned back and started the swing gently in motion. I pulled a rocker up to face them. The sun was behind the ridgeline now. The insects were quiet, but birds had begun their afternoon calling, locating each other, getting ready for night.

The little silver box and the blue envelope were in Michael's hands, which rested lightly in his lap. He held them carefully, as if they were fragile, but didn't look at them. He kept his gaze on us, smiling in a distracted way to me and to Miss Young, but saying nothing.

I nodded to the box. "Was it worth the drive?"

He frowned, then lifted the box and looked closely at it. "This is very old, Theo, very old. Miss Young, how old do you think it must be? Older than the settlement at Lost Creek I would bet, older than the Revolution."

He held the box out to me. It was about the size of my hand, oblong, and heavier than I expected. Its surfaces were plain and so highly polished they gleamed. The hinges that allowed the lid to open were invisible and the line where the sides met couldn't be seen. It was a stunning piece of workmanship. On the cover, time worn, faint, was a small symbol. It seemed the representation of a sailing ship, sails full, heeling slightly as if tacking on a fresh wind and running toward a cross in the clouds beyond. On the underside was what I took to be a maker's mark, indistinct also, but clear enough to be recognizable as the letters CV partially enclosed by a semi-circle.

"Yes, it is very old." Miss Young gently took the box from me. She ran her hand over the surface. "Supposedly this dates to the 1500s. Something special for the safekeeping of precious items. Made for a noble lady, we think. And a good luck token for traveling – see the cross guiding the ship, keeping it safe? It's Spanish or Portuguese. Most likely Spanish. The CV could be for Carlos Vistoramonte, of Seville. He was a well-known silversmith of that era. His symbol was his initials inside a half circle."

"How do you know this?" I asked.

"Aunt Hanna and I often talked about the silver case. We made up stories about it. It was the only really valuable possession she had. The little box had always been in her family, she said, but she didn't know its provenance. I photographed it and sent the photos to friends at the University. This is what they told me."

"Do you know what she kept in it?

"No. She never opened it for me and I never asked. On the afternoon of the day she died she had me put the box in her trunk along with the envelope. I was to keep them both safe until Mr. Dannan could collect them."

"You don't know what was in it?"

"No."

"I'm not sure I do either," Michael said.

It was such a surprising statement that Miss Young stopped the swing.

"But you've seen it," I said.

'I have seen it, but I don't know what it means."

"Tell me," Miss Young urged. "Perhaps I'll know."

Michael took the case back. "She left me a puzzle."

That was all he would say.

He was pensive as we made the drive back up the mountain to Quicksand. It was obvious that he didn't want to talk, so I put on a sweater against the chill in the open car and occupied my mind with watching the stars come out and trying to name them. As we checked into the little motel on the ridge overlooking the river, he said, "This is more curious than I could have possibly imagined, Theo. I need to sleep on it. So hold your questions until tomorrow."

That was all I got that night.

# TWELVE

The silver box held a gold locket.

It was oval in shape and about the size of a half-dollar coin. Inside the locket was a photograph of a young woman and a man, both smiling happily. In the envelope there were four old newspaper clippings and a key.

"Do you recognize the man?" Michael said, handing me the locket.

I took the locket and looked, then looked again.

We were sitting over breakfast in a little restaurant on the road not far from the motel. A few coal truckers were at the counter, caps still on, working on coffee. A table or two of locals, merchants and farmers, were arranged by the window engaged in the bantering conversation that said they were regulars. A few looked up when we came in, curious for a moment, then went back to their stories. We took a booth near the back. A waitress in a green apron was putting fresh baked pies on the shelf above the counter. Another was spelling out the luncheon specials on a blackboard by the cash register.

The man in the picture in the locket was Benjamin Dannan.

He was younger in the photo than in the shots I remembered. But he was unmistakable. Black hair neatly combed, a strong, handsome face, a wide engaging smile. The girl next to him seemed inordinately pleased and proud of herself, delighted with the circumstance of being in the photograph. She had the high cheekbones of a model and eyes so bright they seemed to sparkle out of the old photograph. Her hair was dark and fell in curls to her shoulders. She was an arrestingly attractive young woman.

"Look at the inscription," Michael said.

I turned the locket over. On the back was inscribed, "With the love of Owen, Amos, Llewellyn, and me."

"What...?"

"I don't know," Michael said. "I don't know about any of this. None of it makes sense."

"Who is the girl?"

"Jesse Bristow's sister."

I was too surprised to say anything.

He handed me the clippings.

They had the brittle edges old newsprint takes on. I lifted them carefully.

The first was from the *Lexington Herald* dated June 23, 1939. It was a story about Sue Bristow being named to the faculty of Berea College where she was to be a professor of economics with a special portfolio for research into the economics of mining communities of the Southern Appalachians, particularly the economics of company towns. Miss Bristow was 22 years old and a Berea graduate who, having just completed her work for a master's in applied economics at the University of Kentucky, would become Berea's first female professor in the dismal science. There was a photograph. It was the girl in the locket.

I put the clipping down and picked up the next one. Michael sipped his coffee and didn't say anything.

This one was a faded feature from the *Cincinnati Enquirer* dated May 8, 1931 – eight years earlier – and playing under a four-column head that read *"At The Battle Of Evarts, A Little Angel."*

The Battle of Evarts was the first big clash in the war that broke out when miners in Harlan County revolted against the owners' heavy hands.

The conditions in the coalfields were awful that year. Coal prices were depressed. The mine owners' profits were sagging. To help make up for the loss in income, the owners cut the miners' wages. Adding insult to injury, they raised prices in the company stores at the same time. The company stores were where the miners got their groceries and clothing – at exorbitant prices and on credit at usurious interest rates

Already on the edge of poverty, the wage cuts and price increases were a crushing blow. The miners fought back with the only weapon they had – their labor. They walked out, demanding a living wage and fair prices for food and housing.

More troubling to the owners, they started to form a union.

That couldn't be tolerated. My God, man, that's communism! That's un-American! No, by damn, no unions!

To underscore their displeasure, the owners kicked the miners out of company housing. In company towns, and all the mining communities were company towns, the only housing available was company housing. Rents were outrageous, but the miners had no other option, no matter how high the rent.

And for good measure, to be certain everyone understood who buttered whose bread, the companies cut off the miners' credit at the company stores.

Homeless and hungry, their families suffering and the men feeling almost helpless, a sense of awful outrage began to grow among them. Bad trouble had to follow.

It would be a lopsided contest. The companies ruled the political structure of the county. They controlled the police, the courts, and the few social services that were available.

There was nowhere for the miners to turn – no allies, no protectors, no advocates.

The only possible countervailing force would be a union.

But the sheriff and his deputies broke up their organizing meetings and roughed up their leaders. Soon, gangs of toughs from the back streets of Cincinnati and Wheeling were brought in and deputized to add more muscle to the sheriff's presence.

Men were pulled from their homes at night and beaten. Property was burned. Death threats were made. It was a nasty, bitter time.

Many of the evicted miners found their way to Evarts, a non-company town about twelve miles from Harlan. They could find a little shelter for their families and a bit of credit there.

Bloody violence was inevitable.

It came on the morning of the fifth day of May.

An ambush.

Ten sheriff's deputies were escorting scabbing workers in three cars up the road from Evarts to the Black Diamond Mine. About two hundred yards outside town, the miners attacked the convoy. In the ensuing gunfight, three deputies, one of the scabs, and more than a dozen striking miners were killed. No one knows how many were wounded.

The story I was reading told of the immediate aftermath of the battle, while the dead and wounded lay scattered in the ditches and along the road.

Among the first non-combatants on the killing field was a young girl of about fourteen. She immediately began to care for the wounded. Whether miner or scab or sheriff's deputy made no difference. She staunched blood flows with what she had with her and with what she could scavenge off the wounded – handkerchiefs, scarves, cloth torn from shirts.

One man, a deputy sheriff, bleeding badly from a punctured artery in his thigh, thought she saved his life, and though she was from the other side, called her "a little angel." The first doctor to arrive, the company doctor from Harlan – there were no doctors in Evarts – thought that description was right.

The girl had helped save a number of lives. It turned out that she was Sue Bristow, young sister of Jesse Bristow, one of the striking miners.

Forty-three of the miners would be charged with murder. Jesse Bristow was not among them, but he was nowhere to be found. He had disappeared up the ridges.

The reporter asked the young girl why she rushed to the aid of men who were the enemy of her brother and her friends. "They were hurt," she said. "You can't just let people suffer. Jesse wouldn't expect me to stand by."

"And how did you come to be there?" he asked. "Did you know about the ambush?"

Sue Bristow wouldn't say.

The interview was conducted in Hanna Collins' house in Evarts where Sue and her brother lived with their aunt while he worked in the mine. The reporter was favored with a cup of tea, hot biscuits, fresh butter and strawberry jam, "better than a high tea at any posh hotel" and left thoroughly charmed.

There was a photo also – of a younger Sue Bristow, dark hair tied back with a ribbon, a solemn stare unwittingly warm, standing at the edge of the Evarts Cemetery. I recognized the eyes.

The next clipping was a two-paragraph brief from the *Jackson Herald*, the small county-seat weekly, noting that Sue Bristow, age eight, and her brother, Jesse, age sixteen, had taken first place in the Lost Creek Music Festival that spring weekend. They had won the folk song competition. Sue sang; Jesse accompanied her on the guitar. The song was "Over Yandro."

The last clipping was a small boldface death notice from the *Jackson Herald* announcing the death of Sue Bristow, age twenty-three, on Tuesday, Oct. 22, 1941. The body was at Carson's Funeral Home in Jackson. Visitation was to be from 4 p.m. to 8 p.m. the following Wednesday and Thursday nights. Funeral services would be held at the Lost Creek Baptist Chapel at 2:30 p.m. Friday, Oct. 25, interment to follow in the cemetery there.

I put all the clippings carefully back in the envelope and handed it to Michael.

The waitress came over and began clearing the table. We both sat quietly, considering, while she poured hot coffee.

When she left, Michael said, "I suppose there's a message in all this, but I don't get it."

I wasn't sure whether he didn't get it or didn't want to get it.

"Hanna Collins wants you to know there is a connection between your father and Sue Bristow. And she wants you to appreciate that Sue Bristow is special."

"Why?"

"What about the key, what's it to?

"A safe deposit box at a bank in Berea."

"Maybe what's in it will tell us."

"We would have to go to Berea for that. There isn't time now. We have a date with banker Arnow in Ashland. So tell me what you think?"

I didn't know what I thought. I hadn't thought about it in any organized way yet. Michael had been given glimpses of Sue Bristow as a young girl, as a young woman, and dead. He had been shown that she was tender and bold and talented and bright – and that there was a connection between her and his father. And that she was Jesse Bristow's sister.

Why? Why did Hanna Collins want Michael to know this?

The mystery annoyed me. I was apprehensive that it might have some unforeseeable negative implication for the campaign. I thought we should give top priority to unwinding the secret. I would get to Berea as fast as I could. That's what I told Michael.

"How do you read it?" I asked.

He took a sip of coffee, swirled the remainder around in the cup and stared into it. Smiling for the first time that morning, he said, "I knew I couldn't do without you."

"Berea, then?" I said.

"After Sattis Arnow," he said. "Arnow's support takes priority now."

He took the picture up and became somber again.

"They're more than acquaintances."

He spoke slowly. It seemed almost as if he was talking to himself.

He looked up at me.

"She must be a student he met somewhere, or helper on some project he was involved with."

"Probably," I said.

"Did you notice," he said, "they died in the same week?"

## THIRTEEN

We drove, snaking that little red car across mountains of east Kentucky, our nose set toward Ashland, the only town of any size on the state's entire eastern border.

From Quicksand we headed up to Salyersville, then jogged a little west of north to West Liberty, then cut back on a northeasterly slant to Grayson. We hit Highway 64 there, the main road east from Lexington to the West Virginia line. From there it was a straight shot into Ashland and our meeting with Sattis Arnow.

You may wonder why I am giving you so much detail on the routes we followed. I want to show a bit of the way Michael's mind worked. He felt he should know the country. He wanted to experience what it felt like and smelled like, wanted to get an idea of the little towns and how people lived.

For most of his adult life, Michael had been dropping in and out of world centers, jetting around in fancy airplanes and big limousines. He was a big-time, big-city boy. All he knew of our state was what he remembered from his youth and most of that was limited to the Bluegrass. We had made some short hunting and fishing excursions out into west Kentucky and down toward the Tennessee border on a few of his trips home, but we were playing then, not on a serious mission. And so far as I knew, he had never been in the eastern mountains.

If he intended to play our game on our playground, he felt he needed to know the territory and its ways.

In those first few weeks after he returned, making our calls on what would ultimately be his senior team, we saw the state from east to west and north to south. Saw it first hand. Got the feel of it and the people. It was cursory, but it was enough to get us started. You would be surprised at what happens driving little two-lane country roads – how the character of the land and the mood of the people seeps into you.

A few truckers were standing around the car in the gravel parking lot outside the restaurant in Quicksand when we came out from breakfast. At first I thought we might be in for a little hassling – city boys, fancy car – sissy stuff. But they were simply interested, asked how fast she would go, and shook their heads admiringly.

The sun wasn't high enough when we left to throw light into the deep hollows we were driving through. Michael seemed honor-bound to make the whole run with the top down come everything but rain and even though it was summer, it can be cold down in the basins in the morning chill. But on the straight stretches where the sun could reach us, it was warm and glorious.

We talked hardly at all. Both our minds were occupied with the strange bequest of Hanna Collins and the riddle of Sue Bristow.

After a long while, somewhere near Grayson, he asked me "How would you write it?"

We were on a straight stretch and I was watching a hawk hunting on the ridgeline above us, hanging motionless on a little thermal, ready to dive.

"Write what?" I said.

"What story would you write on the basis of what we've learned so far?"

I kept my gaze on the hawk and took my time answering.

"I wouldn't write anything," I said finally. "I don't know enough."

The hawk flicked its wings and glided out of the thermal, gained altitude and began its circling hunt again. The target of the moment must not have broken cover, or the hunter became impatient.

"If you used your imagination to fill in some of the blanks, what would you write?"

"I don't write fiction," I said.

But I had been asking myself the same question. If I were writing from what I then knew, what would I write?

The key to all this, I thought, was what Hanna Collins wanted Michael to know. And *why* she wanted him to know it.

"What are you going to tell Rhae and Paul Isham about what you found?"

He didn't answer.

I turned my gaze back up to the sky, searching for the hawk.

## FOURTEEN

Sattis Arnow was about 5'6", wiry, and dressed in black – black suit, black vest, and narrow black tie knotted in a tight four-in-hand against a starched shirt so white it was almost blinding. He stood at the side of his desk in the far corner of the open floor at the Miners & Merchants Bank of Ashland, rocking on his toes, watching us, his hands clasped behind his back, a slight scowl on his face.

His area, the platform side where the loans were made and the business done, was separated from the teller stations across the way by a waist-high partition of highly polished mahogany. There was a swinging entrance gate with a guard beside it. We identified ourselves, but Arnow was already walking toward us. He recognized us, or recognized Michael. They had not met, so it must have been from Michael's pictures in the newspapers or on television.

Impatience flowed from the little banker. We were a half-hour late.

It was early afternoon and the bank was relatively empty. Only a few people were in line for the tellers. A young man and his wife were at a desk two down from Arnow's, sitting quietly while a pompous-looking middle-aged man in jacket and tie studied a folder of papers before him. The couple looked uncomfortable and embarrassed. Supplicants for a loan, I guessed. Why else would you be sitting so exposed in the house of the great god Mammon?

I had always thought bankers to be guilty of the grossest of indignities – forcing people entreating for loans to sit in full public view with no privacy at all. What is there to like about people so insensitive. But then, you see, I have this feeling that having to borrow money is embarrassing, a sign that you can't make it on your own, a marker of inadequacy. I know that's not the case. I know without banks and borrowing, homes wouldn't be built or educations paid for. Still, the feeling hangs on. It must be something I learned, or ingested at home as a child. My dad never borrowed money.

I smiled encouragement at the young man and his wife and fell in behind Michael to shake hands with Arnow.

He took a pocket watch from his vest and glanced at it, then took Michael's hand.

"Punctuality, Mr. Dannan, is next to Godliness," he said.

"It is, Mr. Arnow," Michael said, "and something which I practice religiously. But sometimes even the righteous, though they have allowed themselves wide margins of extra time, can't levitate over farm wagons and coal trucks on two-lane roads. I apologize and hope we've not inconvenienced you too much."

Arnow humphed and turned to me.

"Theo Clark. I read your column every now and then. On occasion you get things right." His hand was surprisingly big. He gave me a powerful squeeze and motioned to the chairs on either side of his desk.

"What's on your mind, Mr. Dannan? I don't assume you need money."

Michael laughed and started to reply. I stopped him. I wasn't comfortable to have this discussion in an open room within earshot of anyone who happened by. I said so.

A hint of a smile crossed Arnow's face.

"You can trust me to be smarter than to put myself in a position where others can overhear my private conversations," he said. "You are a suspicious man, aren't you? I like skeptics. They keep us honest." The small smile expanded into a broad grin and his whole appearance changed. Rather than a sour little man in black, he seemed warm, even likeable of a sudden. "Unless you intend to shout, this desk is positioned far enough back in the room that no one can overhear us. You don't intend to shout, do you?"

I stammered. Michael laughed. Arnow, too. It was a nice little break-the-ice-at-my-expense moment. Arnow gestured to the chairs on either side of his desk and we sat down.

I still wasn't entirely comfortable that our little corner was as secure as Arnow thought it to be. Michael had no qualms about it, though, and he began to lay out our plan and the role he hoped Sattis Arnow would play.

The little man listened intently, not interrupting, not nodding or offering any facial expressions that were decipherable. The work of the bank went on around us. He was right about the privacy such an open space could afford if properly engineered.

It was instructive to watch Arnow read Michael. Arnow was one of that rare breed of businessman who becomes successful despite looks, personality, or lack of physical presence. His Miners & Merchants Bank, which he had slyly assembled by picking off one little country bank after another and merging them into a money machine, was the biggest in the eastern end of the state. Arnow's more physically impressive, more personable business competitors were no match for his determination or intelligence. He ate them up. No hard feelings, nothing personal so far as he was concerned. He held mortgages on most of the major commercial real estate in Ashland and was the principal banker to the tangle of oil and chemical companies that flanked the Ohio River on the Kentucky side and spilled east toward Huntington, West Virginia. And the mines. And the railroads. And the public utilities. He carried the Commonwealth's deposits for a third of the state, and had on his books more home mortgages, auto dealer paper, and farm loans than his closest three rivals combined.

If there was anyone more powerful in that end of the state, we couldn't find him. And because he was an economic power, he was a political power – bigger than anyone in the mountains except Jesse Bristow. Maybe bigger than Jesse, but that hadn't been tested yet.

Arnow didn't make many waves. He was far less identified in the public mind with the political process than Dace Havershamp or Judge Blue or even Jonathan Wilson in Louisville. He left the fancy footwork and the notoriety to others. All he wanted was what he wanted and he usually got it quietly and with little fanfare.

I watched Arnow watch Michael and understood why his competitors failed. He concentrated. You could almost hear his mind digesting what Michael was saying, judging it, filing it away in neat little trays to be studied later. But that was only a part his process.

Arnow didn't ask questions. He didn't fill the silences between sentences. He waited. He listened without reaction. He was a sponge, a vacuum. From a turn of words, the inflection of voice, the attitude of the body, he seemed to be sucking out all the said and unsaid meaning that was there. If was as if he were listening for the unconscious tunes that run inside people's heads. Know the tune, call the dance.

"That's our plan," Michael finished. "We have Dace Havershamp in west Kentucky, Judge Blue for the county courthouse crowd, and Jonathan Wilson in the Bluegrass for the business interests. If you join us, with your prestige and your influence with the unions, we would be unbeatable. But Jesse Bristow won't be happy if you do."

"You know Jesse, do you?" It was the first question Arnow had asked.

"No," Michael said, "but we know his record and his reputation. And we know he intends and expects to be Governor."

"You know him?" Arnow said, turning to me.

"No, sir," I said. "I covered the Buford hearings and the Sattler trial, and I have had some casual contact with him on one story or another, but I haven't spent any time with him or interviewed him directly. He would never sit still for it and I never had an interest strong enough to push it."

Arnow leaned back in his big leather chair and looked around the room. The young couple had left, I hoped with the money. There were people at two of the teller cages. The man who had been at the desk with the young couple was shaking hands with a neatly dressed man in a double-breasted blue suit and ushering him to a chair – a man of some importance it seemed, since the only deference being shown was coming from the loan officer.

Sattis Arnow turned his attention back to us.

"Jesse Bristow..." he said, with something like admiration, or maybe it was accusation, in his voice, "...Jesse Bristow could charm a bird out of a tree."

He nodded his head in agreement with himself, and said," Yes, a bird off a limb even if he looked like a cat. Or whip a panther barehanded and never be winded."

He paused thoughtfully again, and then said, "Let me tell you a little about Jesse.

"Jesse was already six-foot tall by the time he was fourteen. He was thin as a rail then, but tough. Nobody pushed him around. He is what…six-two, six-three now and must weigh two-and-a-quarter. Imagine how much harder he is to push now.

"He went into the mines full time when his father died. His mother was already dead and he and his little sister Sue were living with their aunt Hanna Collins in a cabin Jesse's father had built back up one of the hollows just outside of Evarts. Jesse was their only source of income, except for what Hanna Collins made from taking in washing from the wives of the mine officials and some of the single men.

"He was a bright boy. His teachers at the county school didn't want to see him drop out, but what could he, or they, do?

"Jesse lied to get the job. He was big enough that he could pass and the bosses didn't care. They knew he was underage. Jesse's father had worked in the same mine. Died in it. In a cave-in. So they knew Jesse, or knew about him. Maybe they gave him the job because they knew he needed it. I wish I thought that. I don't. I never knew a mine owner to give a rat's for anything but making money.

"Anyway, I first met Jesse when he was fourteen. I was twenty-four and a circuit loan officer for a small bank in Harlan, making a regular swing out to the little towns, that is, the towns that were littler than Harlan, which was none too big itself. This was a very unusual practice for its time. No one else was doing it and since I had no competition, I could charge whatever interest I liked. It was profitable business and almost risk free. Mountain people always paid their debts. It was a matter of pride with them. Nothing is more important to a man of these mountains, or was, than his reputation.

"I was feeling good about myself. The circuit-riding thing was my idea and I was taking a lot of pride in having been considered strong enough to get the job over some of my more experienced colleagues. It didn't occur to me that they might not want it. You had to travel in all kinds of weather and the accommodations in some of the places weren't all that good. But it was the best job I ever had, and the smartest move I could have made, because I got to know the country and could see opportunities that my more comfortable colleagues didn't notice.

"I kept a little office in Evarts and I was in it one Wednesday afternoon, my regular scheduled time for Evarts, when, as I say, this very big boy came through my door and introduced himself. I am not sensitive about my size. I was at one time, as a child growing up, but I had moved past it by then. I would like to be taller, but I am not. Being small can sometimes be an advantage. People think you're no threat. They aren't intimidated by you. So they don't pay you much attention. That can be an advantage.

"I had hair then and was more personable, I imagine, being so young myself. I wasn't attractive by any means, but I had a good smile – people tell me I have a good smile – and people warmed to that. You can get away with a lot if you smile just the right way at just the right time.

"Anyway, this really big boy comes into my little office and when I stand to greet him it's as if I am looking straight up a tall pine tree. The boy realized this, was sensitive to it, and I think it embarrassed him because he thought I was being embarrassed, and without asking or thinking, he sat down immediately. I never forgot that.

"I smiled my best smile, shook his hand, sat down myself and asked him how I could help him.

"He was nervous and not quite sure of what to do, but he didn't seem intimidated and he knew what he was there for, so he told me straight and simple. He wanted to borrow enough money to buy his aunt a sewing machine she had seen in the Sears' catalogue. She intended to take in sewing for the town's unmarried males, but more important, to became a seamstress for the community – making baby clothes and children's outfits and women's dresses, and maybe even the occasional wedding dress. People who knew her knew she was a good seamstress. She was respected, a hard worker, and strong in her church. He could pay the money back in a year, and with the profit from her work, his aunt would be able to shoulder more of the family's financial load. Her idea was that he could then cut back to one shift at the mine and enter school again. He explained that this wasn't his idea, but his aunt's. He was perfectly willing and capable of working and supporting the family, but she was determined that he have a chance at something better than the mines and she thought education could be a ticket that could get him out.

"It was against bank policy to lend money to a minor and outside its lending guidelines to put out funds on any project offering no more security than this one did.

"But I liked the boy. I gave him the loan.

"They paid it off in less than a year."

The banker's manner softened while he was telling us this. He spoke with fondness, and yet there was a sadness to it.

"Jesse says I was the first person to ever really trust him. We were the closest of friends. Yes, the closest of friends for quite a long time. But nothing ever stays the same, does it?

"You know Jesse was very active in the mine wars? Despite his age, one of the leaders? Do you know what the Battle of Evarts was?"

I nodded my head.

"Jesse lived in Evarts with his aunt and his little sister, in the cabin up Hawk Creek that his father built for the family when he came down from the village to go to work in the mines. Jesse's mother was alive then. She couldn't abide the idea of living in a company town, he told me. So they lived on their own land under a roof of their own. It was her Melungeon pride. Did you know that Jesse's mother was Melungeon? No? I don't think anyone outside the immediate family knew except me and I didn't know until Jesse told me when he came to me after the ambush to ask me to look after his sister and aunt while he went to ground. His Melungeon kin would hide him until things blew over, he said. No one in the mountains, no one, could find him while he was with them. He would be safe.

"Anyway, Jesse and his sister and aunt lived in Evarts and were spared the humiliation of being evicted from their homes when the owners started putting the miners out the week before the battle. But his friends weren't spared. One of Jesse's best friends, a cousin on his mother's side, older than he, but not by much, refused to leave his home. The mine owners burned him out. When Jesse and the others saw the flames rising late that night on the ridge above town, they rushed up the hill, but it was too late. The wife and the baby boy lay dead in the ashes of the cabin. Outside, from a white oak tree on the edge of a hill looking down into town, they'd hanged his cousin. Slowly. They hadn't used a hangman's knot. I don't know whether they didn't know how to tie one or were that sadistic. They had just tied a simple loop. The poor boy choked to death watching the flames take the cabin and his loved ones.

"When I got there, Jesse was so calm I was frightened. He should have been fighting mad. Or half crazy.

"We tried to keep the women away, but they gathered around the cabin and on the hill almost as rapidly as we. If the women up here think someone needs help, there is no stopping them. They were too shocked to cry...a thing so horrible the women couldn't find tears for it. Imagine that.

"Jesse held up the weight of his friend's body while others cut him down. We collected what was left of the mother and the child from the ashes. The women were crying by then. They took the bodies away to get them ready.

"Jesse told everyone to go home. He stood in the light of the dying fire ram-rod stiff with such a fury on him that everyone felt it. Yet his voice was steady and his manner composed. He told them to go home, that things would be seen to. There were men who were senior to him there, men more experienced and more mature in a culture where experience and age were honored, men who had been their leaders for years. Yet no one questioned him. That night Jesse Bristow took command. Once he stepped out of the shadows, his right to lead was never questioned – then or since.

"No one had any doubt about who had done this. There were six men, thugs, brought in from Wheeling by the owners and made deputies by the sheriff. They were big ugly bullies, mean and crude. Their job was to clear the cabins. They wore badges and carried axe-handles and wore Colt .45s on their hips. They were the law. People feared those ax-handles more than the pistols. A bullet was sometimes better than being left crippled after a beating with an ax-handle.

"After the others left, Jesse and me and two others he picked headed for the deputies' cabin. It wasn't really my fight. I was just one of the businessmen that lived off the miners. But Jesse was my friend, and so were many of the others, and I was outraged beyond comprehension.

"By the time we got our stuff and got to their cabin, it must have been three in the morning. We found them inside, drinking and laughing, savoring their night's work. Jesse put two of us at the back of the cabin. He and I took the front. I remember that it was a clear, moonless night. Cold. I remember thinking that frost would be on the ground at daylight.

"Jesse kicked open the door and pumped two rounds into the table where the men were sitting. He had an old Winchester Model 94 – a 30'30' – his deer rifle. I had a 12-gauge shotgun. The deputies were startled, then frozen, then scared to death.

"Jesse made them stand with their hands up while our other two came in. Then he had us tie one of the men to the stove and another to the ice-box. We marched the other four outside. Jesse took the kerosene can that was sitting by the lamps and doused the inside of the cabin. The man tied to the stove was wide-eyed. The man by the ice-box began crying. Jesse backed out and threw a match in. A moment passed, then the cabin started burning.

"The remaining four began to plead. An hour earlier we would have laughed to watch them grovel, but with the screams of the burning men in our ears, all we wanted was to get out of there.

"But not Jesse. We marched the others, their hands tied behind their backs, about twenty yards down the path to a little clearing around the well. Jesse made three of them kneel on the stone by the pump handle, and one by one, he shot them through the back of their heads.

"I don't remember what the last man, the chief deputy, looked like, or what he said or what he did, I must have been in shock myself, but Jesse hanged that last man from an old elm that in the summer gave shade to what was now the burning cabin. I suppose he would have found a white oak if he had time, but we didn't know who might come upon us, or when. Still, Jesse didn't hurry.

"He looped the rope around the man's neck, tied a simple knot, a choking knot, threw the rope over a high limb, and then pulled him up kicking and screaming till his feet cleared the ground. It takes a mighty strong man to do that, to lift a man's weight on a rope and hold him off the ground until he chokes to death. The rest of us just watched. The heat from the burning cabin felt good as we stood there in the cold. I was glad the screaming had stopped.

"I took no pleasure from any of this. I had at first...when we found them and burst in and knew we had them. But they were too easy. There was no fight in them. Now, with retribution taken, I was sickened. Six men died that night. Two of them at Jesse's command. Four of them at Jesse's own hand. He was terrible. Absolutely without mercy. He didn't speak except to give an order. He didn't hesitate in his decisions. He was swift in his execution.

"When Jesse let that last deputy fall to the ground, he told us all to scatter. Hide. Lie low. If the owners find out our names we're dead. There won't be any arrests or any trials, he said. Don't speak of this to anyone. Get up the ridges. Hide.

"His advice didn't apply to me. No one would be suspicious of the banker. Even so, I felt nervous and ashamed that we had done so savage a thing. The deputies were guilty of a barbarous, unforgivable act. We were right to take revenge. If we hadn't, there would have been no justice done at all. But that we had been so animal disturbed me greatly. It still does.

"Before he left us that morning, Jesse said he had one more thing to do. And he said to us, 'From now to the end, an eye for an eye!'

"Then we scattered."

Arnow told us this story in a soft and level voice. No emotions crossed his face. He told it as if he had been telling it to himself for so long that he was tired of it. He told it as if he wanted to be rid of it.

"The one more thing turned out to be the ambush at Evarts."

Michael and I sat motionless on either side of the big mahogany desk, dumbfounded at what we had been told. Arnow had implicated himself in four killings and accused Jesse Bristow, as powerful a man as there was in the state, of cold-blooded murder. He hadn't sworn us to secrecy or seemed to be concerned that we might make all this public.

I had seen men start out on a story and be so caught up in telling it that all at once more things started spilling out that they ever intended anyone to know. But I had never been party to a confession by a man of Arnow's prominence to crimes as startling as these.

Trying to find a way out for him and us, I said, "We don't need to know these things. We don't want to know these things." But before I could offer up a lame promise to keep the secrets, he said, "Don't excite yourself, Mr. Clark. By the time the mine wars were over, no one wanted to go back and plow that ground again. As far as the law is concerned, nothing happened on the hill that night. No reports were filed. The missing deputies weren't the kin of anybody local. They were imports, riff-raff. The company didn't care when they disappeared, and the sheriff had a lot more to worry about than what happened to some hired guns from Wheeling when the whole county started coming down around his ears."

Arnow repositioned himself in his chair and leaned back again.

He massaged his temples with his fingers, blunt, working-man's fingers and, looking past us to the big plate glass window across the room, said, "I don't feel guilty that what we did was wrong. I don't think it was. If we hadn't done it, the owners would think they could get away with anything. After that night they knew they couldn't. No, we were right."

He turned his gaze back to us. "Jesse became a hero that night. Then a legend. Once Jesse tasted power, once he came to understand the kind of power he had, he changed. He began looking for power, relished using it. To him, his way was the right way. If you questioned it, it meant you didn't trust him. If you didn't trust him, you were against him. If you were against him, you were in the way. Some good men got hurt not getting out of Jesse's way fast enough.

"I have never been around a braver man, or one so considerate of people's feelings. You don't expect to hear such a man called tender. He was, though. He could be almost motherly tender with people who were hurt, or down, or in trouble. But beginning that night, when Jesse took life and death into his own two hands and gave no thought to any judgment but his own, when he started becoming so righteously arrogant, everything between us changed."

The bank was almost empty by this time. The tellers were locking up their cages. The loan officer had already put his desk in order and was standing up to leave.

Arnow paused, then leaned forward, put his hands on the desktop, palms down, and looked directly into Michael's eyes. "I wouldn't want to risk him with the kind of power the Governor has."

Michael returned his stare, then leaned forward himself.

"But you would risk me," Michael said.

Arnow held his pose. Finally, he nodded his head slightly and said, "I would risk it."

"Why?" Michael said.

"I got to know your father a bit when he was up here. I worked some with him and Jesse. The two were friends then, did you know that? No? Well, no matter. Your father was a fine man. I am one of those who believe that bloodlines tell. And I am in the business of gambling on people. That's what bankers do. We gamble on people. But we don't gamble much. We take collateral. The collateral you're going to give me, Mr. Dannan, is your name. You're going to sign a statement saying that you are depositing one million dollars in my bank in return for my support of your candidacy. If ever you turn out to be a bad risk for me, I'll make the paper public, saying that I demanded it as insurance so that if it ever seemed to me you were working against the best interests of the people of this state, I would use it to bring you down. It would work, don't think it wouldn't."

"Blackmail?"

"You have the same advantage of me," Arnow said.

Michael looked at me amused, then back at Arnow and laughed. "Well I'll be damned," he said. He stuck out his hand to Arnow, shook it, and said, "Done and done!"

So Sattis Arnow joined our side.

Dace Havershamp, Judge Blue, and Jonathan Wilson had come aboard for power – power they wanted for themselves and for their own purposes. Arnow, though, had joined our little team not for power for himself, but to deny power to someone else. That's what Michael understood that I didn't, and that was why he had no fears that Arnow would turn at some point to blackmail. He said that being able to deny someone that you hate, or fear, the thing they want most can be as sweet as having your own fondest dream come true. I didn't think Sattis Arnow was afraid of Jesse Bristow, or hated him. I thought that whatever the relationship was, it was far more complex than either hate or fear. But it made no real difference. Arnow was on our side for now. We had the four. We had enough.

## FIFTEEN

By noon the next day, we were back at the farm, dropping almost due west down Highway 60 through Moorehead to Mt. Sterling, the mountains melting into foothills, then into rolling pastures as we ran past Winchester to Lexington and into the Bluegrass.

Michael drove with the top down and the radio up.

I had to admit I was impressed. He was less than a month home from the corporate wars and already had convinced four of the most powerful men in the state that he could be Governor and that they ought to put their power and their reputations at his disposal.

His father's name helped some. And his mother's clout more still. His own personal fortune made a difference. And so did his reputation. But what hooked them was himself. You couldn't be the focus of Michael's undiluted attention and not be seduced.

Though I had been writing my column regularly while on the road and filing from wherever we happened to be (the one from Ashland about the ambush at Evarts and how the militancy of the miners' union grew to be a force in state politics was particularly good, I thought), I still owed the *Journal* my attention. I had sources to stroke and people to stay current with.

I spent the next few days returning phone calls, making the rounds at the Capitol and around town, but not much was happening. I needed to be where I was, but it meant I had to delay following up on what was then my highest priority, which was to find out what secrets lay in Hanna Collins' safe deposit box.

Unfortunately, we couldn't get into it. Michael had the key, but banks will let only the actual owner of the box or a legally designated representative have access, regardless of who has the key. The signatures of those authorized individuals are kept on file on little cards and whenever anyone wants access to the box, their signature has to match one of those on file. Neither my name nor Michael's was on any of those cards.

Marne seemed the only safe possibility to me. Hanna Collins had trusted her and as she realized she was dying and confined to Mountain Home, she may have turned to her for some of the getting-things-in-order chores she could no longer manage and put Marne's name on the approved list.

I phoned for her on Friday, but found she had gone down to Lexington for the weekend. Reverend Jamieson gave the name of the small hotel near campus where she was staying. I called again that evening. I tried again on Saturday morning. Finally I gave up and left word.

## SIXTEEN

Sattis Arnow was there for the first full meeting of the Inner Council when I arrived. He left Ashland around five a.m., peeling down those two-lane roads through the fog and the mists of a still black morning to make it to the farm by breakfast time. Jonathan Winslow had the drive from his home in Louisville and Judge Blue was coming from Lawrenceburg where his sister lived. Dace Havershamp had spent the night in town, so he was only a half-hour or so away, as was I.

There was country ham and red-eye gravy, eggs the way you liked them (fried, scrambled, poached or boiled), pancakes and maple syrup, buttermilk biscuits, home-churned butter and milk fresh that morning from the farm's own dairy, homemade strawberry and blackberry jam, and jiggers for the Jim Beam to go in our coffee if we liked it that way.

Michael did.

I did.

A jigger of Jim Beam in a cup of black coffee with a half-spoon of sugar gets the day started right.

Who taught us that?

Rhae!

Rhae Dannan did, the summer of our senior year in high school, after we'd had been out all night at the dances and were coming in to change to go right back out to the summer jobs she had given us at the farm. She taught us. We didn't drink then. And she didn't want us to. There would be time for that. But just a little touch of bourbon wrapped in a cupful of caffeine as we shoveled down breakfast got our motors started again and gave us a good outlook on the day.

As I tipped a jigger into my coffee, I looked over to her and smiled.

We were assembled around the big oval table in the kitchen. The kitchen was the biggest room in the house, bigger even than the formal dining room. The dining room was for social occasions. If an important decision was to be made, a course of action to be considered, it took place in the kitchen, around the big oak table made from the tree that had stood on the hill where the house now stood.

No one knew how old the tree was. Over one hundred, to be sure. It had served as a marker for the Shawnee before settlers pushed up this arm of Elkhorn Creek and killed them off

The story is that a massive lightning bolt flashed out of a clear blue sky on an autumn afternoon and struck the tree down intact. There was no fire or scorching, the tree was simply knocked over, as if a giant hand had pushed it to the ground. There it lay, a few leaves already beginning to turn brilliant red, branches intact, in otherwise perfect condition but for the fact it was lying on its side.

All this was puzzling. Trees usually split when struck by lightning, or, at the very least, give signs of burning. No such signs were present. More curious, lightning isn't common in autumn in this country... and never strikes out of a cloudless sky.

This all happened shortly after the end of the Civil War. Rhae Dannan's great-grandfather Thomas Hopkins, a young man then, not yet the successful land-owner and publisher he was to become, not yet the Senator, a young man home from the war, just putting the farm together – expanding from the few hundred acres on the creek his father owned to the several thousands he was buying and acquiring from the smaller landowners around him. Where he found the money at a time when the economy of the state was in tatters and none but the carpet-baggers were flourishing isn't clear. His father, though one of the landed gentry, was not rich and the war had been hard on his enterprise.

Those were uncertain times, superstitious times. People gave credence to signs and portents. The lightning strike was seen as one.

The Senator-to-be, being Irish and superstitious, agreed it meant something. But he was a practical man too, so he doubted God worked his wonders in quite so spectacular a way now as when the Children of Israel had walked on dry land across the Red Sea and the Walls of Jericho had fallen. He wondered if here, indeed, if not a sign, was at least an event which a smart man could turn to his advantage. After all, people far and wide knew of the happening. The story of the bolt out of the blue had been told at church socials and wondered about on court days in the county seats throughout the Bluegrass.

So he waited a bit, and watched, letting the event mix with superstition to become a local myth. After several months, when nothing outside the ordinary run of changeable weather and minor tribulations descended, he declared the event a demonstration of God's mighty wonders. He said he took it as a sign that nothing can stand against His power and that we are to abandon our egos and our pettiness and work for the glory of God and the welfare of our fellow man. He said he, for one, intended to do just that. It was clear the Lord wanted his attention and it did not take lightning to strike twice to give it.

Thomas Hopkins made that little speech at church one Sunday night. Word of it spread, as he had intended, like wildfire.

Since the tree was an omen, he meant to hold on to it. So he had it sawed into boards, and from the best of these he had his carpenter build him a table, a table around which he could gather his family and his friends, and where he could assemble his peers to consider the important matters that concerned them all.

It made a grand table. The carpenter, a Frenchman with woodworking in his blood, fashioned a graceful oval out of the finest of the boards that had been planed from the heart of the oak. The table was the color of dark honey, sturdy and stable, and smooth as a small pond's surface on a windless day. Ten could be seated around it quite comfortably. The rest of the boards went into the building of the Baptist Church in Peaks Mill in 1872.

Oddly, or perhaps appropriately, Thomas Hopkins luck began to change after that. His crops came in more bountiful. His thoroughbreds began to win. The land deals he wanted to put together fell in place without a breath of difficulty. He couldn't seem to lose a hand at poker.

People took notice. Thomas Hopkins talked about all this modestly, but widely. He was wise enough to know that people thought a lucky man was as good a man as any, and better than most, to be sitting in the Senate making laws. They noted how his fortunes had improved since the lightning strike. They thought perhaps he might be favored in some special way. The luckier everyone thought he was, the luckier he became. He was elected to the Senate almost by acclamation and never had a serious challenge afterwards.

Thomas Hopkins took to stroking that old table each day as left for work.

Over the years, the table became something of a special anchor for the family...and stroking the table a family habit.

Rhae told me this story. It had been told to her by her grandmother, the old Senator's daughter.

She stroked it now, unconsciously, as we waited for Betsy to clear away our dishes and pour fresh coffee all around.

The kitchen was at the back of the house. It was a large, open, high-ceiling room that spanned the width of the house and opened on to a roofed porch of similar width. The porch, in turn, opened onto a broad and carefully mowed grassy yard about half as large as a football field. Beyond this was a big bluegrass meadow, then a thin band of trees, and then the creek.

The eating area of the kitchen, where the oval table sat, took up about a third of the room at the end opening onto the porch. Four big screened windows, two on either side of the door leading out to the porch, let in light and air.

Michael sat in the center of the oval with his back to the porch. Next to him, on his right, was Dace Havershamp, and on his left Sattis Arnow. Rhae and Paul Isham sat at either end of the oval and Judge Blue, Jonathan Winslow, and I sat across. This happened naturally. We had discussed where each of us would sit – Rhae and Paul anchoring the ends, Michael and I the centers, but left it to natural selection to see how the others would arrange themselves.

We watched carefully for signs of tension or jealousy among the players. Disharmony would kill us and these were powerful and prideful men. But we saw none. They all seemed peaceable.

While we were laughing and telling stories across the table, getting easy in each other's company, the sun cleared the highest of the ridges to the east and full morning was on us.

Michael turned from his conversation with Sattis Arnow, looked out to the rising day, looked at his watch, and then with everyone well fed and relaxed, he tapped his spoon on a half empty glass to get our attention. We all turned toward him.

Taking his time, he stood. He let his fingers rest lightly on the table. He looked thoughtfully around, holding each of us, one by one, in his steady gaze, his eyes locked to ours, assessing us, assuring us, offering an unspoken bond. In the silence of the moment, we all felt it. Then smiling easily, he said to all of us,

"Thank you."

And that was perfect. For that group...on that day...that simple statement said exactly what needed to be said.

And so it began – the planning and maneuvering and manipulating that was to take Michael Dannan in to history.

## SEVENTEEN

Consider.

We had no organization.

None.

Zip.

Just the four of them – Dace, Sattis, Judge Blue, and Jonathan. And the four of us – Michael, Rhae, Paul Isham, and me.

There are 120 counties in this state. For each county we needed a campaign chairman – 120 people with enough weight in their localities to command attention and generate votes. Senior people. People well connected in their communities. People who are respected and listened to. Most of them were probably already picked off by the Party or part of Jesse Bristow's team.

And in each of the 120 counties we needed precinct chairmen. We needed people to raise funds, to nail posters on telephone poles and fences and any place a Vote for Dannan poster could be hung. Drivers to get our voters to the polls on election day. People to knock on doors and hand out literature and man the phone banks.

We needed a top-flight media man, and speechwriters, and advertising pros to produce the print and radio and television ads and make the right buys in the right media at the right time so our budgets would be effective. We needed schedulers and pollsters and people who knew what groups we should be talking with, and when, and about what. This was just to get an organization going – a thousand or more people committed to making Michael Dannan, a stranger, Governor.

Put all this together and make it work in the time we had available? And all this just for starters.

Once we had an organization, then we had a campaign to run and a war to win against experienced foes already in the field and well entrenched.

By any application of the conventional wisdom, it wasn't possible.

But Michael's rock-hard confidence held us. Rhae's stubborn insistence challenged us.

"We can do this," Michael said. "You, Dace, you know the buttons to push. You, Sattis, you know the debts to call in. Jonathan, Judge Blue, you know the names to call. And the money. We have the money. We can make it happen."

There was some yes-ing and no-ing and maybe-ing, but by mid-morning, we all agreed. We could do this.

I say "we" because by then they took me for "we." Michael explained the role I would play. Dace had suspected something like this from our first meeting. Sattis Arnow didn't care. Jonathan Winslow was at first uneasy at having a newsman in the inner circle, and Judge Blue wondered for a moment about the propriety of it. But in the end, they accepted me. If Michael wanted it, they were willing to accept it.

Dace Havershamp was named State Chairman, and Sattis Arnow Treasurer. These were the two key posts. Dace was in charge of the overall campaign. Sattis would collect and dispense the money. Judge Blue and Jonathan Winslow were Co-Chairmen.

What was needed next was a real pro, someone experienced at organizing, running, and winning, major political campaigns – a full-timer, a person who made his career out of getting people elected to office. Not just anyone. The best that money could buy.

That would be Gershon Pope.

Pope was Rhae's idea. The best of the in-state people had already been taken. Jim Ahern, who had handled the senate campaign for Senator Eagle, was Jesse Bristow's man. Mike Dangerfield, the man who masterminded the current Governor into his chair was probably available, but his sentiments were Republican. They were the two best Kentucky men. There was some sentiment that we needed a Kentucky man, that bringing in a hired gun from out-of-state would turn off the local politicians he would have to depend on and make us look too much like a carpetbagger's campaign. But Rhae Dannan would have none of this.

"People trust winners. Gershon Pope is a winner," she said. "If we are going to get people to go up against the Party and up against Jesse Bristow, we are going to have to give them a reason to think they can win. If we lose, we lose a race. They lose their jobs. They know that they, and their families, will be blacklisted for every job the state, or the county, or the party controls.

"We have to offer them more than a hope. We have to make them know they have an advantage. They will take comfort in knowing that Dace, and Sattis Arnow, and Judge Blue, and Jonathan Winslow are with us. But they will want to know we have someone running the campaign who knows how to win big races. That is Gershon Pope. I've already arranged a meeting with him."

Dace shook his head and glowered.

"This isn't your campaign to run, Rhae. You can't go off making unilateral decisions. None of us can. We have to run this thing together. No free-lancing. On anyone's part."

No one doubted his seriousness as he fixed us each in turn with his deliberate stare.

Rhae was taken aback for a moment. We all were. Rhae Dannan's decisions weren't often challenged.

But Rhae saw immediately that she had overstepped. With an apologetic smile, she said, "You're right, of course, Dace. I should have talked with all of you first. It won't happen again. Together. We'll make the decisions together."

Everyone relaxed and the moment of tension passed. But I knew Rhae was wrong. Michael would make the decisions. He always had.

## EIGHTEEN

Marne Young got back to me early Monday morning, the phone nagging me awake.

"Did I mention that people who work on morning newspapers work all night and don't get up before noon," I said when I heard her voice.

"Oh, don't be a grump," she said. "It's a beautiful day and I have resurrected you for most of it." She was laughing.

"I need to talk with you," I said. "Where are you?"

"I'm still in Lexington. I'm not due back at Mountain Home until tonight."

"How about a late lunch, then?"

She hesitated for a moment, then said, "I think I can manage that. Where?"

We decided on a small place on the edge of the UK campus that we both knew, a favorite of English Lit profs and graduate students, with the pretensions of a Cotswold pub, oak-beamed and leather-chaired, complete with a big fireplace, leaded windows and small flower vases on the tables. There were booths where we could talk and have privacy.

I arrived first and took our booth.

As she walked toward me, I realized what an oddly unsettling effect she produced. She had an elegance to her walk. She carried herself with what I can only describe as a sort of chaste sensuality that suggested far more than gospel songs and evening prayers.

Some of this had come through at Lost Creek, but I had been too focused on Michael and the Hanna Collins mystery to pay much attention to Marne Young.

Rising like the true southern gentleman I like to think I am, I let myself imagine what her body looked like under that neat suit. She gave me a smile and her hand, and I bowed her to the seat across from me, calling on what little self-discipline I have to close the door in my mind I was peeping through.

"You don't look so worn out," she laughed. "I am sorry I didn't know about the sleeping habits of morning newspaperman. Next time I'll wait to return your calls until night comes on." Then she shook her head and laughed again. "No I won't," she said, "I would be too curious."

I said. "I was just being self-indulgent. But now that you're here, my day is bright and all's right with the world."

"My, my. Gallantry. I am impressed."

We both laughed.

We ordered our lunch and traded banter, settling down and getting reacquainted. I knew she was aching with curiosity, humoring my little attempts at charm patiently until I got around, or she brought me around, to what I had called her about. I was trying to be entertaining and, I admit it, buy time with senseless chatter to decide whether I could get her to get me into the Hanna Collins safe-deposit box without telling her what I knew.

"Did you know that Hanna Collins was Melungeon?" I asked.

"That certainly changes the subject," she said. "Oh, yes," she went on, "Aunt Hanna was Melungeon ... and not ashamed of it."

"How did you know?"

"She told me."

"And that makes Jesse Bristow a Melungeon?"

"Half. His father was an Irishman. Aunt Hanna was never happy about that. She liked Mr. Bristow's father well enough, but she felt that her sister should have stayed with the clan and married Melungeon. The Irishman was an accident, or an act of God, she sometimes said. He had no business being where he was, she said. He was high up on Black Mountain. The country was wild. There weren't any roads and only a few trails.

"Whatever he was looking for, he must have slipped off one of the outcroppings. A laurel tree broke his fall, but a limb snapped in the process and punctured his chest. He was close to death when one of the Melungeon men came across him at the bottom of a cliff.

"The man – it turned out he was Aunt Hanna's brother – carried him to their settlement. Aunt Hanna and her little sister were put to taking care of him. Everyone thought he would die before morning. He didn't. The sisters nursed him back to health. In the process, the Irishman and the youngest sister fell in love. When he had his strength again, they married. In a Melugeon ceremony. 'In the afternoon mists on the top of Black Mountain,' as Aunt Hanna told it."

She smiled and looked away.

"Mr. Bristow tried to live Melungeon. But after a year or so, it was too much. Young Jesse had been born by then. They left the mountain and Mr. Bristow went to work in the mines. Aunt Hanna came with them to help with the baby, but really because she couldn't bear the thought of her sister in the outside world alone."

Marne nodded when she said that as if agreeing it was the only thing to be done.

"So you see, Mr. Jesse Bristow isn't full-blooded Melungeon."

"Is he the benefactor of Mountain Home?"

"I imagine."

"Why keep it a secret?"

"You'll have to ask him."

I considered that and thought I probably wouldn't. Marne finished her tea and wiped her lips.

"You've been delaying me long enough. What did you ask me here to talk about?" She neither looked nor sounded as if she was prepared for any further delay.

I had to consider again whether I could get from her what I wanted without having to give back what she wanted. I thought it not likely.

"There was a key in the little box Aunt Hanna left for Michael. It's the key to a safe deposit box at the bank in Berea."

"Yes." It was both a question and a statement.

"You knew?"

"I knew Aunt Hanna had a safe deposit box at the Farmer's Bank in Berea. She had me sign one of the signature cards that would allow me to get into it if ever she needed something from it and couldn't go herself. I don't know why she left it for Mr. Dannan."

"The Farmer's Bank?"

"Yes."

"And you can get into it?"

She looked at me frowning, then after a minute; she smiled a big smile and clapped her hands together.

"You can't get into the box," she said. "You have the key but you can't get in. I can, though. How wonderful."

Miss Young was about to become a player.

Odd that that's the way I thought of it, but I did. It was a game still. We were the players. At the moment, only two of us – me and Michael. Now add Miss Marne Young.

Aunt Hanna's game.

What was it? Why did she make it so puzzling? If she had something to tell Michael, why not tell him? Why stage this little mystery?

Marne sat quietly while I told her what I knew.

I described the locket and the photo of Benjamin Dannan and Sue Bristow smiling happily with their heads together. I told her about the envelope with its clippings of the "Angel at Evarts," and the newly appointed professor of economics. And I told her about the obit, about how Sue Bristow died young and in the same week as Benjamin.

When I finished, she sat for what seemed a long time, not ignoring me but not particularly aware I was there. Whatever she was seeing, it wasn't the room we were in. She looked toward the light coming through the leaded windows near the door, half shivered, then turned her face to me. I could see the faint track of a tear on her cheek.

"That is so sad. So very, very sad," she said, and reached across the table and took my hand, whether to comfort me or herself I couldn't tell.

Her hand was small and warm, and made me think of walking at night across a quite meadow with a half-moon lighting our way. We sat like that for a moment, and then she became aware of what we were doing, our hands joined like that across a table in a public restaurant, and she dropped her eyes and slipped her hand away..

She raised her eyes again and the faraway look was gone. She was back from wherever she had been.

"Aunt Hanna never mentioned Michael Dannan until that night the television carried the story about his coming home. It was just after supper. We were watching the news on the set in her bedroom. 'Good Lord,' she said. The TV was showing a news clip of Mr. Dannan at a plant of some sort while the announcer read the news about his retirement.

"What is it, Aunt Hanna?"

"She seemed puzzled and confused. 'Nothing, child, nothing.' She fussed about for a minute or two, then began to settle down. We read from the Bible a bit, as we often did, and she began to get ready for the night. I helped her kneel by her bedside to pray. Then, as I was helping her into it, she said to me, 'I have to talk with this Mr. Dannan. I want you to write him for me and invite him up here.'

"Do you know him, Aunt Hanna? I said. She didn't answer me.

"So I wrote the letter for her. The next day she organized the things she wanted to give Mr. Dannan, and had me put them in the chest in her room, where you found them. What a pity she passed before Mr. Dannan could get here."

"Do you have any idea of what she wanted to tell Michael?"

"She said she had something she had to tell him before she died, that she couldn't die easy until she did."

## NINETEEN

Berea is about fifty miles west of Jackson and perhaps forty miles southeast of Frankfort, just south of Lexington in the high foothills leading to the Appalachian escarpment – a drive for us both. I was coming from Frankfort, Marne Young from Jackson.

The town grew up around the college there. In pre-Civil War days the area was a remote collection of small farms peopled by families sympathetic to emancipation. When the college was built, in 1855, it was dedicated to providing a solid education to the children of the mountains, the kids who were too poor to afford a college education and too far away to be in the reach of any of the established schools. All Berea students are on scholarships. You can't buy your way in. If you can afford the tuition, you go somewhere else. Berea takes only those who can't afford it and who are willing to carry a full academic load and work ten to fifteen hours a week for the privilege. I'd never been there, but had heard of it for years and was impressed.

The bank is on the northeast corner of the block facing the main entrance to the campus, a building separated from its neighbors by a small rose garden on the right and a little parking lot on the left. The rose garden had been put in by the wife of the bank's founder sometime in the late 1880s and tended ever since by students from the college. It was a local landmark. There were a few benches where passersby could pause and rest or talk, a little sanctuary. Marne Young was waiting there for me. I never am late to meetings, always a few minutes early if possible. But Marne Young was earlier. Not want to know? She could hardly wait.

She had the card, I had the key. We went in.

We were directed to a teller at a little window at the back. She handed him her card and was given a blank card to sign in his presence. I stood beside her. The teller compared her signature with the one he had taken from the file box at his side, looked carefully at her, at me, at the card, back at the card, then said, "Follow me."

He led us into a large, narrow room, the walls of which were lined from top to bottom with slots into which the respective safe deposit boxes fit. The boxes were ranged in numerical order with the lowest numbers at knee level and the highest at arm's reach. He held his hand out. She seemed puzzled.

"The key," he said.

He put it with an identical key he had, inserted them both into the lock of a box about a third of the way down the room on the left-hand side, knee high. He turned both keys, extracted the box, and handed it to her.

"You will want a room," he said, and led us out of that room down a little corridor to a hallway with a series of small cubicles on either side. The cubicle walls were green and there was green carpeting on the floor. He motioned us into one. It was Spartan – a small table with a single chair and overhead fluorescent lighting.

"Call me when you're finished," he said, then closed the door, and we were alone with the box.

The box sat on the table – a black metal rectangular with a flip-open top. It was large enough to hold letters and papers, but not large enough for a hoard of gold or a stack of greenbacks.

There was monumental quiet in that little cubicle. No outside sounds intruded. Our breathing seemed unnaturally loud. We talked in whispers.

"Well?" she said, looking from the box to me.

"Well," I replied.

Carefully, as if she expected something might spring out it at her, she lifted the top.

Inside was a wallet... a man's wallet – the type men carry in an inside jacket pocket.

No papers. No letter or note. No photographs or documents.

A wallet.

We looked at each other with surprise and disappointment. I reached for the wallet and brought it out into the light. I held the box up and shook it just to be sure nothing was lodged in a corner or stuck in a way we couldn't see it.

There was only the wallet.

It was a rich burgundy leather made in the size and shape of a letter envelope, designed to be carried in the inside pocket of a suit or sport jacket. It folded open. On one side was an opening for currency and a pocket for cards. The other had a similar opening and three flat vertical pockets in which tickets or some such could be carried. The whole thing was so slim in design, I doubted the user could even feel it in his pocket. I turned it carefully and looked for markings. On the inside right panel there was a small, gold-embossed monogram. It read "BD."

The currency section held ninety dollars – four twenties and one ten.

I continued the inspection, taking the cards out one by one and laying them on the table.

There was a driver's license made out to Benjamin Dannan. His vital statistics – his height (5'10') and weight (180) and color of hair (black) and eyes (blue). The date of his birth and his address were noted.

There was a Kentucky State Police Press Pass, also made out to Benjamin Dannan; and membership cards to the National Press Club in Washington and the Clendenin Club in Louisville, and others of this use or that – all in the name of Benjamin Dannan.

There was a photo of Michael with his mother. He looked to be about eight or nine.

And six engraved business cards reading: *Benjamin Dannan, Publisher & Editor-in-Chief, The State Journal, 401 Main Street, Frankfort, Ky. Phone CAPITOL 3-2838.*

Benjamin Dannan.

Dead and buried almost thirty years.

His wallet in a safe deposit box in a little bank in a small college town on the western edge of the Appalachians.

It made no sense.

I collected all the cards and put them carefully back in the wallet. We both stared at the box. Finally, Marne looked at me so puzzled she was speechless.

All I could do was shake my head in ignorance.

"Wasn't his wallet with his body when they found it?" she said.

"'I don't know.''

"Mr. Dannan's body was found near Harlan?"

"Yes."

"That's a hundred miles from here?"

"I know."

"How did the wallet get in this box?"

"Somebody put it here."

We called for the clerk, returned the box, and walked outside into a softly misting morning rain.

## TWENTY

*I am …five, six? The fields are wet and the leaves are dripping. I stand on the porch listening.*

*Momma had put me to bed in the big feather bed in the room we always stayed in when we came to Pap's farm. Just her and me. Dad couldn't get away. I liked it when Dad was with us, but I didn't get to sleep in the big bed with her when he did. I was too big, he said. I should sleep in my own bed.*

*She is still asleep.*

*The rain woke me, misting through the open window by my side, or maybe the sound. I am not sure.*

*It is warm in the bed, and sweet.*

*I can hear Mam in the kitchen starting breakfast on the big wood stove. I think to snuggle, then think of pancakes with maple syrup and get up quietly so as not to wake Momma.*

*Mam gives me a kiss and sends me out on the porch with a glass of milk. The milk is fresh from the milking pail and still warm. Pap and my uncles, the two still at home, are out in the barn getting the before-breakfast chores done.*

*The sound comes again. Out in the woods near the creek. A hurt kind of sound. Very weak.*

*And then again.*

*The men in the barn are too far away to hear it. Mam is singing to herself in the kitchen.*

*And again. Longer this time. Weaker. Like someone sobbing.*

*I put my milk down and start through the field to the woods. If someone is hurt, Momma would want me to help. Pap would expect it.*

*The rain has stopped, but wading through the grass gets my socks wet and my pants soaked to the knees. At the tree-line, I wait and listen. When the sound comes again it is so sad it almost makes me cry.*

*I push my way through the brush and the low branches. By now my shirt is wet too and I am shivering.*

*I can hear the tumble of the creek on the other side of the trees and over the sound of the water, that sad cry. Close.*

*I step out of the trees onto the cobbles of the creek bank.*

*Just ahead of me, not far from the water, I see a calf. He seems to be kneeling... down on his knees... moaning. When he sees me he tries to rise. He expects me to help him. I can tell from his eyes.*

*His front legs straighten, then wobble. Then he drops and I can see guts spilling grey from his ripped open belly and what is left of a hind leg twitching helplessly.*

*I guess I scream. I know I run. Pap and my uncles are halfway through the field when I bust out of the tree-line. He grabs me, picks me up and holds me.*

*Afterwards, with all of us around the big table in the kitchen and hot coffee steaming from the cups and the sun out bright, Pap says what had happened. A pack of wild dogs had been running the ridges at night. They must have cut the young calf out before daylight. Pap shot the calf. It was the only thing to do. He and my uncles and the others from farms on both sides of the creek would gather soon. They would have those dogs before nightfall. Don't worry about that!*

*"It was a bad thing to see, son. You were brave to go out. Everything is ok. Eat your pancakes, now."*

*I tell him alright, but I can't.*

## TWENTY-ONE

This misty rain of the morning turned into a full-scale downpour on the way back, but eased off to a steady drizzle by the time I started down East Main Hill into town. A white mist hugged the river. I parked in the little lot in the alley behind the courthouse and managed to make it to the back shop door without getting too wet. There was a chill in the air brought on by the rain.

I went immediately to Paul Isham's office.

He was standing at the small conference table across the room from his desk, studying the layout for tomorrow morning's front page.

He looked up, smiled, turned back to layout. "Find out anything interesting?" he said.

Leaning over the table and studying the layout while he waited for my answer, he looked, as he always looked, relaxed and in command. A tall, lanky, man with a patrician face and slightly graying hair, he personally laid out the front page each day – a job he would delegate only if he was traveling, or ill, both of which occasions happened rarely. As managing editor, he didn't write much any more – an occasional think piece or a signed editorial – so this was the way he kept his hand in on the physical production of the paper. He straightened up. "It needs more punch," he said, gesturing to the page, then turning to me. "Well?'

"I don't know," I said.

"Meaning?"

"Are Michael and Rhae back yet?"

"They were going to spend some time with Jonathan Winslow after their meeting with Pope. I don't expect them until later tonight."

"It's just as well."

"Meaning?"

"Maybe we better close the door," I said.

Paul turned with a puzzled look on his face. Then he nodded an okay, closed the door to his office, and gestured me to the chair in front of his desk.

"All right," he said, "lay it out."

"Michael told you and Rhae about everything that was in the stuff Hanna Collins left for him."

"The little silver box and the bank key? Yes."

"The locket with the photograph in it…and the clippings?"

"No, nothing about a locket or any of that."

I wasn't surprised. I hadn't expected that Michael would bring up the matter of the photograph of his father and the young girl… or the clippings… with Rhae just then. There was something unsettling about that photograph. But I wondered why he hadn't told Paul Isham. Paul was Benjamin Dannan's best friend. He had gone through the mine wars episode with Benjamin and must have known some of the people Benjamin Dannan worked with there.

So I told him what Michael had found…about the locket with the photograph of Benjamin Dannan and Jesse Bristow's sister together. About the press clippings. And I told him what I had found in the safe deposit box at the bank in Berea.

Paul was silent while I related all this. He hardly looked at me. He sat with his hands folded on the desktop, leaning slightly forward.

When I finished, he stayed silent for a long moment, then he looked up at me as if I had said something incomprehensible. "A wallet? Benjamin's wallet?"

I nodded yes.

"Damn!" he cried, beating his fist against the desk, "and damn! And damn again! She knew! She must have known! And she never came forward. Damn her to hell!"

Paul jerked to his feet. He paced to the door. Opened it. Started through. Then stopped. Turned back. Closed it. And came back to the desk, standing over me. I didn't know what to say. I had never seen Paul Isham out of control. I had never seen him even lose his temper.

"Benjamin Dannan was the finest man I ever knew. Somebody killed him. It wasn't an accident. He was killed. I want that somebody. I've wanted it since the day he died." He said this with such a threatening intensity that I instinctively pulled back.

He sat down again, breathing heavily, eyes unfocused, seeing something I couldn't see – watching, I supposed, those days roll by. I don't know how long we stayed this way. Finally he took a deep breath, and then another, and turned to me.

"Thirty years ago and I'm still this outraged about it! My God! I wonder what it will be like for Rhae, bringing the whole disaster fresh again. Awful! Michael doesn't know about the wallet either, does he?"

"We were to get together later tonight," I told him.

"The wallet opens every thing up again. It wasn't with him when his body was found. The sheriff up there made the identification by the watch Benjamin carried, a gold pocket watch. It had an inscription on the back. The staff gave it to him the year he won the press association prize for editorials. There was no jacket, no coat, no wallet. Just Benjamin in his shirt-sleeves in the snow. The sheriff called the State Police. The State Police called me. I had just gotten in from putting the Sunday morning paper to bed.

"Benjamin and Rhae lived in town then, up on Shelby Street, near the Capitol. I got the car out and drove over there. It was a little after seven. Light enough to see outside, but still dark enough that you needed lights on in the house. A dismal morning, cold and foggy. Rhae answered the door, in her robe, sleep still in her eyes. When she saw it was me, she started to smile, then realized that whatever would bring me to her door at daylight on a Sunday morning couldn't be good. Michael was still asleep."

Paul Isham paused. "You've heard all this?"

"No," I said, "I know some of it from having done the story on an anniversary of Mr. Dannan's death – just the basics. Plus what I remember."

"What you remember?" said Isham. 'You were about nine then, weren't you – you and Michael?"

"Nine, yes."

"I don't remember how I told her…what words I used. She got dressed and was making coffee by the time the State Police captain got there. The 'official' notification. Captain Jenkins. I remember what Rhae wore. A long sleeved white blouse buttoned to the neck and a dark skirt that fell to her ankles. Her hair had been brushed to a sheen so high it glistened in the lamp light. How did she find time to do that, I wondered.

"We were in the kitchen. The kitchen was the heart of the house, just as it is now at the farm. Michael came down dressed for church. He had on his blue blazer and slacks. His loafers were shined and his hair was brushed. It was as if, not knowing what to expect and unsure or what he should do or how he should act, he had put on the costume of maturity. Rhae poured us all coffee, then motioned for Michael to come sit beside her at the table. She was clear eyed and in control.

"The State Policeman told us how the line crew found Benjamin. It had been snowing since the previous afternoon, began to slack off around midnight and then quit altogether about three a.m. It was still an hour or so before daylight when the crew came across what they thought was a deer laying at the side of the road. They couldn't tell much until they got close with their flashlights. The State Police and the Sheriff went over the scene as carefully as they could in all that snow. They found nothing. It could have been a hit and run, they said. What else could it have been? But what was he doing there...without a coat, without a hat...on that lonely road...in a snowstorm?

"They searched that morning and then for the next four days every inch of the road within two miles of the scene. They found nothing. They never even found his car.

"We couldn't figure out why he was there. None of us had any idea. Rhae hadn't. He was over one hundred miles from home. What was he doing? He hadn't told me of anything that would take him to the mountains. It made no sense."

Paul had the confused and helpless look of a man who had been over the details a thousand times and still couldn't understand.

"Maybe he was following a lead, working a story," I said.

"No," Paul said. "If something important enough to cause him to drop everything and rush off to the mountains on a Saturday had come up he would have told me. There was no story."

Paul's voice was rising, anger mixing with frustration. He pounded the desk again.

"Dammit! Captain Jenkins put a special team of State Police investigators on the case for over three months. I would have crucified him if he had done less. Nothing. I put Jake Slade on it, the best reporter we had. Jake spent months up there and found nothing. I sent him back four times, knowing that people will talk with reporters but won't talk with police, knowing that the miners up there took Benjamin for a friend after he stood with them in the mine wars, knowing that mountain families looked out for their friends. Still nothing. We ran ads in the newspapers in the area and had announcements read on the radio stations asking anyone who had any information at all to come forward, offering rewards, promising the names would be kept secret.

"The road they found him on wasn't heavily traveled even in the best of weather – two lanes of pot-holed blacktop used by coal trucks and the few locals who lived up in the hollows. Everyone in the area knew about Benjamin dying on that road. Even without the radio and the newspapers, the mountain grapevine had spread the news everywhere.

"Only five people responded to our ads. Two had gone into Harlan for groceries. One went to visit relatives. One had business in the Court House. The bus from Pineville made its regular run. It got into Harlan about 3:30 in the afternoon, a half-hour late. So far as is known, it was the last vehicle on that stretch of road until early Sunday morning."

He shook his head and continued in a quieter voice, "Jake Slade talked with the line crew that found Benjamin and with the Sheriff's men who were on duty that day. He must have spent three or four months up there, poking around, asking questions. Jake made friends with the moonshiners and with the guys at the union hall. He sat around coon hunters' fires. He listened to the tales and the gossip. Nobody was better at that than Jake Slade. Nothing. They all knew it had happened, but that is all they knew. Slade talked with the men in the little garages and backwoods body shops all over the area, hoping to pick up something the State Police missed. A repairman who remembered an odd dent? A strand of cloth? A bloodstain? A running deer tears up a car when it's hit. A walking man must do the same. Perhaps he wasn't walking. Maybe he was standing still. Maybe it wasn't even a car or a truck that did it?"

That surprised me. "What do you mean?"

"All the coroner could say was that he had been hit by a vehicle of some type – or dropped from a great height."

"Paul, you're not..." I didn't get to finish.

"Benjamin Dannan had real enemies. You know that. He used the *Journal* like a weapon. He made a lot of people uncomfortable, put a lot of politicians out to pasture, sent a few of them and their cronies to jail. These were powerful and ruthless men, with powerful and ruthless friends. It's not unreasonable to suppose that Benjamin was killed by one of them, or that one of them arranged to have him killed, and his body dropped where it was found."

His look dared me to challenge the thought.

I didn't. I knew about the speculation. It had been widespread at one time. But it seemed to me an inordinately complicated way to kill a man, when a hit and run could have been arranged on one of the back roads of Franklin County just as easily as 100 miles away in the mountains. I didn't say that, though.

What I did say brought us back around to the wallet.

"So you think the wallet might lead somewhere?"

"I don't know how long fingerprints last, but I am certainly going to find out. And I am going to find out all there is to know about Hanna Collins and particularly where she was and what she was doing the week Benjamin died."

"Thirty years ago? The people she knew might not even be alive now!"

"Well, Jake Slade is. I'm going to put him back on it."

I felt very uneasy about this. "With Michael's candidacy about to take off? This could be a Pandora's Box. Let's leave it alone until we're in the Governor's mansion. It's been thirty years. We can wait another ten months for the answer."

With a jut-jawed look of stubborn anger, Paul said, "I can't!"

The tension around him was electric.

As calmly and in as reasonable a tone as I could manage I said, "This isn't your call is it, Paul? It's Rhae's and Michael's."

He jerked up sharply, started to rise, then sank back slowly in his chair. He kept me fixed with a cold stare, said, "You can't..." then stopped, held a long pause, took a slow breath in and out, calming himself. "We'll discuss it at the farm when they get back tonight."

Paul stood up then and went back to the table. In the break I could feel the tension easing out of the room. He leaned down and inspected the layout, then looked back at me with a half smile, "It hasn't gotten any better."

When I didn't make any move to leave, he asked, "Is there something else?"

"The girl in the locket," I said.

## TWENTY-TWO

Paul Isham never figured in the reportage done on the Michael Dannan affair, so his role went unrecognized.

Michael, Rhae Dannan, Jesse Bristow...Allie to some extent, and me. These were the names people read about. But Paul was almost as central to the action as I was.

He had grown up in Lexington. He had aspirations to be a poet and he had the look for it – tall and lean with soulful eyes and the bearing of a patrician, which he was. The Isham family name was as old and honored among the Bluegrass aristocracy as any. He had followed the family tradition of military school. Most of the male Ishams had made their mark at the Virginia Military Institute. Paul chose The Citadel where he was Commander of the Corps of Cadets and a marksman of Olympic quality. All Kentuckians think they are great shots. Many are. Paul was superb. His weapon was the handgun, his particular niche the twenty-two caliber. He captained the Citadel team and won the Creedmoor Cup in national competition.

His talent as a poet turned out to be only mediocre, but his abilities as prose writer were considerable. He opted for journalism and qualified for the graduate journalism program at Columbia. That's where he met Benjamin Dannan. Dannan was in New York speaking on his experiences during the coverage of the Scopes Monkey Trial.

By the time they finished talking, Paul Isham wanted to come home to Kentucky and he wanted to go to work for Benjamin Dannan.

They were only four years apart in age and they worked hand-in-glove as if they were cast from the same mold – Paul as a reporter, Benjamin as Editor. Paul was as outraged as Benjamin Dannan at the abuse of power and the arrogance of station. He fought at Benjamin's side against both and thought Benjamin Dannan was the finest newspaperman he had ever met. When Benjamin was made Editor-in-Chief and Publisher, Paul succeeded him as Managing Editor.

Paul Isham was Benjamin Dannan's best friend. His knowledge of Benjamin Dannan's actions, or Benjamin Dannan's mind, that last week of his life, should have been better than anyone's except Rhae Dannan's.

"You were up there with him?"

"Only once. I had to be here to run the paper."

"You met Jesse Bristow there?"

"Yes."

"And you met Bristow's family?"

"No, I wasn't there long enough."

"The girl and the aunt?"

"I didn't know about them."

"After the fighting was over? After the miners got their union?"

"Benjamin went back. He did several stories from there."

"Did he see Bristow?"

"Yes. Jesse was his contact."

"And the girl?"

"I wasn't there."

"What did he have to say about Bristow?"

"He liked Jesse. Thought he was a real leader."

"They were friends, then they became enemies?"

"It's a long story."

"Tell me."

"Not now."

"Should we bring Rhae into all this?"

We pondered that, then decided that since Michael had chosen not to tell his mother about the photograph and the clippings, then we shouldn't either. They bothered Michael. They bothered me.

We were still in Paul Isham's office, the door still closed. Outside, through the large glass window that made up the whole north wall of Paul's office looking out on Main Street, the street lights came on.

## TWENTY-THREE

*They come from everywhere for the funeral. The Governor is here, and both United States Senators, and the President of the University. The movers and shakers in politics and business crowd in; and people, plain people whose lives had been helped by Benjamin Dannan – the wronged, the mistreated, the abused; the ignored and taken-advantage-of, the forgotten – they are here. And newspapermen – from New York and Washington, from all over the state – they are here to see one of their own safely to ground.*

*Bishop Grimes drives down from Covington to say the Mass.*

*After the ceremony, the long funeral cortege winds slowly through town and up East Main hill to the cemetery. Traffic stops to let it pass. People along the streets stand silent.*

*It is a magnificent place, that cemetery, beautiful and peaceful beyond compare. It commands a large rolling meadow at the top of the high limestone cliffs that line the east bank of the river looking down on the city. Among the headstones, large oaks and maples rise, seeming older and more lasting than time.*

*Daniel Boone is buried here, and the soldier-poet Theodore O'Hara, after whom I am named, and the heroes of many wars. But for the most part it is a place for the dead of no particular distinction – other than that they were loved by this one or that and missed by those who remembered them.*

*The Dannan family plot is on a slight down slope in the Catholic section near the bowl-like meadow at the front of the cemetery. The hearse and the cars park along the sides of the road above it for there is no closer access. Rhae and Michael go first. A black veil hides her face, but she is steady as she walks, holding Michael's hand tightly in her own. When they are seated, the pall bearers swing the double doors open and roll the coffin slowly out. It is a long carry to the gravesite. They move slowly for they are not all young and the downhill walk is difficult with the weight of the coffin pulling on them and the footing slippery in the shadowed places where frost still lies. The mourners stand respectfully until the casket passes, then follow in a ragged file.*

*A low overcast filters the sun, strong enough to throw shadows, but not strong enough to dull the October chill. The women pull their coats about them. Men hunch their shoulders and shuffle.*

*The family is seated under a small canopy to the side of the open grave. Flowers are all around and a blanket of roses drapes the coffin. The dank smell of freshly turned earth is in the air.*

*Paul Isham walks out of the standing crowd. He leans down to whisper to Rhae Dannan and speaks briefly to the Bishop. He walks to the side of the coffin. The light murmur that has been running through the crowd begins to hush.*

*Isham stands with his head bowed for a moment. When he looks up, he lays his hand on the edge of the coffin and begins to speak.*

*"I ask your pardon for this presumption, Benjamin. Your colleagues at the Journal felt we couldn't let you go without a word. They nominated me to do the honors. I asked Rhae just now and she said it would be all right.*

*"There is no need for me to say much. Your life and your work speak well enough. And there is no way for me to say what is in our hearts. I don't have the words. You were a man of principle. You believed there is good and evil. And right and wrong. Not concretely drawn always, but clear enough that we should be able to see the markers no matter the circumstance. You believed that good should be rewarded and evil fought. You believed that right must prevail and the wrong must be shunned. You lived by those principles and you fought for them. We are all the richer for that.*

*"You were no paragon. You sometimes let your passions cloud your judgment. Your temper was now and then too quick. You were stubborn and prideful. But there was no kinder man, or fairer, or more loyal. There was no better friend."*

*Isham stops and looks around. He is not used to speaking in public. His voice is thin and in the open air it carries poorly, but the big crowd is silent, their eyes firmly on him, straining to hear.*

*He turns back to the coffin. "There is nothing more to be said. Your loss is a terrible thing and I, for one, will never forgive it. Rhae and Michael know they have our deepest sympathy and they know that whatever service we can do for them will be done."*

*Isham lowers his head and puts a hand back on the coffin. "Now old friend, good friend...good-bye."*

*He stands motionless for moment. Then he reaches out and takes a rose from the coffin and puts it in his lapel. He walks over to Rhae Dannan and kisses her gently on the cheek.*

*His movement breaks the spell. Sound begins to rise again. People shuffle to ease the strain of their standing. Muted conversations begin. A few sobs are heard. The Bishop moves forward. Holy water is sprinkled, the final blessing intoned. The pallbearers, who have been standing together at the foot of the grave, take their places on either side of the coffin. Bracing themselves, they begin to lower Benjamin Dannan slowly into the ground.*

*Throughout this, Michael has maintained his poise. He has not cried. He told me he would not. And he has not. Then the first spade of earth falls on the coffin below and he begins to sob heavily against his mother's shoulder. He is embarrassed to be crying, I can tell, but he cannot stop. Rhae puts her arms around him and, lifting her veil, she draws him to her. She whispers to him and strokes his hair. After a moment he is quieted. When he is ready, Rhae rises and takes his arm and they walk slowly to the waiting car. The crowd, then, begins to disperse.*

*At the crowd's edge, near the top of the slope where the cars are parked, a lone man stands watching. His hands are jammed into his overcoat pockets and his shoulders are hunched forward to the wind. He has stayed apart from the crowd. He is a big man, taller than any one around. Many seem to know him. The Governor walks over and takes his hand with easy familiarity, as do several others. Conversations are exchanged, shoulders patted, but in the somber and respectful manner as is proper on such occasions. But for these brief interruptions, the man's attention is riveted on the work at the gravesite below.*

*"That's Jesse Bristow, isn't it?" my mother says to my father. He looks up, then nods, "Yes."*

*We walk on.*

*Jesse Bristow watches the earth close over Benjamin Dannan.*

## TWENTY-FOUR

Even though it was late July, Betsy had a fire going. There was a chill on the night that the rain, which had started again, brought with it.

We were in the library at the farm, Rhae and Paul Isham on the couch in front of the fireplace and Michael and I in the big leather armchairs on either side of it. An oval hooked rug in soft hues of gray and red, the kind the mountain women make that wear like iron, was at our feet. Coffee and sandwiches were on the sideboard. The walls were books.

The only light in the room came from the fire. It was comforting and we could see each other well enough. We sat quietly, watching the play of the flames, considering.

Michael's and Rhae's meeting with Gershon Pope earlier in the day had been covered. It was successful, but there was friction that needed smoothing. And I had done my report on the opening of the safe deposit box at the bank in Berea.

Now the matter of the wallet held our minds.

Could a little oblong of leather, after all this time, unlock the mystery of the death of Benjamin Dannan? After having dealt with the pain and the misery of it and found a way out of the dismay and the despair, did Rhae and Michael want to open that door and go back over all of it again?

I had watched Rhae carefully as I told how we had found the wallet and what it contained. She looked at me directly, intent on what I was saying. No emotion betrayed her until I mentioned the photograph of herself with young Michael at her side. A little sob escaped and she reached across for Paul Isham's hand.

Michael watched the fire, not me. I couldn't tell how this news hit him. He seemed relaxed, but when he heard his mother sob he flinched as if drawing back from a blow. Otherwise he showed nothing outwardly.

Now, with all of it having been told and us sitting in the silence and shadows, waiting for someone to speak, it was as if we were at a moment no one wanted to go beyond, as if we all shared the feeling that it might be best to let what we didn't know remain unknown. Marne Young had felt that way before we went to Berea. I had, too, a bit.

Paul Isham broke the silence.

"We have to, Rhae," he said.

Rhae Dannan patted his hand, whether comforting him or her I couldn't say. She sighed a little sigh, and said, without looking at him, "Yes, I know." She turned to Michael. "Well, son?"

Michael had been splayed back in his chair, half withdrawn into whatever scenes he was conjuring in his mind. Rhae's tone was so plaintive it touched me deeply and I realized how little any of us knew of what they had gone through in losing Benjamin Dannan. We never really feel any loss but our own, never bear any grief but our own. Michael was just a child; Rhae just a young woman. What could we know of what they went through?

What I remember of that time is that Rhae stopped singing. She used to hum to herself and sing softly under her breath when she was deep in work that she enjoyed. That stopped.

And I remember that Michael was angry. Furious. Why did his father have to go to the mountains that day? Why couldn't he just stay home? It wasn't fair. It just wasn't fair!

None of us knew how to treat him. We all still had our fathers. None of us had known a death. Sorry for him? Yes. Uncomfortable around him? Yes. Able to treat him as if nothing had happened and go back to playing the way we had played before?

No.

I could understand that he didn't feel like playing. I just didn't know what to do about it. At first I honored his feelings, but after several days, with nothing improving, I decided to ignore them, to simply roll over them. I wouldn't let him off. In the afternoons when the time came for the choose-up games of touch football after school, I made him play. "We don't have enough boys without you. We need you. Come on." I'd say it loud enough and keep saying it strongly enough that sooner or later he'd be too embarrassed not to give in.

We played a rough game of touch – you weren't down until you were knocked down. With all that running and yelling – and hitting, Michael got better. The games gave him a way to vent, a way to hit, to smash someone and it be okay. I accompanied him home that first afternoon apprehensive that Rhae would be on us both and ready to explain that it was my fault, that Michael had not wanted to play, but that I had shamed him into it.

Michael's lip was split and his clothes were dirty. I wasn't in much better shape. But we were laughing and jostling as we came in. Rhae Dannan understood almost immediately. She laughed and hugged us both and made us hot chocolate that Michael had to drink through a straw.

In time, Michael's anger went away. Rhae Dannan submerged herself in the work of the farm and the newspaper, and in nurturing Michael.

She sold their place in town and moved them to the farm to be with her father, though he was to die within the year, adding even more to Rhae's sense of loss. But the farm was good for them both. Everyone on the place was like family to them and there was enough to do and enough going on that they had little time for brooding.

Michael had to ride a bus to school each day, rather than walk as he used to when they lived in town, and that left us with less time to play after school, but I would often ride the bus home with him in the afternoons and we'd play around the farm. Sometimes I stayed for supper. Sometimes I would spend the night.

When summer came, I almost lived there. We helped with chopping weeds in the tobacco fields, feeding the thoroughbreds, even mucking out the stalls. We fished every inch of the creek from the farm to its mouth near Strohmeir's Camp at the river.

It was a glorious summer. We were sun-browned and work-hardened, so happily tired at night that sleep came easily, and so excited about what the next day would bring that we could hardly wait for the nights to be over.

Benjamin Dannan never intruded on my thoughts. But not so for Rhae Dannan and Michael. He was with them – in Rhae's voice as she said the grace, in Michael's silence when I sometimes found him sitting in his father's chair in the den looking off into space. They put on a brave face, but it took a long time for the two of them to put the death of Benjamin Dannan behind them – if they ever did.

"Son?" Rhae said.

In the shadows, I couldn't see his face, but his voice was calm. He waited a moment, then said, "We don't have a choice. If there is a chance we can know what happened, how it happened, why it happened, we have to take it. Paul is right. We owe it to Father."

He sat forward in his chair, his face fully in the light now, looking like a man with no alternative but to do something he didn't want to do.

"But Theo is right, too. I don't want this to overshadow the campaign. I don't want this to become a media circus or a campaign issue. Whatever we do, we must do privately. We must not involve the police. At least not yet, not until we know what we have."

Paul Isham broke in, "But, Michael, I don't see how we can investigate…"

"Find a way," Michael said. His tone was not one that invited argument.

## TWENTY-FIVE

Jake Slade was retired.

He had been wooed away from the *Journal* to work as press secretary for the state highway department, which job he held through three administrations, a fact that speaks well for either his competence or his cunning, or both. When he could qualify for early retirement he took it.

At the time we went looking for him, he lived alone on the second floor of a time-worn brick office building on the short street that flanks the eastern side of the Old Capitol Building just a block or so from downtown. He'd bought the building, converted the upstairs to an office and apartment, and rented the downstairs out to a plumbing supply company. Rent from the tenant, occasional fees from free-lance writing assignments that still came to him, and a generous pension from the state seemed to accommodate his needs and wants with ample comfort.

Jake was a small man, not much larger than a jockey, given to bow-ties and snap-brim hats. Like many small men, he offset his size by an abundant aggressiveness.

Jake Slade had worked for Benjamin Dannan and Paul Isham for almost twelve years, hiring on at the *Journal* after a year at a weekly in Tennessee. When Benjamin Dannan was found dead in Breathitt County, he was the man Paul Isham assigned to the story. Jake spent the better part of a year digging at it, living in the county, walking the roads and the hollows, talking with everyone who would talk with him, but in the end he knew nothing more of any substance than everyone knew two days after the body had been found.

This was hard. This was bitter. He took it personally. To fail at this, to fail Benjamin Dannan and Paul Isham embarrassed him so badly it made him almost physically ill. But there was nothing to be done for it. The mystery was unyielding.

Over coffee in his kitchen looking out on the Old Capitol grounds, Paul Isham outlined what we had in mind.

He told Jake about the wallet and how we believed that knowing where Hanna Collins was at the time of Benjamin

Dannan's death and afterwards – knowing who she was with, what she was doing – would almost certainly help lead to his killer.

We would try for fingerprints off the wallet, Paul told him, but odds were that none were still legible. Our best shot was to be able to track Hanna Collins. This must be done discretely. We had to attract no attention, raise no suspicions.

Was it possible, did he, Jake, think, to conduct such an inquiry in that tightly knit country and not raise alarm?

And if it was, would he be willing to take the assignment?

Jake sat a long time before answering.

"It was tough up there, Paul. I never worked so hard at anything in my life. You know how private they are. You know how much they distrust strangers.

"But I kept at it and finally they began to open up to me a bit. Not all of them. Not even most of them. But enough that I had the feeling that nobody really knew anything. That's why we could never get a lead. Nobody knew anything. Hanna Collins? I never heard of her. I never even heard that Jesse Bristow had an aunt.

"Could I go back up there now? Ask questions about something that happened thirty years ago? Without raising a stir? Get any better answers than I got thirty years ago?"

He sat his coffee down, got up from his chair and walked to the window. We kept silent, waiting. After a while he turned back to us.

"Hanna Collins? Well, she's more than we had before. When do you want me to start?"

We shook hands.

Little Jake Slade was headed for the mountains again.

## TWENTY-SIX

The strategy was to have Michael's name surface as a possibility for the Governor's chair as if carried there by the unconscious will of a thirsting electorate, bursting on the scene like a comet propelled by natural forces, so right an idea and so clear a fit that the people would have it no other way.

Michael Dannan for Governor. Yes, by God, he's the answer! He's what we need!

The problem was that we were the only people who had such an idea – and we had to get it planted in enough minds that we could fan it into the conflagration it needed to be.

That was my task.

Plant the idea.

Fan the flames.

We had decided on the approach at the first full-scale strategy meeting with Gershon Pope. We met in a suite in the Taft Hotel in Cincinnati, overlooking the Ohio, with a view back over the river to Kentucky. Cincinnati was ninety miles away. We ran less risk of being noticed.

The setting was symbolic. There we were, standing on the bank of a river looking across to the Promised Land. Could we get in?

My column would be the instrument.

In it, for the Sunday paper, I would report that I had it on unimpeachable authority from a highly placed but unnamed source, that Michael Dannan, lately CEO of McKinnon Industries, one of the most respected and successful of American business executives and a Kentucky native, is giving serious thought to making a run for Governor.

I would write that I had been so far unable to confirm this with Dannan himself, but that the source said Dannan's energy, his charisma, and his record as a man who could get difficult things done while working with people of contrasting backgrounds and interests, would make him a golden candidate.

Not yet forty, a vital and handsome young man with a personal fortune that could put him out of the reach of special interests groups hoping to buy influence, Dannan might just "represent the fresh approach and incorruptible leadership the electorate wants after decades of self-dealing party politicians enriching themselves while the state's interests go to hell in a handbasket."

The story would say that if he announced, Michael Dannan would announce as a Democrat and run in the Democratic primary, even though it was a foregone conclusion that Jesse Bristow had the nomination already won.

Dannan was a political amateur with practically no name recognition. Bristow was one of the best known and most politically powerful men in the state. He owned the state Democratic Party machinery. His campaign was well financed, well organized, and well underway.

"On the surface," I would write, "it might seem no contest, but if Mr. Dannan is indeed brash enough to throw his hat in the ring, the state might be in for the most exciting political contest of modern times."

Even though the idea was Pope's, we all liked it.

I have to say, though, that I didn't care for Gershon Pope any more than Michael had on their first meeting. He was an arrogant little man, too soft to be fit and too fashionably dressed to be manly, with just enough New York accent to grate on the ear. His face in profile reminded me of an iguana with its hooded eyes and cold stare and flabby throat.

I had serious questions about his ability to work effectively with the people who would make up the day-to-day staff, but Pope had managed it successfully in Louisiana and Virginia.

Perhaps the secret was Lida McBain, his assistant. She who would be the go-between at the working level.

I liked Lida. She was almost as tall as I. Her hand, when I'd taken it on being introduced, was firm and she looked me in the eye with no artifice. She had a swimmer's broad shoulders and narrow hips and I had the feeling that the very proper gray pinstripe suit she wore hid a body that would be a distraction. She was all business, self-assured and serious, intent on being taken as a professional, but with a flash of humor that leavened Pope's stiffness and put us all at ease.

Pope had begun the meeting by informing us that it was important that we understood the strengths his organization brought to the campaign and to understand that if we followed his lead, Michael would be elected.

"You are a highly saleable product," he told Michael. "You won't take offense if I use that metaphor? Elections are marketing exercises and candidates are the products. In politics, as with any marketing problem, if you have a superior product and a superior marketing strategy that is executed with skill, you always win." He smiled his lizard smile. "You can quite frequently win with an inferior product if the marketing is skillful enough."

"And you're skillful enough," Michael said, half amused.

Pope's little smile flickered again. "We have a great deal of work to do in a very short time and it is very important that we understand each other."

"I'm to dance to your tune?" Michael said, no amusement this time.

"This isn't a dance, Mr. Dannan," Pope replied. "It is a deadly serious undertaking with a prize of considerable value. I have been asked to help you. I am doing that," Pope said. "In return, you must trust my judgment."

"I trust results," Michael said.

Pope pulled his hands together on the tabletop and made a little temple of them. "You are going to be a challenge, Mr. Dannan, but if you are smart enough to put your ego on hold and follow our lead, you will be Governor."

Under hooded eyes, Pope smiled. Michael smiled back.

Lida McBain, acutely aware, as was I, of the rising tension in the room, broke in.

"Oh, not all your ego by any means, Mr. Dannan," she said with a laugh. "Only the part that may want to be stubborn about good advice just to show who is boss. That sometimes happens and never with good results.

"What Gershon is saying is that we need the authority to run your campaign without being second-guessed. You must have had a similar arrangement with your subordinates at McKinnon Industries. You made policy and you let the experts do the work. This is the same. We're the experts. You are delegating authority to us. As for your ego, the part of it that reflects your self-confidence and your drive, that's one of our biggest assets. We're going to use it aggressively."

She turned brightly to Pope. "Isn't that right, Gershon?"

"Of course that's right. See how much more palatable a delicate matter is when run through a woman's filters, Mr. Dannan? Or at least through Lida's?" He smiled his half smile at her.

Well done, Lida, I thought.

## TWENTY-SEVEN

I had all of Saturday to craft my story.

I knew it would play big.

Michael's decision to step down as head of McKinnon Industries had been one of the major business stories of the year, covered in far more detail in New York and Los Angeles and the other major business and financial centers than in our state.

The chief of one of the world's largest and most powerful multinational firms vacating the CEO's chair for no apparent reason – no take-over looming, no failure in sight, no scandal brewing – why? Men didn't walk away from that kind of money and power except for reasons of health, internal coup, shareholder dissatisfaction, or age. None of these applied to Michael Dannan. So the riddle of why he would do such a thing generated almost as much interest as the move itself.

The big media ate it up. *The New York Times, The Wall Street Journal, The Chicago Tribune,* all the big city dailies, and all the major magazines – *BusinessWeek, Fortune, Time, Newsweek, Forbes* – all of them, gave the story banner play. Even network television was hooked.

They were all mystified.

The story played out over several weeks in the national media, with follow-ups quoting this expert or that about the why of it and where his next steps might take Michael Dannan.

And it played large enough here, but not with the same intensity since the state is neither an industrial nor a financial power. The angle here was "local boy who made good in an extraordinary fashion is up to something new."

Every paper in the state and most of the broadcast outlets carried the story of Michael leaving McKinnon. On the basis of that residue, if his named popped up in local media, it would likely attract attention.

Which I was about to make it do.

I kept my story straightforward and lean.

I didn't try for reaction from the political professionals or from the man in the street. That would be second-day stuff. My story simply reported that a hero might come riding out of the west to save the people from the clutches of the monster and lead the Commonwealth to that storied state of happiness and prosperity which it and its citizens so richly deserved. "Don't despair, ma'am, the cavalry's coming!" That was the message I wanted to get across.

We broke the story as an exclusive in the *Journal* with my byline under an eight-column above-the-masthead banner on page one. The wire services picked it up immediately and by mid-morning, the news that Michael Dannan was considering a run at the Governor's chair had been fed to every newspaper and radio and television station in the state.

By noon it was leading the twelve o'clock radio news. By mid-afternoon, the evening papers had their versions ready for their front pages. Reporters for the other morning papers in the state, who would be almost twenty-four hours behind by the time they got a story in print, began a frenzy of phone calls and contact milking to try to add new information to the piece or a new slant, guaranteeing a strong second-day play. TV newscasts that night led with the story on both the six o'clock and eleven o'clock shows.

The first day stories concentrated on the excitement of a political unknown coming out of nowhere to challenge the machine and steal the prize from an all-but-certain winner.

It grew in the second day into a running examination of whether that which was almost impossible might be possible after all.

By the third day, the experts were not willing to say it couldn't be done.

Throughout all of this Michael was unavailable to the media. This was a key part of the strategy. Keep him off-stage and let the demand build.

There were so many media calls to the farm asking for comment and interview time with Michael that Betsy wanted to turn the phones off.

Every caller was politely told that Mr. Dannan was out of town and would be back late Sunday night. He would certainly return their calls as rapidly as he could. Michael *was* out of town, in west Kentucky with Dace Havershamp, a contrived trip, but our fundamental rule going in, Michael's and mine, was "no lies." We would tell no lies to the media. We would tell no lies at all. We might be very thoughtful in the way we phrased an answer, but we wouldn't lie.

Lying is dumb.

Lying in public is crazy.

So without direct quotes from Michael Dannan, the follow-up stories were built on the speculation and guesses of the usual crew of political pundits, party officials, and "informed sources," who knew no more about what was happening than anyone else but never passed up an opportunity to get their names in print.

"Inconceivable," said one widely respected expert. "Jesse Bristow has the Democratic Party machinery in his hip pocket and the machine delivers the nomination to its candidate like clockwork. But this Dannan character, well, he has some appeal."

"He's young," said another. "He has a good record in business. He photographs well. His lack of political experience could prove an asset – no debts owed, not beholden to anyone. He's the sort of candidate you could get excited about, and we haven't had one of those since Happy Chandler."

'If anyone thinks an amateur is going to beat Jesse Bristow and the machine, he's crazy. But I'd give a month's salary to see him try," the *Courier-Journal's* political columnist wrote. "It's time the politicos in this state get a wake-up call. Maybe Dannan is the man to shout it."

A few nay-sayers noted the obvious. "He has no organization, no funding. The race is already underway and Dannan is entering it late and as a dark horse against a man with money to spare and no lack of friends or know-how. It's a joke, isn't it? A rich man feeding his ego trying to play Jack the Giant Killer?"

Fair comment, but no one much picked up on it. People were interested. Michael Dannan was interesting.

Gershon Pope could not have been more pleased.

As we sat down together that weekend to review the report of the press coverage that Lida McBain had assembled, he smiled his little hooded smile, lifted his glass of Glen Livet in toast, and said, "Gentlemen, and ladies, I believe we have a horse race."

He sipped, sighed in appreciation, put his glass down, and turned to Michael. "And this is the way we will come out of the gate." He darted a fast glance around the table to see if we got his racing metaphor. Lida was smiling slightly. Michael looked pained. I smiled, too, knowing that it was expected.

Fixing on Michael, he said, "You will start returning the media calls first thing Monday morning. Each call will result in a story – a local story, not one picked up off the wires and shared with media state-wide, a story by 'our guy in our paper' – *The Paducah Sun, The Hardin County Independent, the Corbin News, the Lexington Herald, the Winchester Sun* and all the others."

Lida McBain jumped in. "The question all the reporters will ask is, are you running?"

Pope nodded. "And your answer to all will be the same, 'Should I?' Reporters aren't usually asked for their opinions. They will be flattered…and we might get a useful answer. In any event, it will stroke the reporter's ego."

Lida came in again, "And you won't elaborate or guess or respond to what-if questions. You'll smile and be engaging and keep repeating in various ways that the questions that are being asked are valid questions *to be put to a candidate*. But you're not a candidate… yet. When, and if, you became one, you'll be happy to answer all the questions anyone wants to ask."

Pope leaned back in his chair and finished what was clearly a well planned exchange. "Lacking a Dannan answer to a specific question, the media has no recourse but to put the question to the various observers and experts out there who will be all too eager to share their views as to what they think Michael Dannan's answer to issue X or problem Y might be, how they think he will handle the key problems facing the Commonwealth. This has the advantage of identifying high-interest issues and possible courses of action for us without putting you at risk in any way. We will test all these ideas with extensive polling later, take the good ones and work them into our campaign."

Pope was obviously pleased with himself. Lida McBain, too. I couldn't fault them. It was an excellent strategy. I could see Michael bristling at being told what he would and wouldn't do, but he saw the sense of the plan.

And that's the way we "came out of the gate."

Michael was golden on television. And just as good with print. He did all the interviews asked of him that week, using the strategy we had agreed upon. He was self-effacing, humorous, and thoughtful.

He came across as a man you could trust, a man you could put your faith in. He looked like a winner.

## TWENTY-EIGHT

By Monday of the following week, Michael's non-candidacy was as well launched as we could have hoped.

If you lived out of the reach of newspaper, radio, or TV you might not have heard the news that a native son had come home and might soon be taking on the rich and powerful to get back for the people the prosperity and the respect that was rightfully theirs... a man to right the wrongs... make sure there were jobs, and schools, and housing....to make sure there was decent treatment for all.

Even if the media didn't reach you – and you would have had to be blind, deaf, or in solitary confinement to have missed it – word of mouth would have.

One man against the system!

One man on our side!

One man to champion us, to fight for us and get those dirty, bloodsucking bosses and bankers and politicians and corporations off our backs.

And isn't the state in awful shape? Just look at the roads. And the hospitals! Lord, lord, they are a disgrace. And don't we need someone to get things back together again? Don't we need to get rid of the courthouse gangs that are stealing us blind? Don't we need to clean out those party hacks in the Capitol that are selling us out to the special interests?

Don't we?

Don't we need it now?

Mightn't this Dannan be the man?

Did you hear about him?

Ain't he grand?

The media didn't say these things directly. But the coverage started people wondering, and guessing, and speculating and running the idea through their collective minds that maybe someone who could make things better was standing close in the shadows, not one of the political barons, not someone who would dance to the party machine's tune, but someone who, honest-to-God, would be on their side.

It had appeal.

It had resonance.

That weekend, Lida McBain quietly began assembling a staff, mostly locals, people who knew their way around county courthouses, who could navigate the halls of the Capitol up in Frankfort. People who were on a first-name basis with the editors of the local weekly newspaper and the presidents of the local school boards. Pros, all of them, but not on the Party favorites list, or who didn't make the cut with the Bristow team. People who were a little bitter, a little anxious.

Jonathan Wilson and Dace Havershamp had recruited them, sworn them to secrecy, promised them the fruit of the spoils when they had won the state.

Their mission was to create the *spontaneous* "Draft Michael Dannan" campaign.

Student groups on college campuses would all at once begin to form, chanting for Michael Dannan. Letters to the editor would begin to appear in the dailies and weeklies that dot the state, urging that Michael Dannan run. Women's clubs and garden clubs would find themselves discussing it. Michael Dannan and his possible candidacy would be talked about at the Lions and the Kiwanis and the Rotary. Rallies would be held. Small at first, then larger and larger until they were being talked about by everyone. All this would generate more stories in the local newspapers and on the radio.

Television would pick up the rallies. Soon, it would be a self generating. Letters would spawn more letters, rallies would fire more rallies. All demanding that Michael Dannan run. All insisting the state couldn't do without him.

Oh, *spontaneous* is very effective.

Lida McBain was a genius at creating it.

How could Michael ignore this, how could he stand against so much honest, passionate public demand?

How, indeed?

Clearly it would appear that Michael Dannan had no choice. He had to run. The public demanded it.

That's what I wrote in my column that Wednesday.

That column took the A head spot on page one of the *Journal* and played on the front pages of all but two of twenty key papers in which I was syndicated.

It opened the door.

It lowered the floodgate.

Maybe my reportage in those first few weeks was less objective than it might have been. Perhaps I painted a more appealing picture of Michael in my stories than a stand-apart observer would do. I had opinions and I expressed them in my column. That's what columnists do. But in my reportage, I kept it straight. My critics are right when they say that my early stories helped set the tone for the way a good portion of the media subsequently presented Michael. I acknowledge that. I don't apologize for it. I intended it to. I believed what I wrote.

Pope and Lida McBain thought it would take Jesse Bristow's people a couple of weeks to figure out what we were doing and then maybe another week to digest it and get concerned about it.

"They won't take you seriously," Pope told Michael. "Why should they? Jesse Bristow has the machine behind him. He has the organization, the backing, the money. A Johnny-come-lately rich kid with no experience and no constituency isn't going to steal the nomination away from Jesse Bristow! No, they won't take you seriously…at first. And by the time they begin to, we'll have so much momentum they can't turn us back."

Another week passed. Across the state "Draft Dannan" signs appeared on telephone poles and fence posts, sprouted from people's lawns. Banners were strung on city streets.

Understand, some of this may truly have been spontaneous. Most of it, however, was Lida McBain and her team working in the trenches. *Spontaneous* is too important to be left to chance. *Spontaneous* take organization.

Seasoned political observers around the state called what was happening an avalanche, a runaway locomotive of public opinion. Whether this represented true enthusiasm for Michael or disgust with the status quo was beside the point. The point was that here was drama, here was excitement. Here was Galahad!

That's what I wrote, and it was true and it was straight.

# TWENTY-NINE

A note was waiting for me when I got to my desk at the *Journal*. By then the column had played in the other papers in the syndication. The syndication contract gave the *Journal* an exclusive right to run it on Sundays; once it had run in the *Journal*, the other papers were free to use it at will.

The note was handwritten, rolled under the platen bar of my typewriter. I recognized the hand: Governor Justin Curtis.... *former* Governor Justin Curtis... previous resident of the Mansion, who had been unable to run to succeed himself since Kentucky limited its Governors to one term at a time. Curtis had been embarrassingly unable to engineer the election of a Democrat to succeed him, so he had to surrender the post to the Republican Warren Parsons, who now sat in the chair at the top of Capitol Avenue. Ex-*Governor* Justin Curtis, now titular head of the state Democratic party was the chief endorser of Jesse Bristow to win the Capitol back for its rightful inhabitants.

Governor Justin Curtis, my old friend.

He had summoned me frequently in this manner when he was Governor and I was writing about him. He liked it personal. He liked it private. No intermediaries. A handwritten note. A discreet meeting. Only the two of us knowing what was discussed or what was said.

"Theo, old friend," the note read, "spare me a moment, please, and come talk with me about a matter of mutual interest. Say around six-thirty this evening? My office? Just us." That's all there was. That's all that was needed.

I called Michael and then Lida.

"I think the balloon is about to go up," I told Michael. "Governor Curtis has summoned me and I have no doubt what the subject is." Michael was delighted. He was ready for the formal battle to begin. Lida was less eager, but not displeased. "Michael is cresting now. All the polls say so," she said. "We'll never be in stronger position to announce than in the next week or so. It will be a dead-run, but fine. Let's get our dancing shoes on and crash the party."

Governor Curtis' office sat at the top of Shelby Street, in an elegant two-story white frame house of early 1900's vintage that overlooked the Capitol. An old fashioned roofed porch wrapped all the way around and there was a widow's walk on top. The first floor housed the Kentucky Democratic Party and its staff. The second floor was given over to the Governor.

The downstairs offices were closed when I got there. An outside set of wooden stairs gave private access to the second floor. I took those, paused at the top to look out over the dome of the Capitol and down to the town and the river winding through it. The sky was still light, but it was darkening in the valley and street lights were beginning to come on. A small breeze had sprung up, pushed in by what looked like rain clouds advancing up the valley. I took a deep breath and thought as I watched the early September twilight fade and the mist rise off the river, "My God, what a beautiful place." I might have stood longer, watching the rain come up the river, but a voice said, "Come on in, Theo. No point in standing there and getting wet."

The Governor stood behind me. I hadn't heard him open the door, though he must have heard me coming up the steps. I laughed, "No sir, no point in it," took his extended hand and entered.

He took a seat behind his desk and motioned me to a chair.

There was an innate decency about Curtis, a quality that all his years as a politician had not managed to erase. Had he been able to run for election again I would have supported him. But I couldn't support the man he had chosen to succeed him...a posturing, pretentious little prosecuting attorney from Louisville who had a modest reputation as a crime-buster and a born-again Christian. I've never been comfortable with people who pray aloud in public or see no conflict in taking large donations from interests they have sworn to oppose.

Governor Curtis should have put his weight behind Jesse Bristow in '67, not "Little Jimmy" Nugent. Jesse Bristow wanted the nomination badly and probably could have won the general election had he got it, but Curtis backed Nugent, with how much urging from the gambling interests in northern Kentucky I was never able to determine. The decision cost the Democrats the governor's chair.

"Little Jimmy," crime buster and preacher extraordinaire, won the Democratic nomination but lost the election to Republican Warren Parsons, whose cause I helped by exposing Nugent's faults as often and as loudly as I could in my column.

So now ex-Governor Curtis found himself in the painful position of titular leader of a defeated party whose members were not in awe of his political judgment and having to back Jesse Bristow who, for good reason, disliked and distrusted him. He was like a toothless tiger with a new ring-master cracking the whip – still roaring, but not being taken too seriously.

I waited.

The only sound was the wind running through the trees outside.

He eyed me sternly for a minute, then lifted his glasses and rubbed his face with both hands, eyes closed, gently working his fingers back and forth across his forehead, then slowly in small circles around his temples.

When his eyes opened, he sat back. "You didn't run into any of your reporter friends on your way here?" he asked.

"Not a one."

"I wouldn't want anything made of this meeting. This is purely between you and me. Private. Confidential. Understand?"

"You look tired, Governor," I replied.

"The work of the people is wearying work, but it is the work of the Lord and I do it gratefully."

I had to smile.

"Your friend Michael Dannan is making quite a stir."

"He is, indeed," I said.

"You are making most of the noise."

"I'm only doing my job, Governor. Just trying to report what's happening."

"Of course," he said. "The fact that he is your friend doesn't have anything to do with it."

"You're my friend, Governor. Did you ever feel I went out of my way to make things easier for you?"

That got a bigger laugh than I expected.

Still chuckling, he leaned down, reaching for something in the desk. He came up with a bottle of I.W. Harper. One hundred proof. Nearly full. He sat the bottle on the edge of the desk along with a silver jigger that had the University of Kentucky emblem on it.

He carefully filled the jigger, put it to his lips and drank it down. And another. Followed by a sip of cold water from the carafe on his desk. "Water of life, Theo, water of life."

"You?" he asked holding the bottle toward me.

I shook my head no.

"Know the secret to drinking?" the Governor said. "Take two fast poppers. Then don't take another drink for an hour. Take another popper then and one every hour after that. Builds a pleasant glow. But you never get tight. You're drinking with everyone. You're one of the boys. You're staying with them. But they're getting drunk and you're not." He nodded his head as if confirming something to himself. "Takes discipline."

He reached for the bottle again and capped it.

"How do you take your bourbon when you take it, Theo, neat or watered?"

"I like a little branch in mine, Governor."

That seemed to corroborate what he had already concluded. He wiped the silver jigger with a starched white handkerchief from his hip pocket, then put the bottle and the cup away.

He leaned back, his chair protesting the weight, folded his hands over his comfortable stomach and said, "Now tell me what Mr. Dannan is up to."

"He's listening to the people," I said.

"He isn't thinking seriously about running!"

"He is."

"He couldn't win in a coon's age. Hell, he can't run anyway. You've got to be a legal resident in this state to run for office. He isn't."

"I'm afraid he is, Governor. His company kept moving him from place to place so often that he decided to keep his legal residence here, at his mother's farm.

"That so? You suppose that's luck or has he been planning this?"

"For over twenty years? Come on, Governor, not even you are that calculating," I said.

"What does he really want? He must want something?"

"He wants the job you used to have, Governor," I said.

"You know what will happen if he enters this race, Theo. Everything he has ever done, or his family, or the company that he works for, anything that can in any way be made to appear venal, immoral, irresponsible, or just plain dumb will be made to appear that way."

Outside we could hear the start of the rain pinging off the windows.

"That company of his? McKinnon? It can't have an absolutely clean record. Somewhere they've cheated customers, or mistreated employees, or raped the environment. His family? Rhae's little empire? Is everything there on the up and up? No corners cut on taxes? No favors given to get a state printing contract? His father's death? That's still a mystery. Something there doesn't make sense. Dannan can't want this whole Pandora's Box of unknowns opened up. And if it can be made to appear that you're using your influence as a newspaperman, putting out propaganda to get him elected, you'll get crucified."

"Dace Havershamp and Sattis Arnow and Judge Blue and Jonathan Winslow are already in Michael's camp," I said. "They seem to think he can win it. Dace will be the campaign chairman."

He looked surprised. He reached for the desk drawer and brought out the I.W. Harper again. He held a glass out to me.

"Has it been an hour?" I said.

He didn't deign to laugh.

"I don't want this fight, Theo," the Governor said. "It will be scorched earth and the Devil take the hindmost. There won't be any prisoners taken or wounded spared."

He tipped back his shot.

"I like Rhae. I don't know Mr. Michael Dannan but I imagine he's a fine young man. I didn't know his father. But I know his reputation. Why put that at risk? Jesse Bristow is ready to assign a dirt team to this if Dannan enters. They'll find everything there is to find and if that's not enough, they'll manufacture whatever else is needed. Tell Dannan to back off."

"I don't think he'll do that."

"Find yourself a bomb shelter then," ex-Governor Curtis said, reaching for the bottle again.

I left the same way I'd come, out the side door and down the wooden steps onto Shelby Street.

It was full dark.

The rain had passed.

Through scudding clouds I could see occasional patches of black sky, and, now and then, stars.

I walked slowly down the hill to the broad stone parapet at the front of the Capitol, savoring the night.

Before me spread the full length of Capitol Avenue, its broad expanse glistening in the streetlights, straight and regal, all the way down to the river. There were no office buildings along the route, no stores, no shops. It pleased me immensely that the Capitol of the Commonwealth sat at the end of a street on the slope of a hill surrounded by homes.

White globed lights on fluted green lamp posts ringed the slender sidewalk that circled the Capitol grounds, making little luminous spots on the wet pavement and sparkles on the edges of the grass. Beyond the lawns were dark trees, steady in the night.

As boys, Michael and I played hide'n'seek among these trees. That was before Michael's father's death, before Michael and Rhae Dannan moved out to the farm.

They're scared, I thought. Then I caught myself. No, Jesse Bristow isn't scared. But he wants to scare Michael.

A lone car moved up the avenue. I watched its headlights grow larger, then it turned on Todd Street and the avenue was deserted again. Well, I said to myself, I guess the battle is joined.

## THIRTY

Michael Danna announced his candidacy for Governor the following Monday – Labor Day, September 7, 1970.

No point in waiting. They knew and would be coming after us. Strike before they could, that was the strategy.

He chose Perryville, population 6,000, a little farm community on the edge of the outer-Bluegrass, an hour or so due south of the Capitol.

Convenient for no one.

One of the bloodiest battles of the Civil War had been fought there.

Gershon Pope argued against it. "The wrong associations," he said, "war and death, a state divided, blood and suffering. It's a turn-off. A negative. There are no votes in it."

"No," Michael argued, "we'll make it a symbol of courage and causes, of honor and sacrifice, of coming together after a time of great conflict and disaster, a symbol of a new state rising from the ashes of the old."

In the end, Pope gave in, partly because Lida liked the idea and partly because there would be more important issues to fight over later and he wanted the leverage of having been reasonable.

The press grumbled, but Lida organized a special bus for them and made arrangements for radio and television feeds which could be taken live or taped for later use. Reporters for the *New York Times* and the *Washington Post* joined the local entourage. The idea that a political unknown had come out of nowhere at the last minute to challenge an entrenched machine was the big political story of the waning year.

Rain fell that morning in drops so small it seemed a mist. The U.S. Weather Bureau in Lexington offered hope of clearing by noon. The ceremonies were scheduled for two p.m. With the three speeches, Michael's and two endorsers, it should all be over by three. Which meant the story would be perfectly positioned for the six o'clock television newscasts and reuse at eleven, and that print reporters would have ample time to work their copy for the next morning's papers.

Paul Isham escorted Rhae Dannan and together they roamed the crowd of well-wishers and supporters, welcoming them, stroking them.

Michael waited alone in a plain car in the deserted parking lot of a Tastee Freeze on the Danville side of Perryville. There was a "Closed" sign in its window. A few soggy wrappers lay limply on the pavement.

Michael's entrance needed to be properly timed.

The press should be assembled and in place, the guests and supporters arranged, an air of expectation and excitement building.

Then he should arrive.

Alone. Driving an everyday, three-year-old blue Chevrolet. Park at the Visitor's Center lot.

Be met by Rhae, and the two of them, son and mother, arm in arm, walk up the hill to the flag-draped platform to the sound of applause and camera's clicking.

When the time was right, Lida would call Michael on the field-grade walkie-talkie purchased for that purpose.

The rain stopped just before noon. Though no longer dripping, the sky stayed somber. No sun shown through. Lida was delighted. The soft, gray light was just right, more dramatic than sunlight. Sunlight is for victories and endings, for bands playing and banners snapping proudly in the breeze. It is for heroes come home and bold objectives achieved.

For beginnings, for the start of momentous matters, the cold light of destiny is to be desired.

Michael moved the crowd even more than even Lida or I had thought he could.

He stood under darkening skies on the hillside where the 16th Tennessee came yelling up the gentle rise into the mouth of the Union cannon in the opening charge of the battle of Perryville.

Neither side picked the ground. It was a chance encounter. Skirmishers out searching for water ran into each other around the stagnant puddles that were all that remained of Doctor's Creek. A withering drought lay on the land and both armies were suffering from thirst.

The Confederates, 16,000 strong under the command of General Braxton Bragg, had invaded from Tennessee, hoping to take control of Kentucky and with it, control of the war. General Don Carlos Buell of the Union moved out of Louisville with an army of 58,000 to repel them.

The fight started about two that afternoon. Surging back and forth through the trees and across the meadows and up the hills, they fought into the twilight. When night came, a full moon rose and they kept on fighting by its fairy light.

By midnight it was over.

The dead and the wounded numbered seven thousand six hundred and ninety-two. In a few hours of an autumn afternoon and part of a moonlit night, almost eight thousand men and boys were shot, bayoneted, ripped by artillery, cut down by saber. Their bodies lay twisted among the dry corn-stalks, on the drought-bleached grass, on the split-rail fences.

Though the ground was parched, it couldn't soak up the blood. It ran in streamlets down the hills to make crimson pools in the dry bed of Doctor's Creek. Even the generals took notice.

Had Bragg been bolder, he might have won Kentucky and dealt a crippling blow to the Union. At that stage of the war, Kentucky was the linchpin for victory. President Lincoln had said when informed of the Confederate incursion, "I hope to have God on my side, but I must have Kentucky. To lose Kentucky is to lose the war." The South's chances to tip the scales were never better than at Perryville.

Bragg and his outnumbered troops had won the battle, but he hadn't the daring to press his advantage. He disengaged and began to withdraw.

General Buell let him.

Had Buell given chase, he might have demolished Bragg's army and brought the war to a swifter conclusion. But he hadn't the resolve.

So with that soft October moon beaming down, and by unspoken agreement, the armies collected their dead and their wounded as best they could, sometimes walking side by side among the broken bodies searching for their own.

Behind Michael, just beyond the tree line, the Corn Field Ambush took place, and to his right was the pit where the

Confederate dead that had been left on the field were finally buried.

The Union dead had been collected the day after the fight and interred along the Springfield Pike. Many of the Confederates still lay where they fell. Their general, a cautious man, left them. As soon as it was light, he gathered his remaining forces and headed south as fast as he could, leaving the dead and the wounded to the mercies of enemies and strangers.

A local farmer, moved by pity at the sight of it and fear of the growing stench, began to bury those he could. Others joined him. Between them, sweating in the heat of the day, swatting through clouds of green flies, they carried the boys from Tennessee and Alabama and Georgia, the boys from Louisiana and the Carolinas and Kentucky – over three hundred of them in all – to thee spot near where Michael stood and buried them in a common grave. Their names are unknown still.

Michael spoke about the battle, about the courage and the suffering and the heroism on both sides. He spoke how bitter it must have been for father to fight against son and brother against brother on home ground, for no state had been so divided as Kentucky.

He told them what a glorious disaster it had been and made them see how tragic the failures of both sides were – not the failure of the soldiers, they fought magnificently – but the failure of the commanders.

"My great-grandfather fought here," he said. "Many of your forefathers fought here, too. Whether they wore the Blue or the Gray isn't important now. What is important is that they fought for their beliefs and after it was over, if they survived, they found a way to come together and rebuild this state and this country. They fought their common enemies. They raised the Commonwealth back to its feet again.

"We must do the same. We must come together against our common enemies. Our enemies are sickness and hunger and despair. Our enemies are poverty and ignorance and joblessness. Greed-blinded leaders and gutless government, these are our enemies, our common foes. They impoverish us all. We can tolerate them no longer. We can pay their price no longer. The price is too high. We must come together to rid ourselves of them. Now! We must put this Commonwealth back on its feet again. Now!

"I didn't come home with any idea of doing this. But I have listened to what you have had to say. I have read your letters. I have heard your call. And in response to that call, with great humility and the promise that you will have from me all that I have to give, I offer myself to you today as a candidate for the Democratic nomination for the office of Governor of the Commonwealth of Kentucky."

Silence.

The wind in the trees.

Silence.

Then they were on their feet cheering and yelling. The field erupted in a wave of sound.

Michael stood on the small raised platform, erect and unsmiling, lost in the seriousness of the moment. Some began to push forward up the hill to be near him. That broke his concentration. He began to smile and wave and it seemed the whole crowd surged and soon he was engulfed in a sea of coats and embraces.

It was made for television.

In the midst of the crowd around Michael, a well dressed, elderly woman holding a young boy by the hand edged toward him. Her hair was silver and her back slightly bent. The boy seemed excited, but shy. Finally she was close enough to Michael to touch his elbow. She tugged at it and he looked around. He saw her and with a broad smile leaned down to hear her clearly. She whispered something in his ear. He smiled again, looked at the boy and offered his hand. The boy took it bashfully. The boy said something, then stepped back. Michael smiled and nodded. The woman stretched up and kissed him on the cheek.

The cameras never left him during this exchange.

When he straightened up again and looked out over the milling crowd as if searching for someone, the cameras came in tight on his face. He looked like the leader they had all been waiting for, whether they knew it or not. Here he is, the images said, this is him. Don't fail him. Follow where he leads.

Michael's gaze finally fixed on the object of his search. There, at the foot of the hill, was Allie.

The crowd was still around him. He was talking and laughing, but watching her. When their eyes met, he smiled and kissed his fingers to her and bowed quite formally. At the bottom of the hill, with a crowd around her, too, she laughed and made a dignified curtsy.

The mist-like rain began again toward evening.

Michael had gone off for television interviews in Louisville. I looked for Allie, but couldn't find her. So Rhae Dannan and Paul Isham and I waited for Rhae's car out of the weather in the little visitor's center near the entrance to the memorial. I had already filed my story, had written most of it, in fact, before leaving for Perryville.

A black Buick, its windshield wipers going, pulled up in front of us and the driver popped out to open the doors.

Rhae Dannan looked apologetically at both of us. "It does seem a little pretentious, doesn't it?" she said. "A driver after all these years. But I became tired of looking for places to park. Do you think so? Do you think it seems pretentious?"

"For a woman of your station? Not in the least," said Isham, helping her into the car. He followed and sank back in plush wine leather seats. I climbed in front with the driver. "Seems a very smart thing to me," Isham said.

The driver turned out of the property onto the Mackville Road. The headlights cut into the mist like yellow lances.

"I think it went well today," she said.

"It went very well," Isham said.

"I suppose the whole thing will have to come up again. It will come up again, won't it, Paul?"

"I'm afraid so," Isham said.

The car turned off the county road onto the main road to Danville. The Buick's suspension system worked like a cradle and we seemed to float through the misty night, lulled by the sound of the road and the wipers and the rain.

## THIRTY-ONE

So it was done.

Official. No longer a plan or a possibility or a conjecture.

We were committed.

From that day on the gloves would come off, the knives would come out, and nothing would ever be the same again.

The prospect exhilarated me, I admit... Michael and I stepping off on an uncertain road to the conquest of a kingdom. Adventure. Danger. Power and glory and the envy and gratitude of the people, bless their hearts.

That's what I thought, lying there in my bed half asleep that Sunday morning while the Baptist Church bells ringing across the river kept reminding me that the faithful were already up and out and doing God's work.

Well, we might be doing it, too. We were going to do *good!*

It was a sophomoric idea ... an idealist's fantasy. I still hadn't been fully disabused of either then – the idealist's certainty that good works will eventually produce good results, the romantic's conviction that fairness and justice is everyone's due. I'd seen the blood and suffering in Korea. I'd touched the rot and smelled the corruption of politics and big business. I am a newspaperman, for God's sake.

But that morning, with Michael's words on the battlefield at Perryville still in my mind, words I'd helped write – that Sunday morning in the warmth of my bed, I believed.

I listened to the bells awhile, lazing in bed – the baritone of the Baptist soon accompanied by the alto of the Catholic, the two churches less than a block apart, their calls melding and harmonizing while their congregations brushed past each other on their way to entreat the same God in separate houses.

I had the apartment above Pete's Restaurant on the corner of Bridge and Second Streets. The perfect location for me. Down the stairs, around the corner and up a block to the Old Bridge. Cross the river. Nod to the Baptist Church. Turn left past the Catholic Church and go a half block to Workhouse Alley. Take a right down the alley to the side entrance to the

*Journal.* I could be at my desk in ten leisurely minutes or less. Or if the Capitol was my destination, down the stairs, left up Second Street to Shelby and straight up Shelby to the East Wing entrance. Eight easy blocks under sheltering oaks and maples, past well kept lawns and neat houses with big front porches.

I liked the walk best in the dark of the early mornings coming home after the paper had been put to bed. The town belonged to me then. No one else was about. The only sound was the sound of my footfall on the pavement. Sometimes a distant bark. Sometimes the faint whistle of the morning train coming up the valley from Georgetown. There might be a full moon with its light filtering through the trees and making patterns on the empty sidewalks. Or white fog folding through the bends of the river. Sometimes a hard rain blowing. Sometimes snow falling so gently that the separate flakes could almost be counted as they floated down. It was a fine thing to have all this to yourself alone.

By the time I finished my coffee, those of the church crowd who lived in South Frankfort were already strolling past the corner – their Sunday morning obligation filled. Some would be stopping in at Pete's for lunch. I pulled back the curtain and watched the procession – couples coming down off the bridge, families, a few children running ahead. Peaceful. Reassuring.

When Michael and I were boys, Pete's Corner was where we all gathered...after school if there was no football practice, after dates on weekend nights, after church on Sundays. Our high school was just four blocks up Shelby Street. The Catholic high school was just across the bridge. It was a natural magnet.

It was there we first saw Allie.

I put my empty cup in the sink and thought about calling her.

I didn't. Instead, I squared away the kitchen, dressed, made my way down the steps and to my car. Jim Colby and his family were just rounding the corner on their way home from church as I hit the pavement.

"Theo, hold up a minute," he called to me.

I stopped and waited for them. His two boys were running ahead. His wife Julie had their little girl by the hand beside them.

"Great news this morning," he said, a big smile on his face. "We read your story first thing. He's really going to do it!"

"It's so exciting," Julie came in. "He'll get all the women's vote!"

"Let's get everybody together, all the old gang, get the ball really rolling." Jim was beaming. "Governor! One of us! Get everybody behind him!"

"Yes," Julie said, "a party – a big party. We can host it. We could do it down at the camp on the river. Like old times. Oh, that would be so much fun. Getting everybody together again!"

"What do you think, Theo? Sound good?"

"I think it's a great idea," I said.

The boys were almost at the far corner now, looking to dart across the street.

"Gotta go," Jim said. "Hold up, boys, don't you go in that street," he yelled. Julie smiled one of those what-can-you-do-about-boys smiles, "I'll be in touch," Jim said over his shoulder as they hurried off.

# THIRTY-TWO

*Allison Boatwright Sinclair.*

*Allie.*

*An April morning.*

*Sunday.*

*I'm standing on the corner with Jim Colby. Michael has just joined us. The Catholics always seem to take longer at service than we Baptists.*

*Most of the church crowd is past us, though people are in no hurry. It is a glorious morning, the first real spring morning of the year and everyone is enjoying it. The girls have broken out their pastels and, chattering and laughing, flow toward us in little eddies of color. It is close enough to church time that for proprieties' sake we still have our jackets on and our ties knotted, but in another hour we won't.*

*A warming sun. A sky as blue as you'd want with a few chubby white clouds to give it character. The silver arch of the Old Bridge rises above the new green leaves of the sycamores along the river. Back a bit farther, with just their tops visible, are the red brick tower of the Baptist Church, the marble cupola of the Post Office, and the tall white spire of the Catholic Church.*

*Bridge Street on Sunday morning in the spring of another time.*

*We flirt with the girls as they come past. That's the point of being here. We know most of them. We know all of the pretty ones. Most of them know us. We're the reigning jocks. Class officers. Jim Colby is on his way to Vanderbilt with a basketball scholarship in the fall. Michael and I share All-Conference football honors. In our small town, almost everyone knows us.*

*A group of about five or six girls approaches, animated, engrossed in their conversation, paying us no attention, concentrating instead on holding the attention of a girl in the center of the group, a girl we've never seen before. Her hair is the color of spun gold. She is no taller than the other girls, but she moves with such grace that the others merit no notice. A white straw hat with a broad brim and a red ribbon frame her face and set off dark blue eyes.*

*She's past us before we can react. We watch her all the way down the block, transfixed.*

*Finally, Michael turns to me and says, "Who was that?"*

"I don't know," I said, "but I'm going to find out."

"After me," says Jim Colby.

"Get in line," Michael says. "I saw her first. She's mine."

That night I call Julie Espy, who was in the group with our mystery girl. Julie is a friend since grade school. Nothing romantic. Just a good friend. "That was Allie," she tells me, "Allison Boatwright Sinclair. They moved here this week. Her father is the manager at the new plant out on Georgetown Road. I think he knows Mrs. Dannan."

"Is she going to our school?"

"Enrolls Monday."

"Put in a good word for me," I said.

Michael did his own detective work.

But I got there first.

## THIRTY-THREE

It was to be a quiet Sunday supper to celebrate Michael's announcement of the day before – a family supper, Michael, Rhae, Paul Isham and me.

They had come to seem like family to me. My dad had passed when I was in Korea. My mother, four years ago. Lord, how I missed her. I have no brothers or sisters. Mom's family is large and spread throughout the county. Farmers mostly. I have cousins and aunts and uncles and am welcome at every one. But we haven't much in common except the blood. The blood is enough for Christmas and Thanksgiving and the family reunion every year. But not enough for every day.

The evening was mild. We ate outside on the big porch looking down to the creek. A whippoorwill was calling in the distance and specks of starlight were appearing overhead.

Candles flickered lazily. A light breeze carried the gentle sound of water flowing over rocks. We had a fine cabernet from Michael's California collection in the glasses before us. Oh, we felt good. We felt confident. We felt invincible.

Lida McBain had called earlier with an appraisal of the statewide reaction to Michael's announcement collected by her contacts in the major cities. From every location the report was essentially the same – enthusiastic response, excitement at the prospect of his candidacy.

The press play had been universally positive. The David-Goliath aspect of the story appealed to the great mass that had been routinely given candidates vetted by the party machine and supported by the establishment. The idea that a political virgin was game enough to take on a man already anointed by most as the next Governor – that a man with no obligations to special interest groups and no fear of entrenched interests was ready to do battle with the people who had been running the state for ages – all this resonated broadly throughout the Commonwealth, just as we thought it would. And was applauded. And was embraced.

And, as we hoped, Jesse Bristow and the machine functionaries were caught off guard. They just couldn't bring themselves to believe that someone with no experience and no organization would actually mount a challenge. Or imagine that if Michael finally deluded himself into trying, that the decision would come as rapidly as it did.

So there was no chorus of criticism, no objections raised about experience or fitness to lead or personal integrity. Those would come in time. But for that day, for the start of it, we had the field to ourselves.

Oh yes, we felt very, very good.

After Betsy cleared the plates and brought the coffee, we turned to the matter of how, with the initiative on our side, we took advantage of it.

There were less than eight months to the primary in May.

As I looked at it, it seemed to me that we were going to have to build Rome in a day. We had to put together an organization, finalize a strategy, and get a full scale state-wide campaign launched and running.

"Anyone think we'll get bored," Michael said after I'd gone through my little litany.

Everyone laughed, maybe a little nervously.

The biggest initial challenge was the organization.

The hard hitting television commercials and snappy newspaper ads and catchy slogans on banners and roadside signs all have their place. But you win elections by getting people to mark their ballots with your candidate's name. You win elections by knowing who is for you and who might be convinced to be for you and getting them to the polling place. You win elections by knowing who can be bought and counted on to do what they've been paid to do, and by knowing who is against you and how to neutralize them.

This can't be done long distance. This takes personal contact. Handholding. Stroking. The making of promises, the twisting of arms, the application of a little grease.

This takes people on the ground who know the territory.

Lots of people.

Kentucky has one hundred twenty counties. For each county we needed a campaign chairman and a campaign treasurer –

people of consequence, people who were known, who were respected and trusted, and if necessary, feared. We had to identify them, recruit them, sign them up right away – two hundred forty of them.

And precinct chairmen. There are over twenty-five hundred precincts in the Commonwealth. We needed precinct chairmen and precinct workers in each of them, men and women working to convince every Democrat in their precinct that Michael Dannan is their man, to make sure each voter gets to the polling place and casts his vote the right way on election day.

Figure twenty-five hundred precinct chairmen, then, and say two workers per precinct. That's five thousand or more precinct workers.

So we needed two-hundred-forty county chairmen and treasurers, twenty-five hundred precinct chairmen, five thousand precinct workers – eight thousand people at the absolute minimum!

"Jesse Bristow already has his team together," Rhae said.

"He's picked off the best people," Paul Isham added.

"Maybe," I said. "What he really has is the usual crowd. Are they the best people? They know their way around, no doubt about that. But maybe there are still enough good people out there who are fed up with the machine and ready for a new face and a new leader. The question is can we find them and get them signed up rapidly enough."

Michael stood up and walked to the edge of the porch.

"I don't think I fully appreciated the management challenge we face. To build an eight thousand person organization and get it running effectively in less than eight months – that's going to take real skill."

He turned around smiling broadly. "This is gonna be fun! So how do we do it?"

"We leave it to the experts," Rhae Dannan said. "If I know anything at all about Dace Havershamp, he started thinking about who he wanted as County Chairmen and who he could get even before he said yes to your invitation. If he didn't believe he could build a winning organization in the time we have, he never would have taken the job. Between him and Sattis and Jonathan and Judge Blue, they'll get the people we need.

"And it will flow down rapidly from there. The County Chairmen will recruit the Precinct Chairmen. The Precinct Chairmen will assemble the precinct workers. Lida McBain will pull the rest of the headquarters team together. Two weeks and you'll have your organization."

"What's going to cause all these people to come rushing to Michael's banner in the teeth of the machine and at the risk they'll be on the outs forever if Michael loses?" I had to ask.

"Power, Theo, that's bait," Michael said with such conviction I had no doubt he was right. "And influence. The kind of influence that strokes egos, generates admiration from friends and family, strikes fear into the hearts of enemies.

"Power and influence. They're impossible to resist. They're our currency. Not money. The heavyweights, the movers and shakers, want power. If others want money, wonderful. We have plenty of that.

"And some will join us because they're true believers, because they can't wait to right the wrongs they see.

"And some because they've been fired or ignored or insulted by the machine and they want revenge."

Rhae nodded in agreement.

"Two weeks," she repeated.

"One thing, though," Michael said. "The most valuable lesson I learned at McKinnon was never leave it to the experts. Their tunnel vision is too blinding. Their egos too big. The experts can build the structure. We'll make the decisions."

I looked at them. Mother and son. Michael assertive. Rhae reflective.

"Okay," I said, "sign me up. Just don't make those kinds of statements in public."

Paul Isham laughed at that, and Rhae did, too. Then Michael. Then me. For what reason I know not. It was late. We'd had a long day this day and a long and emotionally and mentally fatiguing one the day before. We were tired. We were looking for relief, I suppose. Why we all thought that statement funny was something I didn't fathom. We needed to laugh, I guess. Anyway, it relaxed us, so we talked a bit longer, idly, of nothing of importance, then said our goodnights.

Michael walked with me on my way out. We paused at the top of the front porch stairs, taking in the night. The air had become cooler, but not unpleasant, and the night deeper. Across the road, the ridgeline was outlined by stars.

We stood in the silence, listening for wings of owls hunting the country night, of bats darting past the cliffs above the creek. We stood shoulder to shoulder, listening for what we couldn't hear but could see in our minds' eyes, shedding the fatigue and the tension of the past forty hours. It was a good moment.

Into the silence I said, "Allie?"

"What?"

"Allie was there yesterday."

Michael kept his face toward the ridgeline.

"I know," he said.

He turned to me then. The faint light from the lamp still on in the living room lined both our faces in shadows. He put his hand on my shoulder. It seemed to me he was smiling, I couldn't be sure.

"Have you talked with Allie recently?"

"No."

"I've been seeing her," he said.

Surprise kept me silent.

"After we got back from the trip to see Dace," he said, "I thought about what you'd said. I called her. I was ready to feel guilty, but Allie's mood wouldn't let me. It was as if no time had passed. We seemed simply to segue from that last spring at college into the present."

He seemed to be nodding his head, confirming the wonder of it to himself. I caught just a glimpse of his face in the lamplight. Yes, he was smiling.

"I've been careful not to be seen," he said.

When he could, he would slip out to her little cottage on the Bridgeport road late at night, he told me, taking an old car from the many at the farm, one that couldn't be recognized. She always had the garage open, waiting. He met her daughter. He told her stories about his travels. They laughed together. Allie made a late dinner sometimes. Sometimes they sat out back on a blanket on the lawn, looking at the stars.

"It's like a dream I shouldn't have awakened from," he said.

Rhae knew nothing of this and he had taken special care to make sure that I didn't.

"Why?"

"Allie," he said, "Allie didn't want you to know."

"Why," I repeated.

"I don't know. Maybe she's shy. Maybe she feels you might feel, I don't know, an old remorse from all those years ago."

Allie remembered.

"Is this going anywhere? Not like last time? You get close and then back-off?"

"Come on, Theo. Don't spoil this."

"Have you ever had — have you ever been really close to a woman. Close enough to...."

He cut me off, laughing.

"Not that close."

"You were that close to Allie once."

No laugh this time, a silence.

"Then you left her. You quit," I said.

"It wasn't going to work, Theo."

"Is it going to work this time?"

"This is different," he said.

"What's different?"

"Dammit, Theo," he said, "This is a different time. There is nothing I have to prove now. I can give Allie a priority I couldn't then. Dammit, Theo, don't spoil this!"

"You're not going to leave her behind again?"

"How can I know what will happen?"

He put his hand on my shoulder.

"How can anyone know? Pull for us. Light some candles."

## THIRTY-FOUR

Allison Boatwright Sinclair.

The odd thing is that Allie isn't beautiful.

She almost is, but not quite, and that makes you look twice to be sure. After the second look, the word you use makes no difference.

Her hair is the color dandelions take on when the morning light first hits them. Her eyes are fairy blue, like the skies of soft summer afternoons. Watch her walk and know you've never seen anything so graceful, or any form so desirable. She is nearly as tall as I, tall enough that she has only to lift her chin slightly to put her lips in line with mine.

Allie is…comely. Comely is the word. She is so comely that you mistake it for beauty.

Did I love her?

I know I was entranced, enchanted, absolutely taken with her. Some of whatever that was has stayed with me all these years … under the surface, present but not pressing. I still take pleasure just in the sight of her. But it isn't the aching want it was then. I can look and not touch. We are friends. She is my very good friend. And I try to look out for her in my own selfish way… not giving much of myself…not inconveniencing myself; still, though, attentive to her circumstance.

What might have happened between Allie and me isn't clear. Michael intervened.

I began dating Allie the weekend after that first sighting on Pete's Corner. By the next week, Michael had made his entrance. Through the rest of the spring and on into the fall, we both competed for her.

Best friends competing for the same girl? It was the sort of situation that blasts friendships apart. It didn't ours. Things got tense at times. We rode it out.

Allie was very good at balancing between us. But Michael had a car. Michael had money. Not that a car or money were that important to Allie. They were to me, though. Michael could take her places I couldn't in a style I couldn't. If I wanted to take

Allie to the movies, we walked. To a dance, we doubled with one of the guys who had a car. Which was okay. But it wasn't like going in your own car on your own schedule with the freedom to make of the night what you would or could. I didn't take her to restaurants in Lexington or to the touring Broadway plays that came to Louisville that summer.

In time, not a very long time at that, certainly before the end of the summer, I became embarrassed at this...and frustrated. I stopped asking.

I stepped out of the race for Allie.

Michael sprinted on.

Michael and I didn't speak of this. It was the way things were.

They made a fine couple. You only had to see the two of them together to know this.

I had to admire the person she had made of herself. Nothing had been easy. She didn't run home to her mother after leaving with the baby. She found a job and a little apartment and did for herself. The divorce was abrasive. The boy she left didn't want to give her up. He cajoled, threatened, fumed, and drank. He fought about alimony. He and his family tried to get the baby away from her.

Allie prevailed. The judge trusted her. She worked as a waitress until a job opened up in the law office of a local attorney who was a friend of her late father. He hired her as a secretary. In a very short time, she became his assistant. She worked hard and kept learning. She was the office manager now. If she had a social life apart from her mother and a few aunts, I didn't know about it. All her free time seemed to be taken up caring for her daughter. Without complaint.

I saw her from time to time, of course. I was making decent money by then and could afford the good restaurants. We'd go out to dinner now and then. Sometimes we'd go dancing, just to talk and enjoy the music and to get her away. As friends. Nothing more. But when I walked in with her and all the men in the room looked up, my ego swelled.

I can't help wondering how my life would be different if I had ignored my pride and stayed in the contest for Allie.

Outside, I could hear Vince Cervelli's old truck pulling up to deliver the day's fresh vegetables to Pete's restaurant downstairs. Morning was coming. I tried to put Allison Boatwright Sinclair and Michael Dannan out of my mind and manage a few hours' sleep.

## THIRTY-FIVE

The plan was to formally kickoff Michael's race at the Penrod picnic.

Jesse Bristow would already have organized his splash. Michael and Lida McBain set about engineering Michael's.

I still had my ongoing newspaper chores to attend.

I called Bristow's campaign manager, Deke Hasselton. I wanted an interview with Bristow on his reaction to Michael's candidacy – and his plans to blunt it – for my Wednesday column. Bristow hadn't responded to any press queries following Michael's announcement.

So far he had been silent and unavailable. It wasn't a bad strategy. Let the media blow itself out on Dannan coverage then come back with your own counterattack when you can command the stage. If I could get the interview, I'd score a clean beat and, not incidentally, acquire useful intelligence for Michael's campaign.

I pointed out to Deke that the Wednesday column would offer Mr. Bristow a statewide platform to make his points in support of his candidacy – and damn Dannan if he chose to do so. I promised straight reportage. No editorializing on my part. Just the answers in Bristow's own words in whatever way he chose to phrase them.

Deke told me I was crazy. "You've got a lot of balls to expect Jesse to sit still for you after you practically single handedly planted Dannan in the public mind."

"You give me too much credit," I told him. "But if I'm that good, maybe I can do the same for Jesse Bristow."

"We know what side you're on, Theo," Deke said.

"I won't pretend I don't favor Dannan. We were boys together. I know him well. I don't know Mr. Bristow. Maybe if I did, I'd love him. If he'll do the interview he'll get a fair story. Take the chance. It could pay-off for him."

"Regular rules? You'll honor off-the-record? You'll take stuff for non-attribution?"

"Absolutely on the first. We'll have to talk about the second. It depends on what he wants to get in print without being tagged as having said it. No accusations. No character digs, that sort of thing."

"I'll see what Jesse says," Deke said.

That afternoon, Jesse said yes.

We set the session for the next morning, Tuesday, to give me time to write the piece and get it set for distribution to the full network of papers on my syndicate on Wednesday.

I spent the rest of Monday in the files, researching the life and works of Jesse Bristow to the extent the information existed on the public record. A surprising amount did. Jesse Bristow didn't climb to prominence invisibly or unremarked upon.

He'd grown up poor and hard working in the mines of eastern Kentucky. Mother and father dead. Raised by a maiden aunt. One sibling, a sister, younger than he, who died young. Was active in the mine wars of the 1930s. Was still in his teens then, but emerged as a leader of the miners and one of the top officers of the new union. Moved from being secretary of the union to its presidency. Highly popular with the rank and file. Highly unpopular with the executives of the out-of-state corporations who owned and ran the biggest of Kentucky's mines and from whom he wrested ever higher pay, ever more adequate health care, and ever more effective, and consequently costly, safety practices.

In time he became an owner himself, buying up a collection of low-volume truck mining operations throughout a four-county area, consolidating them and turning the agglomeration into a competitive mining operation employing almost 800 people. His company was still acquiring and expanding into west Kentucky when the big four mining companies decided to form a statewide umbrella organization to "protect and expand the interests of all the state's mines and mining suppliers" The latter category "mining suppliers" was a stroke of genius, I thought – it took in the big automotive and truck manufacturers, the railroads, heavy equipment makers, manufacturers of all kinds, the electric utilities, anyone who sold, or wanted to sell, their product or their services to the mining industry in Kentucky. It covered almost the whole universe.

They asked Jesse Bristow to head it.

That was fifteen years ago. With the money, the muscle, and the influence of the Association at his command, Jesse Bristow became a power. He expected, soon, to become Governor.

I looked for dirt, but the record didn't have any. There had been a run of negative stories during Bristow's second year as head of his own mining company, the year Benjamin Dannan died. The state legislature seemed ready to impose a 10% excise tax on each ton of coal mined in the eastern mountains – a tax Bristow claimed would put him and all other small miners out of business. The measure failed on a close vote in the House. Bribery was charged. Jesse Bristow was accused. Nothing was proved. That, and his participation in the Battle of Evarts was all there was. No women, no arrests, no lawsuits – no closets, much less skeletons.

He was 61, never married, a member of the board of regents at Eastern Kentucky State College and a deacon of the Buck Run Baptist Church at Forks of Elkhorn.

An all-around self-made solid citizen.

Of course there was more. The public record never has it all, most of the time not even the most interesting stuff.

There was nothing of what Sattis Arnow had told us about the hangings, nothing about how Bristow managed to become such a power with the miners at such a young age, or how he got the money to start his little, soon to become big, mining company. There is always more to the story, much more, than the public record holds.

This wasn't the sort of story I was after, though. Maybe later, but not now. For now I had promised a straightforward report of Mr. Bristow's reaction to Mr. Dannan's entry into the race for Governor and what his plans were, given this unexpected development. And a balanced, straightforward story I intended to produce. I could afford no less. If I expected to protect my credibility as this race unfolded and I wrote about it, I had better be seen to be fair to Mr. Jesse Bristow.

I arrived at his office ten minutes before our appointed time. I try never to be late. Being late is rude. It is self-indulgent. My mother didn't raise me to be either.

Deke Hasselton was waiting for me.

"Jesse will be with us in just a minute," he told me. "Anything you need? A cup of coffee?"

"How much time will I have?"

"He can spare an hour."

My question list was already prepared. I'd worked through it last night, making sure I had the questions framed clearly in my mind and arranged in the order I wanted to put them. Managing a good interview is a lot like an attorney handling a good cross examination. You do your research. You know your subject. You considered your questions and the way in which they should be ordered to build on each other and lead to the conclusion you hope you'll get. An hour would be plenty.

Exactly at ten o'clock, Jesse Bristow came striding through his office door, all energy and smiles. He took me up in a big handshake and led me toward his office. "Theo Clark," he said, "I've been looking forward to talking with you." Turning to Deke he said, "Make sure Mabel holds my calls." He steered me to the large window that made up one wall of the room. "What do you think of that view?" he said.

The window looked down the valley to the river and the town beyond.

I answered with the only word that came to mind. "Magnificent!"

"It is, isn't it? It cost a fortune to clear the cliff and do the excavating, but worth every penny of it. We're ten minutes from the Capitol. Only a few minutes from the interstate to Louisville and Lexington. Convenient for our members. Convenient for our work."

"But you're looking to leave it," I said.

He smiled. "Come sit down, Mr. Clark. Let's talk."

He directed me to a chair beside a large oak desk in the center of the room. The window with the view was to my left. There was another large window behind him, looking out to a vista of trees. To my right was a floor-to-ceiling wall of books.

My inspection was cut short.

"Theo?" he said. "An unusual name. How did you come by it?"

Taking the initiative, I thought. Smart.

"My father. He liked Theodore O'Hara. The soldier poet. You know him? The full name is Theodore O'Hara Clark. Theo for short."

Bristow smiled.

*"On Fame's eternal camping-ground*
*Their silent tents are spread,*
*And Glory guards, with solemn round,*
*The bivouac of the dead.*

"I'm surprised I still remember that. We learned it by heart in my school days."

I was surprised he knew it, too. But now that he had opened the door to the past, I decided to step through.

"That was in Evarts?"

"Oh, come on, Theo – may I call you Theo? And call me Jesse, like everyone else does and we can drop this formality and get to it. I know you've done your research. You probably know my background better than I do. So don't waste time on inconsequential questions."

He sat back in his chair, pulled out a lower desk drawer, propped his feet on it and offered me that big and inviting smile again. Totally relaxed. Ready for the contest.

If there are matters of consequence involved, an interview really is a contest between the journalist trying to extract information that will shed light on an action or an issue of importance, and the subject trying to put the best possible light on things. The journalist is trying to get the "real story." The subject is trying to tell only the story he wants told.

I nodded and returned his smile.

"Last week it appeared you had a relaxed and unopposed stroll right into the Governor's office. Now it looks as if there might actually be race, with the outcome not at all certain."

"You're talking about Mr. Dannan's announcement of Saturday?

"Yes."

"I'm not quite sure what to make of that. That someone with no experience and no organization, someone who hasn't even been a resident of the state for, oh, I don't know how many years, that someone like that would consider himself qualified to be governor, well, that seems quite an ego to me. And not only that, but that he would imagine he could enter a race already underway and win it? I assume Mr. Dannan assumes he can win it or why go to the trouble in the first place?"

"It is bold," I said.

"Should I be concerned?"

"Are you?"

He considered that, with a look that bordered on amusement. "I'm not sure. No. Not yet. It's a nuisance that he's done this. A factor that has to be considered. I imagine it will work out, though."

"He has a name. He has money."

"Those are big assets. I knew his father, you know. At one time Benjamin Dannan and I were very good friends. During the mine wars. You know all about that? That changed. We found ourselves on opposite sides of an issue very important to me. The friendship didn't survive it. But I liked Benjamin. I admired his courage."

"And Michael?"

"I don't know the young Mr. Dannan. I had hoped to get to know him, but it seems this little piece of business got in the way. I imagine I'll get to know him."

"And he has four very savvy players serving as his brain trust – Dace Havershamp, Judge Blue, Jonathan Wilson, and another old friend of yours, Sattis Arnow."

"Ah, Sattis, bless his heart. He was very important to me at a certain stage in my life. I have great affection for Sattis and great respect. And Dace and Judge Blue and Jonathan? Yes. That is a formidable team."

"So are you concerned?" I asked.

He laughed. "You present me with a situation in which an unknown, an amateur, has thrown his hat into the ring very late in the game. Granted, he has a family name that is well known in this state and what I'm told is considerable personal wealth. And yes, he has four very prominent men in his corner who know their way around Kentucky politics. Is all that something I need to be concerned about? Not yet. Not yet.

"It is something I should pay attention to, and I will certainly do that. It would be foolish to do otherwise. I'm not so egotistical as to think the nomination is mine and all I have to do is claim the Governor's chair. I know there are minds to be won and votes to be earned. I do think, no, I know, that the people know that I am the man for this job at this time.

"They know that I can and will do it better than anyone else can and that I will do it to their benefit. Michael Dannan is only a distraction. Possibly a very useful one. I'm glad he's entered. His candidacy will give me a chance to present my agenda, display my credentials more dramatically than I could possibly have done in an unopposed race. Mr. Dannan may have done me a favor."

He rose as he said this. "Yes, you can say in your column that Jesse Bristow says, 'Welcome, Mr. Dannan. Welcome to the race. And may the best man win.' "

It was a fine performance. I almost applauded.

My column that Wednesday reflected this. I played it, as promised, absolutely straight. I reported what Jesse Bristow told me. I didn't elaborate. I didn't fabricate. I didn't speculate.

And I reported, straight, the impressions Jesse Bristow made on me. A man of considerable strength. A man with a remarkable record of achievement. Tough. Smart. Articulate. Capable. Very serious about what needed doing to bring, if not the good life, than a much better one, to every man, woman, and child in the Commonwealth.

And a man deadly serious about winning.

# THIRTY-SIX

Jake Slade was back.

I was at my desk at the *Journal*, staring blankly at my typewriter while trying to come up with a lede for a story on a new prison reform bill that had been introduced in the House when I got Paul Isham's call. Meet him at Jake's place as fast as I could make it.

The lede is the most important part of any story. That first paragraph has to hook the reader, make him to want to read on. Yet it has to be so carefully crafted that if the reader goes no further than that graf, all the most important information has been presented – the *who* of the story, and the *why*. *How* it happened, and *where*, and *when*.

It is a demanding protocol. No dancing around or fancy footwork. The unvarnished facts presented as concisely as possible. Lean. Tight. Accurate. Phrased in understandable words. All wrapped up in one paragraph, one short paragraph.

There is more leeway with a column. The hook needs to be set in the first line or two of copy or the reader might migrate elsewhere. But once the hook is in, a more leisurely approach is possible. A little dancing around and fancy footwork is permissible, even advisable. In a news story, the readers want solid information and want it fast. In a column, the reader is looking for a little enlightenment or entertainment, for clever writing and provocative thinking.

Dancing around is always easier than heavy lifting.

When Paul's call came, I stopped playing with possibilities. "There are probably fifty ways to write that lede," one of my first editors told me as I sat, like today, staring out over my typewriter trying to find the perfect one as a deadline neared, "Pick one and write it. We've got a newspaper to get out."

I picked one, wrote the story, and headed out the door for Slade's apartment.

"It's open," Jake called out as I knocked at the door.

They were sitting at the table in the kitchen, the side away from the front windows where the sound of kids playing on the

Old Capitol grounds filtered through. Light was coming in from the back windows, but no lights were on in the room. A movie set for a spy movie, I thought. Two men leaning toward each other talking quietly over a table in the half-light of a high-ceiling room. Somber. Serious. Sensitive information being imparted. Important plans being made.

Paul motioned me to a chair.

"He made a connection."

Jake nodded. He looked exhausted but pleased with himself.

"The aunt was the opening. Once I had the aunt's name, I had the lead we needed."

I waited.

"Hannah Collins is remembered in Evarts. I found only one old lady who knew her personally. But there were a couple of men and four women who remembered her from their childhood. They remembered Benjamin Dannan's name, too. None of them could recall ever seeing him around there, but they remembered the name. They had heard their folks talking about him. Most of these people are in their sixties now. They lived through that time as kids. The names they hold are Benjamin Dannan and Jesse Bristow. Bristow was a hero to them, Benjamin not far behind. The stories their parents told made them that. And Hannah Collins, Jesse Bristow's aunt...she got the respect and admiration that came with Jesse Bristow's reputation."

"Where does that lead us?" I said.

"Because she was the aunt of a hero, the people in that little town kept a watch over her as they do in those mountains.

"So?"

"Be quiet, Theo. Let Jesse get this story told," Paul Isham said.

Slade laughed, "You can't change a reporter's habits."

"So," he said smiling at me, "one of those men happened to remember Jesse Bristow coming to Hanna Collins' house about suppertime the night that Benjamin died. The aunt and Bristow left together. Later, he saw Bristow again, without the aunt, but with one of the men who worked for him at the mine. He remembers it because there was a big snowstorm and no other cars were moving. The man in the car with Bristow was a fellow named Lucas Gwynne."

My impatience must have showed.

"I'm getting there," Jake said. "They were heading out on the Pineville road."

"The road where Benjamin's body was found," Paul Isham said looking at me with a quiet fury in his eyes.

"I'm not following all this," I said.

"Lucas Gwynne is still around. He doesn't come into town much, but he's around and he's ambulatory. If Gwynne and Jesse Bristow were on the road to Pineville the night Benjamin died, they said nothing about it at the time of the inquiries. Why? We've got to talk with Gwynne."

"You didn't?"

"Couldn't get to him. He stays back up the mountains. The only road in isn't much more than an old wagon trail. When I started up it, a mule pulling a broken-down wagon blocked my way. The two men with it explained to me, nicely, that visitors weren't welcome and that I had best turn around and go back down to Evarts. They didn't care what my business was or who I wanted to see. The settlement wasn't open to outsiders. I tried again the next day. Same result."

"Is Gwynne a Melungeon?"

"I don't know. I can check it when I go back."

"Not you, Jake," Paul Isham said. "I don't think the third time would be charm for you! We need someone who can get into that Melungeon settlement, someone they won't feel threatened by."

Jake and I looked at him, puzzled.

"Marne Young," Paul Isham explained, "she might manage it."

## THIRTY-SEVEN

I had to tell her the whole story, or at least all that we knew of it.

She listened quietly, sitting with her hands in her lap in the swing on the porch at Mountain Home, looking somewhere off into the distance.

"So we have to find this man. We have to talk him. Hanna Collins had Mr. Dannan's wallet. Did she get it from him before he died? Off his body after he died? From someone else? There has to be a connection. She had to have known something about his death."

Marne Young looked up.

"Going to rain," she said. I followed her gaze. Along the ridge line, a rising wind was picking at the few remaining leaves still clinging to the oaks. The sky, though, was clear and blue.

"I've been to the settlement on Black Mountain," she said, still not looking at me, watching the wind.

"Aunt Hanna took me. I had told her about my research on the Melungeons. She wanted me to meet them. She wanted me to see how her people lived."

"Can you get in again? Will you take me?"

She didn't answer.

"Please, will you take me?"

"It's just a small settlement. On the banks of a creek back up one of the hollows on Black Mountain. Hard to reach. They try to keep it secret. They don't trust outsiders."

A long silence, just the sound of the wind and the creak of the chain as the swing moved slowly back and forth.

At last she turned her eyes to me. "I have a very sad feeling about all this."

She gave a little sigh.

Then the rain came. We watched it march across the ballfield, big fat drops kicking little splats of dust as it came, the wind rising and turning cold, black thunderheads spilling over the ridge line.

"We'll go tomorrow," she said.

## THIRTY-EIGHT

They had always been there. Ghosts in the forests. Myths taken shape.

They had powers. Some could see the future. They could cast spells and change form. With just the touch of their hands they could heal the sick and close wounds. They had unbelievable treasures hidden in caves high up under the ridges. The men moved as silently as catamounts in the forests and could see in the dark. The women were stunning.

No one knew where they came from. Or how they came to be.

"Or that's what people believed, what a few still believe," Marne said.

I listened, fascinated, as we drove.

"The first settlers expected the land to be empty. It was all wilderness, from the Gulf of Mexico to the Great Lakes.

"But there were people where no people should have been. Strange people. People who dressed like the English. People who had Christian names, who spoke English with an accent that was almost Elizabethan. But they didn't look or act English. They had darker skins. They lived in remote little settlements. They didn't tolerate strangers.

"As more settlers pushed in, these strange people withdrew, west and north, up out of the Carolinas and Virginia, in small groups, into the folds of the Appalachians."

We'd been driving since before daylight. The sun still wasn't up. Our headlights cut a tunnel through the darkness. I could imagine strange men with yellow eyes tracking us from the trees.

"For a long while they were able to maintain their seclusion. They had every reason to need to. The new settlers wanted their land, their treasures.

"They were outnumbered, outmaneuvered. In a few places they were even barred from owning land. They withdrew deeper into the mountains, coalescing into tight little communities of people like themselves.

"For a long while they were feared. The myths and the stories about their powers spread through the whole region. Today, they are largely ignored. That suits them fine, both those still trying to live separately and those trying to assimilate into the white culture."

"Where did they come from?" I asked.

"I doubt that anyone will ever really know," Marne said. "Trying to find that answer is part of what my research is about.

"Some think, even some of them think, that they are the children of the Lost Colony. You remember about that? The first English settlement in the New World, the one that disappeared from an island off the coast of what is now North Carolina in the late 1580s? Eighty-five men, seventeen women, one with a baby in her arms, and eleven boys went ashore. No trace of any of its people ever found?"

I nodded.

"The Roanoke Colony. Virginia Dare, the first English child born in the new world," I said, remembering vaguely.

"Others believe they are the survivors of a shipwreck of a Spanish galleon that was carrying Moors and Spanish and Portuguese Jews who were fleeing the last stages of the Spanish Inquisition. Still others that they come from a tiny group of English indentured servants who couldn't stand their bondage and fled into the forests where they met up with Spanish deserters from Florida that had already merged with a small group of African slaves – and that all of them were taken under the wing of some friendly Cherokees."

"What do you think?"

Out of the corner of my eye I could see her frowning as she considered it.

"The Lost Colony theory could explain a lot. Whatever happened to them on Roanoke Island, the survivors could have made it to the mainland and easily could have been taken in by the Croatoans, who were known to be friendly. But I think that's only part of the story.

'Two other groups had already been dropped off on Roanoke Island before the Lost Colony arrived. A small group of Moors and Portuguese were put ashore on the island by Sir Francis Drake. They had been slaves of the Spanish, captured on the high seas and taken to Cartagena, one of Spain's major South American treasure seaports. Drake freed them after a raid he made on Cartagena and was taking them back to England. But a major storm came up and he headed for Roanoke Island where he knew a small English garrison to be.

"Once there he found the garrison had run out of supplies and the men who manned it were in danger of starving. So he put the Moors and the Portuguese off, loaded the English garrison on, and headed back out to sea. The Moors and Portuguese, who thought they were on their way home, were instead left to whatever fate awaited them on a strange island off the coast of strange land.

"About a year later, another small force of English soldiers was sent out to make another try at establishing a garrison on Roanoke Island. They were supposed to be waiting for the Lost Colony group, but when the Lost Colony's ships arrived, the island was deserted. Everyone had disappeared. No Moors, no Portuguese, no English garrison."

Marne tucked her legs up beneath her on the seat and turned to me.

"The Moors and the Portuguese who were put off on the island by Drake had no reason to want to stay there. They hadn't set out to be colonists and they were a long way from home. I think they made their way to the mainland almost immediately after Drake's ships left. They hadn't made enemies of the Indians and were probably taken in by the Croatoans.

'The Englishmen of that second detachment probably ran out of supplies just as the first garrison had done, looked around and considered their situation, and took off for the mainland, too.

"Then finally, the Lost Colony settlers. I think they made their way to the mainland as well. All this was taking place in a time span of a little less than three years. All three groups, the Moors and the Portuguese, the Englishmen of the garrison, and the survivors of the Lost Colony, I think, came together at some point there on the coast of Virginia off Roanoke Island, lived among or with the Croatoans for a while, then struck off inland, taking a few Indian wives with them.

"In time, this small group of English and Moors and Portuguese and Indians intermingled with other lost souls – indentured servants, deserters from the English or Spanish military, slaves. The English were almost certainly the largest single group. Their language and culture probably prevailed, which would explain the Elizabethan speech pattern and the manner of dress that so surprised the incoming settlers. The mixed blood of the others would explain the skin color. They became the Melungeons."

"And ultimately wound up on Black Mountain in Kentucky?"

"Some of them did, a few, yes. And others in places in Tennessee and Virginia and North Carolina. Not many of them now. They're being absorbed into the general population. A few, like those in the village we're going to, choose to continue to live isolated and they stayed as separate as they could, but more and more they're intermarrying into the white culture and moving into the towns. I imagine a pure Melungeon is fairly rare now.

"The name Melungeon, what does it mean?"

"Some say 'cursed soul' from the Arabic. Others say 'abandoned by God' from the Spanish.

"What do they say?"

"They don't say anything. It isn't a name they gave themselves. There are other groups like them spread around the South that might have had similar beginnings – the Brass Ankles of South Carolina, the Redbones of Alabama, the Lumbees of North Carolina."

"How did you get into all this?" I asked.

Marne shrugged.

"I was at Sophie Newcomb. I met a boy, a graduate student at LSU. He was from a little town in mountains of east Tennessee. We became friends. After a while, after we got closer, he said he felt he should tell me that he was half Melungeon. He seemed both proud and ashamed of it.

"I had never heard of Melungeons. I was just floating around, not concentrating on anything. My father wanted me in business school. I'll inherit the farm and all the property when my folks die. He expects me to manage it and wanted me prepared. I found the Melungeons more interesting. That led to cultural anthropology and to a graduate degree at the University of Georgia, then to the research grant for the study of the Melungeon culture, then to Mountain Home and Aunt Hanna Collins, and this ride with you today down to the settlement."

I looked over at her. Her eyes were fully closed and she had her head back against the seat rest.

"Did Hanna Collins tell you anything about the Lost Colony people, about the Moors and the Portuguese?"

"She talked of some of it, of their legends and of the stories she heard the elders tell. Remember the silver box, the one she said had been in her family forever? I think it was the possession of one of Aunt Hanna's Moorish ancestors, one fleeing from the last grasp of the Spanish Inquisition, saved by Sir Francis Drake at Cartagena and delivered to the future at Roanoke Island."

"Would the box get us in to the settlement?"

"We don't need the box. I'm known there. Aunt Hanna took me once."

"Will there be a problem getting Lucas Gwynne to talk with us?"

"Yes," she said. "I imagine that will be a problem"

## THIRTY-NINE

That we found the village at all seemed a miracle. It is hidden in the diamond-shaped slice of mountain and forest bounded by Evarts in the northwest, Louellen in the northeast, Holmes Mill in the southeast, and Dizney in the southwest…wild, practically inaccessible country. Marne, thank God, knew the way or I would still be stumbling around lost.

We rode State Route 38 from Evarts toward Holmes Mill. About eight miles before Holmes Mill, a gravel road cut off to the right. We took it, plunging into the deep forest, up a high ridge and down again and back up again. We gained the spine of the mountain and followed its twists east. As we neared the crest, a narrower trail of dirt and rock cut off to the north. We left the gravel and committed ourselves to this, crawling slowly over the occasional boulder that threatened the car's undercarriage. Barely a car's width wide, the trail curved and climbed still higher, angling through the mist around the mountain summit and then dropping down rapidly through a thick canopy of trees to reveal an unsuspected valley.

The village was there, set on the far bank of a small creek. The trail we were on ended at the creek. A narrow wooden bridge spanned it. There were some buildings spread in a line along the creek and, moving back toward the tree-line, a scatter of cabins.

No one was about. The village seemed deserted.

The bridge was wide enough for a wagon, but not for our car. I stopped and we started to get out. As we did, two men appeared on the far side and began walking toward us.

"You stay there," Marne said to me. She got out and moved up by the front fender, smiling, her arms folded and standing relaxed.

The men were tall and lean. They were dressed like farmers, in long-sleeved cotton work shirts of faded blue rolled up on their forearms, jeans, heavy, low-cut boots, and wide brimmed felt hats with sweat-stained headbands. They walked with an easy, swinging grace, like men accustomed to moving over rough ground and through forests, taking their time, no haste, but coming on steadily, watching carefully, each cradling a rifle hunter-style. As they got closer, it became apparent they were of about the same age, early thirties probably. The man on the left had a scar running across his forehead that stood out like a white slash against his dark skin. They looked stern, unwelcoming.

When they were about ten yards away, Marne stepped away from the car and toward them. They hesitated. She raised her hand, a gesture somewhere between a wave and a benediction.

"Hello," she said. I could hear the smile in her voice.

"I am a friend of Aunt Hanna Collins."

The men paused.

"Aunt Hanna brought me here last year and introduced me to the elders. I was told I could come back whenever I liked."

She walked on toward them. The men stayed still, waiting.

When she reached them, she put her hand out. They were too far away for me to hear the conversation. They talked for a short while, then Marne turned and walked back toward the car. The men stood, waiting, while she did.

"Don't get out," she said as she approached. "It's all right. They know about me and Aunt Hanna."

I started to protest, but realized no purpose would be served. They wouldn't let me in and Marne would go with them whether I thought it safe or not.

By now it was mid-afternoon. Through the canopy of trees, the sky was clear and the sunlight warm. I could hear water running over stones in the creek. Nothing was moving except the occasional pine bough as a light breeze flicked it. I could feel the rich, sweet pull of drowsiness in the warmth and the quiet and had to consciously force myself up and out of the car to shake it off.

I was sure I was being watched, so I stayed with the car and didn't move closer. I walked to the front and leaned back against the fender. Easy to be seen by the watchers, if there were any, and clearly not presenting a threat of any type.

I was perhaps a hundred yards from the village. From where I stood I could see four large structures strung out along the creek to the left and the right of the bridge. The building nearest the bridge to the right looked to be a store of some type. Further on, almost to the edge of the clearing, there was a larger building with a tall church-like tower. At the other end, down to the left, sat a squat, one-story, weathered building with a shed to the side that looked as if it might be place where tools and equipment were repaired.

The area directly in front of the bridge was clear of buildings of any type. It had the appearance of an unfenced pasture, but was neater than a pasture, well tended, almost like a lawn. In its center were two very tall wooden posts with a large bell hanging from a cross beam.

Back from the creek, twelve or so cabins were spread at random around the clearing. Further back, being reclaimed by the forest, were the shambles of a number of other cabins, giving evidence this had been a much larger settlement at one time.

I scanned it all very carefully, looking for movement, looking for a flash of color that might indicate a person lurking in the shadows. Nothing. No sign of people. No animals. No voices. In the bright sun of the early afternoon, silent and deserted.

I waited.

After a while, the door to the building I took to be a store opened and Marne stepped out. She was alone. She turned and said something into the dark opening, then started back across the bridge. As she walked, the two dark men stepped out of the doorway and stood watching her, hands at their sides, unmoving, statue-like. A third man joined them, white-haired, not quite as tall.

At the end of the bridge Marne turned back, waved to them, then came on toward me. The men on the porch remained motionless.

I couldn't read the expression on her face. Surprised. Confused. Not disappointed, but not satisfied. Questioning.

"You're okay?" I said, standing and starting toward her.

She nodded yes. Smiled at me and shook her head in that gesture that says "I don't know what to make of this."

"Get in," she said.

I walked around and opened the door for her. Then returned to my side of the car and slid in beneath the steering wheel.

She gave a little laugh when I turned to her.

"They gave me an RC Cola," she said, "an RC! Out of the ice-box. In the bottle. With a straw. They thought I might be thirsty."

Which made me realize how thirsty I was. We'd nothing to eat or drink since leaving Evarts that morning.

"They couldn't have been more polite." She smiled again.

I put the car in reverse and backed around to start up the trail out of the valley.

"The white-haired man was Lucas Gwynne," she said, looking back out the rear window.

"He remembers the night Benjamin Dannan died. He remembers where he was and what he was doing. He remembers it all very clearly. And he will tell it to no one but Michael Dannan."

"Oh, hell," I said.

"And he would not even speak to Michael except for Aunt Hanna. She sent a message the morning after she learned Michael Dannan was coming home, carried by mouth by an old friend. A person known to them both. For his ears only. "

"Lucas Gwynne told you this?"

"To explain that he was waiting."

"Waiting?

"Aunt Hanna was an elder of the village. The wishes of the elders are honored among the Melungeons. But she was more than that to Lucas Gwynne. She was his godmother."

"How...?"

"Gwynne's mother was the best friend of Aunt Hanna's sister...the mother of Jesse Bristow."

"The message?"

"That Michael Dannan, the son of Benjamin Dannan, was coming home. That she had a story to tell Mr. Dannan about the night his father died. That she was trying to get in touch with Mr. Dannan. That if she didn't succeed, if time ran out for her, she wanted Lucas Gwynne to tell Mr. Dannan the part of the story that he knew. He was to wait for Mr. Dannan to find him, as she was sure he would, and then he was to tell Mr. Dannan all he knew of that night. Lucas Gwynne was to do this without fail. He was to do it for her. Her soul couldn't rest until this had been done."

"He told you no part of it?"

"He didn't want to talk to me at all. This is something very difficult for him. But he realized I'm a way to get to Michael Dannan…and a way to get Michael Dannan to the village."

"He expects Michael to come up here?"

"Gwynne won't leave the village. Michael will have to come to the mountain."

## FORTY

The moon was waxing gibbous.

We passed an occasional car, but for the most part the road was empty.

The night was cold coming through the forests and we drove with the heater on.

Both of us were famished. There was a little diner on the road outside Hyden. We stopped there. The gravel parking lot was unlighted, but the humpback moon was bright enough to cast shadows. Except for a trucker sitting at the counter, we had the place to ourselves.

Meatloaf, mashed potatoes and gravy, green beans, cornbread. Hot black coffee. Cherry pie and vanilla ice cream.

Not much conversation. Our minds were still in the valley, replaying the day, looking for what we'd missed, trying to understand what we didn't understand.

We expected to be back in Lost Creek before midnight. I'd drop Marne Young off at Mountain Home. It would be pushing two a.m. before I made it to bed.

I couldn't shake how strange the feeling had been in that little valley – as if time had stopped, or was about to begin, as if there was no other world but the valley, no other time but then. Yet there was expectancy in the air, a sense of formless apprehension.

"How long do you think that settlement has been there?"

"The village? Since before the Revolutionary War. Daniel Boone and the Long Hunters were beginning to explore into Kentucky then. Settlers were pushing up from North Carolina and Virginia. The Melungeons would have been moving ahead of them."

"How big was it, do you suppose?"

"In those early days? Maybe thirty or thirty-five families. Not nearly so many today. Many of the younger ones have moved in closer to civilization – to the schools, the stores, to jobs. Maybe ten or so families now and a few unmarried men, men who want their hunting, who probably raise a little corn and make a little moonshine on the side."

"Gwynne will expect Michael to go in there alone?"

Marne had her head back on the seat, dozing or lost in thought. She didn't change her position.

"There's no danger," she said.

"Those two who walked you across the bridge looked fairly menacing to me. How do you know what else, or who else, is in there? Or what they've got in mind for Michael?"

She sat up at this and turned to me. "There is no other way to find out what Lucas Gwynne knows."

"I don't like any part of it."

She turned and started fumbling with the heater controls. "It's getting chilly," she said.

The moon was behind the trees. The road ahead was dark and twisting. Except for the tunnel our headlights carved through the night, we were surrounded by black.

She slept. I drove.

It was well after two a.m. by the time I made it home. No matter how I turned the situation in my mind, it was clear that Michael would have to go to the village.

## FORTY-ONE

We were back on the road to the mountains by nine.

I'd gotten home, sat the alarm for six, went immediately to sleep, jumped up at the bell, showered, and called Michael. I told him the story over a very early breakfast at the farm. He didn't hesitate. He called Lida McBain and told her to cancel all his appointments for the day. It was to be a full campaigning day, meetings with party functionaries in two counties, a visit to a nearby county school and a veteran's hospital, a drop-in on the editor of one of the more influential of the Bluegrass country weeklies.

Lida was not happy. She insisted on knowing why Michael was canceling and what excuse she should give. He didn't tell her why, told her to make up whatever excuse she thought acceptable.

Rhae was coming down for breakfast just as we were leaving. Michael kissed her on the check, told her that he and I had to see some people that Jake Slade's visit had flushed out and that he would fill her in when we got back. Asked her to tell Paul Isham.

We filled a couple of thermoses with black coffee and left. We picked up Marne Young at Mountain Home. She took over the front seat with Michael. I climbed in back, stretched out and dozed. What little sleep I'd had was fitful and the tension of the trip to the village was still in my bones.

I half listened to them and half dreamed. Soon I wasn't sure whether I was awake or sleeping. I caught snatches of Marne telling her story of the Melungeons. Not enough new to keep me awake.

I dropped down onto the rim of a dream, and there was Allie, sitting alone beneath the big oak on the lawn near the campus chapel. It was autumn, late afternoon, red and gold leaves brilliant in the fading light. She had on a blue skirt over demurely folded legs and was looking beyond me to someone I could not see…listening intently to something I could not hear. She started to reach out, then stopped. I heard it then. Someone crying so softly you knew that pain was sucking all the breath away.

I thought of a nine-year old awakened on a cold morning to be told his father was dead.

We boys didn't talk about each other's fathers. We knew them, knew they were there. When we stayed for supper or slept over they were nice enough, but distant. They had other things on their minds. We did, too. There was nothing to talk about. They were just there, like the trees.

But not Mr. Dannan. He paid attention. He listened. He asked questions. He laughed and teased us. We liked that. We liked him.

After Mr. Dannan died, some of us, among ourselves, talked about him. About what had happened to him, and about what would happen to Michael and his mother.

After the funeral, Michael put his father away somewhere in his mind and never talked of him again. We learned not to raise his name.

"Theo, you awake?

Michael rolled down his window to let some of the morning air flow in. It was cold and damp. Marne Young shivered and he noticed and put the window back up.

I sat up slowly. A high mist clung to the tree tops.

"Where are we?"

"About an hour away, I guess," Marne said. "Can we stop for a minute to stretch, maybe have a little more coffee out of that thermos?"

"Better than that," Michael said. "Betsy put in some of her doughnuts and packed them to keep them warm. Quick energy so we don't run down," he said.

We pulled off onto a little turnout and had our coffee and doughnuts while the sun worked on drying out the morning.

"They're really expecting us?" Michael said to Marne.

"They're expecting us."

"You made no commitment. We've made no contact. There are no phones there. Yet they are expecting us?"

"Yes, they're expecting us."

"Why?"

"Aunt Hanna said you would come."

"How do they know when?"

"They'll know when we get there."

We drove on, talking of what could be expected when we arrived at the village.

The three were waiting, Lucas Gwynne, his white hair marking him, and the two from yesterday.

They must have had lookouts, or guards, somewhere along the road in – and some way to get word ahead to the village.

"Not to worry, Theo," Michael said.

He parked the car in the meadow where I had parked the day before.

"You stay here," he said. "Marne, make the introductions."

They got out and walked toward the bridge where the three waited in the noon day sun. I climbed out of the back seat and stood by the front fender, an unwilling spectator again.

And then said "To hell with it," and ran after them.

I wasn't going to sit there voluntarily while Michael put himself at risk and while the story of what actually happened to Benjamin Dannan might be unfolding.

They had just started across the bridge when one of the men caught the motion of my moving, or heard the sound of it, and turned. He called something I couldn't hear and racked the rifle up into both hands.

Almost simultaneously, a bell began to ring. Full, urgent peals filled the valley and absorbed all other sounds – the wind in the trees, the thrum of the heart in the ear, all were absorbed by the voice of the bell. Full. Commanding. Clamorous. I stood stock still, too surprised to move. Michael and Marne Young did, too. And so did Lucas Gwynne and his escorts. We all stood rooted to the grassy path.

"What is it," I whispered to Marne.

"Some sort of alarm," she whispered back.

The bell stopped as abruptly as it started. It was as if its voice had sucked all sound out of the valley and we were surrounded momentarily by a profound silence. Then the breeze began to rustle again. And the trance-like inertia the bell had cloaked us in began to lift.

"The Jonah Bell," Lucas Gwynne said in a hushed voice. He turned to Michael, "The village." He moved nervously nearer the two men with him. "Hell's fire, I didn't expect this."

"It's okay," the man on his right said. He put his hand on Gwynne's shoulder. "They know you have to do this."

"But the Jonah Bell…"

"It's done. He's here," the larger of the two men said.

The other herded me to the side of Marne Young and started us all across the bridge. Lucas Gwynne looked jumpy and agitated. Michael was beside him in the lead, then Marne and me, and behind us, the two with the rifles.

## FORTY-TWO

It was not a long bridge…from bank to bank perhaps thirty yards…raised high enough that the occasional tree uprooted by storm shouldn't take it out with the spring flood. And it was not a wide bridge, just broad enough for a wagon with some walking space left on the sides. Logs for the superstructure. Planks for the roadbed. Plain. Large manila ropes anchored in boulders on either side provided the suspension that held the bridge up. I imagined no problem in hacking through them and dropping the bridge into the creek if a threat to the village demanded it.

A tall old man, an ancient old man, waited at the far end of the bridge. His hair was raven black and to his shoulders. His skin was weathered and the color of copper. He wore a faded blue work shirt tucked into an equally faded set of overalls, both clean and freshly pressed. He stood ramrod straight.

Lucas Gwynne darted forward and started to speak. The old man raised his hand. Gwynne stopped. Everyone stopped. And oh was it quiet then. There was a feeling of menace in the air – a sense of apprehension.

The old man motioned Michael to come to him.

When Michael stood before him, the old man looked him over slowly and stared hard into his eyes.

Finally he spoke. His voice was weak, as if it wanted air, but clear.

"Your presence here isn't welcome, Mr. Dannan. You are here because Hanna Collins wanted you to be."

The old man stopped and looked at Lucas Gwynne, who stood off to the side.

He waited for Lucas Gwynne to speak, but when he didn't the old man turned back to Michael.

"We want you gone quickly. You attract attention. The bell you heard rings for danger. You are a danger to this village. The sooner you are gone, the sooner the danger goes."

The village seemed deserted. There were no sounds except our voices. No movement except our shifting. The long lone street was empty. There was no mutter from the string of cabins, no movement in the fields.

"I'm sorry for all this," Michael said. "None of it is my doing."

The old man didn't say anything to that, just stood looking into Michael's eyes for a long moment, then he turned back to Lucas Gwynne.

"Take him to the chapel. Tell your tale there. The men with you will see that no one intrudes and that no one hears what you hold in secret except Mr. Dannan."

Michael spoke up then. "I'd like to take this young lady with me," he said, motioning to Marne Young. "She understands your people and she can help make sure that I don't muddy the story with misimpressions or illusions I might have."

"It is your secret. Take anyone you like."

"Then my friend here, too" he said and motioned me to join them.

The chapel was the large building with the church-like tower I had seen yesterday as I stood waiting for Marne Young to reappear.

Inside was an amphitheatre, with four rows of benches joined to form a descending square around a circular open space in the center of the room. Rising in the center of the circle, which was the focal point of the room, was an elegantly worked standing lectern. In the corners of each of the four walls there were long rectangular windows of stained glass that collected light and spread it softly over the interior. The windows looked ancient. They were telling stories I didn't know. How the glass was transported here and assembled, because surely these windows could not have been created here, was beyond my imagination.

Lucas led us to a bench on the first row in front of the lectern. "The elder stands there," he said pointing to the lectern in explanation, "When he tells the lesson. We listen. If one of us has a thing to say or a story to tell, we stand there, too.

He stood up and took the six paces to the lectern.

Lucas Gwynne appeared to be in his late forties. He hadn't the tall, slim build our escorts with the rifles had. He was short and frail, his eyes pale blue and his skin too fair. He had the look of someone taken in by the clan, not born to it. This sometimes happened, Marne Young said. It had been the case with Jesse Bristow's father. But the elder Bristow didn't stay. He left and took his Melungeon wife with him.

Lucas Gwynne was a Melungeon, though. He was of the blood, by both mother and father. Hanna Collins had said so. Marne said the Melungeon look didn't always run true, that fair skin and blue eyes were not all that uncommon, or blond hair, or complexion sometimes as light as a Scandinavian's. Nothing more curious than genes of a long heritage at work was the explanation. I wondered what other differences might appear among them and how Lucas Gwynne's differences affected his standing with the others, if his looks gave him lower status, like a mulatto in white society, or made him special.

We seemed insignificant in that big, high-ceiling room. It would seat perhaps eighty. The men with the rifles were not in sight. There were just the four of us in the quiet and the muted light from the windows.

Lucas Gwynne went to the lectern. He stood behind it, facing us, gripped the edges firmly as if to steady himself, and bowed his head. Michael and Marne Young sat together. I moved down to the far end of the bench, putting distance between us, not wanting to distress Gwynne further with my unexpected presence. I imagined that he might be comfortable enough with Marne Young. He had met and spent time with her the day before. She had brought Michael to him. She was part of it now. I, though, was another stranger. Not needed. Not wanted. An intruder in a private matter.

When Gwynne at last lifted his head this is what he told us.

## FORTY-THREE

Hanna Collins was a mother to him. When his real mother died and his father already gone, Hanna Collins was the one who brought him from the village into town and arranged the job and found him a place and helped him begin to build a life outside the valley.

He was fifteen then, but even before, back in the village, she had been the one who declared that the strange fair skinned baby was special, a gift to the village, its good luck blessing, and who doted on him and was his special protector.

She got him the job with Jesse Bristow. Mr. Bristow had the mine out Jackson's Hollow just outside of Harlan. A good size mine. One of Mr. Bristow's first. Lucas started as a helper, picking up spilled coal and loading it back onto the trucks that made the run to the railroad yard in Middlesboro. The work was too hard for him, too physical. Mr. Bristow thought he might make a driver. Though he was small, his reflexes were quick and his hands strong. The trucks were enormous. At first, the sheer size of them scared him. They took up most of the two lane roads they had to travel and moved at top speed all the time— a 60,000 lb projectile hurtling down a narrow track. The drivers were paid by the load and the more loads they hauled the higher their pay. Oncoming traffic was well advised to pull over or get off the road.

He was good at the driving. He came to like the danger of it, the thrill.

In a very short time he was as good as any of the drivers. They were a hell-for-leather lot, competitive, combative. Hard drinkers. Hard players. He didn't drink and he didn't play what they played. He had to sit on a special cushion to be high enough to see over the dashboard, but he held his own on the road and in the competition for loads. They respected him. Soon he was accepted. He liked that very much.

He had been driving almost a year. He had a place in Harlan, a used Ford pick-up, and a little money. He was still too shy for girls. He went to church twice on Sundays with Aunt Hanna and always had Sunday dinner with her. Sometimes Mr. Bristow was there. Mr. Bristow was his hero. Everyone knew what Jesse Bristow had done. Everybody knew where Jesse Bristow was going. All the way to the top of whatever mountain he wanted to climb. That he worked for Jesse Bristow, sometimes had Sunday dinner with Mr. Bristow, well, that was a matter of considerable pride and satisfaction to him.

That day it was cold, even for October, and overcast.

He had dumped his load at Middlesboro and was heading back to the yard at Harlan when the first of the snow began to mark his windshield.

Too early in the year to snow, he thought.

By the time he reached the turnoff to Highway 119 just south of Pineville, maybe a third of the way to Harlan, the snowfall was so heavy he could barely make out the road. It was getting darker and colder. Night was coming on.

He punched on his headlights and turned up the heater. The blast fogged the windshield. He wiped at it with his gloved hand. He wasn't worried about getting stuck. The big wheels of the truck could pull him out of snow up to the hubcaps. The thing that worried him was ice. Icy roads were difficult. So long as the fall continued like this, soft and dry, there should be no problem.

The road ahead seemed empty. Nothing coming toward him. Nothing visible ahead. No nervous drivers sliding into him or stalled on the inclines. A trackless field of white before him.

He slowed some so as to not outrun his headlights, but kept up a speed he thought respectable for a driver who knew his stuff. He didn't detect that the road was slick or that ice was forming. He didn't intend to be foolish, but he also wasn't going to run the risk of appearing a sissy if any of his peers should come upon him. Maybe he was driving a little faster than he should have been.

The road from Pineville to Harlan snakes its way over the top and down the sides of a mountain spine that runs for some thirty miles through almost unbroken forest. On clear days it is a challenge. In a blizzard it is hellish.

The constant fogging of the windshield had him sometimes controlling the truck with one hand while he used the other to clear a spot to see through. What he saw when he had done this was a curtain of snow blowing directly at him. He could barely make out the edges of the road and could see perhaps a truck length ahead.

He topped a rise and started through a left turning curve when he caught a glimpse of a car off the side of the road up against the cliff. He started to stop to see if anyone was in it, but he was running downhill and the road was too slick. Braking would throw him into a slide.

As he brought his gaze back to the road, a form materialized in front of him. Before he could register what it was, he felt a thump. Then he was past it. The road twisted again, became steeper. He checked his rearview mirrors, but saw only his tire tracks in the snow. A deer, he told himself. Or was it someone trying to flag him down for help?

Should he try to stop and go back and check? No. It was only a deer. Even if he stopped there was nowhere to turn around. He kept moving.

What kind of car was it? No telling how long the car had been there anyway. It could have been there for days.

It was only a deer.

He'd tell Mr. Bristow about it and see what he thought.

An hour later, he was at the truck yard in Harlan. The storm had eased into a gentle snowfall by then....big lazy flakes drifting softly down, coating everything, making even the coal waste look clean.

Mr. Bristow wasn't there. So he waited in the office, watching the snow fall.

About a half-hour later, Mr. Bristow came in. Lucas Gwynne told him what had happened as well as he could. Keeping the truck on the road and trying to see through the blizzard with things happening so fast made most of it seem like a dream. He didn't remember it all clearly.

"It must have been a deer," he told Mr. Bristow.

"We'd better go see," Mr. Bristow said.

So they got Mr. Bristow's pickup and headed back out the road through town. The snow was a foot deep, but the truck's big tires and weight were all they needed.

The road was as empty as when he came down it...and as trackless. Even the tracks he made with the big coal truck had been covered by the still falling snow.

They found the car easily enough, a black 1939 Buick coupe – up against a cliff in the curve where Lucas Gwynne thought it would be, its right fender smashed where it had come to rest against the rock. The driver must have lost control in a slide. The keys were still in the ignition.

They searched forward from there, one on either side of the road, shuffling through the snow with their big flashlights piercing the icy dark.

They found no deer.

Gwynne was freezing. He had on only a light jacket and his feet were wet and cold.

About four hundred yards further down the road, up on the left-hand bank, almost to the tree line, the beam of Mr. Bristow's flashlight swept across a snow covered mound that didn't look to be a part of the natural landscape.

When they brushed the snow away, a man lay there, twisted and bloody. He was unconscious. Mr. Bristow stared at him for what seemed a long time, then knelt and put his ear to the man's mouth.

"He's breathing," Mr. Bristow said.

Lucas Gwynne was shivering uncontrollably... not from the cold, from distress that he had caused such a thing.

Mr. Bristow remained kneeling by the unconscious man, watching him.

"This was an accident. Nothing you could have done."

He rose, not taking his gaze off the man.

"You go to the village, Lucas. Stay there. Take the Buick. Get rid of it somewhere."

Together, they managed to struggle the car out of the rocks and on to the road. Despite the crash and the cold, the Buick started with the first turn of the key and when the motor warmed, ran smoothly.

"A hit and run is bad enough. If he dies..."

"Don't let him die, Mr. Bristow, don't let him die," Lucas Gwynne pleaded.

Bristow looked down at the form in the snow at his feet. He knelt, studying the man's face.

"Not much time."

Looking up to Lucas, he said. "Go! Now!"

Lucas Gwynne made it to the village a little before daylight. He got rid of the Buick at the abandoned rock quarry outside Evarts. He drove it off the cliff into the deep quarry pool and watched it sink out of sight.

From there he walked, ten, maybe twelve miles in the dark and the snow all the way to the village. And all the way he was in agony thinking of the hell that prison would be. He was tired and freezing. When he finally reached the village he collapsed.

Aunt Hanna came from Evarts in the afternoon. She got him up, got him washed, treated his cuts and his frost-bitten toes, fed him, got him dressed, listened quietly as he told her all he could remember, crying sometimes, embarrassed, but not able to control it. Oh he hurt so, with such shame and remorse ...and fear.

Mr. Bristow came that night.

The man died before Mr. Bristow could get him off the mountain.

The impact of being hit by the truck, the loss of blood, the snow and the cold were too much.

"He was dead before I could move him," Mr. Bristow said.

There was nothing to do but leave him there to be found when someone came upon him after daylight.

"The man is a stranger. There is nothing to tie you to this. We'll keep it that way."

Mr. Bristow put his hands on Lucas's shoulders. "Stay out of the way. Stay in the village. You'll be safe in the village."

Aunt Hanna agreed.

Aunt Hanna and Mr. Bristow were family. They looked out for him. He was so touched to be so cared for that he almost cried. But he would never cry in Mr. Bristow's presence.

So he stayed.

From that day to this.

The black Buick is still in the quarry pool.

# FORTY-FOUR

"That's the story the way Lucas Gwynne told it to us," I said, laying my notes down and waiting for the reactions.

We were ringed around the table in the kitchen at the farm, Rhae Dannan, Michael, Paul Isham, Jake Slade, Marne Young, and me.

Three of us had already heard it from Lucas Gwynne himself. It was obvious he had never told the story before and equally obvious that he was living it again it as he brought it into words.

We couldn't help being caught up in his feelings and so might have missed points that would have registered in a less emotional telling or heard things that weren't really there. A sensitive young man caught in a nightmare he couldn't wake from. Suffering guilt beyond measure. Tormented by fear of prison. Deathly afraid of stepping outside the protection of his native village. A self-imposed life sentence being served in a remote mountain valley in the wild Appalachians. All that could very much influence the way we heard what Lucas Gwynne told us.

Marne Young and I talked about it all the way back. Michael was silent. He concentrated on his driving, kept his thoughts to himself.

I saw Rhae Dannan reach for Michael's hand as soon as I began. She hardly breathed. Paul Isham kept muttering "damn" beneath his breath. When I finished, he slammed his fist against the table. Jake Slade listened intently, then nodded at the end as if it made sense to him. The reason he couldn't get the story was because no one knew it.

We all sat quietly, waiting for someone to speak. The twilight was fading and night was growing. We let the dark come in. Peaceful. Comforting. In a moment we'd turn on the lights, but not yet. We weren't ready for light yet.

"Did Benjamin die, or did Jesse Bristow kill him?"

That jolted us out of our reverie.

Paul Isham said it again.

"Did Benjamin die or did Jesse let him die? Did he just sit there waiting for Benjamin to bleed to death? It shouldn't have taken long."

"Paul," Rhae said in shock, "how could you say such a thing?"

"They were as close as brothers during the Mine Wars," Jake Slade said in disbelief.

"That changed. Men change." Paul Isham replied.

"Not enough to sit by and let an old friend die. Surely not that much," Rhae Dannan said, still shocked.

Paul Isham didn't reply. After a long moment, his face flushed with anger, he said. "I'm sorry. I'm so damn mad my suspicious mind takes over. But, why the hell didn't Jesse put Benjamin in that truck and try to get him down the mountain. He didn't even try!"

None of us knew how to respond to that.

Marne Young had been making herself inconspicuous. She had never been part of this circle and seemed embarrassed to intrude, but Michael and I had insisted she be part of this conversation. She knew as much about this matter as any of us. She had been at the village and heard Lucas Gwynne for herself. More important, she knew Hanna Collins. Marne Young could explain things we'd have to guess at.

She was losing in her attempt to be a part of the background. She almost raised her hand as she said, "Please excuse me for jumping in uninvited." She looked around the table. Michael nodded for her to go on.

Looking directly at Michael, she said, "Aunt Hanna wanted you to know something. Lucas Gwynne's story was part of it. And the picture of the girl and the clippings and wallet, they are part of it. There must be more. Something's missing. Something very important. Something that ties all this together."

She's right, I thought. Hanna Collins had been too thorough in directing Michael to this odd collection of facts and clues to chance that he would miss her message, and I suspected that when her message was finally delivered in its entirety, none of those involved would find any reason to rejoice.

I realized then that we had to let this alone. I admit I was the one pushing to find out what this was all about so it wouldn't be problem for the campaign. But now I saw that it was already a major problem for the campaign. If the press got hold of any of this story it would wind up going places none of us would want it to go. Was Jesse Bristow involved in Michael's father death? Did he sit coldly by while Benjamin Dannan bled to death? And we still don't know what Benjamin Dannan was doing on that road that night. Why was he there? The answer might not be one we wanted to hear.

"We haven't time for this," I broke in. "We've got to let it lie. Our focus has to be on putting Michael in the governor's chair. None of this is going to help us do that." I turned to Michael. "That's why you came back, right? To be Governor? That's why we're all here, right?"

Michael ignored me. He leaned across the table to Paul Isham. "Why would you think Jesse Bristow killed my father?" His voice was as cold and demanding as I had ever heard it.

Paul was seated next to Rhae Dannan. He looked up and found her eyes. He seemed to deflate then. He sighed, "I'm so mad I might say anything. Even believe anything. Forget I said that. Theo is right about focus. Keep it on the campaign."

"No, Paul," Michael said. "Tell me about Jesse Bristow."

Before Paul could respond, Rhae Dannan spoke. She put her hand over Paul's clinched fists and looked across the table at her son.

"At first, Benjamin and Jesse were like brothers," she said. "Benjamin the older brother, Jesse the younger. They were only five years apart in age. You remember how it was, Paul."

Paul Isham nodded, remembering. The room was almost dark by then. No one had bothered with the lights. "Ah, Rhae, we have to live it again do we?" He stood up slowly, sadly.

"The lights," he said. "I'll get the lights."

His movement broke the tension in the room and bought him time to collect his story.

"It started with our stringer," Paul Isham began, returning to his seat beside Rhae. "Benjamin left as soon as he heard what had happened. The boy's fingers were broken and both hands stomped on and crushed. There was no mystery about who did it. The mine owners didn't like the story he wrote about the ambush at Evarts. He was told as much by the men who snapped his fingers one by one. 'No more of that' they told him."

Rhae Dannan joined in. "The call about the stringer must have come about four or five in the afternoon. Benjamin came home immediately. I had never seen him so outraged. He told me what had happened, barely controlling his fury. 'I have to see to this, Rhae,' he told me.

"The idea to rough up the stringer had to come from the local goons," Paul Isham said. "The owners were much too smart to risk antagonizing Benjamin Dannan themselves. But that's what happened. Nobody could abuse Benjamin Dannan's people. No one could intimidate the *Journal*."

"Benjamin didn't know anyone up there," Rhae Dannan continued. "He had no contacts there. He had never even met the stringer. Harlan was at least a six-hour drive, Evarts perhaps another hour. If he left right then, he would be getting into a strange town, a hostile town, in the middle of the night, with nowhere to stay and no support anywhere near. I tried to talk him into waiting and leaving in the morning. He saw the reasonableness of it, but no, he had to go right then."

Paul Isham cut in. "I tried to convince him I should go with him. Give him some company on the drive. Be extra eyes and ears once he actually got on the site. No sale. He wanted me here, running the paper. He said he didn't know how long he'd be gone. Like Rhae, I was concerned that he was going into a very unsettled situation, a potentially dangerous situation, with no one around who could give him any help. I didn't even want to call the stringer to let him know Benjamin was on his way because I assumed the phone was tapped. You have to understand how it was then," he went on. "This was 1931. The roads were bad. Telephone communication wasn't very good and almost never private because the local phone operators routinely listened in on calls. In the mining counties, the local sheriff was a power who answered only to the companies. The companies were the law. Housing, groceries, doctors, paychecks, they all flowed from the companies. The companies ran everything. Benjamin was going to be trespassing on their turf. They weren't going to like it."

"We didn't hear from Benjamin again until just before supper the next evening," Rhae Dannan said.

"Paul and I were on tenterhooks the whole time. The suspense had become so great for me that I went down to the *Journal* to wait there for word. I assumed that's where Benjamin would make contact first and that's where I wanted to be. I sat in his office and waited. He called from a phone booth outside a gas station on the road into Harlan. He had made contact with the stringer. The stringer had put in him in touch with some of the striking miners. He was going to their meeting that night. He'd file a story on it the next morning. That's where he met Jesse Bristow. At the meeting that night."

It was eerily quiet in the kitchen. We hung on the story Rhae and Paul were telling, barely breathing, huddled around the table like we used to huddle around the radio on Sunday nights long ago, letting our imaginations give form to the tale we were hearing.

I whispered to Michael, "this must have been just a night or two after the events Sattis told us about, the shooting and the hanging."

Paul Isham picked the story back up, muffling Michael's response.

"We didn't see Benjamin for almost three weeks. He filed six stories from the war zone. Yes, it became a war zone during that time. His first story almost blew the dome off the Capitol. The last five stories were syndicated nationally by the *Washington Post*. All at once the mine owners' private little fiefdom in the mountains of east Kentucky was being overrun by reporters from out of state and the battle of the little miners of Harlan County against the goliaths of the coal mines became front-page national news"

"When he finally came home, Benjamin had Jesse Bristow with him," Rhae Dannan took the lead again.

"I was asleep. I heard noise in the kitchen, then smelled coffee brewing. I knew it was Benjamin. Always, when he came home in the early morning after having been up all night, he made coffee and fixed himself breakfast. He always had coffee waiting for me when I came down. On this particular morning Jesse Bristow sat at the table beside him. I didn't know who he was at the time – just a young man sitting at the kitchen table with his back to me while Benjamin poured him coffee."

## FORTY-FIVE

The tale of Benjamin Dannan and Jesse Bristow's relationship took almost until midnight to get told. Rhae Dannan and Paul Isham alternated in the telling, one breaking in on the other, injecting, adding, re-living it as they remembered it.

That early morning in her kitchen Jesse Bristow was touchingly embarrassed at having intruded on her home at such an hour, Rhae said. He was dressed in jeans and a long-sleeved, blue denim work shirt. A leather jacket hung across the back of his chair.

He stood politely, as well-mannered young men do when ladies enter a room, and looked sheepishly from coal-black eyes while Benjamin introduced him. They seemed of a kind, he and Benjamin – young men certain in their youth and their strength. Eager. Ready to challenge anything. Benjamin was just twenty-seven, Jesse only twenty-two. Rhae sensed a natural chemistry between them. She liked Jesse Bristow immediately, as obviously Benjamin did.

The poor stringer with the crushed hands and broken fingers had arranged their meeting. If Benjamin wanted the story of what was happening, he needed be in the action. The action was Jesse Bristow. Jesse Bristow's actions the night he took retribution for the death of his friend and later his conduct at the Battle of Evarts had already put Jesse Bristow in the front of the fight against the owners.

At first Benjamin and Jesse saw in each other a tool that could be used to get what they wanted. Benjamin wanted to avenge his stringer, but it was more complicated than that. His sense of right and wrong was outraged. He wanted the owners' blood. Drawing intense public attention to their excesses through the stories he could write and the stories his coverage would stimulate in other newspapers was the way to draw it. Jesse Bristow was the conduit to the stories.

Jesse was smart enough to know that outraged public opinion was one of the strongest allies the miners could have in their fight. Benjamin Dannan was the way to get their story out. They began by needing each other. They ended up fast friends.

That much was obvious the morning in Rhae Dannan's kitchen.

Their plan was to see the U. S. attorney in Louisville and try to get federal marshals sent into the area to protect the miners as they continued to try to organize a union despite the owners' brutal opposition.

After that, they were going on to Washington to engage the senators and start building federal pressure to guarantee that the miners could form their union. Benjamin would get them the necessary appointments. Jesse would supply the facts and describe the situation as a first-hand participant.

Their mission was overweight with danger. If the miners were successful in establishing a union, the hit to the companies' profits and operating autonomy would be dramatic. The beatings and the burnings were evidence that the owners wouldn't tolerate such a thing.

Benjamin, for his stories, and Jesse, for his role as a leader of the miners, were highest on the list of people the owners wanted silenced. Now, by taking this aggressive step to secure federal government oversight and intervention, they were putting themselves at even greater risk.

There had already been two attempts on Jesse Bristow's life – ambushes that failed. Poor execution on one that should have worked as he walked on foot down a lonely ridge following a midnight meeting at a remote cabin. The shooter wound up shot. Then they tried to run him down with a speeding truck on the street in front of the courthouse in Harlan, but he was too agile. Benjamin, too, had been targeted. His car had drawn rifle fire on the road from Evarts.

The dangers drew them closer.

The strike collapsed. The muscle of the owners was too much, but the union organizing push didn't stop. Benjamin and Jesse kept working despite the threats and the dangers, with Benjamin making frequent trips to the mining communities and keeping the effort alive in print while Jesse did the on-the-ground work. Shrugging off pressure from the federal government, the owners held out for another seven years. But finally the day came when the union was organized. Jesse Bristow was elected secretary-treasurer. His reputation for honesty, intelligence, and courage was golden throughout the mountains of east Kentucky.

Jesse stayed with that long enough to make sure the union was on solid footing, then he began looking. The union job wasn't big enough for Jesse Bristow. Everyone knew that. He decided he would try business. He started with a small truck mine, financed by Sattis. He treated his people right and paid them well. Showed them respect and was attentive to their families. He made deals like he played poker – he never left a dollar on the table.

The big companies took notice. Jesse Bristow had been a nemesis as a union organizer. Now he was making a nuisance of himself as a competitor. They tried to buy him out. No luck. They tried to hire him with offers of more money than Jesse Bristow thought any one man would ever be worth. Jesse wasn't above taking their money, he just couldn't accept the idea of answering to anyone other than himself. He kept doing well and soon had small string of mines working both the underground shafts of the eastern mountains and the strip mining area in west Kentucky.

Then the Big Sadie tax bill hit. A no-name member of the legislature, an idealistic teacher from the Bluegrass who had somehow managed to slip in and get elected, introduced a bill intended to begin repair some of the damage done to the state by the ravages of the mine operators. He wanted to stop the pollution the mines were putting into the creeks and rivers and reclaim the land destroyed by strip mining. He was going to make the owners foot the bill through a special tax. The bill he introduced, The Big Sadie tax bill (named for the infamous mine of the same name), put a ten-cent a ton excise tax on all coal mined anywhere in the state by any method, with the monies collected earmarked for reclamation efforts. It had some resonance.

Jesse opposed it passionately. Benjamin supported it just as passionately. Jesse said the tax would put him and all miners like him out of business. Bad enough for him, he said, but disastrous for the men and the communities that depended for their jobs on the mines.

Benjamin said the rape of the land by the mining operators had gone on far too long. The state was at risk. He didn't believe the mine owners would go out of business or that many jobs would be lost. Benjamin fought for the bill as hard as he could. He even formed a coalition of publishers in favor of the bill who were to put their editorial pages behind it. Jesse joined forces with the big mine operators and brought the rest of the small operators with him.

For the first time, Jesse Bristow and the owners were on the same side of a fight.

Benjamin and his allies worked the public with words and reason. Jesse and his colleagues worked the legislature – with money.

The bill was defeated. Jesse won. Benjamin lost.

Rhae Dannan finished the story for us.

"That fight ended their friendship," she said. "Benjamin was both saddened and angered at Jesse's stand. Jesse couldn't fathom that Benjamin had turned against him. Benjamin was convinced that the owners had bought the vote and that Jesse was the man who did the buying. He said as much in print. Jesse sued for slander. Benjamin couldn't produce enough legal proof to sustain his charges. His sources were fearful of coming forward and he was honor bound not to reveal their names. Jesse couldn't prove malice. The judge dismissed the case. There was considerable ill will on both sides."

She paused, then began again.

"I missed Jesse. Often when he was in town he stayed with us. He was good company. Polite, thoughtful. He and Benjamin seemed to enjoy each other so. After the trial, Jesse was in my house only once again. That was after the funeral. All Benjamin's old friends came by. Even Jesse. I remember him saying how he wished things could have turned out differently, how sorry he was for the distress he knew I must be feeling. He said that if I needed his help in any way, I had only to ask."

Paul Isham: "There was the trial, yes. And that ended the friendship. But there was something else in Jesse's craw."

I knew almost instinctively. "The girl in the locket!" I said.

"Theo!" Paul cut me off. But Rhae Dannan's soft voice quieted us both.

"It's all right, Paul," she said, "I know."

She stood up.

"I'm cold. Let's go in by the fireplace."

Slowly, we all rose and followed her.

## FORTY-SIX

Sue Bristow was the prettiest thing those ancient mountains had produced in a hundred years, said the miners who had seen her.

She was tall for a girl, slim and lithe and as graceful as a doe. She had a model's high cheekbones, or a Cherokee's, depending on who was doing the describing, hair as black as the blackest coal and eyes as blue as the deepest blue of the winter sky. When she spoke, it was like music. And when she laughed, which was often for she was of uncommon good nature, everyone within earshot felt good.

No one was as sure of foot or as fast on the trails and the paths as she, which is how she came to be at the meeting that night when Benjamin Dannan came in with Jesse Bristow.

It was 1935 and she was Jesse's messenger that fateful spring. Panther like, she moved along the ridges and through the hollows, silent and unseen, the connection between the small groups of men meeting secretly in remote cabins to plot their union into existence.

These are the things that were said about her, and are still said about her by those who remember her, Paul Isham told us as he sat beside Rhae on the couch by the fireplace trying to capture what had happened and how it had happened that long time ago.

Sue Bristow was eighteen, on spring break from her freshman year studies at Berea College and excited to be helping with her brother's fight for justice. Benjamin Dannan was thirty-one.

How is what happened between them to be explained? Is it enough to say that they were drawn to each against their wills? That the attraction they felt was a force of nature, arising spontaneously and once felt, irresistible? That though they wanted to resist it, knew they should resist it, neither could?

Benjamin was Jesse's friend. He was a man from outside – powerful, famous even. She was flattered to be working with him, proud to be working with him. No man was more proper with women, or courteous, than Benjamin Dannan. She was his friend's little sister. He was polite and attentive and strictly observant of the protocol such relationships required.

That was the first year. As the fight went on, moving from remote cabins on lonely ridges down into the towns and into meeting halls and small offices, their mutual defense began to erode, then eroded completely. Their attraction was intensely physical and their minds engaged as neither had experienced with any other. They fit. In all ways. They began to meet secretly, she slipping away from school to rendezvous in places they felt no one would know them.

Their pretext was uncomplicated. For her, the demands of family, or as her studies progressed, research for special projects. For him, special meetings of one of the many organizations to which he belonged, or on the trail of a story he was pursuing. A weekend. A night. Whatever could be arranged. They were alone together perhaps six times. They went on this way for almost four years... until the week they both died.

Benjamin carried an awful burden. He loved Rhae dearly and cherished Michael. But the need he carried for Sue Bristow was something he could not put away. He was sure he was damned, for his Catholicism was real and deep.

Sue Bristow loved only Benjamin. She carried no particular guilt in that regard, except for the deception of her brother, whom she worshipped and for the certain disapproval of her aunt, whose staunch Baptist creed would be scandalized. Her only fear and apprehension was that her actions might bring dishonor to the family. That would have been a tragedy for her.

"Benjamin's guilt was so great that he had to confide in someone," Paul Isham said in so soft a voice we almost couldn't hear him.

"That someone wasn't a priest. It was me.

"Benjamin trusted me. He trusted me to hold in confidence anything he told me and he trusted me not to judge.

"The knowledge has been a torture for me," Paul said, his voice becoming stronger.

"I could, and would, forgive him the weakness. He knew that. Benjamin's passions were part of what made him the great man he was. What hurt me, Rhae, was the hurt of I knew it would bring to you if any of this ever came to light. I wasn't going to let that happen if I could prevent it.

"I listened. I didn't remonstrate. I didn't judge. I heard him out and didn't say a word.

"When he finished there were tears in his eyes.

"Oh that tore at me. Who was I to advise such a man at such a time? Who was I to say what should be? But I did. I knew the course that had to be taken almost from the beginning of his confession.

"I told him that the risk that he was running was insane. If knowledge of the affair become known to Jesse Bristow, he would kill Benjamin as surely as the two of us sat there talking. Bristow's family honor would demand it. His temper would compel it. It was miraculous that Bristow hadn't stumbled on to them already.

"More important, I told him that the risk of hurt to you, Rhae, and to Michael, and that the damage such a revelation would do to his reputation if it became public, was a risk he had no right to run.

"You have to end it, Benjamin. Now and completely.

"I told him this with as much understanding as I could muster, but with as much force as I could command in talking to the man I respected and admired above all others.

"We drank over this through a long night at my place up on Bald Knob. When morning came, Benjamin made the decision he knew he had to make. Three weeks later, his body was found on the side of that road in Breathitt County."

So said Paul Isham, all of us sitting there around the fireplace with the chill of the night pushing against the windows.

Michael almost never showed his feelings. Remarkable, isn't it, how people who can be so sensitive to others, whose personal antennae can pick up the hurt or sorrow or fear of others can be so private into themselves.

That was Michael. He sensed what others were feeling. He could react to comfort or console or inspire. The empathy he carried was a gift, a talent. It gave him a remarkable instrument with which to manipulate people if he chose to do so. I suppose the gift could also be a curse. He had to feel what they were feeling and that must have often been distressing.

But how he felt within himself was almost never evident. He wasn't readable in the way that most people are readable. He didn't send signals. He didn't betray himself.

I could read him better than most. Better than Allie. Better than anyone but Rhae. He showed nothing after Paul Isham finished. Outrage? Anger? Hurt? Nothing was revealed in his face or manner. I didn't know what I expected, but then I remembered the nine-year old, how he cried at the cemetery – and never did again; how his anger consumed him when he came back to school – and how he controlled it.

Rhae, though, poor Rhae. She hadn't the discipline her son had worked at. The hurt showed in her eyes. Her misery that Michael had learned the father he thought a paragon was as weak as the most common of men was so evident that even those of us without a sharpened sense of empathy felt her pain.

Michael reached out for her hand and took it and held it tight. He was calm, controlled. His manner seemed to strengthen her.

"Thank you, Paul," she said. "All these years that I thought I was protecting Michael and you, you were protecting me. Benjamin told me the week before he died."

She turned to Michael, "Son, I…"

He stopped her.

"Don't explain."

Michael then nodded to me. "Theo is right. We haven't time for this now. We'll unravel it later. I have an election to win."

And that was that. There was no more talk of it. We were too drained to talk of anything else so we said our goodnights, feeling oddly embarrassed and in a strange way outraged.

It was too late and we were too tired to drive Marne Young back to Mountain Home so Rhae Dannan insisted Marne spend the night at the farm and settled her in one of the guest rooms there.

Paul Isham and Jack Slade left together, grim faced and silent. I tarried a bit to be alone with Michael.

"Can you stay focused on what we have to achieve and not let this distract you? Will you? Because if you can't, you'll lose."

We were on the porch, the night starless and cold. His face was just barely visible.

"Can you wait? Can you put all this away until we've won?"

He nodded.

Well, hell, I said to myself. No man on God's green earth has more self-discipline than Michael Dannan. Here we go on the wild dog's back. High-low-Jack and the whole damn game.

## FORTY-SEVEN

I occupied myself during those next few weeks with the business of newspapering. I covered my beat and wrote my columns and tried to put Sue Bristow and Benjamin Dannan out of my mind.

That fall was as mild as any I could remember. The days were crisp, but never uncomfortable. Like Camelot, it never rained until after sunset, and then only often enough to keep things green. And the nights, ah the nights were clear, and though often cold, the stars sparkled.

I walked the streets in the early morning dark after the paper was put to bed and let the magic of the sleeping city take me…watching the play of shadows on the sidewalks and the flow of the river under the bridges. Lord, what a lovely place this is. Why would I want to leave it? And leave it I would if Michael won. For as certain as day follows night, if Michael became Governor, he would become President.

Oh, I would miss it. I missed it badly while I was in New York. We Irish are bound to the place where we are born, anchored to the land where our people lie, where they made their lives and gave us ours. Blood and earth. Those are the ties. We are bound to homeplace.

The pull of it is the principal reason I came back. Some think it was because of remorse that the girl died. Or that I was afraid a knife would find me.

It is true that if I hadn't written the story in the way I did, using her name, she might have gone unharmed. But there was no way to expose the ring without naming names – and stupidly, as it turned out, I thought the protection the police promised would be enough. Her brother vowed revenge. I wasn't afraid. I was just tired…tired of the dirt and the noise and the avarice and the indifference of Manhattan. I wanted to go home. Home called me.

I am so very, very sorry about the girl. She didn't want to be involved, but she was my proof. She was one of the few of the young Filipino girls who had escaped the ring and the only one willing to talk about it. Without her, there was no story. I can't change what happened. However hard I try, I cannot change the past. But I ache from it in the lonely dark.

Michael was as good as his word. He was focused, tireless, and relentless. Dace Havershamp and his co-chairmen had done the unthinkable. They had knit together a cadre of leaders in every county who were rapidly creating the local organizations needed. Michael would have an effective organization in place and at work well before the middle of January and certainly well in advance of the primary in late May.

I did a story on this, a nice, long Sunday feature which played in the syndication. I checked with the Bristow camp, too, and made sure Jesse Bristow's organization was covered in the story. What Bristow had was the old gang, the establishment, nothing very exciting about that. But Dannan, well, this Dannan thing had some excitement to it. Not so crudely stated as that, but that was the drift of the piece.

Lida McBain and her organization had the "Dannan Clubs" already energized – putting up signs and making phone calls. As important, she was only a week away from monopolizing the broadcast air-time and newspaper print space that would be crucial in the final weeks of the campaign. The strategy called for Michael to own, literally own, all the prime-time television minutes available on the state's four major television stations the three weeks prior to the election. And to have locked up space for full-page ads in every daily newspaper in the state for the four Sundays leading up to the vote. By the time Bristow's people got around to buying their air time and newspaper space, the Dannan campaign would have all the best of it taken.

The only real break Michael took was over the Thanksgiving weekend.

Jim and Julie Colby had followed through on their idea to get the old gang together for a big, like-it-used-to-be party at her camp on the river, the one they had suggested to me when we ran into each other casually the morning my story on Michael's announcement ran.

The old Admiral, Admiral J. J. B. Espy, Julie's grandfather and single heir to the Espy tobacco fortune, had built the place on twenty acres fronting the Kentucky River about five miles north of town. He was buried there, beneath the flags of the United States and the Commonwealth of Kentucky on the highest point of the ridgeline. From there, if the day was clear and the season was right, the tip of the dome of the Capitol Building could be seen down the valley cut by the river on its way into town.

The main building was a gracious, two-story log structure nested on the hillside behind a big veranda that ran down to the river. The upper floor was the sleeping floor – seven rooms outfitted as comfortably as the best rooms in the best hotel downtown. The lower floor was the cooking, eating, and drinking floor with a great room in the center, dominated by a fireplace large enough for eight big men to stand-side by side and still have turning space. Like most of the places on the river, only bigger and more grand, it had a sitting porch that ran the front and the sides. There was a sandy beach in front of the veranda, a boat dock, and a swimming platform anchored out in the river.

The best of it was the cottage that sat back up the hill. It was built to look like a New England cottage with pointed dormers and a white-picket fence. This was the Admiral's personal place, the den he retreated to when the presence of visitors or family became more than he wished to enjoy further. There was a sitting room, its walls lined with river maps and books, and a small bedroom in back that opened out to the ridge. I'd stayed in it before. So had Michael.

We all had spent many fine weekends at that Camp. Julie's parties were frequent. Some of us learned to smoke there (not Michael or me, we didn't smoke) and some learned to drink (again, neither of us – we weren't drinking then.) And there was the intoxication of young, eager, tantalizing sex. On warm summer nights with a full moon high, a light breeze blowing, and soft music fingering through the deep black shadows all around, we did a lot of exploring. And we learned a lot.

The "we" that Julie invited for this party was our high school graduating class from near and far wherever they lived. Almost all came, even George Weld and his wife from Florida and Jackson Kane from Alaska. His wife was tending a sick child and couldn't come, but he came. And the eight others who had moved out of the county but not out of state. No one was ill. No one had died.

Oh, it was a grand night and a grand party and Michael was still the king of the class and Allie the prettiest and we danced and drank and talked and sang and the whole lot of us, by damn, would beat the bushes for every vote that could be scared up and carry Michael to the Governor's mansion on our very own shoulders come the day.

That's not why I put this in the story.

I put this in the story because of Michael and Allie.

Daylight came. We had been going that long. There was fog on the river and a mist on the ridgeline above the Camp. Everyone had left but Julie and Jim Colby and me and Michael. We were standing around in the kitchen, yawning and yearning for the coffee Julie had just put on the stove. I looked around for Michael but didn't see him, hadn't seen him for quite some time, but he could have been anywhere – in the head, down at the river watching the light on the water, walking up to the top of the hill to see the sunrise.

Jim Colby was poking up the fire in the big fireplace to take some of the morning chill of the room.

"Seen Michael?" I asked him.

He stopped and looked over at Julie. She tried to hide a smile.

"I haven't seen Allie, either," she said in that I-know-something-you-don't-know voice that women employ when they have a secret that want to tell you. She turned back to the stove looking more pleased than she should have at the prospect of making breakfast.

I knew then.

For some reason I can not fathom, some reason beyond any rational explanation, I felt betrayed. I was the one who had backed off all those years ago, not Allie. She hadn't chosen Michael over me. I had stepped aside and left her to him. How could I possibly be the betrayed? Still, I felt it.

I took a cup of hot black coffee from Julie and walked out on the porch to wait for them.

After a while, through the mist, I saw them coming down the hill from the Admiral's cottage. They were hand in hand and in the rising light looked as young as when they walked hand in hand across the campus at UK. They had always made a handsome couple, but never more so than on the pathway that morning. They hadn't seen me and probably wouldn't have noticed anyway until there were right on me, they were so focused on each other. Allie was laughing and Michael looked more at ease and relaxed than I had seen him since he came home. And relieved. He had the look and the easy walk of a man who has put his burdens down and seen the light.

They fit together so well, complemented each other so thoroughly that I was immediately ashamed of my earlier feelings.

"Gonna be a beautiful day, Theo," Michael said with an enthusiastic smile as he stepped onto the porch with Allie's hand in his.

Allie smiled, too, almost shyly. She knew I knew where they had been, what they had done, or could intuit it. She hadn't lost the modesty of the times she grew up in and would still believe that such matters were private. But the proprieties of her girlhood didn't override her happiness that morning. And she knew I was her friend and Michael's friend and would be happy for them both and protect them both.

She kissed me on the cheek and slipped on by into the kitchen to help Julie with the breakfast. Michael stopped and stood beside me. We watched the fog leave the river as the sun rose.

Michael put his arm around my shoulder. "Good times coming, buddy. Yes, indeed, good times."

He looked so happy we both laughed, laughed just because it felt good to feel good. And went inside.

They should have never been apart. I knew that. They seemed to know it, too.

I was happy for them. I hoped the future would be good to them, and I expected that Michael was right, that good times were coming.

## FORTY-EIGHT

During those next few months, Michael was inexhaustible. He traveled the state relentlessly – north to south, east to west, or on any diagonal Lida's schedulers cared to suggest.

That was the drill. A full-court press. From start to finish, get Michael Dannan face to face with as many voters as possible in as many places as possible.

No Lions Club, or Rotary, or Kiwanis was too small for his attention, nor any garden club or church group or Chamber of Commerce.

He did coffees and drop-ins and hospital visits. He went out of his way to call on the editors of the small weekly newspapers and the little local radio stations that dotted the state and barely reached beyond their own county's boundaries. They were local and listened to and read. And flattered to be shown such attention.

People in towns so small that never in anyone's memory had a candidate for governor come to call found themselves stopped on the street by a handsome young man with an engaging smile and a strong handshake and asked for their vote. Personally. By the man himself.

Bandana, Maynard, Four Oaks, Honeybee, New Zion, Red Fox – if the road was paved and he could get to it by car, he made every crossroads village and rural community he could hit on his winding way through the Commonwealth. "I'm Michael Dannan and I'm running for Governor. Give me your vote, I'll give you your hopes," he told them.

They were surprised and impressed. Michael Dannan cared. Michael Dannan was for them. Michael Dannan was their man!

I made a few of these runs with him. Not many. I was excess baggage on these trips, of no real use except as company to Michael. For the most part, it was him and Lida McBain, a driver, and the local county chairman. The four filled up a car. Like Pony Express riders, they changed county chairman as they passed from county to county.

He kept up this pace through the wet, cold winter. Low pressure systems keep sucking moisture up out of the Gulf of Mexico and dropping it as rain and slushy snow most of December and into January.

As benign as the fall had been, the winter was dark and grumpy.

But Michael pushed through it, refusing to be put off by conditions and determined to keep his humor. The people responded.

He took a few days off for Christmas at the farm. We had rain all three days, a chill, driving rain that blurred the colored lights strung around downtown Frankfort and left the crèche at the Methodist Church floating in a small lake on the lawn.

The fire in the big fireplace at the farm was grand, though, and the big old house so cheery and warm that none of us gave a thought to the weather once we were inside.

Allie was there for Christmas dinner, radiant and happy. Rhae was at the head of the table, with Michael on her right and Allie on her left. Allie glowed in the candlelight and basked in their attention.

I was interested in Rhae's manner toward Allie. Rhae seemed to have accepted her without question and to be pleased with her company. Then I remembered that Allie wasn't a stranger to Rhae, that Rhae must have known her and possibly have been with her at games or concerts when Michael was in school and Allie and he were a couple.

Rhae Dannan had invited Marne Young, too, but Marne had made the trip back to Glasgow to be with her parents for the holiday.

Paul Isham and I filled out the table, me next to Allie, Paul across from me next to Michael.

It was a relaxing, luxuriant evening. We ate too much. Drank very well, and talked not of politics at all.

Those few days at Christmas were the only days Michael took away from the campaign that long winter.

I stayed on the periphery of the action during this time, catching up with Michael at a rally or a speech to file or story or get material for a column – not overdoing it, but providing enough press attention to make sure his candidacy sustained a reasonably high public profile in what were usually down months for campaigning.

Jesse Bristow must have figured he was far enough ahead in the race that he needn't inconvenience himself unnecessarily in the wet and the cold for his campaign was relatively passive those winter weeks. He made a big speech at a Teamsters' Union convention in Louisville that got good coverage and did a round of radio interviews in Covington and Newport, but largely kept to his office in Frankfort and out of the weather.

He was pointing, I assumed, as were we, at the Penrod Picnic.

## FORTY-NINE

Penrod.

Michael had never been there. I'd been only once – four years ago to do a feature for the Sunday paper.

The village of Penrod, never larger than 800 or 900 souls, sits off in the western end of the state, too far from the centers of power to be of much consequence and too small to be noticed – but for the Picnic.

No other event anywhere in the Commonwealth is like it – probably nothing like it anywhere in any other state.

The picnic had begun in the long ago of the village, in the time before the Civil War, always on the first weekend in March, the month when the fields were beginning be rid of winter's hold and ready for the plows to cut furrows for the first crops of spring.

The war halted that, but the town resumed the practice afterwards. This would be the 90th in an unbroken chain. In that time the picnic had grown into an institution – a weekend that was part reunion, part festival, all spectacle…and the unofficial kick-off of the state-wide political games.

The entire community took part. Those who had left to try their fortunes in greener fields came home for it, bringing their growing families with them. Bluegrass and country music filled the air. There was dancing and laughing into the night. There was a parade and games and the best barbeque anyone ever tasted, honest to God, they all agreed.

Politicians took over in the early afternoon. How they came to discover it, no one remembers, but all at once they started showing up. At first, just candidates for local offices took advantage of it. They had all those potential voters together in one place. They worked the crowd, made speeches. And then the press began showing up, giving the candidates a way to get their messages before bigger audiences, which lured candidates for state-wide office, which then generated even wider coverage.

In gubernatorial years and the years when the big races for the U.S. Senate were on, all the candidates came. There they were, face to face, to be measured against one another. The crowds loved it. The press ate it up. The smart candidates used it to great effectiveness.

In time, the attention of the whole state focused on the Penrod Picnic and the speeches made there.

Happy Chandler said the Penrod Picnic launched his political career. Back in the thirties he showed up, a relative unknown, running for Lt. Governor. He came dressed in a white suit to make sure he'd stand out. Happy kissed every baby in sight, danced with every woman in reach. Kept that big smile on his face and sang a song or two.

And he orated. Happy was a mighty orator. On election day that year the people of the grand and glorious Commonwealth of Kentucky sent Albert B. "Happy" Chandler to the State Capitol – the first step on a path that took him to the governor's chair twice, to the U.S. Senate, and finally to Commissioner of Baseball.

Happy said the secret to getting elected is, "Tell 'em what they want to hear."

The trick is knowing *what* they want to hear. Happy could intuit it. Like Michael, he had a feel for the people. He had the gift of empathy.

The Penrod Picnic could be the most important day in Michael's young candidacy.

Gershon Pope was skeptical of the event and thought it inconvenient. Lida McBain, though, was Kentucky bred and born. She understood.

So Michael had drawn us all together to make sure the plans for the event were solid.

It was a full gathering of all the top people involved with the campaign: Dace Havershamp and Sattis Arnow and Judge Blue and Jonathan Wilson. Rhae was there, as were Paul Isham, Gershon Pope, and Lida McBain. And even Marne Young. After the Melungeon exercise, Marne had grown on all of us, on Rhae Dannan particularly. Rhae liked her strength and her confidence and above all, her spirit. Gershon wasn't happy that an "outsider" and a "non-professional" was admitted to the inner circle. "Can she be trusted? Will she waste our time with inane questions?" Rhae Dannan overrode him.

We met at the farm. The importance of the meeting was underscored by the presence of Dace Havershamp and Sattis Arnow. They had to come from either end of the state making long five to six hour drives over twisting and often two-lane roads.

Because Michael had a passion for meetings that began at the break of day, or as near to it as he could browbeat people into making, we were to meet at eight, so they had to come in the night before. So did all the others except Lida, who was nearby at Georgetown. Pope came the furthest. By plane from New York to Cincinnati and by car from there, but none of us cared.

The sun was barely up when we sat down around the large table in the kitchen.

I took a seat beside Sattis. "How does it look?" I asked him.

"We've hardly started," he said. "Ask me after Penrod."

We expected Penrod to be the spot where Michael's state-wide career would take-off. But he wouldn't come in a white suit, as Happy did.

That was among the things decided at the meeting around the kitchen table that February morning. Many other things as well, but that is the one that stands out in my memory.

Dace Havershamp would be Michael's escort. Penrod was less than sixty miles from Dace's place at Kentucky Lake. Dace knew almost everyone in town and we were sure that with Dace's influence, Michael would get a preferred spot in the speaking order. We weren't sure how many office seekers would be there; the forum was open to all, but we knew Jesse Bristow would be there. And the two men running in the Republican primary, plus, most likely, five or six others vying for elective statewide offices like Secretary of State, and Treasurer, and such.

It was important that Michael be slotted after Bristow. We wanted him to have the advantage of the last word.

Lida McBain was to take care of the "touches" – placing supporters in the crowd to clap and cheer at appropriate times, getting a supply of Dannan t-shirts and buttons and placards spread around, arranging for a special bus load of "Students for

Dannan" from Murray State to make a strong impact as they unloaded yelling and waving banners.

We wanted all of the Dannan power brokers to be there, circulating through the crowd and standing together when Michael took the podium, so everyone could see the quality of the team he had behind him – Dace Havershamp and Sattis Arnow and Judge Blue and Jonathan Winslow.

Jesse Bristow couldn't trump that. He'd have the party regulars, but not men of this stature.

Michael wanted Allie to be there, but everyone, Rhae and me included, convinced him this was not a good idea.

As for me, I would go down on the Wednesday before. I'd stay in one of the cabins at Dace's marina on Kentucky Lake. My plan was to be on the water before daylight, however cold it might be, and see if I could scare up a bass off one of the rocky points. I hadn't put a line in the water since Michael came home. I needed the therapy. Later I'd drive down to Penrod and do a special feature from there for Saturday morning's paper. I'd make it a "Ready for the Kick-Off" story, trying to catch the flavor of the town as it waited for the whistle to blow.

## FIFTY

Noon was approaching when Michael and Dace Havershamp arrived at Penrod. We wanted him to make an "entrance," the way he had at his announcement speech at Perryville – materialize on the scene in a dramatic fashion, get everyone's attention, dominate the space.

Figuring out how to make this happen in the midst of the carnival already underway was more than a challenge.

But Lida McBain came through.

Michael would helicopter in.

While people were in line getting their barbecue and Pepsi or beginning to settle comfortably at the big trestle tables spread around, a white helicopter would come in over the trees from the west, loop around the spire of St. Jerome's, and land on the road in front of the church.

Everyone would stop what they were doing. They'd look up, wondering. A helicopter at Penrod would be a sight. They crowd would watch it touch down, nudging each other, speculating on what was going on. The blades would stop. The 'copter would sit mysteriously for a moment, and then out would step Michael Dannan, candidate for Governor of the Commonwealth of Kentucky, accompanied by Dace Havershamp, known to all.

Lida would have the students standing by.

As soon as the helicopter door opened and Michael stepped out, they'd rush forward, waving big Dannan signs and yelling and cheering. He'd come forward to the picnic ground surrounded by enthusiastic kids and happy noises. There is no way all this wouldn't command the attention of the whole encampment – no question people would be listening for what he had to say.

Everyone else, all the other speakers, Jesse Bristow included, would come in the usual way, the ordinary way – by car. Michael Dannan would be, for at least those fleeting moments, the talk of the day.

Dace's influence had been as good as we had hoped. Jesse Bristow would lead off the speaking. That was fine. That was good. It was the spot Bristow wanted and it fit perfectly with our strategy – give people, and the television cameras, the opportunity to see the two of them, one after the other, in context, see how they measured up against each other. Let Bristow speak first, give Michael the closing shot.

Bristow was good.

He told them why he wanted to be governor and why they ought to vote for him. He said he was one of them, an everyday, hardworking God-fearing man who had fought for all he had and earned all he possessed.

"Nobody gave me anything. No one has a leash around my neck. I'll look out for you. I'll see that you're well served. Schools, roads, hospitals, I'll get them for you. I'll see to it that there are jobs good enough to keep your young people at home. And no new taxes. You're already paying too much. You'll see no new taxes with me."

He said it well. He hit the chords. Nearly everyone knew his reputation. Nearly everyone knew he usually delivered what he promised. I was impressed.

Following him to the podium, Michael seemed a boy.

Jesse projected maturity. He came across as father-like. Strong. Stern. Capable.

When Michael took the platform, you thought of a brother – an older brother who would keep you safe from bullies and look out for you. A brother you could put your faith in and trust with your life.

That was the difference, that and the way he said what he had say.

Michael's agenda for the commonwealth wasn't all that different from Jesse's, except in his plans for an environmental renaissance and the matter of taxes. Michael made no promises about taxes. The difference was the way he said it. Have you ever heard the truth spoken and know it to be gospel? Have you ever heard a promise made and know it to be golden? A hush settled over the crowd when he finished.

They believed.

I think Jesse Bristow sensed as much. The Bristow camp hadn't taken Michael very seriously up to this point. The look on Jesse's face when Michael finished, though, was that of a man beginning to grasp that a possibility might in fact be a probability. That look was still on his face as he moved through the bunch pressing around Michael. Several were reporters, me among them. I was at Michael's elbow.

I saw Jesse Bristow coming. Jesse was smiling. He was bringing his congratulations, as any smart candidate would in that crowd.

I moved aside. Michael was talking animatedly with a man who had his hand on Michael's shoulder.

They both looked up as Jesse stepped in front of Michael. The man nodded and smiled at Jesse and stepped back, making room. Jesse Bristow started to extend his hand. Just as he did, Michael turned back to the man he had been talking with, cutting Jesse. It was as rude an action as I had ever seen Michael take and it shocked me. It had the same effect on those standing nearby, but on Jesse more than any of us.

He stopped stock-still, almost in disbelief, then turned and walked rapidly away, shouldering through the crowd like a heavy wind through grass.

Michael's move was so spontaneous I knew it was an automatic reaction, not something he had planned. It was as if he was recoiling in revulsion from contact with the person of Jesse Bristow. I knew then that whatever any of us had thought this race for the Governor's chair might be about, it was now about something very personal on both their parts and that the race would be mean and unforgiving.

It was a dumb move on Michael's part. The candidate from out-of-nowhere snubbing the front-running candidate in the midst of the Penrod crowd. That act was more newsworthy than anything either of them had said in their speeches and would play high in all the stories written that day, probably even dominate the coverage.

I started thinking immediately about how to contain the damage. What if the act wasn't a calculated insult? What if instead it demonstrated that Michael Dannan wasn't one of the good old boys, that he didn't play by their rules, that he didn't fraternize with the enemy, and that he wasn't afraid to throw down the glove? What if it said that Michael Dannan wasn't intimidated by Jesse Bristow and not awed by the party machine?

That would be my spin. That's the point I'd try to make to my fellow journalists as we discussed the events of the day and began to put our stories together. It was a very long shot, but I had nothing better. Some might like the irreverence of it. Some might write it that way. But the act worried me considerably. Michael had let his emotions affect his actions – in public. That was troubling.

I managed only a few private moments with Michael that day, just as he was leaving to reboard the helicopter and head back to Dace's place with Rhae and the rest of the first team. We stood under the tail of the craft and talked briefly.

"That wasn't a very smart move with Jesse Bristow," I told him.

He knew it.

"I couldn't bring myself to shake the man's hand," he said. "Can you handle it with the media?"

I said I didn't know.

"Well, what happened happened. This is what I want you to do. I want you to find Jesse Bristow and tell him I want to talk with him. Privately. He can name the place and the time. But soon. Tomorrow. The next day latest."

"You're not going to apologize," I said. "That's the worst move you could make."

An apology would only feed Jesse Bristow's ego and make Michael look weak and apprehensive. I said as much.

"Arrange it, please, Theo."

They all got back on the helicopter and flew away. I walked off to find Jesse Bristow.

He was with a small group standing around a big white Buick in the parking lot by the church, apparently getting ready to leave. They seemed cheerful enough. I walked up to the edge.

"Can I see you for a minute, Mr. Bristow," I said into the group.

Jesse Bristow looked over the heads of the circle around him, recognized me, and nodded. We walked off to the side.

"Your boy Dannan doesn't seem to know his manners, does he? I thought Rhae would have raised him better."

I let it pass.

"You two grew up together, didn't you? How do you explain his actions?"

I let that pass, too.

"People don't turn their backs on me, Mr. Clark."

I could feel his lingering anger.

"I'm not Michael's keeper and I don't make apologies for him. I'm just a reporter. I've played it straight with you."

He gave a dismissive laugh. "What do you want?" he said.

"Michael wants to talk with you. Privately. Any time or place you say, but soon."

He looked surprised. Then laughed out loud.

"Well I'll be damned. He's not as tough as I thought." He laughed again, pleased with himself.

"Well, of course, I'll be happy to talk with young Mr. Dannan," he said. "Of course. Everyone makes mistakes. I understand that. Yes. Well, the sooner the better. I'm leaving now for my place at Lake Cumberland. I'll be there tomorrow and Monday. Make it Monday. Sunday ought to be a day of rest. Even for sinners. I'll see him at my place on the lake Monday anytime in the afternoon. Tell him to show up. I'll be there."

He laughed again, wrote the address and telephone number for me on the back of his card and turned and walked jauntily back to the group waiting for him at his car.

## FIFTY-ONE

We stayed at the lake Sunday, all of us, in cottages at Dace's marina. The cottages were set on a cliff above a private cove about a mile from the dock. We had an excellent view up the lake. The day was clear, the morning warming. A few white sails moving on a nice breeze were angling up toward the bridge at midlake. Lida McBain's people had phoned in to read to us the play in the big papers in Louisville and Lexington and in the Cincinnati area.

In general, they were fair. Michael's snub of Jesse Bristow led the stories but it wasn't the major negative it could have been. But in the eastern papers – in Ashland, Harlan, Middlesboro, all throughout the mining area – the play was universally critical of Michael Dannan's lack of civility and his apparent immaturity and bad judgment.

Sattis Arnow sipped his coffee and shook his head as the stories were read to us.

The coverage in the west Kentucky papers, the ones we could get ourselves, was fine. They were impressed with Michael and satisfied with his program.

So while the campaign kickoff at Penrod wasn't the soaring success the Dannan team had hoped it would be, had thought it would be, it was good enough. Michael Dannan's candidacy was fairly launched.

In the post-mortems we did that morning no one lingered over Michael's snub of Jesse Bristow. There was no need. Michael realized how close he had come to an opening disaster. I had the feeling, though, that he didn't really care…that given the same circumstance, he would act exactly the same. I think Rhea Dannan had the same feeling.

This was a reason for more than passing concern. During the hard campaigning to come, Michael Dannan and Jesse Bristow would share many platforms. They would encounter each other in various venues. If Michael acted toward Jesse Bristow on those occasions as he had at Penrod, and Jesse could hold his temper, Jesse would benefit. The public will stand for a great deal, but repeated insults in time begin to look surly and reflect badly on the perpetrator.

Not much would be required to paint Michael as a spoiled, petulant rich kid with an inflated opinion of himself and no respect for his betters. This wasn't the sort of persona that would get him elected.

Yes, they would cast him as a "kid" against Jesse Bristow's maturity and as "rich" against Jesse Bristow's reputation as a self-made man. The more I thought about this, the more uneasy I became. It was not something to take up with Michael at the moment. Later, when the time was right.

When all had been said that anyone had to say about yesterday, we sat over a late lunch on the patio outside Rhae's cottage, those of us still there.

Lida, Judge Blue, Jonathan Winslow, and Marne Young had left immediately, expecting to get home before dark. The rest of us would head back tomorrow – Michael and me by way of Lake Cumberland. Michael asked me to go with him. I didn't question why. I assumed he wanted company on the long drive.

As the others drifted away from the table, I moved closer to Sattis Arnow. He was smoking and idly stirring the cup of coffee before him. He smiled wryly as I scooted in closer. "Well, son, I think we have our work cut out for us."

"That bad?" I said.

"So Michael is going to see Jesse tomorrow?"

"That's the plan."

"Do you have any idea of what he has in mind?

"None."

Sattis shook his head again in the rueful way he did as the coverage from the east Kentucky papers was read to us.

"Jesse Bristow is a very proud man. Michael insulted him in public yesterday."

"I know."

"That was a dangerous thing to do."

"Dumb, yes – but dangerous?"

"Twenty years ago Jesse would have beat him senseless on the spot."

"Oh, come on," I said.

"None of you realize yet what you're dealing with. You can't apply the rules of the polite society you know to Jesse Bristow. He has a different set of rules."

"But this isn't twenty years ago."

"Wake up, Theo. The way Jesse was raised, the culture he comes from, the hardships he's overcome…all that formed him. His code is absolute. There are just three things important to Jesse Bristow. His honor. His blood kin. His mission. I've told you what he's capable of. Michael spit on his honor yesterday and is threatening his mission."

"His mission?"

"Jesse is the messiah. He knows what's best — for you, for me, for the poor and mistreated of this grand Commonwealth, for the moneyed and the famous. He has his heart set on being governor. In his mind he's earned it. In his way of thinking, he deserves it. Michael stands in his way. I know how Jesse's mind works. This is what he believes."

"What should Michael do then?"

"Be very, very careful."

## FIFTY-TWO

I was anything but relaxed when we left for Lake Cumberland the next morning.

We followed the route we'd earlier taken to see Judge Blue – across the bridges of the two big lakes, through the Barrens and across the Pennyrile, dropping down to Jamestown.

Michael's mood was unsettling. He bounced between being happily upbeat and morosely quiet. We didn't talk much about the campaign. We were talked out on that. We talked about fishing and about how good the quail crop would be at Ft. Campbell when hunting season came this year. Mostly we listened to the radio, pulling in the small local stations as we came in range. Waylon Jennings and Crystal Gayle and Johnny Cash sang us on our way.

As we neared Jamestown, I began checking the map for the turn-off to Jesse's place.

"We'll be there in about half an hour."

Michael shifted his hands on the wheel. His face clouded.

"Is there anything you want to tell me about this, anything I should know about what's going on?"

"I won't be long," he said, leaning forward and turning the radio volume up a bit.

Jesse Bristow's cabin was on the west side of the lake, on a high cliff looking out toward Wolf Creek. We turned off the state road onto narrow gravel trail through a dense pine forest. The trail ended at the cabin. We parked in the little half-circle in front of the cabin headed back the way we had come.

There was a note on the door. "I'm down at the dock. The door is open. Go on through and make yourself comfortable on the deck. I'll be up shortly." Not addressed to anyone. Not signed by anyone.

We did as it suggested, crossing through what was obviously the main room of the cabin to a set of sliding doors leading out onto an expansive deck with an astounding view of the main lake. A large round table was off to the side. On it was a cooler and glasses.

We looked around, but could see no one. The only sound was the wind through the pines and, off in the distance, the buzz of an outboard motor as a boat made its way up the lake. Apparently it was just us and Jesse Bristow.

We'd had a long drive and the afternoon sun was warm. I went for the cooler. Little rivulets of condensation ran down the sides of the icy green bottles and the silver cans. I chose a Falls City beer and silently applauded Jesse Bristow's hospitality. Michael took a Coke. We stood on the deck admiring the view and waited.

It was a view that deserved admiration. The day was clear, the sky cloudless and of that delicate blue wash of early spring. The sun behind us laid a silver shine on the flat of the lake. I recognized the entrance to Wolf Creek. I had fished it before, but we could see well beyond that, further than any view up the lake I had ever seen. I was almost disappointed when we heard steps coming up the outside stairs.

Jesse Bristow's head and shoulders appeared above the railing. He was smiling.

"There were a few things to do on the dock," he said. "Sorry to keep you waiting." He went to the cooler and opened a beer and tipped the bottle toward us in an unspoken toast. He had the manner of a man who has won, who is satisfied he is superior, and is fully prepared to be magnanimous to his foe.

If he was surprised to see me with Michael, he didn't say so. I think he was too pleased with the turn of events to care.

"Well, young Mr. Dannan" Jesse Bristow began, but Michael interrupted him.

"This isn't a social call. I have a question to ask you. I want a truthful answer."

Bristow was taken back by this…his welcome disdained, his hospitality rejected. I could see his anger rising.

"I'm not accustomed to lying." There was a certain menace in his voice.

"Lucas Gwynne told me a story," Michael said.

"Lucas?"

"About the night my father died."

"Ah," said Jesse Bristow.

"Did you let him bleed to death?"

I flinched involuntarily at the question. Jesse Bristow didn't.

There was a long moment of silence, and then he said, "Lucas Gwynne is a fine boy. Not a very bright boy, but a fine one. He gets confused."

Michael pressed. "Did you sit there watching, waiting while his life spilled out on the snow?"

Bristow didn't seem outraged at the thought that he would do such a thing. His voice didn't rise. His temper didn't flare.

"Lucas told me he talked with you. He told me Aunt Hanna wanted him to do it. Why did she want that?"

"Answer me!" Michael said in a voice almost a shout.

Bristow turned to me. "Maybe you ought to give us a chance to talk this out privately. There's a boat tied up at the dock. You could take a run up the lake."

Though the prospect of listening to this drama play out was almost overwhelmingly compelling, I felt that whatever was to be said was so personal and private a matter that no one else should intrude. I was embarrassed to be there. Michael must have wanted a witness when he confronted Jesse Bristow. To what end? There couldn't possibly be a way to prove the charge and even if Jesse Bristow admitted to it to Michael, in any public arena, it would be Bristow's word against Michael's. And what actual crime could Bristow be accused of? Murder by inaction? To let a man bleed to death by taking no action, by standing idly by and watching – that would be an awful thing. But would it be a crime at law?

I nodded to Bristow in agreement and started to the stairs.

"No!" Michael said. "I want you here."

He turned to Bristow.

"You understand? He's here to make sure I don't hear things you don't say."

Jesse Bristow shook his head in disgust.

"There is no reason this side of sanity that I ought even tolerate you, much less answer you."

Jesse walked to the railing, looked out over the lake, collecting himself, then said bitterly into the quite afternoon, "Damn you, Michael Dannan, and damn your father! I was through with this. You want the full story, the true story? All right. Listen. When I'm done, you can go to hell!"

## FIFTY-THREE

I am not sure how to present this. The way Jesse Bristow told it, the anger flowing out of him, the pain he felt, is as important to the grasp of his story as any fact he offered. I can't approach the intensity of it with words, nor the effect it had on Michael.

I could not take notes, did not even entertain the thought in a situation so charged and intimate. Later we talked it through, Michael and me, every part of it, on the drive back. And since returning I have committed it to writing and have carefully examined each part, purging anything of which I am uncertain, deleting anything which smells of conjecture.

The story Jesse Bristow told was sad.

And brutal.

And maddening.

It began with a call from his sister, his dearly beloved and much cherished sister. She called him early that week for the use of his hunting cabin on Johnson Ridge. She was working on a project for her class at Berea College, she told him, and needed privacy.

Sue Bristow was in her first year of teaching at Berea. She was the first female economics professor on the faculty. He was inordinately proud of her. As proud of her as he was of himself.

His cabin was remote, reachable only by an infrequently traveled Forest Service road. He wasn't concerned for her safety. He knew she knew what she needed to know to take care of herself. And no one in those mountains would harm her.

He wasn't concerned until Aunt Hanna called. She was apprehensive. Some said his aunt had powers. He believed she did. He knew she could heal. He had seen it during the mine wars. Wounds closed at the touch of her hands. And she had premonitions, sensed things coming. She didn't have them often, but when she did he never knew her to be wrong.

"I have a feeling about Sue," she told him, "a bad feeling."

He left immediately for the cabin, going up from the Evarts side.

It was night by then and an unexpected snow that had been falling since early afternoon was layering the roads. On the ridge, the accumulation would be deepening. He took the big truck.

There was a dim light showing through the cabin windows when he reached the top.

Sue Bristow's blue Ford coupe was parked in back, but no movement. Even allowing for the muffling effect of the snow, the sound of his approach should have brought her to the door.

A low log fire was barely burning in the fireplace when he entered. Except for the glow from the fire, the big room of the cabin was dark and cold.

He called for her. No response. Again, more loudly. Still no response.

Down the hall, a light slipped out from under the closed door to the bedroom.

She was there. On his bed. Lying still. Her eyes open. Staring at nothing.

The sight of it stopped him cold.

Blood soaked the lower part of the bed and the quilt that covered her. Only a man's coat that was pulled up tight around her shoulders and tucked close to her neck was bloodless. He stumbled to the bed, took her cold wrist in his big warm hand searching for a pulse.

He knew she was dead, knew it when he entered the cabin. He held the hand anyway, for how long he didn't know. In time, he placed her hand back beneath the covers. He went for the telephone to call his Aunt Hanna. The phone was dead. The storm must have downed the line.

All alone in the silence and the cold, pain racked him, grief consumed him. He had not cried since his mother died. He did not think he remembered how. But oh, he did. He cradled his head in his hands and his body shook and he cried. He cried until he could cry no more.

He lifted the coat gently from her shoulders, pulled the quilt slowly back and saw how the blood streamed from beneath her gown. On the table at the bedside he saw the instrument. The shock of what she was trying to do dropped him to his knees. Oh, Lord, he groaned. Oh, my poor, poor Sue.

In the place where the pain had been, an awful rage began to grow.

He grabbed the coat. A man's coat. Not his. Whose? He began going through the pockets. Inside he found a wallet. The wallet was Benjamin Dannan's.

He didn't understand. And then he began to. When a couple of his men told him they thought they had seen Benjamin and Sue together, at a time and in place that led to inferences that were revolting, he told them they were wrong. He told them to shut up and forget it. Benjamin had turned against him by then, but he still considered Benjamin family. Sue was like a little sister to Benjamin. Benjamin wouldn't. Benjamin couldn't. Whoever his men saw, it couldn't have been Benjamin and Sue. Not Sue.

But it was Benjamin's coat.

Jesse covered her with a clean quilt, stoked the fire to warm the cabin for when he would return with Aunt Hanna, and left to find Benjamin Dannan.

Snow was up to the hubcaps of the truck as he came off the ridge. He hadn't passed Dannan on his way up, so Dannan must have taken the road down the other side. Jesse drove as fast as he could without losing control. The big truck was heavy enough to hold traction on the upslope and he used the gears to brake coming down.

He saw nothing of Dannan on the Forest Service road. He turned on the road to Harlan and hadn't gone far when he spotted a spun-out car. He pulled up, got out and went over. The car was a Buick, a new black Buick, the hood smashed against the cliff face. Apparently the diver had tried to back out, but to no avail. The rear wheels were mired in snow up over the fenders. The car was empty, the keys still in the ignition.

He thought it the kind of car Dannan might drive. Dannan must have lost control, skidded off the road, then mired the car in his haste to get free.

Abandon the car! Flag down the next vehicle by and get off the mountain! That's what Dannan would have done.

Jesse ran back to his truck, rushing to catch up with the car he thought Benjamin Dannan might be escaping in.

Snow was falling heavily again. Visibility was awful. Still, he pushed it. He came up a small rise, drifted into a tight curve and as he was coming out of it, saw a man walking in the road.

The man turned, saw the truck, raised his hands and started waving to flag it down. The man was too far out in the road. Jesse was moving too fast to stop.

Jesse skidded, felt a bump, fought for control, pulled to a stop. He jumped out and ran back.

The force of the hit had thrown the man off the road and into a shallow ditch to the side. He lay there, face down in the snow, his left leg bent grotesquely beneath him.

Jesse knelt down and turned the man over.

The truck's bumper must have caught him just below the rib-cage. Blood soaked his white shirt and flowed from his mouth and nose.

As he knew it would be from the moment he saw the coatless man waving in the center of the road, the broken body he looked down on was Benjamin Dannan's.

Adrenalin and anger made his head ache and his hands shake.

Jesse knelt motionless in the snow doing nothing, just watching.

Bleed, you bastard, bleed, he said soundlessly into the gusting wind.

When the shaking stopped, he got back in the truck and drove away. After several miles his mind cleared and the madness lifted. He wondered if he should go back. He thought about it. He decided no.

The rest of the story tracked almost exactly with what Lucas Gwynne had told us.

Lucas waited in Jesse Bristow's office that night until Jesse got there. Lucas told Jesse about coming down the road in the blinding snow and hitting something, something he thought was a deer, but couldn't be sure. Jesse listened.

"We have to go back up and be sure," Jesse told him. They climbed in Jesse's big truck, forded through the snow, and found Benjamin Dannan's body just as Jesse knew they would.

Lucas Gwynne did hit something coming down that road that night, and it most likely was a deer, but Lucas came down the road after Jesse Bristow had already traveled it. The coincidence was the sort of luck that Jesse Bristow had had most of his life.

Jesse told Lucas to get rid of Benjamin Dannan's car and then to go to the village and stay there. After that, Jesse went back to Evarts to get Aunt Hanna.

"Was he still alive when you drove off," Michael pressed.

Jesse Bristow answered, "I don't know. I didn't care."

At that, Michael groaned and leaped at Jesse. I tackled him to stop him. We lay sprawled on the deck. Jesse Bristow stood over us, glaring.

I had Michael pinned. He struggled to get up, but couldn't. Fighting against me, Michael hurled this promise in Jesse's face.

"I'm going to win. I'm going to be Governor, not you, and I'm going to expose you for the murderer you are! I promise. I swear!"

Bristow spun and walked away.

It isn't clear who took the most pain that night, Michael or Jesse.

I felt for them…but mostly I felt for Sue Bristow.

## FIFTY-FOUR

Sattis Arnow's caution kept coming back to me as we drove home through the night. "Jesse Bristow doesn't play by rules you play by. He's capable of anything."

Michael's insult to Jesse at Penrod was bad enough. But this "promise," this threat to charge Jesse Bristow with the death of Benjamin Dannan, was hotheadedly reckless.

Michael didn't care. He would do exactly as he said on both counts. That's what he told me and that's what he meant. Nevertheless, I endorsed Sattis Arnow's advice: "Be careful."

Michael dropped me on the corner by my apartment. He wanted to see Allie. It was two o'clock in the morning by then. Only the White Signal, the little hamburger joint by the alley, was open at that hour. I got a hot cup of coffee and a fresh sweet roll, and walked back across the street to take a seat on the stone wall that skirted the ball field and wait for whatever might happen – just as we did when we were boys after our dates were home but we were too charged to give up on the night.

Except no one else would be coming.

The others were themselves home in bed with their wives, or lost in Korea, or losing to illness, or the bottle, or luck. I was alone in the shadows. There was no traffic, no one out on foot, just the stutter of the stoplight at the corner.

I thought of Allie. Of the darkened garage and the open door. Of soft light inside. And warmth. And the touch of lips.

I thought of other nights on the wall, of how sure we were the world was ours, that whatever door we needed to step through was standing open waiting for us and that if it wasn't open we'd kick it down. Through that door was whatever we wanted. We didn't know what we wanted, but whatever that turned out to be, it would be ours.

I looked around at my surroundings. This is what was on the other side.

Is this what I wanted? I still didn't know. I wondered if Michael did.

Governor? So he said.

Revenge on Jesse Bristow? He'd promised to take it.

President? Did he really believe he could be that? Did I believe it?

Allie? Ah, Allie, where was she on the Michael Dannan scale of wants and needs?

My coffee was cold, the stone wall colder. I crossed the street and climbed the stairs and went to bed...except I couldn't turn off the images of the day.

So now we knew almost all of it. We knew how it was that Benjamin Dannan came to be on that lonely road that snowy night. We knew why he was abroad in a snowstorm in only his shirtsleeves. We knew why he had no car and where the car could be found. We knew how he died. And why he died.

What we didn't know was why Hanna Collins, dear Aunt Hanna, started it all. Her nephew Jesse Bristow didn't know. Her godson Lucas Gwynne didn't know. Her friend and caregiver Marne Young didn't know. So far as I could tell, no one alive knew or would ever know.

Considering Jesse Bristow's temperament and present state of mind, the result of what she started could be the death of Michael Dannan. Surely that couldn't have been her plan?

I fell asleep wrestling with the thought.

I drove out to the farm the next morning and told Rhae about our encounter with Jesse Bristow.

She cried.

For the girl, I think, and for Benjamin.

Michael hadn't come home yet. That wasn't good. I began to wonder if Michael might be losing his discipline. I had no difficulty imagining how hard it might be to leave the warm bed of Allison Boatwright Sinclair, but he should have been there at the farm, focused and ready for the next step in this *danse macabre*.

The more I thought about his promise to Jesse Bristow, the more apprehensive I became. If pinned, I couldn't specify what I was fearful of. Call it presentiment. We Irish have a bit of the mystic in us, too.

I told the whole story to Paul Isham. I hadn't to Rhae. I told her what I thought she should know, but left out the parts I thought would give her unnecessary grief. If Michael felt compelled to be more complete, that was his prerogative.

Paul was ready to organize a mob and orchestrate a lynching.

"He admitted it? He ran Benjamin down and left him to die in the snow? My God! He ought to be strung up from the nearest tree and left for the birds."

In fairness I had to point out that it wasn't entirely clear that Bristow had intentionally hit Benjamin Dannan on that snowy night. He was driving fast on an icy road and Benjamin Dannan all at once appeared in the middle of it. It could have been an accident. Jesse had presented it that way. I doubted it was, but it could have been.

Paul Isham would have none of it. He wanted Michael to press charges immediately. "Start writing the story. You were there. Make it first-person. We'll play it as the banner in tomorrow morning's paper. We'll do a big follow-up the next day. The full front page. Pictures of Bristow being arrested, carted off to jail! We'll stay on it so long and so hard he'll cry for mercy and we won't give him any!"

I let Paul blow himself out. We wouldn't do a story. We didn't have one unless and until Michael actually accused Jesse Bristow of murder. And I didn't think Michael would, at least not now. Despite his promise to Bristow, Michael had no proof. All he had was conversation. If Michael intended to charge Bristow, he needed hard proof and that would take time and real effort to produce – if indeed, any hard proof existed.

I made these points to Paul after he calmed down. Of course he agreed. He knew real proof would be needed. He was just so outraged that his fury overrode his judgment. I was sure that if this had been an earlier time, he would have called Jesse Bristow out and shot him down in the street.

When we finally did sit down with Michael the day was almost gone. He didn't explain where he had been and we didn't ask.

Putting Jesse Bristow on trial wasn't the agenda item of the moment. The Governorship was.

"What do you think my father would want," he asked, "revenge on Jesse Bristow or his son in the Governor's chair? I've thought long and hard on that. I've discussed it with mother. I think the way to best honor Benjamin Dannan's name and reputation is for his son to become Governor. First! Then I'll have Jesse Bristow!"

Despite his rage, Paul Isham could find no practical ground on which to take a stand to the contrary. Outrage, justice, retribution, the sheer satisfaction of seeing evil defeated, none of these prevailed. The objective was to elect Michael Dannan Governor of the Commonwealth of Kentucky, the necessary stepping stone to the larger post he sought – the one that would lodge the Dannan name in history.

This was Michael's objective. This is not the way Michael would phrase it. It is far too crudely ambitious. But this is what he felt. He did not tell me this. It is what I knew. We had been eager fans of the Star Trek television series when it began airing. We were addicted to the most creative science fiction we could find, written or otherwise. Star Trek was the pinnacle. We sometimes traded phone calls about the shows

At the end of one call, Michael asked me, "What do you want to be when you grow up?" Before I could think of an answer, he said "Let me tell you what I want. When I grow up I want to be Captain of the Starship Enterprise. If I can't be that, then I want to be Governor of the Planet Earth."

I'd never forgotten that. It was so true to Michael's personality.

The captaincy of the Enterprise wasn't available. Governor of the Planet Earth it would have to be then. The Presidency was just a stepping stone on the way.

Paul caged his anger and agreed that Jesse Bristow's retribution would have to wait upon Michael's ascendancy. In the meantime, he would set to work to gather the proof needed to make it stick. He would assemble a small team, a discreet team, under Jake Slade. They would turn over every stone that still existed to find the damning secrets that lay beneath.

I doubted they'd find much and was concerned that their actions would attract too much attention, attention that might be more than counterproductive if any hint of it became public.

Paul understood my uneasiness. He promised the team would be invisible and, in any case, untraceable to Michael.

The point that only I seemed to be sensitive to in all this is that the story of Benjamin Dannan's death couldn't be told without telling the story of Benjamin Dannan's affair with Jesse Bristow's sister, the abortion attempt, her death, and Benjamin Dannan's culpability.

None of this would reflect positively on the Dannan name or reputation. And the pain and embarrassment it would bring Rhae Dannan, and yes, Michael, was too high a price to pay for the satisfaction.

Michael heard me out.

"Comments noted," was all he said in reply.

The next morning the Michael Dannan express began rolling full speed again toward the big white building on the hill in Frankfort.

## FIFTY-FIVE

The Dannan campaign developed a momentum after Penrod that was truly astonishing. The old-line politicians, the good old boys, and the power brokers watched in amazement.

Dannan groups sprang up everywhere. Everywhere – even in the heart of Jesse Bristow's mountain redoubt. His comings and goings, his meetings with the local Rotary Clubs and Ladies Guilds, his speeches at the county courthouses and the rallies for him at the American Legion ball fields – all these were covered extensively, as if it was real news. His name seemed to be in every newspaper, commented on in every nightly newscast, always favorably – young Galahad riding out of the west to save the countryside.

Lida McBain and her crew of college kids, growing into an enormous young people's crusade, knocked on doors and stopped people on the streets to tell the Dannan story.

Jesse Bristow's people were overrun and outclassed. The polls at the end of the March had Michael leading Bristow by twenty points and winning the general election going away.

Consternation gave way to concern at Party Headquarters. Their anointed was getting waxed. The machine was being derailed. Somebody do something!

At Jesse Bristow's headquarters, an air of disbelief prevailed. And anger. That an inexperienced, overly privileged, undeserving whelp of the rich and the entitled, an outsider, by God, should come in here and presume to take the governor's chair away from the man who had earned it and rightly deserved it, well, that was beyond indignation.

Jesse Bristow's people called us all in for a big press conference the day after the poll results were released – a damage control exercise.

Everyone was there – all the major dailies, the wire services, a goodly representation of weeklies, radio and television crews, a couple of correspondents for national publications. The Bristow team had the platform they wanted. The question was did they have a message that would work.

For a backdrop, Jesse chose the Old Capitol in downtown Frankfort. A small platform had been raised on the sidewalk leading up to it. It was great staging. There stood the candidate in the embrace of history, Mr. and Mrs. Ordinary Citizen strolling by, perhaps stopping to listen.

Some did, mingling with us working reporters and in general getting in the way. When the crowd was large enough, Jesse stepped up on the platform. He stood with his hands on his hips, looking around, making eye contact, saying nothing, unsmilingly serious, like the opening scene in a well mounted play – waiting. When all eyes were on him, when the talking stopped and jostling ceased, he began. No fanfare. No introduction. Just Jesse Bristow.

Jesse is an impressive man, I've said that – physically commanding and a persuasive speaker. Not an orator, nothing fancy, but very effective with simple words delivered sincerely

Jesse congratulated "young Mr. Dannan" for his fine showing in the latest polls. His tone was that of an indulgent parent showing appreciation for a nice double by the visiting team in a high school game. He applauded Michael's effective use of the funds available to him in creating a grass-roots organization and placing effective advertising, implying that anyone with as much money as Michael Dannan had who couldn't buy a gang of hired-hands to do his dirty work ought to be committed and that the poll numbers were a result of all the advertising the Dannan campaign had splurged on, not the appeal of the candidate nor the quality of his platform.

While he didn't exactly use the word carpetbagger, he emphasized that Michael was a "new face" in the state and certainly hoped that "young Mr. Dannan's" experience as a corporate executive could prove useful in trying to run a state government.

"My friends," Jesse said, "Polls results are only a snapshot in time. Don't be misled by them. There is a long way to go before the actual voting takes place. The only poll that makes any difference is the one taken on Election Day at the ballot box. I'm confident that the good people of Kentucky will exercise sound judgment on that day and choose me to represent them as Governor of Kentucky"

It was a great opening statement. There was applause. There is no applause at press conferences. The media don't applaud. But this was an event staged in the open air in a public place. I was sure Bristow had seeded the crowd. Nice touch. The print media would ignore it, of course. But TV wouldn't pass it up on a bet.

After the opening statement, Jesse took questions. Nothing startling came out of it. Jesse was in control, kept his temper, answered only the questions he chose to answer. I put forward no questions. I didn't want to be noticed. But Jesse saw me. He fixed a chilling stare on me. I was fairly sure I understood the message.

I came away from that session convinced that the Bristow campaign was hurting. The poll numbers said so, but more important was Jesse Bristow's manner. He was working too hard at trying to make the case that the Michael Dannan candidacy was only a diverting interlude on Jesse Bristow's march to the Governor's chair. That's the way I wrote it.


With the poll numbers buoying them and certain that the Dannan campaign had real momentum, Gershon Pope and Lida McBain wanted to carry the battle into Jesse Bristow's home territory.

They chose Harlan.

Bloody Harlan.

The town and county had been at the center of the mine wars that raged throughout the 1930s and that some said were still being fought. A current of violence underlay the culture.

For his bravery and leadership in that long conflict and for the success he'd made of himself, Jesse Bristow was a local hero. I couldn't see the sense of putting Michael in that caldron. Even at his most persuasive, Michael would be very unlikely to sway many votes. And the crowd might get nasty.

Lida McBain reminded me that the Dannan name had currency in those parts, too, that Benjamin Dannan was remembered and honored. More importantly, she was going to mount a made-for-TV event. She was going to stack the crowd with "Dannan for Governor" students from two small nearby mountain colleges—busing them in from Williamsburg and

Cumberland. They'd be enthusiastic, energetic, and loud. And there would be enough of them to outnumber the Bristow supporters unless Bristow's people took this seriously and put real effort into turning out a hostile crowd.

TV would love it. The whole point of the exercise was to show that the Michael Dannan candidacy had solid support, even in Jesse Bristow's stronghold. This would do it. If he got the right kind of press play out of it throughout the state, the result would be disastrous for the Bristow campaign.

I saw the possibilities. I also saw the hazards. My uneasiness didn't change the decision.

The rally was to take place at high noon on the first Saturday in April in the square in front of the courthouse, the most visible spot in town. The town would be full of people in from the outlying countryside for their weekly shopping.

Michael would make his remarks from a bunting-bedecked stage on the courthouse steps surrounded by such local leaders as Lida and the Sattis Arnow people could assemble, with the students yelling and waving banners ardently in the foreground.

Arranging for this in the heart of Bristow country took some doing, but Sattis Arnow called in the necessary chits and things fell nicely into place.

We went up in separate cars. Michael, Rhae Dannan, and Paul Isham made the drive in a nice conservative blue Chevrolet. Lida McBain would come up on one of the buses transporting the students. I came with Marne Young. She wanted to be there. Her knowledge of the area would be useful. And I enjoyed her company.

We all arrived within twenty minutes of each other.

A crowd had already formed around the stage at the courthouse and was growing, drawn by the banners and the music.

We parked on Central Street, a block down from the courthouse. Sattis Arnow was waiting. Michael would walk up from there, accompanied by Sattis and Rhae, shaking hands, being introduced, kissing babies, and charming young women. Lida had it timed for about twenty minutes. Then Michael would step up on the stage, the music would stop, Sattis Arnow would take the podium and introduce him, and Michael Dannan would proceed to woo and win the local populace. That was the plan.

And it was going as planned.

The sun was shining, the music playing. People were smiling and laughing and being impressed. Michael was in great spirits and top form, with Sattis to his left and Rhae just behind him. Marne and I were trailing about ten paces farther back.

Michael had just stepped up onto the courthouse steps and stopped to shake an old miner's hand in that way of his of taking your hand in his and drawing you closer, intent, interested, when another man edged in between them.

Michael looked up, surprised, then smiled. He recognized the man. So did Marne. So did I. It was Lucas Gwynne. Michael turned to him and reached out his hand.

All of us heard the shot.

And then the second.

And then a string too fast and too many to be counted.

For a stunned moment, everything stopped. Then everyone scrambled.

Except Michael.

Except Lucas.

Michael leaned slightly toward Lucas, disbelief on his face.

Lucas held a pistol in his right hand.

Michael slumped to his knees, looked up at Lucas, then fell forward.

Screams erupted on all sides. The students, the crowd, the musicians, all scattered.

The first shot froze me, but I had begun moving toward Michael by the time the last one was fired.

I knelt in his blood and started to lift him, but knew I shouldn't.

I looked up at Lucas Gwynne, standing above me. His eyes were glazed, his body swaying. I started to stand, rising slowly, my eyes locked on his.

As I rose, his gun hand rose, too. He kept his eyes on mine.

The pistol swung with me as I stood.

To my chest.

To my face.

Lucas continued the rise of it in an unhurried arc, bringing the barrel to his face, to his mouth. With tears on his cheeks, he took the barrel between his lips.

An eye-blink later his head exploded.

## FIFTY-SIX

Michael died just before dawn. Rhae was holding his hand.

That he lasted so long was a tease and a torment. We held to the hope that something miraculous would occur. We knew in our hearts it would not.

Michael was too shot up even to be moved from the courthouse steps to the little hospital in Harlan, but that wasn't an option. He had to be moved.

They have considerable experience with gunshot wounds in Harlan. The medics were very good. They hoped to be able to stabilize him until we could get him airlifted to the hospital in Lexington. Governor Parsons sent a National Guard helicopter from the airbase in Louisville as soon as he heard. The whole state seems to have heard almost at once. But it was no good. Surviving the transfer to the helicopter, much less the flight, was seen as impossible.

I alternated between Michael's room and Sattis Arnow's.

Sattis was behind Michael when the shooting started. One slug passed through Michael, hitting Sattis in the groin. Another caught a woman in the crowd, not badly, a flesh wound in the arm. All six shots had gone into Michael. Lucas Gwynne was practically touching Michael when he began firing. No one misses at that range, not even someone as frightened as Lucas, but at that range, unless the bullet hit bone, it was likely to pass through, slightly spent, still dangerous.

The injury to Sattis was serious but not life threatening. He drifted in and out of consciousness and I kept walking down the hall to his room, concerned for him, but principally to escape the pain of watching Michael die.

I must have been in shock through the move from the courthouse square to the hospital because I remember very little of it. I do remember the sticky feel of my pant leg from kneeling in Michael's blood and the flecks of Lucas Gwynne on my jacket.

Somehow Marne Young found me clean clothes. I washed up in the room the doctors wanted to put me in, but I wouldn't give in to their insistence that I get medical attention, too.

Marne was our buffer. She had been with me and was considered by the hospital staff part of the family group and was allowed the run of the floor and access to Michael's room and to Sattis'. She became the link to the first floor waiting room where Lida McBain was doing her best to keep the media, the concerned, and the plain curious in check.

We took no calls on Michael's floor, not even Jesse Bristow's.

Rhae sat at Michael's bedside, his hand in hers, through that interminable time. She spoke softly to him now and then, so softly we couldn't hear, but otherwise was silent and still. Paul Isham and I hovered in the corners, subdued, pensive, staying out of the way, but there if she needed us.

My imagination wasn't prepared to accommodate what was happening.

I could picture Michael as Governor. I could picture him as President. Even as Governor of the Planet Earth. I could see him and Allie together and living happily. What I could not imagine was that he could die like this, in an austere little room in a small mining town on the outer reaches of Appalachia, shot by a man who had been instrumental in his father's death.

This can't be happening to Michael Dannan. Not to the Pride of Peaks Mill!

I realized I was crying.

Outside, the students clustered in front of the hospital. They had run after the ambulance, crowding and calling disbelievingly to each other. Lida had the buses ready to return them to their schools, but no one would go. Around the students the crowd grew hourly as word spread of what had happened. Some prayed, some cried. A few stood with arms around each other and heads together. The silence that blanketed the crowd made the scene even more somber.

As night came on, an older woman passed candles. Their slender yellow flames reflected off the Dannan signs still being clutched by the students.

Michael died gently.

His breathing slowed.

He seemed to relax.

And he was gone.

Rhae moaned, raised his hand to her lips, then to her cheek. Paul and I backed quietly out of the room to give her the privacy she and he deserved.

Somehow I found my way to the roof of the hospital. The night was clear, the sky punctured by stars. I looked for Orion. In the spring, from my backyard when I was a boy, I could stand at night and raise my left arm to the top of the maple by the fence. There was Orion. He moved around the sky as the seasons changed, but I could always find him. When I could find Orion, I could find home.

I stayed staring at the sky while the dread of what I had to face spread through me.

Rhae was still at the bedside. I walked in quietly, tried a comforting hand on her shoulder. She looked up, waited while recognition came, nodded, reached out for my hand, and turned back to Michael.

I turned to the job I had to do and hated most. The news moved so fast that Allie would have heard of Michael's death before I could reach her. But I would have to tell her. I was the messenger who would make it real.

I drove through the grey dawn, tired and low, but the sun when it rose was bright and the day sparkling.

"I've been waiting for you," was all she said when she opened her door to me. That almost broke my heart.

There was nothing I could say. I've spent my life working with words and I have never, ever, found any words that are worth anything more than the good intentions with which they are whispered when grief and despair have their hold. We don't have such words.

She had come so close.

I put my arms around her and she learned her forehead against my chest. She began to cry quietly. That broke my heart the rest of the way.

## FIFTY-SEVEN

The investigation of Michael's murder was the province of the local police. They were as thorough as they needed to be and speedily efficient in identifying Lucas Gwynne as the shooter. Pressure to wrap the case up quickly was intense. The nation was shocked. The state was embarrassed. Governor Parsons offered the assistance of the Kentucky State Police. Senator Johnson volunteered to bring in the FBI. Jesse Bristow, Michael Dannan's honorable opponent in the gubernatorial race and the area's favorite son, insisted that no stone be left unturned.

But what stones were there?

Lucas Gwynne did it.

Then killed himself.

There were eyewitnesses. There was Lucas Gwynne's body lying there, head blown away, the killing weapon beside him.

The only thing that gave the investigators pause was motive. What moved Lucas Gwynne to so outrageous an act? So far as could be determined, there was no contact between Michael Dannan and Lucas Gwynne, no known or suspected grievances. Gwynne had never been violent. Or unstable. Or anything other than an obscure and peaceful resident of somewhere back up there in the hollows.

That Lucas Gwynne did it, however, was without doubt. Which was all the Coroner's Jury required.

The investigation was conducted, the inquest held, and the verdict brought in the week between the shooting and Michael's funeral. Perhaps not a record, but a testament to the efficiency of the obvious in apportioning guilt when the public demands swift closure.

Those who wanted answers where none existed were told this was sadly, but simply, the act of a deranged individual. Who knew what was in his head? Who knew what triggered his anger? Who will ever know?

Marne Young wasn't a buyer. She saw it happen. She saw the bodies fall. She smelled the blood. She could not deny the evidence of her own eyes, yet she couldn't let the killing be explained away as the act of a madman. She knew Lucas Gwynne. He wasn't mad. He was timid, and apprehensive, and needy, and shy – but he wasn't crazy. She was sure that whatever propelled Lucas Gwynne, it wasn't psychosis.

I was the only other one of us who had seen Lucas Gwynne. I was with him the day he told us the story of the night of Benjamin Dannan's death. The experience was so intense that I felt I had an understanding of the kind of man he was. I shared Marne's view. You don't have to be crazy to kill. Most of the killing is done by sane men. I've seen it. I've done it. All that's needed is a strong enough reason.

Lucas Gwynne wasn't crazy. He was driven. Something drove Lucas Gwynne to kill Michael Dannan. Marne and I swore to find out what…or who.

After.

After Michael was in the ground.

Rhae buried him from the Church of the Good Shepherd on the street by the river. It is pristine white that church, its pointed steeple rising high above the old section of town as a beacon to guide the faithful, higher than the Baptists Church spire nearby, or any of the other church towers in town. Michael's great grandfather was the principal founder of the church and was buried from it, as was his son, and his son's son, and now his great-grandson.

I was in that church only once before. For Michael's father's funeral. We sat, my mother and father and I, near the back, a bit uneasy. My folks were Baptist and not sure how to act in this strange place where the scent of incense hung in the air and bells sounded at unexpected times.

I was frightened as we entered. I saw the body of Christ hanging painfully from a massive cross over the altar. And smaller representations around the sides of the church of His path up to Calvary – falling, being beaten, harangued. We had nothing like this in my church. The sight of all this scared me and made me sad. If the church hadn't been so full of light reflecting off the pure white walls and magnifying the brilliant colors of the stained glass windows, I would not have stayed in that place. But as it was, with the light and the colors, I felt comforted and then I saw Michael up front next to his mother and forgot about my own unease and wondered about him.

Now it was Michael in the coffin in front of the altar.

Oh, Lord.

It was a grand funeral. The unsettled April weather retreated to give way to an almost spring-like day. Everyone who should have been there was there, and more, from all over the state and the country. The little local airport was clogged with corporate jets. The car rental agencies at the Louisville and Lexington airports were booked out. The church was too small to accommodate all the friends of Michael and Rhae Dannan, so the street outside was filled with a silent, respectful throng.

That great hoard of Students for Dannan, the young and the passionate who had been so important to his campaign, many of whom had been with him at Harlan, turned out in such numbers that traffic had to be diverted from that end of town.

For the politicians, not to be seen at the funeral of Michael Dannan would have been in such bad taste as to be unthinkable.

Jesse Bristow was prominently there, walking down the center aisle after Rhae had been seated, to bend down and offer his condolences. It was mostly theatre, but I watched him closely. I think he genuinely felt for Rhae. He touched her hand tenderly and whatever he said to her seemed to be said with unfeigned tenderness. Rhae was heartbreakingly regal and controlled. She sat straight and tall. Her gaze seemed to be fixed on spot just above the coffin and there was no motion of body or expression of face to indicate she acknowledge Jesse Bristow at all. No one else intruded on her.

The ritual proceeded much as it did for Michael's father...the Mass, the long drive through town and up East Main hill to the cemetery, the graveside service – all of it much the same. Paul Isham and I sat on either side of Rhea on the chairs placed before the coffin.

When the priest finished the blessing and the water was sprinkled, we stood. The overwhelming silence of the cemetery embraced us. Sunlight and shadows played over headstones that rose from the grass in the meadow. For a moment it seemed as if Rhae might sag, but she steadied herself. After bowing her head, she took a small step forward, put her fingers to her lips then touched them to coffin. The single rose she carried she placed tenderly on its surface, then turned and for the first time that day, seemed to see us. Every eye was on her. She took our arms and we walked her to the waiting car. Though all of it she did not speak...or cry. Not there or all the way home to the farm. I wished she had. Her tears might have soothed my pain.

I felt so very sorry. The weight of it pressed me down, sucked the light from the day. I would miss him terribly. I knew that. We understood each other so well, complemented each other's strengths and cushioned each other's weaknesses so thoroughly, had been so close for so long, that to lose him was to lose a part of me I was not sure I could do without.

And I was sorry for all of us. Michael offered such promise, possessed so many talents that, given the time and the support, he might truly have made the difference in people's lives that he thought he could. And Rhae. And Allie. How great the loss for them.

## FIFTY-EIGHT

The work of disbanding the Dannan for Governor organization began the week after the funeral.

There were tears and stories told and promises made to stay in touch as Lida McBain closed down the Georgetown headquarters. Mostly there was great regret at what had been denied the good and worthy citizens of the Commonwealth through the brutal taking of Michael Dannan's life.

All of the staff members were paid their full salaries through November. They would all be on the Bristow black list and unlikely to find work. The volunteers, the housewives and students and others, were likewise compensated. No price could be put on their loyalty and commitment, but the Dannan family could show its appreciation and did.

Toward the end of that week, Dace Havershamp brought the inner sanctum together. Sattis Arnow had been transferred from the Harlan hospital to the University of Kentucky Medical Center in Lexington and was healing well, but had not been released yet. We met there, in a conference room at the hospital. There wasn't much of an agenda. A few papers had to be signed to wind down the bank accounts, that sort of thing. There was no real need to meet, except we all felt that this impossible attempt that had captured the imaginations of so many ordinary Kentuckians deserved a final salute.

Sattis and Dace and Judge Blue and Jonathan were marked men politically as long as Jesse Bristow held power. They knew the risk going in, though, and felt the potential return worth the gamble.

If there was any plus in the current situation it was that the three of them would be looked to as leaders when, and if, a new challenge to the established party machine arose. They had proven what they could do.

For Rhae and Paul and me, the consequence was Michael's death...a risk none of us could have imagined and would have undertaken under no circumstance.

As he ended the meeting, Dace looked around the room at everyone and said, "We would have won it!" All heads nodded in agreement.

I lingered for a word with Sattis as the others left. "What drove Lucas Gwynne?" I asked him.

"Jesse," he replied. "Jesse, damn his eyes!"

Jesse Bristow, of course, had a lock on the Governor's chair. Now unopposed, he would collect the Democratic nomination by virtual acclamation in the primary and roll easily over whomever the Republicans put up as their candidate in November's general election.

As the primaries edged closer, accusations were made, never attributed but widely circulated, that Michael Dannan's killer had been a fanatic supporter of Jesse Bristow and had acted to insure Bristow's success. The Bristow camp labeled the rumor a salacious and contemptible attempt on the part of the Republican State Committee to smear the man they knew they couldn't beat and ignored it.

To try to throw off the depression that grabbed me after Michael's funeral, I jumped back into my work.

I didn't write the story of the shooting.

I was there, on the spot, in a better position than anyone to do the story. But I couldn't do it. No one suggested that I should.

Later though, after the funeral, I did a long Sunday piece, a retrospective on the Michael Dannan phenomenon and what it portended for politics in the Commonwealth. The days of the all-powerful party machine are numbered. The people are demanding, and will have, honest and competent government. My conclusions weren't popular with either party's hierarchy.

I tried to get an interview with Jesse Bristow. Jesse wasn't giving interviews. I tried for reaction to the Lucas Gwynne rumor. No comment.

Paul Isham and I sparred.

I knew he wanted me to do the story of what Lucas Gwynne told us about how Benjamin Dannan died. I knew he wanted me to link it to Michael's death. He was obsessed with justice for the Dannans. Or perhaps it was revenge. Paul Isham's rage was barely contained.

I wasn't ready. I didn't have enough. I needed to be able to conclusively tie Jesse Bristow to Lucas Gwynne's actions at Harlan.

In his calmer moments, Paul realized this.

He sent Jake Slade back to the mountains to try to find a connection between the two, something more current than a long ago truck ride on a certain snowy night.

Remembering the pledge we made to each other the night Michael died, I asked Marne Young to go to the old man in the village. If there had been a recent contact between Jesse Bristow and Lucas Gwynne, the village is the place it most likely would have happened and he would know of it.

I drove Marne as I had done on that first visit to the village. The country was beginning to show scattered wildflowers poking up in the meadows and, as we made elevation, the extravagant pinks and whites of dogwoods and wild cherry were peeping through the deep green of the forest.

We had sun most of the way, but outside Hyden, as happens in the early spring and particularly in the mountains, the day changed abruptly. The wind came up and the sky went black. Roiling clouds surfed over the ridges. Behind the wind came the rain. Water accumulated so rapidly I could barely feel the traction of the tires on the road surface. The wipers were useless. A vision of driving off a cliff and being crushed on the boulders at the bottom of the canyon jumped into my mind. I simply stopped in the roadway. If there were other cars behind me, I hoped the drivers would be smart enough to do the same.

For what seemed a half-hour or more, we sat with rain hammering on the car and the apprehension that any moment somebody would plow into us and throw us over the side. Outside was midnight dark and wind howled in a way that made us think that if a car didn't push us over, the wind would.

Suddenly the hammering let up and the rain disappeared. When we could see, we saw that we had stopped on a straight stretch on a downhill run on the canyon side of the road. I looked out to a freshly washed sky and sunlight so bright it sparkled. We got out and stood in the middle of the road and our spirits lifted.

At the bottom of the hill the road was flooded. Cars regularly get swept away and people drown trying to cross flooded roads in the mountains. We decided not to test either the depth or the speed of the water rushing by.

By the time the flood played out and we made it to the village, it was late afternoon. We'd been stopped twice, once on the gravel road shortly after we left the highway, then again at the crest of the ridge where the gravel road segued into the rock and dirt trail that tracked down through the valley to the village. In each case, grim-faced men with rifles at their sides tried to turn us back. In each case Marne was recognized. She talked us through. At the last stop we waited almost an hour while a runner took a message to the village and returned. The men were agitated, nervous.

"They're frightened," Marne said. "They expect trouble. The best way to avoid trouble is to keep people away like they've always done."

The runner brought back the Elder's message that he would see us and we started down that slippery, jolting little trail to the village as the sun dropped below the ridgeline.

## FIFTY-NINE

The air of apprehension we'd felt so strongly as we dealt with the sentinels hung like a pall over the village.

On the long street that paralleled the creek, we could see people moving.

"How large is the village?" I asked.

"I don't know. Not large."

She stepped out of the car to get a better look.

"They are preparing for something. All these people don't live here. They've come in."

She got back in and we crossed the bridge.

The old man in the blue work shirt that we'd met on our first visit, the Elder, was waiting for us. He caught our eyes, held them with his, then nodded and turned, motioning for us to follow him.

He led us to the chapel, the place where Lucas Gwynne told us his story.

When we were settled, I asked, "What's going on here?"

The old man didn't look at me. He turned to Marne.

"Lucas Gwynne has brought too much attention to us. The country folk know we are around, but they have no reason to bother us. Now Lucas has made us notorious. The village may be threatened. We are preparing."

"I don't understand."

Marne answered. "The local papers must have picked up that Lucas was a Melungeon. The people around here would have heard stories about Melungeons – strange people living secretly somewhere out in the mountains. Now there has been a violent murder...done by one of them. Maybe they are a threat. Maybe they ought to be removed."

"A pogrom!" I said disbelievingly,

"Melungeon history is full of them," Marne said. "Sometimes it was to get their land. Sometimes just because they were different and because people were fearful of them."

"Jesse Bristow has promised he will not let any harm come to the village," the old man said. "I believe he will try. If they come, we will disappear into the woods. Whatever the sin of Lucas Gwynne, it is not our sin and we will not be responsible for it."

"Oh, Lord, pray it doesn't come to that," Marne Young said.

Oddly I felt reassured that the village had Jesse Bristow's promise. The old man only nodded. It was clear he was putting his trust in himself and his people.

He motioned to the benches and told us to sit.

"Why are you here?"

"Lucas Gwynne," Marne said.

The old man started to rise.

"Please," she said. He sat back, waiting.

"None of us who knew Lucas believe that he could kill so brutally and in such cold blood. Or that he could even plan such a killing – in public, in broad daylight?"

"We are as surprised as you," the old man said.

"What could have set him off?"

"Why do you care about Lucas?"

"He was a friend. He gave us something important."

"The secret that Hanna wanted him to share with you?" the old man said.

"It may have triggered all this," Marne said.

"Oh Hanna, Hanna," the old man said wearily. "She could never let things be." He reached over and took Marne's hand. She seemed to relax at this touch. "Tell me what you can."

Marne glanced at me for approval, but whether I approved or not would have made no difference.

So Marne Young told him everything. All of it. From Hanna Collins' first message to Michael Dannan, to the signs she'd left for Michael to follow, to Lucas Gwynne's story, to Michael's confrontation with Jesse Bristow at Lake Cumberland and Jesse Bristow's admissions.

Full night came while we were in that little room and the old man, motioning Marne not to stop, got up and lit a kerosene lamp to give us light. He lowered himself back down into his chair with care. I have no idea how old he was. Ancient. And yet such strength coursed from him that I felt secure in his presence.

Marne was talking very softly and the old man took Marne's hands again and leaned in toward her, consolingly.

When Marne finished, we stayed still. The old man leaned back, folded his hands in his lap, and sat motionless. The hush in the room was absolute and the flickering light from the kerosene lamp cast strange shadows on the walls. A spell-like silence held us.

The old man broke it.

"Why do we abuse each other so," he sighed. Slowly he dropped to his knees and began to pray.

He prayed wordlessly, his face lifted, his arms at his side. When he was done, we helped him to stand.

"You will spend the night," he said. "It is too dangerous to drive back over the mountain in the dark." He smiled at Marne and ran his hand over her hair. "We will talk in the morning."

A while later, a young woman came for us and led us to a cabin beside the creek. There was a loft with a bed and, in front of the large fireplace, a couch with a beautiful old star pattern quilt in blues and greens. Food was on a trestle table in the kitchen. I thought I would be too excited to go to sleep, that Marne and I would talk into the early morning. Marne was almost asleep before she finished eating. I wasn't far behind. As I drifted off, I could hear the muffled sounds of the village still getting itself ready.

Later, toward morning, I woke to the rhyme of showers on the roof, and later still, in the first glow of dawn, to a quiet so intense it absorbed all sound, even my breathing. I pulled the quilt up and sank down into a deep, dreamless sleep.

When I finally woke, a fire was dancing in the fireplace and Marne Young was in the kitchen. A pitcher of water was on the table along with a big tin wash pan, a bar of soap, and a large white towel. I took them out on the porch to wash up and then came back in to join Marne.

The mountain air was magic for her. Her eyes sparkled, her skin glowed. She was smiling, and animated, and radiated such warmth that she was like a magnet drawing the delight of the day. Watching her, I wondered if Benjamin Dannan had succumbed to such enchantment when he saw Sue Bristow on such a morning and no one had come along to break the spell. At that moment, all I wanted was to wrap myself in all that delight.

I might have, but the Elder was walking down the road toward us

Marne brought the coffee out to the porch and we sat there in a patch of sunlight, reluctant to rush back into last night's discussion. The sun was pleasant, the coffee hot and strong. The Elder seemed rested; I hoped he was, I imagined his next few days would not be pleasant. There was no one anywhere to be seen, on the street or in the fields. The cabins seemed abandoned, the village uninhabited. Except for birdsong, and the rush of the creek, there was no sound.

What would a mob coming up on it think? When the ghosts came streaming silently out of the trees and up from the water, blades piercing, bullets boring into flesh – what would the invaders think then?

The Elder sat his coffee down on the porch by his chair. As it was last night, his attention was on Marne, not me.

"We do not have aristocracy. You know that. If we did, Jesse Bristow and Hanna Collins would be at the top of it. There is no man more admired and respected among us than Jesse Bristow. There is no woman whose memory is more honored or loved than Hanna Collins. Do you understand the word "champion" in the old sense – the hero, the warrior, the protector of his people? Jesse Bristow is a hero in that old sense. In the whole history of our people, from the beginning and through the dispersals and travels, we have had only a few. Jesse may be the greatest.

"I tell you this so that you will understand what you have asked of me and why I reply as I do.

"The tale you told me is tragic. Sue Bristow was a treasure, not just to Jesse and Hanna, but to all of us. She was the jewel of the village and the whole village mourned her deeply. Lucas was a simple, gentle boy. An impressionable boy. We all loved him.

"You are looking for an answer to explain why Lucas did what he did. I do not have that answer. The only possible explanation for me and the others with whom I've talked is that Lucas feared that Michael Dannan was a threat to the safety of the village, or a deadly threat to Jesse Bristow. Or possibly both. Such fears could trigger him. He loved this village. It kept him safe and gave him succor. He would defend it. And he worshiped Jesse Bristow. He would lay down his life for Jesse. None of us doubt that."

The old man said very softly, "And you seem to believe that Jesse may have been the instrument that levered poor Lucas."

Marne looked down, embarrassed. "Yes," she said.

The old man continued then, his voice still soft.

"Jesse came to the village the week before the shooting. He and Lucas walked the fields and the ridges all afternoon. Just the two of them. Jesse sometimes would do that. No one intruded. After Jesse left, Lucas seemed unusually withdrawn. No one knows what they spoke of. Lucas offered no explanation and none was asked.

"Make of this what you must. I will not presume to judge Jesse Bristow. Or to justify his actions. He is who he is and what he is. That is enough for us."

He stood then and raised Marne to her feet in front of him. He kissed her on the forehead and left.

I left shortly thereafter. Marne decided to stay. She felt protective of the village.

## SIXTY

All the way back, all the long, dreary way back, I tired to fathom the mind of Jesse Bristow. I could explain the killings on the ridge that Sattis Arnow told us about, even the death of Benjamin Dannan. These were acts of passion, driven by emotion. But Michael's death and the absolute wasting of Lucas Gwynne, these were beyond the excuse of emotion. They were cold, calculating, abhorrent acts. And to use Lucas Gwynne, to manipulate so frail a soul into murder and self-destruction was appallingly evil.

There seemed to be no moral code Jesse Bristow answered to. Yet I believe he was a compassionate man, as Sattis Arnow said he was. And a fair man. His reputation for such was well known. I know he felt for Rhae's pain at Michael's funeral. Yet he seemed to carry no guilt. From what the Elder told us, Jesse held affection for Luca Gwynne. But if he used Lucas Gwynne in the way we thought he had, he would be beneath contempt.

The man mystified me. There was no proof he had let Benjamin Dannan die. And there was only our suspicion to support the idea that he maneuvered Lucas Gwynne into the murder of Michael. He was unlike any other man I had ever met.

"There are three things important to Jesse," Sattis Arnow had said, "his honor, his blood kin, his mission. He makes his own rules. Jesse is the messiah. He decides what is right and wrong. The only power he answers to is himself."

I remembered Sattis saying that just before Michael and I left for the meeting at Jesse's place at Lake Cumberland. Now that it came back to me, I decided I didn't need to fathom Jesse Bristow's mind. Or even understand him. What I needed to do was get the bastard.

And as I thought about how, my little envelope of righteousness collapsed and the real frustration set it.

Jesse Bristow killed Michael Dannan and the instrument he used was Lucas Gwynne. The Elder's information led to no other conclusion. Jesse's motive? He was losing. All the polls had Michael winning the nomination in a walk. Bristow's ego, his "mission" couldn't accept that. He couldn't let that happen. The only way Jesse could win would be for Michael to no longer be a candidate: Dead men don't win elections.

And there was Jesse's concern that Michael would, as he had promised, charge Jesse with murder for the death of Benjamin Dannan. Jesse could probably survive that, but the particulars of his sister's affair with Benjamin Dannan would be made public and he wouldn't tolerate that.

Everything fed the conclusion that Jesse Bristow was responsible for the death of the Dannans, father and son – both of them.

I had the story. It was damning.

But I had no proof.

Lucas Gwynne, the best and most believable witness to the charge was himself dead. The Melungeon elder would never talk publicly. And if he did, to what could he attest? That Lucas and Jesse Bristow had met the week before Michael's murder? Whatever he might think happened between the two was of no consequence. The only thing of consequence is what he knew to be the case.

Oh, I could write the story. I had more than enough for that. I could make the circumstantial evidence so convincing there would be no doubt about Jesse Bristow's guilt in the public mind. I could punish Jesse Bristow. I could take revenge and extract justice.

But who could I get to print the story?

Without proof, the kind of piece I wanted to write would be an automatic invitation to a massive libel suit, a winnable libel suite. With Jesse Bristow's name and reputation at stake, the amount of money involved could bankrupt the *Journal*, do serious damage to the finances of any of the reputable papers that might consider it, if any reputable paper would.

My only hope was that Jake Slade's investigation had found a link that would stand up. I didn't need much.

But Jake had nothing. There were no overheard conversations to be speculated upon. No bank records, no phone calls. The only thing Jake returned with was a description of the murder weapon, an old Colt .45 – the classic Army 4 ¾-inch, 45-caliber revolver. It had been the virtual side-arm of the

mine wars. The local sheriffs and their deputies carried them. So
did the National Guard officers the Governor sent in to try
restore peace. And the miners, if they could afford one, or if not,
take one by combat.

We could have had this information simply by calling the
sheriff's office. They'd taken the weapon from Lucas Gwynne's
dead hand. There was no way to trace its ownership. There were
no records. No one cared in those times and in that country who
bought what firearm or for what purpose.

My anguish was nothing compared to that of Paul Isham. He
had carried his outrage for over thirty years. Paul admired
Benjamin Dannan almost to the point of veneration. His anger
and frustration over all those years of not knowing who was
responsible for Benjamin's death but knowing that someone
was, that was a flame that burned constantly at the edges of his
consciousness.

Now that it seemed that the cowardly, no-good sonofabitch
Jesse Bristow was finally exposed, Paul was exhilarated. And that
Bristow had been living the lie all these years and presuming to
the friendship of Rhae, that made revenge all the more
compelling.

Paul would have printed my story just as I had it, no further
verification needed. He *knew* Jesse was guilty. He would gladly
risk any lawsuit in any amount at any time, so intense was his
rage and so determined his intent to bring Jesse Bristow down.
He'd gamble the *Journal* for that – easily.

But it wasn't his decision to make. It was Rhae's. Rhae
wanted justice as badly as any of us, I believe. But I don't think
revenge was a part of the equation for her.

Rhae was caught up in a great silent sadness. In the weeks
after Michael's funeral, she shunned company. She kept to
herself. It was as it was with the death of Benjamin. She
withdrew into herself. She would heal silently and alone. What
happened to, or with, Jesse Bristow was not a cause for her. She
had seen enough death and felt enough pain to know that more
of it would be of no comfort.

The rest of us, though, seethed in frustration.

We met in counsel one last time. It was my suggestion. We
had to come to some resolution. This canker was infecting

everything else we should have been about. We had to make a decision either to push ahead and damn the consequences or let it lie and get on with life.

Rhae, Paul Isham, Sattis Arnow, now out of the hospital and recovering, Judge Blue, Jonathan Winslow, Dace, and me – we were the cabal. I took the liberty of asking Marne Young to join us. Marne had been our guide into this madness. And our translator. She understood the Melungeon part better than any of us. She wasn't encumbered with political or emotional baggage and might well be the clearest head among us. More important to me, I had come to have great regard for Marne Young. I found her presence reassuring. I found her satisfying.

We met in the conference room of the *Journal*, just after midnight, just after the paper had gone to bed. There were crystal shot glasses at each place around the table and a decanter of I.W. Harper in the center, a beautifully cut piece that reflected shards of colored light. Rhae poured each shot glass full. As we stood, she raised her glass to us and said, "To friends." We held our glasses out to each other and repeated, "To friends," then drank our drinks down. Rhae passed the decanter and we filled our glasses again, then sat.

There were only two options: run with the story or walk away. As much as we wanted, none of us could make a case for printing the story. Rhae had already had a top libel attorney review the piece and he advised that even with proof the story was probably libelous. Without proof it was categorically so. He would be delighted to have the case, he said – representing Bristow. They'd own the *Journal* and everything else Rhae might have.

We knew all we needed to know, or almost all. The only remaining mystery was Hanna Collins. A dying woman writes a letter and scatters a handful of esoteric pointers. As a result, two men die violently. Did she intend that? Did she foresee it?

Marne knew Hanna Collins' mind better than anyone alive. The trust and affection that had grown between them as Marne cared for her during her last days was a special tie.

Marne was lovely that night. It was well after midnight, yet she looked as fresh as if the evening was just beginning. I remember she wore a blue scarf in that way women wear them across the shoulders, the scarf almost as deep a blue as her eyes. She had been sitting quietly, waiting to be invited into the conversation.

When we turned the question to her, she hesitated, collecting her thoughts.

"Aunt Hanna knew her time was near," she said, going slowly, considering what she wanted to say before she said it.

"She wanted a clean conscience when she passed. She needed to be free of remorse."

Turning to me, keeping her eyes fixed on me, she said, "I think Aunt Hanna felt guilty.

"She had known how Benjamin Dannan died, and why, and had kept it hidden from Michael and his mother all these years.

"I believe she wanted Michael to know about Sue Bristow, about how beautiful, and talented and loving, Sue Bristow was and that Benjamin Dannan died trying to save her life.

'She wanted Michael to know she forgave Mr. Dannan because she realized, after her anger cooled, that Sue Bristow was as responsible as Mr. Dannan for what happened between them.

"And she wanted to be forgiven for holding on to her anger for so many years.

"I believe that was the purpose of her letter to Michael. She would have shown him the locket and the press clippings and told him how Sue died, accidentally by her own hand trying to abort the baby that she and Mr. Dannan had conceived, and how Mr. Dannan had been struck down on that snowy night going for help.

"If she had lived, she would have told Michael all this.

"She had no devious plan. She only wanted to be unburdened of what she knew and be forgiven."

Marne paused, turning her head slowly to engage each of us, eye to eye, then said sadly, "But time ran out."

No one moved. No one said anything. We looked around at each other, wonderingly, stupidly.

Something so simple as conscience to explain what to all of us had seemed such a malevolent plan, such a vicious plan, such a hateful plan? Could we accept that after we had built such fine Machiavellian explanations in our minds?

Were we reading evil where none was intended, seeing malice where only a simple urge to right an old wrong was the motive?

It could have been as Marne said. It might have been as Marne said. Maybe it was as Marne said. Who were we to say differently? No one knew Hanna Collins better.

After a moment, Marne collected herself. She looked at me directly.

"Don't do the story," she said.

She spoke of the Melungeons, of how further press attention might intensify the dangers to them and to the village. She thought as I thought – that Jesse Bristow had outrageously made a victim of Lucas Gwynne and detested it as much as any of us. But she would not endorse running a story that would accomplish nothing except soothe our sense of outrage.

As for the politics, the story might not even prove that damaging to Jesse Bristow. It would be cast by the Bristow organization as despicable attempt to smear an honorable and long-serving public servant.

Only Paul Isham held out – for justice, for revenge. Those weren't commodities that bought much that night.

The discussion was sometimes heated but most often merely resigned.

Sattis Arnow kept quiet throughout it all. At the end he snorted and said, "He got away again."

We looked at each other, accepting the bitterness of it.

I lifted my glass.

"Jesse wins," I said.

And drank it and turned down the empty glass.

Nothing more was to be said. We shook hands solemnly with each other and left in silence.

Marne went home with me. She felt sorry for me. I felt sorry for me.

But when I woke the next morning with her beside me, still asleep, breathing lightly with her hair catching the sun from the corner window, I was for that moment, for that short, sharp moment, happier than I think I had ever been.

## SIXTY-ONE

The world went on, of course. It paid no attention to my state of mind. Michael Dannan's killing was a terrible thing. But that was yesterday's headline. New ones were being written every day. Get with the program, Theo, I told myself. Bristow's off scot-free and there is nothing you can do about it.

Jesse Bristow, unopposed now, was rolling inexorably to the nomination. Michael's name was still on the ballot. There was no time to get new ballots printed. He figured in every story.

Could he have won? Would he have won, this upstart with no experience and no organization? All the stories asked that question in one way or another, and kept asking it. But none of the stories, after the first flurry the week after the killing, made any attempt to tie Jesse Bristow to Michael's death.

There was nothing honorable in this restraint. Bristow's people had warned every news organization that if so much as a suggestion appeared that Jesse Bristow had anything to do with Michael Dannan's death, libel suits would be on their desks before their papers hit the streets. Some of the editors balked, but all of the publishers believed. They gave the necessary orders.

So Jesse Bristow was waltzing to the governor's chair. It made no difference which of the three candidates in the Republican primary won. Jesse would be unbeatable in the general election in November and would stand gratefully, and humbly, on the steps of the State Capitol on that day in late December to accept the will of the people – and become Governor of the Commonwealth.

Despite having it locked, Jesse continued to campaign vigorously. Speeches, rallies, meetings, he didn't cut back on any of them. He savored the attention and seemed to be enjoying it all immensely.

I did my routine things. Filed my columns, worked on stories. These weren't my best days. Continuing to cover the campaign was taking more discipline than I wanted to keep trying to come up with.

I had enough experience with time as a healer to know how painfully slow the process is and to understand that the most that can expected is a dulling of the ache, not its disappearance.

Marne kept me sane. She sensed my black moods and would not indulge them. During those weeks she came down from Mountain Home and distracted me with diversions and little entertainments. The spring meet at Keenland was on. Rhae gave us the use of her box and we lost ourselves for a time in the excitement of the races. On other days, she arranged picnics at the creek and long walks along the river. One Sunday we drove down to Louisville for a concert in the park. On occasion, as a surprise to me, she would be waiting for me at the apartment after the paper was put to bed, the sound of sheets rustling when I opened the door. Oh, she distracted me – and she comforted me with her touch and her taste.

So the days rolled on and Jesse Bristow's coronation crept closer.

Derby weekend came.

Though it was only a month since Michael's funeral, Rhae decided she should be there. Main Creek Stables, her stable, had entries in two races that day. She had not been beyond the farm since the funeral, but she decided it was now time. Paul Isham and I accompanied her. She invited Dace and Judge Blue and Sattis and Jonathan as well to join us in her box. I suppose we were making a statement.

On the drive down and even in the box, Paul was restrained. His had been the hardest adjustment to our decision to drop the Lucas Gwynne story. We had gone back to our respective jobs at the *Journal,* each of us, and done them with little enthusiasm and with the complete understanding that the subject was one that neither of us would discuss.

Rhae had not been a presence during all that time. She had kept her own company alone at the farm. Today was, in effect, a coming out for all of us – the first time we'd been together in public since the day of Michael's funeral. To say that we drew attention understates the case.

There is no greater aggregation of color in any spot on earth than at Churchill Downs on Derby Day, the women in pastels of every hue and with hats more glorious than the blooms of any flowers. Even on a dark day, being there is like being in the middle of a living Monet.

This day, this Derby Day, was glorious, just cool enough to be comfortable, sunshine bright and soft, a little breeze to keep the banners waving.

Against that panoply of color, Rhae Dannan was regal in solid black. And she attracted people like a magnet. There was a constant stream to the box, men and women paying their respects, offering their condolences, wishing her well. She was warm and gracious and held her composure like a queen.

The only difficult moment came just before post-time for the Derby. The Governor's box is at the finish line. Rhae's box was three down from that. Jesse Bristow's was back at the home stretch post.

A commotion to our left caught everyone's attention and we saw it was Jesse Bristow making his entrance, stopping and shaking hands on the way to his box. But he didn't stop there. He came directly to Rhae, working his way through the crowd slowly. It seemed the eyes of everyone were following him.

When he got to the box, he leaned in close to Rhae and said something to her that none of us could hear. No emotion registered on Rhae. She looked stonily ahead and sat straight. He looked into her face for a long moment, silently. Then he looked up and offered his gaze to each of us in turn. He made no effort to extend his hand. He understood the risk too well.

For a brief moment I thought Paul Isham, who was sitting next Rhae, would vault the railing and attack Jesse on the spot. But I saw Rhae put her hand on his arm. Paul got control and settled back. Just then the bugler began the call to post and the horses started on the track.

I thought then, and I still hold the opinion, that as crass and obvious as Jesse Bristow's act was, the man was sincere. I think he truly did feel for Rhae's pain and loss. At that moment, I had the uncomfortable sensation of liking the man.

## SIXTY-TWO

There was a huge full moon on Derby night, so bright that we cast shadows as we walked. The breeze was as soft as silk and the air scented with honeysuckle. On such a night, I thought, unicorns should be prancing in the meadows and Puck dropping potions onto the eyelids of slumbering lovers.

Marne was waiting for me at the apartment and we strolled the sleeping streets until almost dawn.

Some of it was sweet and some of it was bad.

Bad because Michael's death kept prodding me.

I had tried, but I couldn't let it go.

Marne knew without me telling her.

"What can you do?" she asked.

"I don't know," I said. "Wait," I said.

"For what?"

"I don't know," I said. "Something. Anything."

We walked on, silently.

I saw Allie the next day.

I was on Main Street, on the corner, just before noon, waiting for the stoplight to change, people moving hurriedly all around me. One of them was Allie.

I hadn't been with her since the day of Michael's funeral. I had no solace to offer so I had taken the coward's way and stayed away.

She saw me and came up and reached out her hand to me.

There was a hurt in her eyes that looked as if it would never go away.

All I could think to say was, "How are you?"

She deflected the question with a small shake of her head.

"He won't get away with it, will he, Theo?"

She held my hand tightly.

"What do you mean?" I said.

"I've heard the stories. Jesse Bristow arranged it."

I could feel the hot anger through her fingertips.

"There's no case against Bristow, Allie," I said.

"He mustn't get away with it."

I had no idea how to reply, but before I could start, she said, "You could write a story. You could expose him."

I looked at her helplessly.

"There's no proof, no way to tie him to it."

She eased her grip on my hand and stepped back a half-pace to lock her eyes on mine.

The light changed.

She squeezed my hand.

"You can find a way, Theo."

She said it with such conviction I almost believed her.

Then she stretched up and kissed me lightly on the lips.

There on the corner of Main and St. Clair.

At high noon.

In the center of town.

And walked away.

## SIXTY-THREE

The primary was just two weeks away. The closer it got, the more restless I became.

During this time I took to staying even later at the paper than usual, getting comfort from the sound of the presses running and the bright lights of the newsroom. Then I'd make a long loop home, going up Main Street to the New Bridge, crossing the river there, then taking my time up Capitol Avenue, drawn like a moth to the lighted dome, making a slow circuit of the Capitol, then back down Shelby Street to home.

Hardly anyone was out at that hour. On occasion I'd run into Father O'Conner on his way to open the church for the early morning Mass. But for the most part, the streets were mine.

I remembered the ancient Celts called those hours before dawn "the time between times." Night hadn't let go its hold, but daylight hadn't come yet. Neither the gods of the night nor the gods of the day held sway. Anything could happen. I liked being one of the few creatures out among the unseen monsters and the unnamed heroes.

The morning of Jesse Bristow's death there was only a half moon. Nothing to compare to the grand full moon of Derby Day but still strong enough to throw shadows on the sidewalk as I made my way home.

I was awake when the phone rang.

"You better get over here."

"What?" I mumbled.

"Jesse Bristow is dead. Theo, do you hear me? Jesse Bristow's been shot."

The call came from Jack Toms, a friend on the Frankfort Police Force.

"A cleaning woman found him. He's at the Democratic Party office on Capitol Avenue."

I was the first newspaperman there. Red lights were flashing from the roofs of the cruisers outside and a uniform was beginning to uncoil yellow crime scene tape and place orange traffic control cones as I arrived.

Inside, the silence was broken only by the click of the shutter as the photographer began to shoot the scene.

The office was on the second floor.

"Jack," I said when I saw him across the room.

He shook his head.

"We don't know. We haven't found the gun. The cleaning woman didn't see or hear anyone. We got here almost immediately after she called. He was dead. Sitting at the desk. A small hole in his forehead. Not much blood. The desk light was on. There was no evidence of a struggle."

The scream of an ambulance rushing up Capitol Avenue grated on the morning. Lights were coming on in the homes nearby and a few people where coming out onto their porches to see what the excitement was about.

Jesse Bristow had bid his chief of staff goodnight around midnight and remained to work on a speech he was to deliver the following week.

No entry had been forced. The back door and side door and windows were locked. So was the front door. Even the door at the top of the outside stairs that led up to second floor was locked.

There had been no threats against him. No rumors of concern.

The murder weapon turned out to be a twenty-two and the bullet a target-round – not one designed to expand and explode but to bore in swiftly on the target and penetrate cleanly.

"Jesse Bristow killed by a twenty-two! That's almost as much an insult as the act itself," Jack Toms said to me. I used the quote in my story.

It was a frustrating case.

Jesse could have let his killer in and probably did. To get close enough to kill with a single shot from a twenty-two, to be close enough to place the shot so accurately in the center of the forehead – the killer had to be someone Jesse knew. But Jesse Bristow knew everybody.

The day dissolved into a kaleidoscope of rumor and speculation. The first rumor was that the killer, John Wilkes

Booth style, had broken an ankle jumping from the second floor landing and was surrounded at the river trying to steal a boat and make his escape by water. But then came word that the killer had just walked into the Frankfort Police station and given herself up. Then there was a report that a night watchman had spotted a red sedan with two suspicious-looking men parked in front of the building with the motor running. The car had been spotted on the Lexington road and the State Police were in pursuit.

By the time the press briefing came late that afternoon, every newsman covering the story was exhausted. None of the "suspects" panned out. The day had been spent chasing smoke.

Chief Mason Stone, the head of the city police force, could only confirm what everyone already knew and suspected. Which was that the combined experts of the Kentucky State Police and the Frankfort City Police had no idea of how the crime was committed or who did it.

They were able, in a general sense, to pinpoint the time of the murder. Based on the coroner's estimate, Jesse Bristow departed this world at about one o'clock the morning of Monday, May 3, seated at a desk in the headquarters of the state Democratic Party in a private office there he often used.

Only one shot was fired. The slug entered the brain at a slightly descending angle, indicating the shooter was standing and Jesse was sitting, and exited into the back of the chair with only a minimum amount of blood and mess spread about. There were no powder burns, so the shooter was within a reasonable remove of the victim. The sound of the shot would not have been enough to attract attention from as close as downstairs. The twenty-two is a nice, quiet weapon.

"Given the placement of the shot, the caliber of the weapon, and the circumstances, we are of the opinion that the shooter is an expert marksman. Amateurs don't pull off shots like that," Chief Stone said.

"A hit," came a question from the floor, "a contract killing?"

"Not likely," Stone replied. "The locked doors indicate that Mr. Bristow must have let the killer in. Which means he must have known him. We don't think Mr. Bristow kept company with professional killers."

"Then who?" came the follow-up.

"We don't know. We'll find out."

That was the first day's story – killer unknown. And the second day's. And the third day's.

Mid-way through the second week the police were no closer to answers than they had been that first morning. They had questioned everyone living within four blocks of the murder site, everyone working at the Democratic Headquarters and the Capitol building the night and morning of the crime, the bus drivers running the South Frankfort route, the street cleaning crews that had been on Shelby Street and Capitol Avenue that morning on the chance they may have seen something suspicious. No one had seen anything.

I was sitting over my typewriter staring off into space trying to come up with a lede for the story for the next morning's paper when Paul Isham walked in. His mood had improved markedly in the past few weeks. With Jesse Bristow's death, he seemed to shed the load of anger and frustration that had been bending him down and to stand up straighter and move about with more enthusiasm.

He looked at me quizzically.

"Can't find a lede," I said. "The police have nothing and it doesn't look as if they are ever going to have anything."

He looked at his watch. We were coming up on deadline.

"Don't force it," he said, a half smile on his face. "If it isn't there, it isn't there."

He left almost cheerfully.

Paul's mood was understandable. He was glad that Jesse Bristow was dead. He believed at long last that justice had been done – that Benjamin Dannan's and Michael Dannan's killer had been punished in the only way acceptable – with death. He could walk unencumbered in the sunlight again. Whether Jesse Bristow's killer was ever found was a matter of indifference to him. I understood that– and I felt good for him.

As all these events unfolded, he and Rhae Dannan moved to a closer stage in their friendship. I think now that Paul must have always been in love with Rhae. His friendship with Benjamin never let him admit it to himself. Now that the mystery of Benjamin Dannan's death had been solved, now that the killer had been found and punished, the restraints that

Benjamin Dannan's memory had wrapped around his emotions were loosening. Paul was a freer spirit.

## SIXTY-FOUR

Jesse Bristow's murder threw the political world into turmoil. His death meant that the rapidly approaching Democratic primary was without a candidate. There had been only two candidates in the race, Michael Dannan and Jesse Bristow. Both were now dead, which meant that Democrats would go to the polls the last Tuesday in May with no one to vote for.

Unless someone came up with a solution for finding a way to nominate a Democrat to run against the Republicans in the general election in November, the Republicans would waltz into the Governor's Mansion unopposed. The situation had never occurred before. No one knew what to do.

I spent my time alternating between these two running stories – the Bristow murder and the Democratic conundrum. Both were big. Both were important.

The Democrats decided that the State Central Committee would name a candidate and that candidate would be the Democratic candidate in the general election in November. This put enormous power in the Party's hands, but it had always had enormous power.

The decision was bitterly debated by the factions trying to erode the machine's power, particularly by the factions that had supported Michael's candidacy, but in the end it proved the only practical solution.

The anointed turned out to be a young lawyer from Prestonsburg. The Party learned something about the mood of the electorate from Michael's campaign. It learned that people wanted change. Real change. This young man was the son of a miner and a native of the small mountain community of Top Most. He was bright enough and aggressive enough to make it through Harvard Law and come home to make his career as a public defender. He was a candidate even Dace and Sattis could support.

As the political drama moved forward, the Bristow investigation came to center on the only facet of the case that seemed to offer any promise at all...the search for a shooter skilled enough to handle a twenty-two with an expert's precision who could somehow be connected to Jesse Bristow. And then to provide a motive. It was not a strategy for which anyone had much enthusiasm.

The FBI's data base came up with eighty-one names – men and women who had won recognition in state or national shooting contests. Almost all of these were with rifles, only six with pistols.

Paul Isham was among them. His name leaped out from the confidential list leaked to me by a man with the investigation who expected he'd need a favor at some point.

I rushed with the information to Paul's office. I didn't want him blindsided.

Paul already knew.

He had, in fact, already been scheduled by the State Police for an interview. He turned to the bookshelf behind his desk. There were six or eight trophies sitting there, all for various things, press awards, that sort of thing. He handed one to me. It was a slightly tarnished small silver bowl with a simple inscription: *The Creedmoor Cup. Paul Isham, National Champion, Twenty-Two Caliber Handgun.*

"I was pretty good," he said, "would have been on the Olympic Team, but I met Benjamin that summer."

I started to speak, but he stopped me.

"Let the police ask the questions," he said.

## SIXTY-FIVE

Of course.

Paul Isham, the Avenger!

If the police knew what Rhae and I knew about the rage and anger that had tormented Paul all these years, it wouldn't be difficult to make the case that Paul had motive. Could a certain long-ago excellence with a small handgun be enough to key a serious investigation and produce a sustainable charge?

But, oh how easy it would have been to do the deed.

*The outside stairs are well shielded by trees. There is no street light on that corner. The odds that anyone would see him on the stairs, even if anyone was on the sidewalk at that hour in that neighborhood, were almost non-existent. Nor was there likely to be any traffic. The Capitol is a block away and buttoned up for the night. Only a cleaning staff would be working and they would be inside. The odd car might come up Shelby, someone on the way home very late, but this is unlikely, and even so, the side of the house with the outside stairs isn't visible from the street.*

*Up the stairs. Knock on the door.*

*Jesse answers. No reason to be apprehensive. No reason to be timid. He's Jesse Bristow, for God's sake.*

*He is surprised when he sees Paul Isham smiling at him through the glass. He can't imagine what business Paul Isham might have at that hour, but he has no reason to fear him, and he is curious, so he opens the door.*

*They go back to his office. Jesse takes his seat in the chair behind the desk and motions Paul to sit. But Paul remains standing. He is holding a small briefcase in his left hand. Calmly, for Paul would have been icy calm at this point, he extracts a pistol and raises it with arms extended in the classic two-hand shooter's pose. Jesse is momentarily taken aback at this, but when he sees that it is a twenty-two pointed at him, he laughs. A twenty-two slug, unless Isham is good enough to place it in his brain or heart, would hardly sting, and he has no reason to respect Paul Isham's marksmanship.*

*But before he can move, Paul fires. One shot. Center forehead.*

*Surprise spreads across Jesse Bristow's face as he dies.*

*Paul puts the little twenty-two automatic back in his briefcase. The shot has rocked Jesse back in his chair. Paul leans him forward and props him so that Jesse is sitting with his arms extended on either side of the piece of paper he was working on.*

*The head won't stay up, so Paul lets it droop forward, as if Jesse has fallen asleep. Only a trickle of blood runs from the small hole in the forehead.*

*He arranges the rest of the papers into an orderly stack on the left corner of the desk and locks the outside door leading to the stairs. He wipes the door handle with his handkerchief, checks that he has left no footprints, and walks down the inside stairs through the darkened offices on the first floor to the front door. He opens it, wipes it clean of fingerprints, too, then steps out on the porch, pulls the door shut behind him, which locks automatically, and walks the few paces down the sidewalk to the waiting car.*

There would have to have been a waiting car. Paul couldn't take the chance of leaving a parked car within walking distance of the office, or the chance of being seen walking either to or from it.

Jake Slade would have been the driver. They would have timed it so that Jake would pull up in front and Paul would walk to the car almost before it stopped rolling – or have arranged a signal, say, the upstairs light turned off for a moment, then back on.

That was a risk, but about the only one. And Jake would be the alibi if Paul needed one. Although the probability that one would be needed was very, very slim. There is no conceivable motive for such an act on Paul Isham's part so far as anyone knows – that is, so far as any one knows other than those of us who have Paul Isham's best interests at heart.

The only known connection between Paul Isham and Jesse Bristow is their brief friendship during the mine wars. Jesse and Benjamin Dannan's subsequent fight over the Big Sadie Tax Bill was between the two of them. Paul Isham wasn't a part of it. To the extent anyone cares to inquire, Paul Isham's involvement with Jesse Bristow is minimal at best and in any event not unfriendly.

Paul Isham a serious suspect?

I had to talk to Rhae.

She would be at the farm. The hour was late, but I didn't call ahead. I gambled she would still be up and that my unannounced arrival would be overlooked. Rhae had always granted me certain indulgences.

The house was dark – a single light glowing in the rear. I knocked and after a long moment, Betsy came to the door. When she saw it was me, she opened it shaking her head in a scolding way, but saying only "You better have a good reason for getting me out of bed at this hour, young man." She motioned to the kitchen. "Miss Rhae in there."

I found Rhae sitting at the big table in an oversize white robe with a cup before her. She didn't seem surprised to see me. Just exhausted. But she smiled.

"Theo. Come sit. I'm not sleeping well these days. Join me?"

She lifted the cup. "My mother's secret potion for the after-midnight willies – a little hot coffee, a little warm milk, a little sugar, and a lot of bourbon."

At that moment, the concoction seemed the most appealing drink I'd ever heard of.

"Please," I said.

I remained quiet while she made it for me, not sure how to begin. I could hear the house creak and faintly, from outside, tree frogs down at the creek.

Rhae sat the cup before me.

"Why are you here?" she said.

"I have a story I need to tell you."

"Not a long story, I hope."

"Not long."

"Is it a story about a perfect murder?"

She put her hand over mine, reassuringly.

"About a man dead in a locked house? No witnesses, no murder weapon, no apparent motive, no suspect?"

"The police are having Paul in for questioning tomorrow," I said.

Rhae patted my hand.

"I know."

"Should we do anything?"

"What would you do? Turn yourself in?"

I sat up in surprise.

"Go home and get some sleep," she said.

The FBI found nothing suspicious in its questioning of Paul Isham. That he had at one time, as a young man, been considered an expert with the twenty-two caliber handgun wasn't germane to the crime being investigated. Isham had spent the early part of the night in question at his job at the *Journal*, and after the paper had gone to press, the rest of it at an early breakfast at the Dannan Farm near Peaks Mill with Rhae Dannan and Jake Slade, who had driven him.

Thank you for your time and your cooperation, Mr. Isham. Next.

Only there was no next.

The investigation hit a wall. No leads. No suspects. Jesse Bristow was the victim of an assailant or assailants unknown.

I checked with the police every day, as a good reporter would be expected to do. No developments. Nothing new. The suspense wore at me, though, like waiting for those damn whistles to signal the start of another Chinese attack up the frozen ridges in Korea.

I kept my focus on my job, on following my usual routine. There was nothing, absolutely nothing, to tie me to Jesse Bristow. I meant to keep it that way. Yet even in the most certain of situations, nothing is guaranteed.

I countered the resulting tension with work and luckily, the political story stayed heated enough to keep my time and my mind almost fully occupied. Not totally, but enough so that only Marne noticed that I sometimes seemed apprehensive and removed.

The primary came, of course, and of course, the young lawyer got the Democratic nomination – though Michael won almost 24% of the vote and Jesse 18%. Their deaths occurred too late in the process for new ballots to be printed, so their names remained in play and some people, for whatever reason, chose them rather than the hand-picked party candidate.

The outlook for the general election in the fall was not good for the Democrats. The party was in too much disarray to recover in the time it had. So it seemed we were going to put a Republican in the Governor's Mansion again.

My fame grew as a result of all these misfortunes. I had better information than most of my peers and more perspective to bring to my stories. The column was picked up by ten new papers. I was asked to do a piece for *The New Yorker* on the Bristow murder and a long article for *Atlantic Monthly* on Michael Dannan's success against the entrenched interests of the state machine and what this presaged for the way campaigns would be run in the future.

The result was that while my psyche hurt and I kept glancing over my shoulder to see if anyone was on my trail, my ego was stroked most satisfactorily and my bank account grew.

So far as I could tell, only Rhae Dannan suspected. No, the truth of it is, she knew. She knew as certainly as she knew Michael's eyes were blue. I didn't question how she knew. I simply accepted that she did. I had confided in no one. Not even Marne. Yet Rhae Dannan knew.

Doing it was amazingly easy – as easy as in my little imagining putting Paul in my place in Jesse Bristow's office that night.

Only I didn't have a car and driver waiting.

I left the *Journal* that night by the alley door just after deadline but before the page forms were locked up and put on the press. No one noticed in the rush of getting that morning's edition ready. Even if any had, no one would have thought anything of it. My habit of rambling the streets was so established that notice would have been taken only if I hadn't ducked out into the night.

I crossed the bridge and strolled casually up Shelby Street, all but invisible in the heavy shadows. One car passed. When I reached the office where I knew Jesse Bristow to be, I climbed the outside stairs and stood on the landing in front of the door. I was uncommonly calm.

Jesse answered my knock and when he saw who it was, opened the door.

"What are you doing here? Well, no matter. I need a wordsmith. This speech is getting me down. Come on in," he said.

He turned and led the way back into his office. He took a seat behind the desk and looked up at me, smiling.

By then I had the pistol out. The shot took him in the center of the forehead. A small hole appeared. He frowned. A trickle of blood started down toward his right eye. He lifted his head a bit, as if to say something, the frown still on his face, then slumped forward.

I stood there only a second, letting a feeling of relief wash over me, the tension going, the tingle of exhilaration building as it does when you've just won a tight game, an important game, in the final minute. And for an instant, just a touch of regret. There was something about the man that I liked. But he had started the game and set the rules.

I put the little twenty-two back in my coat pocket and let myself out the door to the outside stairs.

No one was about.

Shelby Street was asleep.

The only light came from the street lights at the corner of each block. I stayed in the shadows to cross the river at the Old Bridge.

I stopped in the middle of the bridge, my arms resting on the railing that bordered the pedestrian walkway. The half moon was still up, but sliding down toward the ridgeline on Louisville Hill through a scattering of veil-like clouds. Up river, a spotlight on the Arsenal's tower made it seem an old fortress, standing ready to defend the town.

The Court House clock struck one-thirty.

After a while I reached over the railing and dropped the twenty-two into the night black waters of the Kentucky.

No one would ever find it. If they did, it would be untraceable. I'd had the little pistol since I was a boy – a gift from my grandfather, my mother's father, the farmer, when I turned twelve. He thought all young men should know how to shoot and he taught me how to aim it true and never waste a shot. I used it to hunt squirrels in the autumn in the big oaks along the creek at his place. It was the only handgun I ever owned. It meant a lot to me.

I became lethal with that little twenty-two – skilled enough to prepare me to qualify as Expert with both rifle and pistol at

Parris Island on my way through Marine Boot Camp. I got better in Korea.

The presses were running when I let myself back in the alley door at the *Journal.*

If I had been missed, no one mentioned it. Or no one noticed.

I grabbed one of the early editions, the newsprint still warm from its run through the press, stuck my head into the newsroom, shook my head at the guys breaking out the cards for a quick round of poker, and headed out again into the dawning morning.

I had taken care of what had to be taken care of. I had done what I had to do.

## SIXTY-SIX

Rhae Dannan called me to the farm for lunch a few weeks later, after the excitement of the primary died down and coverage of the Bristow assassination had disappeared from the papers. We both knew it would. There is nothing less interesting than yesterday's news. The world forgets.

Betsy had set a table on the far corner of the porch where we could look out over the meadow and the creek. The afternoon was one of those patented jewels of a Bluegrass summer – a pale blue sky and a tender breeze. Roses cut from the wild ones that grew on the fence line were in a graceful green vase on the white table cloth and mint-juleps in frosted silver cups were waiting for us.

We made small talk for a while. I wasn't sure of the reason for the invitation and was both curious and slightly apprehensive. I hadn't talked privately with Rhae since the morning I went to the farm to tell her of Paul Isham's impending investigation by the police.

Rhae was relaxed and gracious.

She asked about the new papers that had subscribed to my syndication and commented on the *Atlantic* article which she had read and with which she agreed.

"And Marne," she said, "Are the two of you together? You should be. I like Marne. I think she's good for you."

I must have looked embarrassed.

"Of course you are. As obtuse as you can sometimes be, Theo Clark, you're not thick. There is no need to share the details. Just nod if you're showing some sense," she said laughing

I laughed, too, and nodded.

"Well, good. Things have a way of working out."

She looked at me with that look people have when they are remembering, seeing through time to the person you were once upon a time. A small, sad smile played on her lips.

"A toast," Rhae said, and lifted her julep cup.

I reached for mine and lifted it.

Her eyes held me.

"To Kings," she said.

I hesitated, unsure of her meaning.

"When you two were together, you were Kings of all you surveyed."

Then understanding, I touched my cup to hers and said, "To Kings. God bless us all, wherever we may be."

When we lowered our cups, Rhae took my hand.

"You were never a complicated boy, Theo, or mean, or vindictive. You spent so much time with Michael that I came to feel as if I knew you almost as well as your mother. Your moods...what you liked and didn't...what you'd do and wouldn't. You were like a brother to Michael. You can't know how you touched my heart by the way you looked out for him after his father died, how you took care of him and tried to ease his way.

"And I knew how the two of you together were determined to win, regardless of the game or the opponent. I worried about that, that being so competitive wasn't good for either of you. But I soon realized it wasn't so much a matter of competitiveness as the opinion you held of yourselves. You were winners. Winning was your due. I hoped that kind of self-confidence would carry you both to great things."

Rhae paused and stared over the meadow. The colts had been turned out and were racing across the grass.

I started to interrupt, but she stopped me.

"The morning they found Jesse Bristow dead at his desk, I knew there were only two possibilities. Paul had finally given in to his rage. Or you had avenged your best friend. Paul was with me. That left only you.

"I knew how close you were to Michael. I knew how much his loss meant to you. I knew, Theo, even before you came to tell me."

Again I started to interrupt and again she stopped me.

"Don't say anything. I don't want you ever at risk because of something you might have told me."

She leaned across the table then and kissed me on the cheek.

There is talk of erecting a statue of Jesse Bristow, to be done in the heroic mold and placed in Evarts. A public subscription has begun.

There is no talk of a statue of Michael Dannan. He blazed like a meteor through the Kentucky sky for a short, mesmerizing time, then was extinguished.

We will never be able to calculate the loss.

He gave people faith in themselves. He could make them feel that they were worth something and deserved respect and fair treatment. He gave them confidence that they could do things none of them thought possible.

Michael Dannan would have made a great Governor. He might even have made a good President. He would have been for the people. He would have done right by them. I would have seen to that.

I don't want the memory of him to be lost.

The story I want to write would take care of that.

But I can't write it.

I can't tell Michael's story without telling Benjamin's. And I can't tell Benjamin's without telling the story of Sue Bristow ... and of how she died and why.

Rhae doesn't deserve that humiliation.

And Benjamin Dannan's honorably won and truly deserved public reputation is worth protecting.

I'm not obliged to tell all I know. Those of us who poke around in the dark places and ferret out the secrets have never told all we know. If we did, the world would stop.

I've talked all this through with Marne, even my part in it. My actions and moods of the past month had given her reason to suspect there was something on my mind that I couldn't speak of. She even suspected it might have something to do with Jesse Bristow. She thought I was concerned for Paul Isham and was trying to protect him.

When I told her I was responsible, she was taken aback, but not appalled.

She saw Michael fall.

She saw Lucas Gwynne put the gun in his mouth.

Her outrage at the way poor Lucas was used and Michael killed was intense and unforgiving.

Waiting for Jesse Bristow to get his due on Judgment Day wasn't acceptable.

She understood.

She understood that I had done what had to be done. Though she wouldn't say so, I think she was middling proud that I had.

For the time being then, Jesse Bristow remains a martyred hero and Michael Dannan the young prince with so much promise whose life was cut brutally short by a deranged gunman.

The particulars of Benjamin Dannan's death are still a mystery.

Rhae Dannan and Paul Isham and Marne feel that a private justice has been done. For them that is enough.

It is not enough for me.

Which is why I've written this.

It will go in to my private files along with the novel I'll never finish and the few scraps of poetry I like enough to keep but am too embarrassed to offer for public scrutiny.

Someone will find this manuscript after I die and be smart enough, I hope, to turn it over to a good reporter who will see its value and finally write the story that I cannot write – the true story of the Dannans and Jesse Bristow.

So that we may know our heroes and our villains.

And understand how little separates the two.

**End**

# Acknowledgements

Though this is a work of fiction and the characters are imaginary, the places, most of them, are real.

There is no Penrod as such and the Melungeon village may or may not be where Theo found it, but the rest are there.

Frankfort is real. I grew up there and love it still.

And all the other places mentioned, they are there, too. You can visit them and enjoy them and I hope that at some point you have an opportunity to do so.

*The State Journal* is a real newspaper – a very good one. And the Melungeons are real. Much still isn't known about them. But much is. I encourage you to go online and find out more. Theirs is a fascinating story.

My references to actual events – the Lost Colony, the Mine Wars, The Battle of Evarts, and others – are as accurate as my reportage could make them.

Getting this story told took a lot of help from a lot of people. I am particularly indebted to my sister Ann Hatterick, whose experience in Kentucky politics, and knowledge of how the game is played, informs the entire narrative, and whose encouragement helped keep me writing.

Darden Chambliss, an old friend from New York days and a former Associated Press newsman, gave the manuscript a thorough and critical read and made many excellent suggestions, as did Charles Hudson, Franklin Professor of History and Anthropology at the University of Georgia, one of the country's leading authorities on the Indians of the Southeastern United States. A much published author, he insisted I get the facts right and write unambiguous sentences. We were boys together so he didn't worry about my ego.

Nor did Don Wheeler, also of the small group of us who grew up together in that little town on the Kentucky River, an ex-journalist and former manager of the University of Kentucky's WUKY public radio station. His comments on dialogue were golden.

The enthusiasm for the story of Carol Ann Hackley of the University of the Pacific and her confidence in its appeal kept me motivated beyond reasonable expectations and her clinical review of grammar, spelling, and punctuation would give me hopes that if this were a paper being submitted for grade it would merit an A. If an error in any of these areas still exists, it's because I failed to make the changes I was told to make.

Finally, editor Linda Hobson's work on the manuscript made this a materially better book than it started out to be or would have been without her and is greatly appreciated.

To all of you, my thanks. I am beholden.